Tim O'Brien

was born in Minnesota, and graduated from Macalester College in St Paul. He served as an infantryman in Vietnam and after graduate studies at Harvard worked as a national affairs reporter for the *Washington Post*. He established himself as one of the leading American writers of his generation in 1973 when he published *If I Die in a Combat Zone*, the compelling account of his own tour of duty in Vietnam. This was followed in 1975 by his acclaimed first novel, *Northern Lights*. In 1979 he received the National Book Award in Fiction for *Going After Cacciato*. *The Things They Carried* was a finalist for the Pulitzer Prize and the National Book Critics Circle Award. *In the Lake of the Woods* was chosen by the *New York Times Book Review* as one of the best books of the year, and was selected as the best work of fiction of 1994 by *Time* magazine.

From the reviews of *Tomcat in Love*:

'One of the best books I've come across in years. My advice is that you waste no more time on this review. Go out and find a copy of *Tomcat in Love*. Now. It really is that good ... a wickedly accurate portrait of obsessive love that manages to be both fiercely comic and profoundly moving. Read it and weep. And laugh.'   DAVID NICHOLSON, *Washington Post*

'O'Brien's jolly jape centres around his outré creation – a six-foot-six professor, whose pomposity is matched only by his verbosity. O'Brien's prose is punchy and glittering; his book a Nabokovian inquiry into the double helix of eroticism and language. Chippering's harmless conquests of the opposite sex are often very funny and take on darkly comic tones as he slips into self-delusion.'   RICHARD SKINNER, *Guardian*

Further reviews overleaf

'Demonically engaging . . . narrative genius. A manic, knife-at-the-throat humour . . . a little like listening to Lenny Bruce. Chippering is wickedly realised. The agility and intelligence that created this pathos-ridden romantic make one marvel at Tim O'Brien's gifts.'   GAIL CALDWELL, *Boston Globe*

'Very funny . . . Both hilarious and touching, *Tomcat* will strike a chord in most males today.'   BRIAN CASE, *Time Out*

'Lust, laughs and literary mastery . . . breathtaking prose . . . playful and funny.'   KATE AURTHUR, *New York Post*

'*Tomcat in Love* is genuinely funny, the humour arising from Chippering's unreliability and acute lack of self-awareness. O'Brien exhibits a new-found playfulness, taking sideswipes at the campus culture of political correctness, poking fun at the artificiality of fictional narration and relishing the liberation from realism that his burlesque plot brings.'
    PHIL WHITAKER, *New Statesman*

'Tim O'Brien is ingenious in making this ghastly man sympathetic, not least by surrounding him with characters so devious, manipulative and stupidly cunning that his highbrow, self-deluding hypocrisy seems almost Quixotic. A successful departure from O'Brien's Vietnam novels, it maintains his high ranking among North American writers.'
    HUGO BARNACLE, *Sunday Times*

'A savage comedy . . . picaresque in its plotting and hyperbolic in the neuroses besetting its characters . . . as they persist in misunderstanding and manipulating one another.'
    BRUCE WEBER, *New York Times*

'O'Brien is unquestionably a brilliant writer. This new novel is a radical, somewhat startling departure from his previous dark works but a quite brilliant and complex piece at the same time.' MICHAEL TIERNEY, *Glasgow Herald*

'*Tomcat in Love* is an extraordinary novel, a sustained and sophisticated comedy that, just as it makes you laugh with appalled disbelief, drips with pain, anguish and loss.' ALEX CLARK, *Guardian*

'*Tomcat* is a complex affair that invites a complex response and offers a complex reward. Whatever O'Brien's motives in changing his style and direction, I, for one, hope he keeps it up. Now that the millennium is upon us, may it rain comic novels all around.' JANE SMILEY, *New York Times Book Review*

'Thomas Chippering may be a neurotic lunatic, but he is our kind of neurotic lunatic. That he both unsettles and appeals to us is an indication of O'Brien's skill. The novel also succeeds with the winning combination of O'Brien's well-tuned, understated style and the hyperactive plot and parade of colourfully deranged characters.' JONATHAN FASMAN, *Times Literary Supplement*

'A brilliant, touching and wickedly funny love story . . . its humour is some of the blackest ever written. Chippering is an extraordinary creation, and his narration of the story is what makes *Tomcat in Love* so hypnotically readable. This is a complex and compassionate comedy . . . the product of a prodigiously talented writer at the top of his game . . . he deserves an ovation for an unqualified success.' ANDREW VINE, *Yorkshire Post*

GOING AFTER CACCIATO

'His irony recalls that of Stendhal, his landscapes have the breadth and scope of Tolstoy's, and the essential American wonder and innocence of his vision deserves to stand beside that of Stephen Crane.'   National Book Award citation

'To call *Going After Cacciato* a novel about war is like calling *Moby Dick* a novel about whales. Tim O'Brien's writing is crisp, authentic and grimly ironic ... a major achievement.'
New York Times Book Review

'*Going After Cacciato* is not only the best novel about the Vietnam War, but among the finest works of fiction in contemporary American literature.'   PHILIP CAPUTO, *Esquire*

NORTHERN LIGHTS

'Written in beautifully spare language, a powerful adventure story set in the frozen wastes of Minnesota.'   *Daily Telegraph*

'Here is a crafted work of serious intent with themes at least as old as the Old Testament – they still work.'
New York Times Book Review

IF I DIE IN A COMBAT ZONE

'*If I Die in a Combat Zone* is a powerful book. Its effect is as devastating as if its author had been killed. But he survived. So through such writing may the American language.'
The Times

'No one has written about the Vietnam War with the elegance of Tim O'Brien. *If I Die in a Combat Zone* may be the single greatest piece of work to come out of Vietnam, a work on a level with *The Naked and the Dead* and *From Here to Eternity*.'
Washington Star

By Tim O'Brien

TIM O'BRIEN

Tomcat in Love

Flamingo
An Imprint of HarperCollinsPublishers

This is a work of the imagination, and the standard conventions are in force. These characters are wholly invented; these events are wholly fictitious.

Portions of this book appeared in *The New Yorker*

Grateful acknowledgment for:
'Camelot', by Alan Jay Lerner and Frederick Lowe,
© 1960, 1961 (copyrights renewed) Alan Jay Lerner and Frederick Lowe.
All rights administered by Chappell & Co. All rights reserved. Used by permission.
WARNER BROS. PUBLICATIONS U.S. INC., Miami, FL 33014.

Excerpt from 'One Art' from *The Complete Poems 1972–1979* by Elizabeth Bishop.
Copyright © 1979, 1983 by Alice Helen Methfessel.
Reprinted by permission of Farrar, Strauss & Giroux, Inc.

Flamingo
An Imprint of HarperCollins*Publishers*
77–85 Fulham Palace Road,
Hammersmith, London w6 8jb

www.**fire**and**water**.com

Published by Flamingo 2000
9 8 7 6 5 4 3 2 1

First published in Great Britain by Flamingo 1999

First published in the USA by Broadway Books 1998

Copyright © Tim O'Brien 1998

The Author asserts the moral right to
be identified as the author of this work

Author photograph by Jerry Bauer

isbn 0 00 655152 1

Typeset in Janson by Palimpsest Book Production Limited,
Polmont, Stirlingshire
Printed and bound in Great Britain by Clays Ltd, St Ives plc

– Even losing you (the joking voice, a gesture
I love) I shan't have lied. It's evident
the art of losing's not too hard to master
though it may look like (*Write* it!) like disaster.

Elizabeth Bishop

Contents

Tomcat in Love

1

Faith

I begin with the ridiculous, in June 1952, middle-century Minnesota, on that silvery-hot morning when Herbie Zylstra and I nailed two plywood boards together and called it an airplane. 'What we need,' said Herbie, 'is an engine.'

The word *engine* – its meanings beyond mere meaning – began to open up for me. I went into the house and found my father.

'I'll need an engine,' I told him.

'Engine?' he said.

'For an airplane.'

My father thought about it. 'Makes sense,' he said. 'One airplane engine, coming up.'

'When?'

'Soon enough,' said my father. 'Pronto.'

Was this a promise?

Was this duplicity?

Herbie and I waited all summer. We painted our airplane green. We cleared a runway in the backyard, moving the big white birdbath, digging up two of my mother's rhododendrons. We eyed our plane. 'What if it crashes?' I said.

Herbie made a scoffing noise. '*Parachutes*,' he said. (A couple of his front teeth were missing, which caused bubbles to form when he laughed at me.) 'Anyway, don't be stupid. We'll drop bombs on people. Bomb my house.'

So we filled mason jars with gasoline. Through July and August, in the soft, grave density of that prairie summer, we practiced our bombing runs, getting the feel of it, the lift, the swoop. Herbie was eight, I was seven. We made the sounds an engine would make. In our heads, where the world was, we bombed Mrs Catchitt's garage, the church across the street, Jerry Powell and his cousin Ernest and other people we feared or despised. Mostly, though, we bombed Herbie's house. The place was huge and bright yellow, a half block away, full of cousins and uncles and nuns and priests and leathery old grandmothers. A scary house, I thought, and Herbie thought so too. He liked yelling '*Die!*' as he banked into a dive; he said things about his mother, about black bones and fires in the attic.

For me, the bombing was fine. It seemed useful, vaguely productive, but the best part was flight itself, or the anticipation of flight, and over those summer days the word *engine* did important engine work in my thoughts. I did not envision machinery. I envisioned thrust: a force pressing upward and outward, even beyond. This notion had its objective component – properties both firm and man-made – but on a higher level, as pure idea, the engine that my father would be bringing home did not operate on mechanical principles. I knew nothing, for example, of propellers and gears and such. My engine would somehow *contain* flight. Like a box, I imagined, which when opened would release the magical qualities of levitation into the plywood boards of my airplane.

At night, in bed, I would find myself murmuring that powerful, empowering word: *engine*. I loved its sound. I loved everything it meant, everything it did not mean but should.

*   *   *

2

Summer ended, autumn came, and what my father finally brought home was a turtle. A mud turtle – small and black. My father had a proud look on his face as he stooped down and placed it on our backyard runway.

'That thing's a *turtle*,' Herbie said.

'Toby,' said my father. 'I think his name is Toby.'

'Well, God, I know that,' Herbie said. 'Every turtle on earth, they're *all* named Toby. It's still just a stupid old turtle.'

'A pretty good one,' my father said.

Herbie's face seemed to curdle in the bright sunlight. He scooped up the turtle, searched for its head, then dropped it upside down on the runway. I remember backing away, feeling a web of tensions far too complex for me: disappointment, partly, and confusion, but mostly I was afraid for my father. Herbie could be vicious at times, very loud, very demonstrative, easily unnerved by the wrongs of the world.

'Oh, boy,' he muttered.

He took a few slow steps, then ran.

If anything was said between my father and me, I cannot remember it. What I do remember – vividly – is feeling stupid. The words *turtle* and *engine* seemed to do loops in the backyard sunlight. There had to be some sort of meaningful connection, a turtleness inside engineness, or the other way around, but right then I could not locate the logic.

The backyard was silent. I remember my father's pale-blue eyes, how he gazed at something just beyond the birdbath. 'Well,' he said, then stopped and carefully folded his hands. 'Sorry, Tommy. Best I could do.' Then he turned and went into the house.

Afterward, I stood studying Toby. I poked at him with my foot. 'Hey, you,' I murmured, but it was a very stupid turtle, more object than animal. It showed no interest in my foot, or my voice, or anything else in the physical universe. Turtle, I kept thinking, and even now, in my middle age, those twin syllables still claw at me. The quick *t*'s on my tongue: *turtle*. Even after four decades I cannot encounter that word without a gate creaking open inside me. Turtle for the world – turtle for you – will never be turtle for me.

Nor this: *corn*.

Nor this: *Pontiac*.

Have you ever loved a man, then lost him, then learned he lives on Fiji with a new lover? Is Fiji still Fiji? Coconuts and palm trees?

At sixteen, in a windy autumn cornfield, I made first love on the hood of my father's green Pontiac. I remember the steel against my skin. I remember darkness, too, and a sharp wind, and rustlings in the corn. I was terrified. *Pontiac* means: Will this improve? And that Indian-head ornament on the hood – did the bastard bite my feet? Did I hear a chuckle? Peeping Tom, ogler, eyewitness, sly critic: the word *Indian* embraces all of these meanings and many more.

The world shrieks and sinks talons into our hearts. This we call memory.

In the backyard that afternoon, alone with Toby, I felt a helplessness that went beyond engines or turtles. It had to do with treachery. Even back then, in a dark, preknowledge way, I understood that language was involved, its frailties and mutabilities, its potential for betrayal. My airplane, after all, was not an airplane. No engine on earth would make it fly. And over the years I have come to realize that Herbie and I had willfully deceived ourselves, renaming things, reinventing the world, which was both pretending and a kind of lying.

But there were also the words my father had used: 'One airplane engine, coming up.'

His intent, I know, was benign. To encourage. To engage. And yet for me, as a seven-year-old, the language he had chosen took on the power of a binding commitment, one I

4

kept pestering him to honor, and through July and August, as summer heated up, my father must have felt trapped by a promise he neither had intended nor could possibly keep.

'Right. I'm working on it,' he'd say, whenever I brought up the subject.

He'd say, 'Pretty soon, partner.' He'd say, 'No sweat.' He'd say, 'Be patient. I've placed the order.'

But a turtle?

Why not broccoli?

The next morning was a Sunday. Maybe an hour after Mass, Herbie walked into my backyard.

'Your dad's a liar,' he said.

'Yeah, sort of,' I told him, 'but not usually,' then I tried to mount a defense. I talked about Toby, what a fine turtle he was, how I could get him to stick his head out from under the shell by putting a pan of water in front of him. I talked about using Toby as a bomb. 'It'll be neat,' I said. 'Drop him on the mailman.'

Herbie looked at me hard. 'Except your dad's still a liar, Tommy. They all are. They just lie and lie. They can't even help it. That's what fathers are *for*. Nothing else. They lie.'

I stood silent. Arguments, I knew, were useless. All I could do was wait – which I did – and after a few moments Herbie strolled over to our plywood airplane, picked it up, and carried it across the lawn. He placed it tail down against the garage.

'It's not a plane anymore,' he said. 'It's a cross.'

'Cross how?' I asked.

'Like in the Bible,' said Herbie. 'A *cross*. Let's go get my sister. Lorna Sue – we'll nail her to it.'

'Okay,' I said.

We walked the half block to Herbie's yellow house. The place was enormous, especially to a child, and it took a long while to find Lorna Sue, who sat playing with her dollhouse up in the attic. She was seven years old. Very pretty: black hair, summer-brown skin. I liked her a lot, and Lorna Sue liked me too, which was obvious, and a decade later we would find ourselves in a cornfield along Highway 16, completely in love, very cold, testing our courage on the hood of my father's Pontiac.

The world sometimes precedes itself. In the attic that day – September 1952 – I am almost certain that both Lorna Sue and I understood deep in our bones that significant events were now in motion.

I remember the smell of that attic, so dank and fungal, so dangerous. I remember Herbie gazing down at his sister.

'We need you,' he said.

'What for?' said Lorna Sue.

'It'll be neat. Tommy and me, we've got this cross – we'll nail you to it.'

Lorna Sue smiled at me.

This was love. Seven years old. Even then.

'Well,' she said, 'I *guess* so.'

And so the three of us trooped back to my house. Impatiently, under Herbie's supervision, Lorna Sue stood against the cross and spread out her slender brown arms. 'This better be fun,' she said, 'because I'm pretty busy.' Herbie and I went into the garage, where we found a hammer and two rusty nails. I remember a frothiness in my stomach; I felt queasy, yes, but also curious. As we walked back toward Lorna Sue, I lagged behind a little.

'You think this'll hurt?' I asked.

Herbie shrugged. His eyes had a hard, fixed, enthusiastic shine, like the eyes of certain trained assassins I would later encounter in the mountains of Vietnam. Herbie gripped the hammer in his right hand. Quietly, like a doctor, he told Lorna Sue to close her eyes, which she did, and at that point, thank God, my mother came out the back door with a basket of damp laundry. The basket was blue, the laundry mostly white.

'What's this?' my mother asked.

'Sunday school,' Lorna Sue said. 'I get to be Jesus.'

At dinner that evening, the hammer and nails lay at the center of the kitchen table. It was a long and very difficult meal. Over and over, I had to explain how the whole thing had been a game, just for fun, not even a real cross. My father studied me as if I'd come down with polio.

'The hammer,' he said. 'You see the hammer?'

'Sure.'

'Is it real?'

'Naturally,' I said.

He nodded. 'And the nails? Real or unreal?'

'Real,' I told him, 'but not like . . . I mean, is Toby a real *engine*?'

My father was unhappy with that. I remember how his jaw firmed up, how he leaned back, glanced over at my mother, then segued into a vigorous lecture about the difference between playing games and driving nails through people's hands. Even as a seven-year-old, I already knew the difference – it was obvious – but sitting there at the kitchen table, feeling wronged and defenseless, I could not find words to say the many things I wanted to say: that I was not a murderer, that events had unfolded like a story in a book, that I had been pulled along by awe and wonder, that I had never really believed in any of it, that I was almost positive that Herbie would not have hammered those nails through Lorna Sue's pretty brown hands.

These and other thoughts spun through my head. But all I could do was stare down at my plate and say, 'All right.'

'All right *what*?' my father said.

'You know. I won't nail anybody.'

'What about Herbie?'

'He won't either,' I said. 'I'm pretty sure.'

But he did. The left palm. Halfway through. Almost dead center.

Accuracy matters.

Herbie Zylstra was not a mean-spirited child. Nothing of the sort. Hyperactive, to be sure, and so impulsive he could sometimes make my stomach wobble, but I never felt physical fear in his presence. More like wariness – a butterfly sensation.

In a later decade, Herbie would have been a candidate for Ritalin or some similar drug, gallons of the stuff, a long rubber hose running from pharmacy to vein.

Accuracy, though.

September. A Saturday morning, two weeks after school opened. Around noon Herbie stopped by. 'I'll need the cross,' he said.

I was busy with Toby; I barely looked up.

Herbie muttered something and picked up the cross and carried it over to his house and set it up against a big elm tree on the front lawn. He found Lorna Sue. He told her to stay steady. He squinted and pursed his lips and put the point of the nail against the center of her left palm and took aim and cocked his wrist. He did not have the strength, I suppose, to drive the nail all the way through, or maybe it wasn't a solid strike, or maybe at the last instant Herbie held back out of some secret virtue, pity or humility.

I was not there to witness it. All I can attest to is the sound of sirens.

Voices too, I think. And maybe a scream. But maybe not.

Later in the day my mother called me inside and told me about it. Immediately, I ran for my bedroom. I slammed the door, crawled under the bed, made fists, yelled something, banged the floor. What I was feeling, oddly enough, was a kind of rage, a cheated sensation: denied access to something rare and mysterious and important. I should have *been* there – an eyewitness to the nailing. I deserved it. Even now, half a lifetime later, my absence that day remains a source of regret and bitterness. I had earned the right. It was my plywood. My green paint. Other reasons too: because at age sixteen I would make first love with Lorna Sue Zylstra on the hood of my father's Pontiac, and because ten years later we would be married, and because twenty-some years after that Lorna Sue would discover romance with another man, and betray me, and move to Tampa.

After the nailing, I did not see Herbie for almost a year.

He was dispatched to a Jesuit boys' school up in the Twin Cities – a 'hospital school,' my mother called it, which was probably close to accurate – and when he returned the following summer, in early June, things were different. I had new friends; Herbie had a new personality. He was a loner now. Silent and self-absorbed. The transformation was remarkable, edging up on radical, and if I were a believer in the Pauline epiphanies, or in divine intervention, which I most certainly am not, I might be tempted to argue that Herbie had been visited by some higher power during his stay with the good Catholics of Minneapolis.

Contrition, so rare in any of us, seemed to have struck Herbie Zylstra as a nine-year-old.

This is not to say that the reformation was absolute. He still had a temper; he could go hard and hostile. In fact, from all I could tell, the new Herbie was wound tighter than ever. The sweetness was gone. The naive, impish exuberance had been sucked out of him, recklessness replaced by qualities much more stern – something zealous and rigid, a severity of spirit that seemed a little eerie.

For the next eight years, until he graduated from high school, Herbie and I went our separate ways. Not unfriendly but never friendly either. He kept to himself, earned respectable grades, played a skillful forward on a basketball team that twice advanced to the state semifinals. In a cautious way, most people admired him, especially girls. He moved well. He was tall and lean, with gray eyes and wavy brown hair, but beneath this handsome exterior was a quiet, smoldering aloofness. There were times, I thought, when he gave off a dangerous glow, like fire in a jar, rectitude squeezed inside muscle – a physicality I envied.

On the surface, at least, things were neutral between us. I lived in one world, Herbie in another, and our childhood was never a topic of discussion. There were no topics at all. In school, or at church, his eyes swept across me as if I were air; he avoided me at parties, rarely even nodded when we happened to cross paths on a sidewalk. In a way, it seemed, my old pal had willfully erased me from memory, along with our joint history, and I have since come to suspect that this was a means of wiping away his own shame, obliterating guilt by obliterating me. I was invisible to him: not even a ghost.

All this changed when I began dating Lorna Sue in the middle of my junior year.

To put it simply, Herbie did not approve.

In the school hallways, in classes and the cafeteria, I could feel him glaring at me like an Old Testament judge, wary and suspicious, alert to sin, his bright gray eyes locking onto me with what can only be called loathing. When I complained to Lorna Sue, she laughed and told me to forget it. 'That's Herbie,' she said. 'That's not us.'

I nodded. 'Maybe. But it feels strange.'

'Just ignore him,' she said. 'Pretend you don't notice. It'll drive him crazy.'

'I don't *want* him crazy.'

Lorna Sue shrugged and went silent. 'All right, I'll talk to him,' she finally said, then hesitated. 'Except I don't think . . . I mean, I don't think you'll *ever* please him. Nobody can. That's how he is.'

'How?'

'You know. The big brother.'

'Okay, sure,' I said, 'but there's something else too. It feels like – I don't know – almost like he *owns* you.'

'Well, he doesn't,' said Lorna Sue, but again there was a wrinkle in her voice, as if she was afraid of something. She held up the palm of her left hand, displaying a small, star-shaped, purply-red scar. 'The opposite, Tommy. I own *him*.'

I nodded and said, 'Right.'

Lorna Sue said, 'Right.'

But what she meant, exactly, was a puzzle to me, and always will be.

From that point onward, well into adulthood, Herbie seemed possessed by a sullen, brooding jealousy, as if I had stolen his sister from him or somehow defiled her. Even when Lorna Sue and I were alone – in a movie theater, in my father's Pontiac – I could sense his shadow nearby: a drop in the temperature, a pressure against my spine.

It's a mystery. Four decades have passed, so much pain, so much horror, yet I cannot begin to understand the causes. All I know is this: I am alone now.

Herbie killed my marriage.

He murdered love. Intentionally. Systematically. He found the weakness in me, and he showed it to Lorna Sue.

Why me? I cannot help but wonder. I deserved better. By any estimate I am a man of some majesty, tall and eye-catching, no paunch, no deficits worth the spill of ink. I am a full professor of linguistics, the author of twenty-one highly regarded monographs; I am beloved by my students,* esteemed by my academic confederates. And, yes – beyond everything – I adored Lorna Sue with every fiery corpuscle of my being.

So why?

In my bleakest moods, when black gets blackest, I think of it as raw perversion: Herbie coveted his own sister. Which is a fact. The stone truth. He was in love with her. More generously, I will sometimes concede that it was not sexual love, or not entirely, and that Herbie was driven by the obsessions of a penitent, a torturer turned savior. Partly, too, I am quite certain that Herbie secretly associated me with his own guilt. I was present at the beginning. My backyard, my plywood, my green paint. And it was my father who had failed to deliver an airplane engine, who had instead brought home a turtle named Toby.

Toby: it's an obscenity to me.

I lie awake nights, mulling things over.

Surely the Catholics were involved.

That's another one – *Catholic*. I fall sick driving past churches. I see a priest, I think divorce.

Catholic. I am full of hatred.

And this too: *yellow*. Even color gets colored. Lemon drops taste like betrayal.

'Die!' Herbie used to yell, then he'd bank into an imaginary bombing run toward his big yellow house.

That house: big and spooky and broken down, three stories plus an attic, and even as a kid I knew things were not happy inside. Too much noise, too much clutter. Its sickly yellowness. The unmowed lawn. The screen windows patched up with newspapers and packing tape. In the hallways and living areas

---

* My celebrated biweekly seminars, I might add, are almost always booked to the limit with attentive, worshipful, ardent young lollipops eager to widen their horizons.

I detected the smell of mildew, a corrupt, musty stink, like the tombs of some abandoned old necropolis. On the walls – in virtually every room – were framed photographs of Herbie and Lorna Sue. In most cases they stood side by side, brother and sister, but in poses that suggested something vaguely beatific, almost saintly, like a pair of child martyrs: fingers interlocked, gazes elevated.

This house – this mausoleum – was *their* place, foreign to me, and sinister.

I hated it. I hated its *theirness*.

Let me offer an instance. A night back in high school, junior year: Lorna Sue and I had parked in her driveway after a late movie. (Radio music, a gauzy half-moon, my father's green Pontiac.) Lorna Sue had pulled off her shirt and bra, always an astonishing moment, and I was lost in all the plenitude. Breasts were new to me – I had not yet mastered my enthusiasm – and some time passed before I realized that Lorna Sue was crying. Not loud. A whimper. After a moment she seemed to shudder, then she pushed me away, hunched forward, and slipped her shirt on. I remember reaching out, half apologizing, but Lorna Sue twisted sideways in her seat. 'Stop,' she said. 'Just please stop.'

'I didn't mean –'

'They're *watching*.'

Lorna Sue motioned at the house. A large bay window overlooked the driveway, perhaps ten feet away, and in the dark I could make out five or six white faces pressed up against the glass. The features were blurry. Like clouded moons: hazy, round, softly lighted. There was a noise, I remember, which must have been laughter, and then the faces began vanishing one by one, each flickering out in turn, like the candles on an altar being extinguished by some ghostly celebrant. After a few seconds only a single face remained, which even in the dark I knew had to be Herbie's.

I almost nodded.

Unnatural, to say the least, and for whatever reasons it occurred to me that this entire family was in love with Lorna Sue, or obsessed by her, or caught up in some perverse form of idolatry. Those faces at the window. The scar on her hand. The evidence of intuition.

In the driveway that night, Lorna Sue sat motionless for a time, cradling her chest.

'That house,' she whispered. 'God, that *house*.'

The next day Herbie approached me after school.

'Hey, Don Juan,' he said.

He stared at me for longer than was comfortable, ice in his eyes, then he opened up a brown paper bag, reached inside, and passed over to me the Indian-head ornament off my father's Pontiac. A cryptic moment. Frightening too. Herbie's eyes – so full of love, so full of hatred.

And years later, when Lorna Sue announced her plans for divorce, she would give me the same cold stare, as if I were an infidel, as if there were things I could never understand.

We were married for two fascinating decades. She divorced me eight months ago.

Why?

The answer is convoluted. (Keep in mind your own tangled history, how your husband flew off to Fiji in the company of a redhead barely half his age. Confusing, yes? Loose ends? Numerous unknowns?) In my own case, I had hidden certain mildly incriminating documents beneath the mattress of our bed – Lorna Sue's and mine. These materials were perfectly safe, I reasoned, for in our twenty years together I had yet to see Lorna Sue turn that mattress, or replace the box springs, or otherwise investigate the regions of our love.

Mattress. The word chills me.

How Herbie came to discover my private papers is difficult to imagine, and I lie sleepless at night, violated, envisioning his stealth.

They're *watching*, she had said. *He's* watching.

The documents themselves were unimportant. Evidence of minor deceit. What matters is how Herbie came to discover such intimate artifacts from my life. If he knew about the documents – their whereabouts, their implications – what else had he invaded? What else did he know?

And by what means?

Did he steal a key? Was he snooping even last winter, while Lorna Sue and I vacationed in Tampa? Outside Tampa, to be literal, at a resort called Seaside Dunes, where we played minigolf and browned ourselves in the sunlight, and where one afternoon Lorna Sue befriended a certain hairy gentleman whose name I have vowed never again to utter. (It is a promise, however, often broken in my thoughts. Kersten. Whom she calls Kerr. Whom I call shit. Preposterous name, oily personality.) At what precise instant, I wonder, did Lorna Sue fall in love with him? And out of love with me? When the gentleman sucked in his belly? When he approached our patch of sand without invitation? When he removed his shirt and puffed out his chest and introduced himself with those two vile syllables that rhyme with Thurston?

I doubt it. Not then. The arms of conscious liaison probably opened later, several months after we had returned, on that humid evening when Herbie retrieved my secrets from beneath the mattress.

I wonder, too, how long Herbie stalked me. Did he steal into my bedroom? Did he open cupboards, sniff my laundry, shake out books, finally take notice of our king-size mattress?

Who knows?

In truth, I must admit, I had been pushing my luck for many weeks, terrified of discovery, aware of the consequences.

No doubt I should have relocated my incriminating cache. Or destroyed it. And yet, as so often happens, ordinary life conspired against common sense. (I am a teacher. I have stress syndrome. I married a woman with a hole in her hand.) The point is this: daily flux presents its own ample store of worries, even without betrayal, and in this instance I postponed an act of simple sanity and self-preservation. I delayed. I forgot.

'There,' Herbie said.

The documents lay on our brass bed like a losing hand of poker.

'There,' said Herbie, 'is your angel.'

My transgression? A misdemeanor by any standard. After our return from Tampa, Lorna Sue had withdrawn inside herself, going quiet and preoccupied, and in a very real sense, I believe, she was still sitting on that sunny beach, still chatting with her handsome new friend, still giggling at the hairy bastard's offensive little jokes. (I was *there*, for God's sake. I feigned sleep. I listened to the frothy sounds of surf and seduction.) In any case, she had detached herself from me, and I felt her absence as surely as I had once felt her thereness, her everness, her absolute and indestructible love. (If a love dies, how can such love be love? By what linguistic contrivance?) And so I began to sound the vastness of Lorna Sue's absence, or the stirrings of discontent, or whatever else it is that a man feels as his wife contemplates a furry, pompous, pre-embalmed, ridiculously well-tanned tycoon.

The signs were everywhere. She was not merely absentminded; she was absent. She was seeking an excuse, I believe, and Herbie promptly provided her with a very tidy one.

On that humid evening he rang the doorbell. He had the nerve to shake my hand. He kissed Lorna Sue. He marched directly to our bedroom, to our brass bed, and without emotion he raided my life. He dropped the documents on our handmade checkered quilt. 'Angel,' he said.

As mentioned, my crime was minor. Certainly pardonable by love.

The documents were these: fourteen uncashed checks made out to one Dr Ralph Constantine. A psychiatrist. A phony psychiatrist, actually, whose name I had invented. What was I trying to prove? My equilibrium, no doubt. That it was unfair of her to suggest that our troubles were caused by my own jealousy and paranoia. And so I had concocted a counterfeit psychiatrist to solve a counterfeit problem – a sacred lie to save a marriage.

Not so horrible, do you think?

'Angel – your deceiving angel,' said Herbie, who then shrugged and strolled out of our bedroom and left me with a future no longer worth pursuing. (Do not forget: Herbie worshiped Lorna Sue. Adoration in the biblical sense. He wanted his sister back.)

For months, especially after our return from Tampa, Lorna Sue had been insisting that I seek help. *Her* phrase: 'Seek help.' And so like my father – like all of us at one time or another – I had issued a promise that could not be honored. I did not need a counselor. I wasn't blind, I wasn't sick. Nor was I crazy. Granted, I had taken to fervent noontide praying; I had begun talking in colors – that's how Lorna Sue described it – at least in my sleep. But she had *left* me. She had absented herself, drifting away, dreaming of a tycoon, and none of this was the product of my imagination. Yet I loved her, so much, and still do, and always will, because that *is* love, the unending alwaysness, and I therefore wished only to please her, to reduce her absence, to pretend I was under the care of a fictitious shrink by the name of Dr Ralph Constantine. All this in the hope of winning back the love I had felt dissolving on a beach outside Tampa.

*   *   *

A few weeks after the divorce I paid a covert visit to Lorna Sue and her new husband. Watched from a distance as she squeezed the gentleman's arm outside a real-estate office in downtown Tampa. He's a high roller. Lorna Sue seems proud of that. She's well dressed. Expensive jewelry, tanned skin, very beautiful. Herbie lives nearby. Watchful. I give the marriage two years.

One last example. The word *mice*. Plural and ridiculous.

When I was twelve, Lorna Sue got angry at me for kissing a girl named Faith Graffenteen. 'I didn't mean to,' I told her. 'It was mostly an accident.'

'You kissed her *face*,' Lorna Sue said. 'You kissed her snotty nose.'

'I didn't mean that either,' I said, then waited a moment. 'So did Faith like it?'

'God, no,' said Lorna Sue. 'She puked mice. And don't ever try it with me, Tommy.'

'Who wants to?' I said.

'You.'

We were walking down North Fourth Street. Past Mrs Catchitt's house. Past St Paul's Catholic Church. It was Christmas break, no school for two weeks.

'It just makes me sick,' said Lorna Sue. 'I mean, you kissed her snot. That's what Faith said – you almost sucked out all her snot. And not just Faith either. You kissed Beth. You kissed Linda and Corinne and Ruthie and Pam and I don't even *know* who else. And you wrote their names down. I found your stupid list.' She handed me a scrap of notebook paper. 'It's pretty sickening. You're not even a teenager yet.'

I tucked the list in my pocket. Lorna Sue had her brother's temper, her brother's sensitivity to injustice. We kept walking.

'So why?' she finally said.

'Faith *made* me,' I said. 'Besides, I'll bet you kissed almost everybody. That time with Dennis in the warming house. That time with Jerry Powell.'

'They love me,' Lorna Sue said.

'Not Dennis. Dennis doesn't.'

Lorna Sue frowned. 'You want to kiss me?'

'No.'

'Well, don't even dare. Herbie'll kill you.'

We stopped in front of her house. Lorna Sue slipped her bad hand into a parka pocket.

'Do you love Faith?'

'Probably,' I said. 'She still forced me.'

'For how long?'

'Just the regular time. Barely a second – it wasn't even real kissing.'

'I don't *mean* that,' Lorna Sue said. 'I mean, how long will you *love* her?'

'I don't know. For a while.'

'But God, she puked *mice*! Rabbit guts and mice.'

'All right,' I said. 'I'll stop.'

'Do you love me?'

'I guess so.'

Lorna Sue laughed. 'Herbie'll kill you.'

Does language contain history the way plywood contains flight? Are we bruised each day of our lives by syllabic collisions, our spirits slashed by combinations of vowel and consonant? At a cocktail party, say, or at a ball game, or at our daughter's wedding, would you feel Death slide between your ribs if someone were to utter the name of your exhusband? Can a color cause bad dreams? Can a cornfield make you cry? Do we irradiate language by the lives we lead? *Angel, engine, cross, Indian, plywood, Pontiac, mattress, rabbit guts and mice* . . . Is your ex still in the tropics? Is he happy? Should you have been there to stop him, or to help him, or to bear witness as he made his way to a new lover and a new life? If the opportunity arose, would revenge be an option? Against whom – a sick family, a jealous brother? Revenge how? Hammer and nails? A pithy sentence, a squeal of outrage? Would it occur to you that your very vows of troth, your wedding pledge, had been a betrayal from the start, that you had been doomed by a crazy lie, that you were never meant to have and to hold?

Would a trip to Florida be in order? Maybe next month? Maybe the month after?

Can a word stop your heart as surely as arsenic?

Turtle. Tampa.

2

Eighteen

Numbers, like words, can become ghosts in our lives. Lorna Sue left me on a Tuesday afternoon, the ninth day of July. She said, 'I'm moving to a new city.'

She said, 'There's someone else – he's innocent.'

She said, 'I don't want a scene, Tom.'

She said, 'Don't be an eighteen-year-old.'

I took off my jacket and tie and shirt and pants. I stood before her in my underwear. I did not cry, because this horror was so far beyond what crying is for, but I took her by the shoulders and led her to our brass bed and pushed myself up against her, as if sex could save me, knowing it could not, and I begged and made promises and said things about the purity and perfection of my love, but Lorna Sue would only stare at me with cold, crocodile eyes and say, 'Don't be an eighteen-year-old.' I told her she was sacred to me. I told her she was holy. I told her I had loved her before either of us had been born. I told her she was my everything – my sunlight, my heartbeat. But it meant nothing to her. She stared her flat, reptile stare and said, 'Don't be an eighteen-year-old' – which meant *what*? – and then she pushed to her feet and went to the door and picked up a blue suitcase and opened the door and left me forever and closed the door behind her – not softly, not loudly, just closed it. For a while I thought about following her down the sidewalk in my underwear, except such behavior was the province of eighteen-year-olds. I was not eighteen. I was ancient. I was a thousand years old. I was aging at the speed of light. I was a creaking, ruined, desiccated, hollow old man in his underwear, but I was no goddamn eighteen-year-old and never would be ever again.

3

Tulip

It is early May, let us imagine, and one glorious morning you stop to admire a red tulip along some garden path. You are conscious of the sky above, the earth below. And so for a few moments, perhaps, you pause to think thoughts about the circle of life, how growth goes to decay and then back again to growth. You recall other May mornings. (Your wedding day. How happy you were.) You review your past, envision your future. You think: Ah, such a tulip!

And me?

My stomach drops.

I glance over my shoulder.

I scan the shrubbery, listen for footsteps, peer up the garden path to where it curls away into the shadows of a forbidding green forest.

Tulips do it to me.

Even the word *tulip*.

Oh, yes, and the word *goof*. And the words *spider* and *wildfire* and *death chant*.

All of us, no doubt, have our demons. One way or another we are pursued by the ghosts of our own history, our lost loves, our blunders, our broken promises and grieving wives and missing children. And a single tulip is enough to remind us. In your own case, remember, it is a Hilton hotel along that busy freeway you take to work each morning. You try not to look. But you do. For it was there, in room 622, that your ex-husband spent his Tuesday afternoons with a tall, willowy redhead half his age. (You found those matches in his pocket.) And now he lives in Fiji, and you do not, and that Hilton will always be there in your rearview mirror.

So please, take this at face value: I am being chased.

I lock my doors at night. I avoid dark entryways, keep my eyes peeled even on bustling city streets.

There is much to be recorded here, much to be weighed and balanced, but in due course I shall elaborate. For the present, let it be understood that I have been ruthlessly pursued for many decades now, partly by a Tulip, partly by the word *tulip*. And do not for an instant try to tell me that words are not lethal.*

Tulip. Tampa. Tycoon.

---

* Exhibit A – a firing squad. The words: 'Ready! Aim!' Who among us, if beneath the black hood, would not celebrate a sudden case of laryngitis? Exhibit B – I have *been* there. I know a thing or two about firing squads. (Again, more to follow.) Exhibit C – Hilton.

4

Roses

In summary, then, my circumstances were these. Something over forty-nine years of age. Recently divorced. Pursued. Prone to late-night weeping. Betrayed not once but threefold: by the girl of my dreams, by her Pilate of a brother, and by a Tampa real-estate tycoon whose name I have vowed never again to utter.

The popular wisdom dictates that in such situations we must 'go forward' at all costs. (At one point or another, we have all chuckled aloud at the pertinent advisories in the pages of *Cosmopolitan*.) Move or die – so say the psychiatric sages. Learn to cope. Face reality. Stay busy. Exercise. Take up hobbies. Find a new partner.

For some, no doubt, this progressive counsel proves rock solid. Not so in my case. In the weeks following my divorce, I did in fact make a halfhearted effort at 'coming to terms' with 'new realities.' I packed up Lorna Sue's belongings, purchased an Exercycle, attended faithfully to my duties as occupant of the Rolvaag Chair in Modern American Lexicology at the University of Minnesota. And while it was traumatic, I also forced myself to spend considerable after-hours time in the company of several droll, well-sculpted enrollees in my seminar on the homographs of erotic slang.

None of this had the slightest curative effect. I cried like a baby in the arms of Sarah and Signe and the tiny, redheaded Rhonda; I gained six unfashionable pounds; I drank myself to sleep. Worse yet, on a professional level, my scholarship came to a complete and terrifying halt. My classroom lectures, once so justly famous, began to meander like the barroom soliloquies of some dull, downstate sophomore. The old academic pleasures no longer beckoned. (During office hours, even as a chorus line of leggy young coeds awaited my attention in the hallway, I sometimes locked the door and lay immobile on the floor, driveshaft idle, my magnificent old sex engine backfiring on grief.)

Modern methods, in short, had failed abysmally. Antiquity beckoned.

Thus revenge.

The word comes to us from the Latin, *vindicare*, to vindicate, and in its most primitive etymology is without pejorative shading of any sort. To vindicate is to triumph over suspicion or accusation or presumed guilt, and for the ancients, such triumph did not exclude the ferocious punishment of false accusers. (Hence *vindicta*. Hence vengeance.) By this classical formulation, there was nothing ignoble about seeking satisfaction through punitive means. To be 'vindictive' implied qualities both honorable and heroic, a fineness of spirit, a moral readiness to strike back against falsity and betrayal.

Sadly, of course, all this is now history. Paladin is passé. Chivalry is a belly laugh.

My resolve, therefore, was to resuscitate the old virtues.

Enough coping, I decided.

Time now to punish.

On three successive Thursdays, immediately after my final class of the week, I flew to Tampa with the purpose of scouting out the terrain. These were costly excursions, to be sure, not to mention excruciatingly lonely, but in no time at all I had acquired a working knowledge of the environs.

Tampa itself brought to mind a great pastel jellyfish beached up along the sea, its flesh gnawed away by salt and sunlight, the remains loosely bound together by a skeleton of bridges and causeways and hotels and shopping malls and multilane freeways. The dominant fact was sunshine. The dominant color was turquoise. All very splendid, no doubt, but as a Minnesotan, a son of Swedes, I found the subtropical air far less than bracing, the tempo sluggish, the smells musty and flower-sweet. (I suffer from hay fever. I cannot tolerate excessive vegetation.)

Tampa: languid, lazy, listless. Nice place to visit, et cetera.

Yet it was here, in the land of Buccaneers, that my unfaithful Penelope and her two salacious suitors somehow managed to survive. In marital partnership with her tycoon, Lorna Sue was cohabitant of a huge, flagrantly ornate mock-Tudor dwelling in the southeastern suburbs of the city; Herbie lived in a handsome little bungalow a half block away. (Cozy arrangement. Wholly predictable.) Under a hot Tampa sun, roasted by sorrow, I spent those long, fuzzy days sitting in a rental car with a notebook and a pair of binoculars. I fumed. I drank and talked to myself. On one painful occasion, for an entire afternoon, I looked on as Lorna Sue planted a bed of red roses along her front doorstep. Here, in tight denim shorts, was the woman I had loved beyond loving, the woman who had eventually traded me in like a battered old Chevrolet. I could scarcely keep the binoculars on her. Barefoot and content, humming to herself, she seemed so casual about putting down roots in the bleached Florida soil. Roses, for Christ sake!* There was not a hint of remorse in her posture, not a tremor of dissatisfaction, and I could only seethe at how quickly and thoroughly my revered

* *Rose*: a word that will forever turn my stomach sour with treachery.

Lorna Sue had adapted to life in the Sunshine State. Healthy and serene. Tanned skin. Hair held back by a checkered red bandanna. I will confess that it choked me up to study those untroubled brown eyes, those pouty lips that had once issued vows of eternal fidelity.

Roses!

I yearned for a hammer and nails.

Say what you will, but the Romans understood these matters. They coined the lingo.

I had no plan in mind, no agenda, but over the course of those three separate visits to Tampa, I trusted in fate and patiently collected intelligence from the safety of my rental car. I watched Herbie mow his lawn, watched the tycoon polish his snazzy blue Mercedes. In the late afternoons, almost without exception, I tailed Lorna Sue to a nearby supermarket – fresh vegetables, expensive cuts of meat. Cocktails were at six. Dinner was at seven sharp.

It was a stressful period, yes, but the notion of revenge kept me going on even the most trying occasions.

Such as:

– A Sunday picnic on the beach.

– Lorna Sue's silhouette against the drawn bedroom curtains.

– An afternoon yard sale featuring artifacts from our years of marriage. (My coin collection. Lorna Sue's homemade wedding gown.)

– Roses.

How, in such circumstances, could any sensitive human being avoid the occasional pinch of gloom? Call me crazy, if you wish, but do not forget your own double-crossing husband, that beloved Judas who disclaimed and repudiated you. Ask yourself this: Is not all human bleakness, all genuine tragedy, ultimately the product of a broken heart?

*   *   *

Late at night, in my ninth-floor hotel chamber, I began sketching out a strategy of reprisal. The least important of my targets was clearly the tycoon. Granted, I despised the usurping bastard, but in a way he seemed incidental to it all, someone to be dispensed with quickly and without fuss. The possibilities were infinite, and I soon found myself giggling as I jotted down some of the more intriguing methods – arson, food poisoning, transudative sailboats.

To look at me, perhaps, one might conclude that I am incapable of violence, rather meek and unassuming, yet little could be more distant from the truth. I am a war hero. I have experience with napalm. No doubt my students would raise their Neanderthal eyebrows at this, even cackle in disbelief, for I cultivate the facade of a distant, rather ineffectual man of letters. Effete, some would say. Imperious.* (Other possibilities: officious, prissy, insufferable.) At the same time, however, I must in good conscience point out that women find

* *Imperious*? What balderdash! Permit me, in this space, to offer an anecdote that goes far to explain how a man of my diaphanous abilities has come to be the recipient of such shameful invective. To wit: On seven separate occasions I had been a nominee for the university's Hubert H. Humphrey Prize for teaching excellence. Seven straight years I went down to defeat. (Payola. Collegial jealousy.) On the morning of my seventh Waterloo, I happened to encounter that year's prizewinner – a professor of biology whose insignificant Cornish name escapes me. This rendezvous occurred, it is crucial to note, in the faculty club men's room, where we stood side by side at our respective urinals. Eventually, job complete, I turned away without a word, scrubbed up, toweled off, and began to depart, at which point the smug, victory-flushed Wellington zipped up and approached me with an outstretched hand. (A damp, unsanitary hand. This a *biology* teacher) Did I refuse to shake? I did not. I bit the bullet, wrapped a paper towel around my fist, and vigorously pumped away. So then: Imperious? Or hygienic? I leave the verdict, as it were, in your hands.

me attractive beyond words. And who on earth could blame them? I stand an impressive six feet six; my weight rarely exceeds one hundred eighty pounds. In the eyes of many, I resemble a clean-shaven version of our sixteenth President, gangly and benign, yet this is mere camouflage for the man within – a recipient of the Silver Star for valor.

In short, I am hazardous. I can kill with words, or otherwise.

And so, yes, first the tycoon.

Late one afternoon, on my third trip to Tampa, I visited a small, exclusive boutique in the hotel, where with the assistance of a personable young salesgirl – Carla, by name – I browsed through a selection of women's undergarments. Quite graciously, I thought, and very boldly, the girl agreed to model several items at the rear of the store, and in the end, after numerous changes of costume, I settled upon a pair of fluorescent purple panties and matching bra.

'For your wife?' Carla inquired.

'For her husband,' said I.

The girl glanced up with interest. (Fascinating creature. Spiked orange hair. Leather dog collar, also spiked. Iron bracelets. Iron anklets. Snake tattoo just below the navel.)

'So you're divorced,' said this punkish, altogether immodest cupcake. 'Fucked over and all that?'

'Sadly so,' I replied.

The girl nodded, then frowned. 'So why the purple shit? I mean, like – you know – why all this expensive underwear for some cocksucker who stole your squeeze? Just yank his nuts off.'

I was enchanted.

And for the next few moments, with pleasure, I proceeded to outline my recent history, including (but not limited to) certain heartbreaking incidents of perfidy and faithlessness. The word *hairy* popped up. Also the following: *mattress, turtle, engine, tycoon, Pontiac*.

Carla studied me briefly and then sighed.

'Okay, I get the picture. Revenge. Sock it to the fuckers.' She stood there for a moment, grim-faced, plainly infatuated, still clad in phosphorescent violet. 'Look, man, if you're really serious, I got some pretty sick shit you might like.'

Swiftly, then, the girl escorted me into a dark, poorly ventilated back room. Instantly, I was reminded of Poe's tales of the macabre. Arranged on the shelves were numerous devices of torture, among which I spotted such items as handcuffs, chains, padlocks, whips, gags, masks, leg irons, car batteries, neck clamps, pliers, assorted pins and needles.

'I keep this stuff for friends,' said the fetching (and plainly dangerous) young Carla. 'Take your time, dude. Browse.'

'Intriguing,' I purred, 'but I am not in the market.'

'You want *revenge*, right? Entrapment? What you do is, you just plant some of this sick shit. They'll be divorced like tomorrow.' The girl eyed me. 'S and M. It's my thing.'

'S and M?'

'Sick!'

'Sick?' said I.

'Yeah, like – you know – *sick*. It means . . . Hard to explain. I mean, you meet this guy, let's say, and he's real tall and ugly and older than shit – sort of strange-ass cool – and you think: Sick! Know what I'm saying?'

I had not the slightest idea. Hence finesse:

'I'll put it this way,' I said cagily. 'I happen to *teach* this sick business. Our American tongue, that is.'

'You teach tongue?'

'Stock-in-trade, my dear.' I reached out and shook her callused, washerwoman's hand. 'Thomas H Chippering, professor of linguistics.'

'No shit,' she muttered, and yawned, and stared vacantly. 'Want me to model something?'

I took a seat.

'Sick!' I said.

And thus, by this bewildering sequence of events, I spent a fruitful, often spine-tingling forty-five minutes as a spectator to the latest in S and M. My plucky iron maiden modeled her entire collection, A to Z, chatting me up, occasionally requesting my assistance with keys and combinations.

'The thing is,' Carla informed me at one point, 'I get tired of selling all those stupid sundresses and Mexican blouses and crap. Like, there's no *pain* in it. You know what I mean?'

'Precisely,' said I, and looked directly into her tongue, where at the moment she was inserting a steel pin in the shape of a barbell.

'See, what people don't realize,' said Carla, 'is that nobody can fucking *hurt* you if you're *already* fucking hurting. Am I right?' She paused thoughtfully. (The barbell impeded her speech not a whit.) 'How the fuck old are you?'

'Forty plus,' said I.

'Sick!'

'And you? How the . . . How old would you be?'

'Lots and lots and lots less,' she said. 'Clamp me, will you?'

'Pardon?'

'The handcuffs. Tight.'

I clamped her; she winced in gratitude.

'You're catching on,' she said, and almost smiled. 'Tall guys, they've got huge dicks, I suppose. Pile drivers?'

This was too much.

I stood up, shot her a rebuking glare, and started toward the door. Carla hooked my arm.

'Hey, come on,' she said. 'All I meant was, I meant like you're into *hurting* people, right? The S part? Which is totally cool.' Her lower lip quivered. 'Revenge – I've been there. My ex-boyfriend, he was this motorcycle asshole, loved his hog more than me.'

'And?'

'And like – you know – I *know*.'

Then she wept.

Not only wept; the little pumpkin virtually fell into my arms. Spiked hair, dog collar, purple panties, purple bra, handcuffs, tongue pin – all irrelevant. She hugged me and shuddered and cried like a little girl. True, I shouldered the responsibility, yet at the same time I could not help wondering why it was that such odd, crippled creatures so often flit through my life. The maimed, the vulnerable, the emotionally disadvantaged.

'There, there,' I said.

She looked up. 'You want to bite me?'

'I do not.'

'It's okay. It's *good*.'

'No, indeed,' I told her sternly. 'This motorcycle chap. You struck back, I gather?'

Carla wiped her tears.

'Well, sure, that's what I'm *saying*. Hurt him bad. Leaky brakes.' She blinked, looked down at her handcuffs, then sniffled provocatively. 'Listen, man, you're not so bad. If you want, I can give you some tips, like helpful hints about – you know – how to really torture people.'

I weighed my options.

'Kind of you,' I said. 'Over dinner, perhaps?'

The girl frowned, then sighed heavily. 'Okay, dinner. Biting. Nothing else. You're way too old for me.'

'Righto,' I said.

'Promise?'

'I do. How much for the leg irons?'

*   *   *

Hours later, after a long and liquid supper, Carla and I exchanged reluctant goodbyes. (I am a flirt, yes. I am also Catholic. I do not freely copulate.)

Exhausted, somewhat melancholy, I embarked on a wee-hour drive out to the southeastern suburbs, parked in front of Lorna Sue's house, sat quietly for a moment, then walked up the driveway and carefully slipped the leg irons and purple undergarments beneath the front seat of the tycoon's ostentatiously upscale Mercedes. (No problem. Unlocked.)

My heart, I confess, was bubbling. Adrenaline was at work, and the aftershocks of young Carla, but beneath it all was a tremor of genuine sadness.

For some twenty minutes I reclined on the front lawn, staring up at the house, barely holding myself together. Behind those darkened bedroom windows, so blind and brooding, the girl of my dreams slept the night away in the arms of her princely new husband. How, I wondered, does the human animal tolerate such torture? That icy self-control of hers. That female practicality. (Flatly, without emotion, Lorna Sue had once advised me against becoming an eighteen-year-old, as if sorrow and rage were the province of children, as if an on-off switch had been built into the deep freeze of her reptilian heart.)

At one point I heard myself declaiming to the stars.

At another point I wept like young Carla.

And then later, on my hands and knees, I plucked a good many roses from their fertile new bed along the front steps. Whole bushes, in fact – yanking them out by the roots.

I recall almost nothing of the drive back to the hotel. Napalm fantasies, I believe.

Over the next forty-two hours I watched and waited. It was a ticklish period: close calls, dashed hopes. At times I feared my late-night handiwork would come to nothing. (For the experiment to succeed, it was vital that no one but Lorna Sue recover the incriminating articles.) The odds were essentially fifty-fifty, yet I felt the tension of a gambler riding a lifelong losing streak. Little has ever come easily for me. Over the years, through trial and error, I have discovered that monkey wrenches abound in this fluky, tricked-up world of ours. (Typos slip into my scholarship. Herbie retrieved fourteen phony checks from under my mattress, plus several other highly compromising documents.)

'Poor unlucky Tommy,' Lorna Sue once said. 'Born to lose.'

To calm myself, I dined again one evening with the punkish young Carla, who had taken the standard shine to me. (No surprise. Why ask why?) Although the girl was twenty-some years my junior, with a mentality to match, I found it relaxing to nod at her callow chitchat, to feel our knees in sporadic contact beneath the dinner table. I explained to her – in no uncertain terms – that my heart resided elsewhere, but this information only served to energize Carla's already vigorous libido. After dessert, on some brash and flimsy pretext, the tart little lemon drop invited herself up to my room, where we spent an agreeable two hours discussing techniques of vengeance. My companion, I must say, was creative in this regard. She knew the ins and outs of physical reprisal; she had a keen, uncanny eye for the possibilities opened by the advent of AIDS. 'The simpler the better,' Carla said at one point. 'Envelopes, for instance. Nothing to it.'

'Envelopes?' I said, and lifted an eyebrow. 'Please elaborate.'

My iron maiden nodded. 'The self-addressed kind. All you do is, you brush a little poison on the flap. Arsenic, maybe. After that, it's easy. Your victim licks the flap, puts on a stamp, and sends you back the evidence. A day later he's in the morgue. You're home free.'

'Elegant,' I murmured.

'You bet,' said Carla. 'And I've got a million ideas just like it. *Better* ones.'

She kicked off her shoes and sat beside me on the bed. For our night out, the sweet little assassin had dyed her hair a blinding shade of yellow. She wore a leather vest, leather skirt, leather earrings, a heavy chain belt at her waist.

'Fingernail polish,' she continued grimly. 'That's another one. Two drops of cyanide in the bottle, maybe three, then sit back and watch your mark start biting her fucking fingernails. Zappo. Funeral time.' She glanced at my lower torso, then even farther southward. 'Think of all the ridiculous shit people stick in their mouths.'

It was appropriate, I reckoned, to change the subject. I waited a moment and then innocently inquired about the serpentine tattoo etched upon her abdomen.

'Oh, that,' Carla said, and shrugged. 'My ex-boyfriend's idea. Like I told you, he's history. Motorcycle wreck, piss-poor brakes.' She sighed and unzipped her leather vest. 'All right, then, if you dig tattoos, I guess you can take a look. But no touchies. You're an old, old man.'

'Forty-nine,' I told her. (Accurately enough for the occasion.)

'Right. Ancient. Hands off.'

As it turned out, my companion amounted to a living mural of the flesh, and for some time I happily toured her bodily flora and fauna. I noted a honking goose at her left hip. A set of fangs on her inner thigh. Dragons (male and female) on the arches of her bony brown feet. A red rose at her breast.

It was the rose, alas, that I impulsively plucked.

Out of sorrow.

Without the least carnal motive.

(And who could fault me? I was the ill-fated Achilles, the rose my tender heel.)

Within an instant I recognized my error, yet the volatile little hellcat had already seized my thumb and forefinger. I will not repeat the girl's language. Inventive obscenities. Strident free verse. The gist of it had to do with allegations of attempted rape – patently trumped up – along with several unwholesome phrases regarding my status as a dirty old man. (Which I most emphatically was not. I was clean as a whistle and far from elderly.)

'No fucking touchies!' Carla yelled. 'Didn't I *tell* you that?'

'Yes, of course, but I assumed –'

'Assumed! Just because I was nice to you. An old fart! And now I suppose you want to bite it, don't you? I suppose you want to *chew*.'

I was perplexed. I shook my head diagonally.

'So what does *that* mean?' said Carla. 'Yes or no?'

I nodded.

'No,' I said.

'Come on, don't be such a namby-pamby.' She arched her back, aimed the rose at me. 'Make up your mind. Which *is* it?'

Here, I realized, was a sweetmeat with difficulties.

I had no inkling as to the proper response – yea or nay, or both, or neither. (What is it that women *want*? I will never know.) In this instance, alas, my dilemma was compounded by the proximity of the rose tattoo. Not to mention its anatomic location. Not to mention the import of the very word: *rose*.

I took what seemed the wisest course. I remained silent. Mute as a coffin.

Yet even this proved inadequate.

'Creep!' cried Carla.

The girl stood up and moved swiftly to the door – a blur of yellow hair and heavy metal.

'Guys like you,' she snarled, 'should be shot through the heart. Butchered like sheep. Someday, man, you'll get *yours*. Maybe tonight.'

37

She departed in haste.

I will confess that sleep came hard that night. For the duration of the evening, and well into the gateway hours of the morrow, I remained vigilant, door chained and bolted, eyes wide open.

The truth, I fear, is that young Carla – like such female forebears as Lorna Sue and the original apple-laden Eve – had presented to me a question that admitted of no appropriate response. *Yes* implied perversion. *No* implied absence of interest. *Maybe* implied weakness. Silence implied creephood.

The game of life had been rigged.

Stacked decks, shaved cards. Lorna Sue had it right: Poor unlucky Tommy.

On my final night in Tampa, all but resigned to failure, I tailed Lorna Sue and her ridiculous buffoon-tycoon to a nearby shopping mall. After my experience with Carla, I was in something of a funk – restless, suicidal – as I waited in the mall's parking lot for the happy couple to complete their shopping. More than an hour passed before they reappeared, each laden with packages. They were laughing, plainly charmed by themselves. As they approached the Mercedes, the tycoon passed over his keys to Lorna Sue, who opened the driver's door and began to slip inside. Up to that point, nothing even remotely remarkable had occurred. But in the next instant I knew with perfect certainty that the evening would turn interesting.

It happened fast – too fast. I could barely get the binoculars focused.

Lorna Sue dropped one of her bundles. She cursed. She bent down, made a short, jerky motion with her shoulders, seemed to hesitate, then reached under the seat and pulled out the purple panties.

It was a pleasure, I must confess, to watch her lips form an oval.

How do I describe my delight as she pressed the panties to her nose? As she inhaled? As the stench of treachery swept into her lungs?

After a second Lorna Sue reached down again, retrieved the matching brassiere, and spread it out across the steering wheel as if to measure its potential occupants. (Unfortunately, even with the binoculars, I could not make out her expression. This was evening, remember, and shadows had fallen.) Perhaps she murmured something. Perhaps she closed her eyes. All I can report with any accuracy is the deliberation with which she draped the panties and bra over the rearview mirror, and how, with considerably more deliberation – at half speed, it seemed – she then pulled out the leg irons.

The tycoon slumped down beside her.

My view was oblique. Profiles, mostly. Nonetheless, I decided that here was a marriage in trouble.

No smooching on the ride home.

Always the reckless motorist, Lorna Sue now outperformed herself at the wheel, and after the first mile or so I lost her in traffic. Not that it mattered. An important event had finally gone well in my life, even better than well, and I was giddy with pride. (So elegant! So simple and satisfying! In times of grief why gobble chocolates and cry your eyes out? Consider the alternatives – maybe a ticket to Fiji.)

For me, of course, it was only a start.

If this modest, impromptu experiment could yield such results, what might be accomplished with proper planning?

I drove slowly, enjoying the night air. The city of Tampa now seemed a more hospitable place. When I arrived at Lorna Sue's handsome mock-Tudor residence, I was not at all surprised to find the Mercedes parked at an odd angle on the front lawn, headlights blazing, doors ajar. For a few transcendent minutes I sat studying the house, imagining the scene that had to be unfolding within: allegations and rebuttals and disbelief. Lorna Sue's reptile stare. Bewildered denials. Acrimony at every turn.

And as I drove away, heading for the airport, it occurred to me that trust was at the center of every successful marriage, and that this particular relationship would require more than the ordinary dosage.

5

Confession

Words, I have discovered, are like embers. They smolder. They drop to the bottom of our souls, where for years they give off only a modest heat, and then out of nowhere a life-wind suddenly whips up and the words burst into red-hot, spirit-scorching flame.

An example: *confession*.

In 1957, the year my father died, the sanctuary of St Paul's Catholic Church in Owago was ravaged by a fire that very nearly consumed the entire structure. A case of arson, it was decided – almost certainly at the hands of a child – and within days the field of suspects had been more or less narrowed down to Herbie and me.

(I was innocent. Play with the mathematics.)

Herbie was an altar boy; I was not. He had a key to St Paul's; I did not. And most important, he had a motive – a religious bone to pick, so to speak – which I did not. How it transpired that I became a suspect, therefore, is beyond comprehension. Granted, St Paul's happened to be located across the street from my house; granted, too, I was seen playing combat games on church property the evening of the fire. But still, with Herbie's history as a wielder of hammer and nails, and with his new religious zealotry, it seemed to me, even as a twelve-year-old, that the case was open-and-shut. After returning from his stay with the corrective Jesuits of Minneapolis, Herbie had displayed all the characteristics of a fanatic. Everything about him had been tightened, his skin and his lips and his slicked-down hair, and at some essential level he had obviously exchanged one extreme for another: exuberance for austerity, devilishness for a stern, self-flagellating religiosity.

This was piety, in other words, beyond mere piety.

In part, I am quite sure, these behaviors can be traced back to the summer of 1952, to a plywood cross and the rusty nail he had driven into Lorna Sue's tiny brown hand.

But there was also a family influence at work, something elusive and unnatural.

For me, this hidden force was embodied in Herbie's yellow house, its musty smell and tomblike corridors, all the religious relics, the anonymous old nuns and priests who came and went like fugitives in the night. Moreover, while neither Lorna Sue nor Herbie ever spoke much about it, there was neighborhood gossip to the effect that their father, Ned, had once been a seminarian, a would-be priest who had forsaken his calling in circumstances tainted by scandal. One story pointed to a previous, unacknowledged marriage; another involved Velva Zylstra, Lorna Sue and Herbie's own mother, who herself may or may not have been wedded to Christ at one point, a woman of habits, so to speak. (Lorna Sue refused to discuss the matter. In our years of marriage, she invariably shunted aside my questions with an irritated sigh, as if I were inquiring about issues of gynecology. 'That's *my* business,' she would say, or words similar. 'Being married doesn't mean you get to cut open my head and poke around inside. I'm entitled to some basic secrets.')

Still, whatever the genesis – biblical or otherwise – the fact remains that the Zylstra household was infected by a virulent and very stubborn godly virus.

It was always my hypothesis, therefore, that the 1957 fire

could be seen as a cruel but not unpredictable outcome of the pressures on Herbie's spirit. A mix of rage and guilt, no doubt, had made him try to burn religion out of his life and perhaps out of the world as a whole. Nor did it stop there. Four days after the fire, a closetful of vestments and choir robes was found cut to shreds; sexual graffiti had been scrawled on the church's front steps, a statue of Christ disfigured in a most outlandish way – lipstick and rouge, a pair of distinctly feminine breasts appended to the suffering son of God.

In the end there was no solution to these crimes, no confession or conviction, and had I not been summoned to defend myself before Father Dern, the entire episode might well have vanished from my memory.

But in fact I *was* summoned. And the injustice of that two-hour inquisition still torments me.

A Saturday afternoon, I remember, and together Herbie and I sat on a pair of folding chairs in front of Father Dern's big oak desk, squirming under a blitz of threats and accusations and medieval Catholic cajolery.

An ordeal, to be sure. The purest humiliation. But what made the experience memorable, beyond the obvious terror and embarrassment, was the fact that Herbie and I endured it side by side, as a team. At one point during the interrogation I glanced over at him with the hope that he might acknowledge this union.

But there was nothing. It was as if I were not present in the room, not even alive.

He stared straight ahead at Father Dern, almost insolently. When he responded to the priest's questions, it was in a monotone, just yes or no. (Like me, Herbie denied all involvement.) And yet his voice – his whole demeanor – seemed flat and inhuman. Rehearsed somehow. No indignation.

On my own part, I could barely stop myself from screaming

43

out protests of innocence, and as a consequence my denials must have seemed less than convincing.

Father Dern's gaze settled on a spot near the center of my forehead.

Relentlessly, the old man grilled me regarding my whereabouts during the hours in question, a span of time for which I had no solid alibi – I simply could not remember.

In the end, to protect myself, I lied. Stupid, reckless lies. I claimed, for instance, that I was bathing when the fire broke out.

Father Dern's eyelids fluttered.

'Bathing?' he said. 'At two in the morning?'

I had overlooked this detail and responded with a woeful little shrug. A few seconds elapsed before Herbie made a noise in his throat.

'Look, Tommy didn't do it. I know that for a fact. He *couldn't.*'

'Couldn't?' said Father Dern.

'He's not the type. No guts.'

The priest squinted at me. 'Well, I don't know. It still seems –'

'Impossible,' Herbie said with crisp finality. 'Tommy wouldn't dare. A little baby.'

Father Dern rolled his shoulders and pulled out a pair of blackened mason jars.

'Look familiar?' he said.

I glanced over at Herbie, whose expression remained neutral. (At that instant the issue of guilt was sealed. Herbie: no one else.)

'No,' I said quietly – another lie.

'You're sure?'

I shrugged and said, 'Positive.'

The priest gave me a long, watery-eyed stare. 'We found these last night in the sanctuary. Exactly where the fire started.'

He paused several seconds to let this message sink in. (The same annoying technique he applied so lavishly in his Sunday sermons.) 'Go ahead, take a whiff. You can smell the gasoline.'

'No, thanks,' I said. 'Never saw them before.'

Right then, though, I could have blurted out the whole incriminating truth. The summer of 1952: Herbie straddling our plywood plane, banking into a bombing run toward his yellow house, one hand gripping a mason jar filled with gasoline from my garage. 'Die!' he always yelled, then afterward he would talk about black bones and fires in the attic.

Now we were protecting each other.

Protecting something.

The bulk of our audience with Father Dern has long since receded from memory, leaving only its gray stain, and after more than three decades only one other detail remains with me. Near the end of our session, for reasons I will never understand, the old priest pushed to his feet, carried one of the mason jars to a spot just to the side of my chair, paused there, then let the jar drop to the floor.

After a moment he dropped the second jar.

'Consider that God's blessing,' he said. 'The police will never see those jars – so be it – but take my word that our Lord Jesus Christ *did* see them.' There was a short silence. 'And he saw both of you. He knows.'

He fixed his liquid eyes on me for a time. I could feel a prayer coming.

'Let us pray.'

When it was over, I caught up with Herbie outside the church. I was partly grateful, I suppose, but mostly I was angry. 'You could've just admitted everything,' I told him. 'I'm innocent – you know that.'

Even then, Herbie refused to look at me. 'I tried to help,' he said quietly, and kept walking.

'But you're the one who *did* it all. What a faker.'

Herbie stopped.

He closed his eyes briefly, then looked at me for the first time that day. 'Just forget it,' he said, his voice sharp, almost bitter. 'You're clean and clear. It's different for me. I have to get messy sometimes.'

'Messy?'

'Right,' he said. 'I do what it takes.'

I laughed. 'Set fires? Put boobs on Jesus?'

'Whatever.'

He turned and crossed the street, moving toward his big yellow house, but after a second I followed him into the front yard. Apparently Lorna Sue had been waiting for him, because she was already starting in our direction. Her face had a dark, strained look.

'So?' she said.

'Went fine,' Herbie said.

I reached out and grabbed him.

'What about *me*?' I yelled. 'They think . . . I mean, they think *I'm* the one. If you're so hot on confession, why not just confess?'

'Because he's not a liar,' said Lorna Sue.

She took her brother's hand and stood staring at me. Her eyes, I thought, contained a pure, distilled defiance, absolute certainty mixed with absolute disdain. In later years, especially as our marriage disintegrated, I would come to know this expression in its numerous forms and applications. Near the end, in fact, it would become the primary standard by which I measured the erosion of her love.

'At least Herbie *tries* to do the right thing,' she said. 'He's not a coward or anything.'

I was astonished.

'Coward?' I said.

'Well, he wouldn't be afraid to admit it, Tommy. Not if he

46

really had to – if there wasn't any other choice. That's the difference between you two.' For emphasis, consciously or not, Lorna Sue squeezed her brother's hand. 'Isn't that right? You're not afraid, are you?'

Herbie looked down at the ground. His gaze fastened on something too large or too small for the human eye.

'Get inside,' he said. 'The subject's closed.'

Lorna Sue pushed up on her toes, kissed him lightly on the cheek, gave me an I-told-you-so stare, then bounced up the steps and into the house. Even at age twelve, she had the moves of a pro.

'What the heck was all *that*?' I said.

Herbie shrugged. 'Just stay out of it, Tommy.'

I started to walk away, but Herbie stepped in front of me.

'I mean it,' he said. 'You're not part of this – not anymore. Leave us alone.'

'Us?'

'Us,' he said.

I nodded. But right then I knew it was more than a brother-sister thing. It was a plywood cross. It was God.

6

Substance

Imagine any object, any person, any human event. Ponder the word *substance*.

As an example I might pluck some random snapshot from memory. A backyard, let us say. Midcentury Minnesota, the summer of 1952, and I am watching my father perform sleight-of-hand for Lorna Sue and Herbie and me. I see him now as he was then, athletic and graceful, utterly adult, standing near the birdbath in that silvery backyard. Sunlight surrounds him. He sparkles with the ferocity of here and now. Proud, but also a little nervous, I watch as my father shakes out a cigarette – a Lucky Strike – lights it with a match, slides it into the opening of his right ear, blinks at the pain, then smiles at me and retrieves the cigarette from his mouth.

All this is like concrete. It has a dense, solid, ongoing durability. Granted, my father died in 1957, of heart failure, yet he has substance even without substance. He lives in the chemistry of thought, an inhabitant of the mind, his flesh reconstituted into those organic compounds we so lamely call memory. I do not mean this in a figurative sense; I mean it literally: my father has substance. Hit a switch in my head, fire up the chemistry, and there he is again, in the backyard, wincing as he inserts a Lucky Strike into his right ear. Herbie's mouth drops open. Lorna Sue squeals with delight. And I am there too, seven years old, snagged in Lorna Sue's brown eyes, her black hair and summer skin – I loved her even then, obsessively. It is indelible. I see the white birdbath before me, the bubbles appearing at Herbie's lips as he demands that my father do the trick once more. 'Come on!' he screams.

He jiggles.

He grabs my father's arm.

'Jeez, come on!' he yells. 'Stick it in *my* ear!'

A painful admission, but it's true: Back then, in 1952, I loved Herbie with the same volatile, high-octane passion that now fuels my hatred. Same for Lorna Sue.

It's been hard since she left me. Late at night I'll jot down things to say to her in the event she calls someday. The word *reptile* is on my list. And *lizard*. And *crocodile*.

I cannot choose from among the three. *Lizard* has the virtue of specificity, *crocodile* even more so, but in the end *reptile* probably makes the strongest claim, most inclusive, most primitive and wicked and dangerous and cold-blooded.

The pregnant point; however, is that by way of memory I can recapture and restore the love that once flooded my childhood, as if emotion were a piece of flesh, as if love were a bodily member subject to both amputation and re-membering. Any example will do: a kiss on some long-ago summer Sunday, Lorna Sue's tongue in my mouth, the scent of her hair, the stern tissue of her lips – all transformed by cellular magic into neuropeptides and sugars and phosphates. It seems reasonable, therefore, to hypothesize that the pain of betrayal can be diminished or eradicated by means of vengeance. We can cleanse ourselves. We can scrape the corrosive love poisons from our memories like bug juice off a windshield.

All it requires is true heroism: the ancient art of revenge.

*　　*　　*

49

Substance: the word gnaws at me.

Late at night, tormented, I find myself sliding up and down the scales of history, first here, next there, and eventually I return to a hot, windy beach outside Tampa, where not so long ago I lay feigning sleep while Lorna Sue chatted up her greasy new friend, a Tampa tycoon.

I was present. I heard it all. I smelled his Coppertone, seethed at his rancid pleasantries.

In the days afterward, almost without pause, Lorna Sue devoted our vacation to a slow, compendious recitation of the man's virtues. (With each glowing item, by way of silent contrast, she was also devaluing and denigrating me.) The cocksucker was witty, she claimed. Generous. Thoughtful. At peace with himself. A good listener. Self-assured. Comfortable inside his own skin. Polite. Smart. A man of substance.

At this – finally – I balked.

We were flying home, I recall, and Lorna Sue had sighed and levered back her seat. 'Most people with money,' she was telling me, 'they're not really comfortable inside their own skins, they're not at peace with themselves, but he's . . . well, obviously he's a man of substance, but he still seems –'

'Who?' I said.

Lorna Sue blinked. 'Well, you know.' (She then intoned the man's name.) 'He's got –'

'Let me guess,' I said. 'I'll bet he's got substance dripping out his nostrils.'

It was shortly thereafter that Lorna Sue suggested I see a counselor. I was paranoid, she claimed. I was irrational.

'First Herbie,' she said, 'and now you're jealous of –' (Again, painfully, she uttered the tycoon's patently ridiculous name.) 'I'm serious, Tom, you need help. It's like you won't . . . like I can't have anybody else in my life. No friends. Not even a *brother*.'

I shrugged and closed my eyes.

Her allegations were without substance.

Tampa: it breaks my heart.

I stare at my airline ticket stubs and feel a great chill in my chest, a frozen sensation. I cannot catch my breath. For you, perhaps, the place might be Boston, or San Francisco, or Fiji, but in any case it strikes me that words, too, have genuine substance – mass and weight and specific gravity. I carry Tampa with me all day long, and to bed each night, and I fear my spirit has been warped by the burden. I dream in turquoise.

An interesting wrinkle. One hot afternoon, while staking out Herbie's new house in Tampa, I happened across a spicy little item in the local newspaper. A Catholic church in the vicinity – Our Lady of Assumption – had burned to the ground three days before my arrival. No surprise: arson. The possibilities for vengeance did not escape me. Immediately, still seated in my rental car, I began composing an anonymous letter to the Tampa police force, alerting them to Herbie's presence in their sunny city, providing key data regarding similar events in the small prairie town of Owago, Minnesota.

Can I be faulted for giggling as I posted my incriminating epistle that night?

(I cannot be.)

Even if by some curious fluke he was completely innocent – in fact, especially so – Herbie would soon be feeling precisely what I had felt on the day he invaded my marriage and my life. He would learn, as I had, the full meaning of such phrases as 'circumstantial evidence' and 'presumed guilt.' Late at night he would wake up screaming the word *assumption*.

A few weeks after returning from my third solo trip to Tampa, revitalized by my successes there, I had occasion to revisit the backyard of my childhood. Easter break, spectacular weather. My students had packed up their Levi's and bad grammar, I packed my Wittgenstein and a pair of suits.

At a gas station near campus, as I took on fuel, a trio of young coeds sped by in a blood-red Camaro, giggling and honking at me, lifting their stubby middle fingers in salutation. I returned the greeting. (My students, it appears, consider me an odd duck. And why is this? Because I can spell *cat* without drooling? Because I refuse to fucking split my infinitives?)

Believe me, I am no duck. I am a man. I sail along with furled feathers, an ardent, lovable, hurting human being. A victim, in fact, of my own humanity. Remember: Herbie destroyed me. Lorna Sue sleeps with her tycoon in Tampa.

Enough – why bother?

Easter break, school dismissed, and I drove south through farm country, past pigs and soybeans, past a huge billboard indicating my arrival in the Valley of the Jolly Green Giant. (Fee-fi, ho-hum.) Two hours later, in early afternoon, I approached the outskirts of my pitiful history, a forlorn little prairie town tucked up against the Minnesota-Iowa border. Owago: Pop. 9,977. Off to my left, as I made the final turn onto Highway 16, I took notice of the very cornfield in which Lorna Sue and I had once bared ourselves to the elements of autumn. Such zeal, such ardor. 'It hurts!' she had cried, and who could blame her? A layer of frost had accumulated that night on the hood of my father's Pontiac.

Now she lives in Tampa. Quack-quack.

Tired and hungry, battered by the road, I found humble lodging at the Shady Lane Motel, just off Main Street. (No shade, no lane. The professor in me shivers at such vacuity of language.) Enthroned in my room, I showered, rested, corrected papers, raged, wept, plotted, napped. Near dusk I returned to my car and executed a slow reconnaissance up

Main Street. Why exactly was I here? In part, no doubt, out of desperation. And because the trail of human misery inevitably leads homeward. And, it goes without saying, for revenge: I yearned to cause hurt where the hurt would hurt most – at the roots.

And so I cruised – tooled, as my freshmen say – up and down Main Street. The town had changed little since my departure thirty-odd years earlier, still bleak, still threadbare. In modern dictionaries, under the word *boring*, you will find a small pen-and-ink illustration of Owago, Minnesota. Flat, bald, windy, isolated, desolate. (How impotent the adjective.) Proudly, a bit ridiculously, the town promoted itself as the Rock Cornish Hen Capital of the World, a grip on fame at once tenuous and pathetic. Firstly, the hen business had fallen on hard times; the graph spiraled downward. Secondly, it struck me as sad that a community's grandest annual celebration boiled down to an event called Rock Cornish Hen Day. (In September of each year a banner is hoisted to the top of the water tower; ministers prepare sermons; housewives bake pies. At midday, a few hardy farmers truck their hens into town, dump them in front of the courthouse, then herd them up Main Street in a great clucking parade. The citizens of Owago watch from sidewalks. Then they go home.)

Odd duck? *Me*?

With these and related memories, I drove past the Rock Cornish Café, Wilson's Standard Oil station, the courthouse, the First National Bank, the Ben Franklin store. Day had passed into dark by the time I parked in front of the tiny stucco house of my youth. There were no signs of animation from within. No lights, no sounds. The place seemed impossibly small, as if shrunken by the tumble of time, and for a moment I considered pointing the car back toward Minneapolis.

Instead, impulsively, I locked my vehicle and strode into the backyard. The birdbath was still there, and my mother's rhododendrons, yet again I felt a curious compressive force at work. My whole life suddenly seemed puny and pitiful. My dreams had shriveled. My spirit too. (I had wanted to be a cowboy, for God's sake, but here I was, a peddler of the English language.) I was struck, also, by the thought that Lorna Sue had represented my one true chance at happiness – my life raft, my lovely bobbing buoy – and now even that gallant vessel had gone to the bottom under the winds of marital treachery.

It made me want to cry.

And I did.

I lay beside the birdbath and made fists and blubbered at the moon.

Imagine my embarrassment, therefore, when only minutes later I was interrupted by a shrill, off-key, distinctly displeased female voice. I blinked away my grief. Above me, haloed by moonlight, loomed a tall, very shapely member of the wholly opposite sex. Stunning specimen, I thought, although at the moment she held a garden spade to my head.

'Trespasser!' she cried. 'Don't budge. Not one muscle.'

My position, of course, was awkward. (Supine. Teary face. Spade at my skull.) To my advantage, thank goodness, I was dressed in respectable garb, a blue wool suit and a silk tie, and with this modest consolation I sat up and introduced myself.

'Thomas H Chippering,' I said merrily. 'Professor of linguistics.'

My captor was not enthused. 'Professor?' she muttered. 'In somebody's backyard? On private property? Bawling like a three-year-old?' She poked at me with the spade. 'What *is* this anyway?'

'Apologies,' I said.

'Sick man.'

'Of spirit,' I admitted. 'May I stand?'

'Not yet.'

The woman appraised me with a blend of fear and curiosity,

perhaps slightly shaded toward the latter, and I therefore seized the opportunity to outline my circumstances: that the world had recently dealt me a number of knockout blows, among them faithlessness and divorce. I explained, too, that I had spent my early youth in this very backyard, a child of Owago. 'Granted, it may seem peculiar,' I said, 'but if we could only . . . Seriously, may I stand?'

She shook her head. 'You could've knocked. Asked permission.'

'Absolutely.'

'And you were . . . Listen, you were *crying*.'

'Right. That too.'

The woman hesitated then withdrew her spade a fraction. 'Divorce, you said?'

'Eight months ago Thursday. Crushed. Heartbroken.'

She nodded thoughtfully. 'So it's like an anniversary sort of? That's why you're here crying in my backyard?'

'More or less. Seeking answers.'

'Well, God. I should call the police.'

'You should not,' said I. 'You should offer me a drink.'

The woman relaxed her grip on the spade. Here came the moment of decision, plainly, and as a signal of good faith I smiled and displayed my huge, pale, innocent hands. (With due modesty, yet truthfully, I must point out that I am not an unattractive man – tall and craggy in the mode of certain stage actors. Virile as Secretariat. A war hero.) No surprise, therefore, that a surrendering twitch came to the corners of my captor's pliant, full-lipped, well-moistened mouth.

'Water,' she grunted. 'One glass. Then you're out of here.'

Home sweet home.

Inside, escorted by this handsome female prototype (who had by now introduced herself to me as one Mrs Robert Kooshof), I stood in the long-lost kitchen of my youth: same gas stove, same breakfast nook, same pink Formica cabinets. Briefly, I had to stave off another wave of tears, and it was fortunate that Mrs Kooshof chose that moment to place a plastic tumbler on the kitchen table. 'Water,' she said. 'Drink up.'

I smiled gratefully, helped myself to a chair. I sensed a turn of mood, a new warmth. (The whole kitchen, for that matter, was positively fragrant with innuendo. Standard stimulus-response. I have grown used to it.)

'And your husband?' I inquired. 'Mr Robert Kooshof. He would be returning when?'

There was a little shift in her eyes. 'Five to seven years. Tax fraud. I've been thinking about divorce myself.'

'I see.'

'You *don't* see.'

'Very true, but I was only –'

'And don't condescend,' she said. 'You're not exactly a welcome guest on the premises.'

'No,' I murmured. 'Nor inexactly.'

Mrs Kooshof shot me a look. 'Right *there*. That's condescension.'

And so once again I found myself apologizing, a form of discourse that has never fallen within the perimeter of my special genius. (Arrogant, I am falsely called. Supercilious.) Cautiously, over a second glass of tap water, I did my best to make peace with my bewitching host, outlining the sequence of events that had carried me back to this squalid piece of the prairie. Betrayal, I said. Marital treason. Once or twice Mrs Kooshof came close to nodding – a definite thaw in progress – and it occurred to me again that I was in the presence of a truly unique representative of the malleable gender. (Mid-thirties. Blond hair. Blue eyes. Busty as Nepal. One hundred fifty well-muscled pounds.)

Here, I recognized, was a Dutch beauty only marginally tarnished by the years. A woman with substance.

'Tax fraud?' I said casually.

She glanced up. 'Don't pry. It's not something I talk about.'

'Certainly not, but if you should ever . . . Well, I'm in your debt. Friends already, are we not?'

Mrs Kooshof shrugged her magnificent shoulders. 'Let's not jump the gun. Anyway, you're the one bawling in the backyard.'

'True,' I sighed. 'Human folly.'

'So you messed her over?'

'Messed?'

'The ex-wife,' said Mrs Robert Kooshof. 'I'll bet the lady left you for pretty good reasons. It's always something.'

'Not in this case,' I said stoutly, but then, in the next instant, I noted my error. The correct course, given her pitiless gaze, would be to temper self-defense with fragments of truth. 'Perhaps one or two minor infractions. Petty nonsense.'

Mrs Kooshof laughed – a loud, fizzy, uncorked laugh. She took a seat beside me at the table. 'Infractions,' she muttered. 'I can't wait.'

'You're sure?'

'The abridged version.'

And thus I sketched out the depressing parabola of my life: Herbie and Lorna Sue, the crucifixion episode, Herbie's incredible jealousy. How for years he had plotted to undermine my marriage. And how with a single stroke he had driven my precious wife into the bed of a two-bit Tampa tycoon.

It was then – unexpectedly – that I choked up.

No tears, thank God, but I was compelled to ask if there were spirits on hand.

'Bourbon?' said Mrs Kooshof.

I would have preferred schnapps, yet even so I moved an encouraging hand to her thigh.

'Bourbon,' I said, 'might be just the ticket.'

*   *   *

57

In short, what a glorious spring break! What a reprieve from despair and self-pity!

I had the run of the house. I had flannel sheets, pot roast, apple bread, chocolate chip cookies, and Mrs Robert Kooshof. Very curious, is it not, how such detours pop up along life's unfolding freeway? How at odd moments we find ourselves tapping the brakes, gearing down, bumping along past spectacular and untamed vistas? Even in times of mental anguish, or perhaps especially in such times, we are sometimes visited by the rare wine, the winning bingo card, the out-of-the-blue phone call from a forgotten old flame.

Diversions, to be sure. The detour ends. The freeway awaits us. My torment, in other words, did not vanish – I am hardly so fickle. Hour to hour, Lorna Sue lingered at the tip of my thoughts like some sour afterscent: Thursday's head cold, last night's cabbage.

The hurt remained, yes, but Mrs Kooshof did much to file off its sharpest edges. We sported between flannel sheets, watched televised crime dramas, depleted her bourbon, recovered with long walks up and down North Fourth Street, past the United Methodist Church and Mrs Catchitt's house and the elementary school where Herbie and Lorna Sue and I had once endured our ABCs. Mostly, though, we commiserated. Held hands. Exchanged horror stories. Mrs Kooshof's husband, I came to learn, was a veterinarian by trade, now serving his five to seven in Stillwater. 'At first it was tax fraud,' she said bitterly. 'I mean, that was bad enough – feds everywhere – but the creep was stealing from *me* too. Spending it on women. No joke, he had the bitches tucked away like spare parts. Over in Sioux Falls. Windom, Jackson, Mountain Lake. Two up in Pipestone. And I didn't have even the slightest inkling. Zero. Stupid me, but I never thought Doc was the type. I thought he was sort of – you know – I thought he was a veterinarian. What a nightmare.'

'Doc?' I said.

'Robert – my husband. And it's a small town too. Everybody knows.'

I assumed my gravest classroom demeanor. 'You have my sympathy,' I told her. 'Hideous, I know, but if you don't mind, may I take a moment to recommend the path of reprisal? Old-fashioned vengeance. In my own case, I must say, I've found it most gratifying.'

'You're kidding?'

'No, indeed. Swift, stern, merciless punishment.'

Mrs Kooshof looked up at me with a pair of hot Dutch eyes. 'Punishment how?'

'By whatever methods you might prefer,' I said, then went on to delineate my own personal program. 'My plan,' I said bluntly, 'is to remarry her.'

Mrs Kooshof nodded. 'That *would* hurt.'

'Break up her marriage. Win her back. And then dump her like a truckload of used diapers. Tell her not to be an eighteen-year-old.'

'You're serious?'

'That I am.'

A short silence followed. We were entwined in bed, Mrs Kooshof's blond curls at my belly. (As mentioned, she was a large, healthy woman, hefty across the upper torso; my left arm had gone numb beneath her bulk.)

'So what about me?' she said.

'You? How so?'

'I *rescued* you, Thomas. Crying like a baby in my backyard. You were totally lost.'

'True,' I said, and slipped my arm free. I thought fast. Pluses, minuses. 'And I am prepared to offer a reward of sorts. Tampa. The two of us.' Winning smile. 'Expenses to be shared, of course.'

Mrs Kooshof regarded me with suspicion.

59

She sat up, lit a cigarette, dispatched three or four smoke rings toward the heavens.

'Tampa,' she said. 'What's in it for me?'

'Sun and sea.'

'Big deal. That's it?'

'Manly companionship.'

'What else, Thomas?'

'Coppertone tan,' I said. 'Payback lessons. I am, after all, an educator.'

7

Jungle

Here I must digress – a tactical transgression, perhaps, but I urge forbearance. The shortest distance between two points may well be a straight line, but one must remember that efficiency is not the only narrative virtue. Texture is another. Accuracy still another. Our universe does not operate on purely linear principles.

Bear in mind, too, the story of your own botched life, its circularities and meanderings, how your thoughts sometimes slide back to that dismal afternoon when you introduced your husband to a lanky young redhead named Suzanne or Sandra or Sarah – let us settle on Sandra – and how you watched the two of them chat over coffee, and how at one point it occurred to you that they might be getting along rather too well – Sandra's saucy eyes, your husband's laughter – but how you said nothing, how you did nothing, and how as a consequence you now wake up screaming the word *Fiji*.

A well-placed digression, though interruptive, can often prove progressive in its effects. We move forward by looping briefly backward.

Thus: the year 1969.

Thus: Vietnam.

*　　*　　*

I was always an inert young man, the reactive type, a tardy and somewhat petulant respondent to the world, almost never an initiator. Events dictated. I complied. By this process, the war sucked me in, and in January of 1969 I found myself filling sandbags at a forward firebase in the mountains of Quang Ngai Province. It was, by any measure, a stressful twelve months. Although my tour involved no formal combat, nothing dangerous, I admit to having had trouble appreciating the wholesome, outdoorsy rigors of warfare. There were no beds. No books. The food was called *chow* – a word that speaks volumes. The days seemed to stretch out toward infinity, blank and humid, without purpose, and at night I was kept awake by the endless drone of mosquitoes and helicopters. (Why wars must be contested under such conditions I shall never understand. Is not death sufficient?)

The year 1969, to put it politely, was not my happiest. I felt marooned; my health deteriorated.

Surrounded by bunkers and barbed wire, sealed off from the real war, I spent that year as an awards clerk in a battalion adjutant's office, where my primary chore was to compose and process citations for gallantry in action – Silver Stars, Bronze Stars, Purple Hearts, et cetera. In the beginning, I suppose, I rather enjoyed manufacturing these scenarios of human valor. I was good with machine gun nests. I imagined young lieutenants leaping upon land mines, shielding their charges, miraculously limping away with mild contusions to the extremities. (*Extremity*, in fact, was a favorite word. I milked it mercilessly.) Still, after a couple of months, I exhausted both my thesaurus and my creativity, and I soon viewed my agency as the purest hackwork.

Why, then, was I there? Certainly not out of moral conviction. Nor to seek adventure, nor to test my masculinity. (Never a problem. I am amply hormonal, a fact upon which clever women often comment.) So why? The brief answer –

the silly answer – is that I was conscripted. Yet I did nothing to avoid this fate. When the draft notice arrived, in my first year of graduate school, I chuckled and promptly returned to my books.

Imagine my surprise, therefore, when our country's claim upon my person turned out to be in earnest.

Passively, inert to the end, I capitulated with scarcely a snarl. I watched myself plod through the humiliations of a physical examination, then basic training, then clerk's school at a dismal installation in rural Kentucky. (My sole fond memory from this period is of a rubbery little Appalachian number by the name of June. Acrobatic tongue. Tooth decay. Illiterate in everything but love.)

Then off to war.

Vietnam itself came as a relatively minor insult to prior injury, almost entirely uneventful. Only a single episode deserves attention, yet this incident goes far to explain the human being I have since become.

To wit: Near the end of my tour, not a month before rotating back to the States, I was called upon to join six compatriots* in manning a listening post several kilometers outside the firebase. Our orders were to move by foot into the mountains, position ourselves along a designated trail, dig in deep, then spend the next four days (and nights) lying low, listening for enemy movement.

None of this was my cup of tea.

Though it is awkward to acknowledge personal inadequacies, I must concede that I was not cut out for the grim business of soldiering. I am a tall, somewhat gawky man. Athletically disinclined. A distinctive stride – pelvis forward,

* I was later to learn that these six filthy gentlemen referred to themselves as 'Greenies,' an abbreviation for 'Green Berets,' itself an abbreviation for a rare condition of mental and spiritual gangrene.

elbows sideward – an intellectual's abstract tilt to the jaw. With no complaints from yours truly, I had been routinely excused from most outdoor ventures, largely out of prejudice against men of accomplishment.

So, yes, with all this, the new assignment came as a shock. How it happened I can only guess. A silly prank, some officer's idea of comedy.

I received my orders at noon. Thirty minutes later I was reporting to a young, dull-faced captain at the front gate, who issued me a military radio, rations, ammunition for my thoroughly rusted M-16. 'Won't be too bad,' the captain said, and gestured at the mountains. 'Like Cub Scouts. Pretend it's a weenie roast.'

My comrades waited outside the gate: six tough, tired, soiled faces. These were grunts. Paddy stompers, real soldiers. They spoke not a word to me, just exchanged glances and moved out single file toward the mountains.

For more than five hours we plodded straight west, then briefly northward, then began climbing through deep, dripping rain forest. The greenery was massive. Triple canopy, foliage stacked upon foliage. This was machete country. Snake country, too, and creatures I dared not imagine. Although I had ridded myself of unessential burdens – a *Webster's Collegiate*, a complete Chaucer – I soon passed into a state far beyond exhaustion. I could smell death in my bones.

At last, in late afternoon, we halted at a trail junction overlooking a wide river below. Immediately, I collapsed beneath a tree. The universe had gone limp along its margins – no definition, therefore no meaning – and it was all I could do to watch the others set up a perimeter and clear fields of fire. Even then, my six ghostly comrades spoke not a word. Soberly, as dusk came on, they ate their rations and rolled out their ponchos for the night. I was aware, of course, that field discipline was critical, yet the muteness of these sour gentlemen seemed extreme. I had been expecting ridicule, the standard snide mockery, but instead I was treated like a piece of insignificant jungle scenery. When dark threatened, I saw no alternative but to approach one of these savage mutes. I chose the smallest, a wiry kid with bad breath and bad posture. Politely, even sheepishly, I tapped his arm and requested information regarding the evening's activities.

The boy stared over my shoulder. Hard to be certain, for his lips did not move, but I believe he eventually murmured the word *shit*.

'My own thought,' said I. (Here was progress.) 'So look, if you don't mind, I'm new at this. What do I *do*?'

'Do?'

'You know. Do.'

There was a pause that lasted half the night. The boy spat, closed his eyes, chewed thoughtfully on a wad of gum, then repeated his almost inaudible ventriloquist's act. 'The usual,' he seemed to whisper.

I nodded vigorously. 'The usual. Very good.'

'Same-same.'

'Got it,' I said. 'Same-same. Many thanks.'

I began to edge away, but with a silky little motion the boy reached out and caught me by an ear.

'Listen!' he hissed.

'Hey, I'm *trying*.'

'Fuckin' idiot.'

'That stings,' I said, 'and I very much wish –'

He gave my ear a twist. 'Fuckin' listening post. So fuckin' *listen*.'

I spent the remainder of the night alone in a clump of bushes. I did not sleep. I listened. And the nighttime sounds were nothing if not compelling: monkeys, tigers, sappers, parrots, fish, Herbie, Lorna Sue, my whole sad history. I heard water evaporating. I heard the tick of my own biology.

At one appalling point, near dawn, I detected what seemed to be the sound of a nail entering human flesh.

At daybreak I was alone.

They were gone – all six of them. The radio, too, and any sign of human presence.

I searched all morning.

I waited all afternoon.

It occurred to me, as the sun sank low, that this had to be a bizarre practical joke. At any instant they would come creeping up on me – jumping out, whooping – but that richly imagined instant never arrived. When dark settled, I retreated to my clump of bushes. *Jungle*, I kept thinking. The word itself seemed haunted, and even now, decades later, those two syllables signify betrayal and panic and helplessness, far beyond anything listed in your standard *Roget's*.

The next morning I set off for the firebase, a vague optimism pushing me along. South, I thought – down the mountain.

Patiently, trying to encourage myself, I took inventory of all the reasons not to panic. I had my weapon. I had rations and ammunition. I had three canteens of water. And common sense. Plenty of it.

In twenty minutes I was thoroughly lost.

Everything had become everything else: trees blending into more trees. To go down I had to go up. But I could not find up.

At midday I crossed an unfamiliar footbridge. Hours later, in a clearing, I came upon an abandoned stone pagoda. I made camp there for the night, a long, drizzly, foggy night, then resumed my march just after daybreak. No left or right, no direction to things, just the dense green jungle kaleidoscoping into deeper jungle, and for the entire day I followed a narrow dirt trail that wound through the mountains without pattern or purpose. Once, I spotted a pair of jets well off to the west;

I heard the dull, distant thud of an air strike. Otherwise, the world had emptied itself. Forward, backward, it was all one thing. No villages, no roads, no structures of any kind. This was wilderness. High, green, shaggy country. Quiet country. Lush country. Landfalls of botany, mountains growing out of mountains. Greenhouse country. Huge palms and banana trees, wildflowers, waist-high grasses, vines and wet thickets and humidity. Enemy country too. Hostile in the most fundamental sense.

Terror kept me going.

All day, as I trudged along, my thoughts were wired to an internal transformer of despair and rage. I yelled at the jungle. I envisioned scenarios of revenge, how someday I would acquire the means to retaliate against my six so-called comrades. Napalm strikes. Grenades rolling into foxholes. I smiled at these thoughts, then found myself trembling.

Perhaps it was fatigue, perhaps madness, but I suddenly allowed myself to collapse in the middle of the trail. I watched the sky; I did not move. Even at dusk, as a wet fog settled in, I lay there paralyzed, wrapped up in my poncho, listening to sounds that should never be listened to. Voices in the fog, other voices inside me.

Lost, I thought. Lost as lost gets.

At this point, as promised, our digressive loop becomes progressive. We circle forward to the present.

Lost then, lost now.

Needless to say, I am a survivor. I found my way out of that spooky jungle, which is a tale I must set aside for the appropriate moment. Here it is sufficient to underscore three salient consequences of the whole experience: my sensitivity to people leaving me, my terror of betrayal, my lifelong propensity for exacting vengeance.

It should be clear, too, that I am not without backbone.

67

The timid scholar inside me perished forever in those mountains. Stung by treachery, I learned how to respond. And in Tampa, abetted by Mrs Robert Kooshof, I would soon be bringing some extremely serious shit to bear.

8

Ned, Earleen, Velva

Mrs Robert Kooshof accepted my no-frills travel offer,* and late the next afternoon I made our reservations for Florida. Afterward, we raised a toast, had supper à la buff, made spicy love, then dressed and strolled down the street to Lorna Sue's big yellow house. Here, at last, was what had brought me back to Owago. To face the foe. To survey defenses and gather crucial intelligence.

Given my history, the Zylstra homestead had always seemed vaguely threatening, at times edging up on eerie, and as we approached the front door I felt my heart doing little somersaults. For an instant I nearly turned away. Courageously, however, I made a fist, risked my knuckles, and was soon rewarded by a loud grinding noise within, succeeded by metallic squeaks, succeeded by a voice yelling, 'Jesus Christ, just *wait* a minute, for Chrissake!' A moment later I was gazing down upon a wizened old lady in a wheelchair: Lorna Sue's paternal grandmother – Earleen Zylstra by name – a creature riddled to the core with spite and mental illness. We had not encountered each other since my wedding day, but the old woman cocked

* Given my paramour's Dutch ancestry, one would have expected her to insist on sharing our expenses fifty-fifty. No dice. Penny-pinching silence.

her head in recognition. 'You,' she said. 'I thought you was ancient history.'

'Alas,' I said, 'I weren't.'

(Such grammar brings out the animal in me.)

Mrs Kooshof whispered the word *condescension*, digging a sharp Dutch elbow into my ribs. It seemed prudent to withhold further venom; I forced a smile, extended a hand, and informed Earleen that she was looking fit.

The old woman's beady eyes glistened. 'Fuck fit. You want in?'

'Splendid,' said I.

'Well, Jesus Christ,' Earleen grunted.

She spun around in her wheelchair and led us down a filthy hallway, through air that smelled of stewed underwear. In the living room a large TV set boomed out at full blather, six or seven brutish relatives camped before it in various states of stupefaction. A few I recognized, among them Lorna Sue's mother and father – Ned and Velva. But no one rose. No one glanced up. Hesitantly, I stepped forward, but at the same instant an ill-shaven old nun – an aunt, I believe – swiveled and made a slicing motion across her throat. 'Wait'll it's *over*!' she snapped. 'Jesus Christ.'

Amazing, I thought.

It was to these garbled chromosomes, this biological catastrophe that I had once cast my marital fortunes.

After a few seconds had ticked by, Mrs Kooshof and I took seats on the soiled carpet, where with the rest of the household we witnessed the concluding minutes of a program that featured homemade videotapes of people falling off curbs and chairs and bicycles. The slack-jawed Zylstra assemblage found these mishaps hypnotic. For a moment I nearly forgave Lorna Sue and Herbie their considerable sins. After all, what else could one expect from this puddle of baboon genes? (During my years of marriage I had done everything possible to avoid the whole loathsome clan, often inventing excuses to explain my absence at family gatherings. One Christmas I was diagnosed with lupus; the following summer I received a rare summons to the Vatican.) Naturally enough, my hands-off policy had caused domestic turmoil between Lorna Sue and me. Antisocial, she claimed. A compulsive liar. The word *pathological* had popped up. In truth, I will admit, I do at times incline toward exaggeration, especially in self-defense, but Lorna Sue's charges were essentially without substance. Prevarication comes in many shades. Mine was true-blue. I loved her. Yes, I *did* – more than anything – and she should not have left me over a couple of snow-white lies, a few embarrassing documents beneath a mattress.

Thus I sat tumbling inside myself, grieving again, full of remorse and self-hatred. My senses were temporarily impaired, and I failed to notice that the television had gone silent, that the room had mostly emptied of relatives, and that Lorna Sue's bovine genitors were now studying me from the sofa. Velva munched on candied popcorn. Ned blinked and massaged his belly. Both parents had reached their mid seventies, yet they seemed to have aged not at all. Bloated faces, dyed hair, pasty white skin. 'All right, so get off the floor,' Ned finally muttered. 'Can't you even sit in a chair like a normal person?'

I shrugged. 'Perfectly comfortable.'

'What the hell you *want*?'

'No wanting in the least,' I said. 'A courtesy call. In the neighborhood, as it were.'

'And there goes the fuckin' neighborhood,' Ned stupidly responded. (A former Jesuit, of all things. A divinity school dropout, now a foul-mouthed peddler of clichés.)

Shrill laughter came from the wheelchair across the room, where Earleen sat stroking a large gray cat. The old lady wiggled her tongue at me, almost flirtatiously, then winked and kissed her cat. (I was at a loss as to what any of this might

71

have signified. Dementia, perhaps – a household virus. More on this later.)

'Anyhow, face it,' Ned was saying. 'You're not even family no more. Barely ever was.' He squinted at his wife. 'Divorced, aren't they? Abe and Lorna Sue?'

'They sure as heck are,' said Velva.

'Bingo,' Ned said. 'Exactly what I thought.'

Mrs Kooshof nudged me. 'Who's Abe?'

'That, I'm afraid, would be I.'

'You told me –'

'A family nickname,' I said brusquely. 'Primate wordplay.'

Mrs Kooshof grinned. 'Abe! I *like* that!'

The topic wearied me. Though discomposed, I managed a pleasant sigh and then turned and inquired about Lorna Sue's well-being.

'Fine, I guess,' said Velva. 'Happy as a clam.' The woman's articulation, never the best, was now flawed by a mouthful of candied popcorn. 'Never saw her happier, not *ever*, and as long as you keep away from –'

'And her new husband? The name escapes me.'

'Yeah, sure, he's fine too. Rich and handsome.' She swallowed and refilled. 'What's it to you?'

'Compassion,' said I.

'Com-*what*?'

'Passion, Velva. Lorna Sue and I were once locked in holy matrimony. Cuckold and wife.'

Velva stopped chewing to sort this out. She was a large, square individual, almost certainly female. 'Well, okay,' she finally said, 'but you never had no compassion about *none* of us. Zilch. Never even showed up for a single Christmas.'

'Untrue,' I replied. 'One, I believe.'

Velva picked her teeth, ingested another mouthful of popcorn, glared at me, then stood up and waddled out of the room. The atmosphere, I noted, had gone sour. Earleen grinned from her wheelchair, Ned gaped at the universe with idiotic and wholly inhospitable eyes. Even more to my discomfort, however, was a large black-and-white photograph on the far wall: Lorna Sue and Herbie standing side by side, hands interlocked, their expressions saintly and mutually adoring. The frame had been draped with white satin, and directly beneath it, on a small table, stood a pair of candles. Like a family shrine, I thought, or some holy sacrarium. It crossed my mind – certainly not for the first time – that my marriage had been in trouble even before it began.

A few moments passed before Ned Zylstra was able to stitch together a coherent utterance.

'All right, asshole, here's the truth,' he said. 'Lorna Sue don't want you near her, not in a trillion miles. She *told* me so. Said you'd come crawling someday, trying to worm your way back. 'Worm' – exact quote. And if you ever showed up here, she said, I was supposed to kick your ass to kingdom come. *That's* where she wants you. Kingdom come.' The man sucked in a breath. (He was a smoker – Pall Malls.) 'Beat it,' he said. 'You and your floozy.'

Mrs Robert Kooshof looked up with interest.

'Floozy?' she said.

Earleen cackled from her wheelchair. 'Floozy! Jesus Christ!'

'Bingo,' said Ned.

A little vein twitched at Mrs Robert Kooshof's temple. To her credit, though, my companion remained poised. 'Well, listen, I've got my problems,' she said softly, 'but I don't suppose flooziness is one of them.' She adjusted her posture. A cool smile came to her lips. 'It's not your fault, obviously – too much time with Velva. All those popcorn farts.'

Ned began to rise, belly wobbling, but something in Mrs Kooshof's demeanor pressed him back into the sofa.

'Floozy,' she murmured.

At that instant our alliance was fully sealed.

'Okay, then,' Ned said, 'but if I was you, I'd be real extra careful. The professor here, he's like your jailbird husband. One more sneaky, lying, womanizing cheat. I thought maybe you'd had your fill of that with Doc.'

There was a short silence.

'Womanizing?' said Mrs Kooshof.

'Hell, yes. He had the *names* written down. These long lists, like account books.'

Mrs Kooshof's eyes slid, measuring me. She rose to her feet. 'With the aid of a garbage truck,' she said quietly, 'I believe we can find our own way out.'

'What's *that* supposed to mean?'

'It means,' she said, 'that I feel filthy.'

Outside, Mrs Kooshof was livid. 'You cheated on her, didn't you?'

'Cheated?'

'The ex-wife, Abe.'

'Please, that nickname,' I said. 'It rubs me the wrong way.'

Mrs Kooshof's glance grazed my forehead and ricocheted up the street. 'A word of advice, Thomas. I won't tolerate this lying-cheating stuff.'

'I never cheated on her.'

'What then?'

'It's complicated,' I said. 'A mattress was involved.'

We strolled the half block to Mrs Kooshof's residence (formerly my own), stripped to the quick, ran water into her large blue bathtub, eased ourselves in, and began scrubbing off the Zylstra grime. My companion's mood was uneasy, even sullen, but as so often happens in such liquid settings, one thing swiftly led to another. Cause and effect. Splashy. And as we locked limbs – face-to-face, more or less – I was surprised by odd stirrings of tenderness, even affection. For the

74

moment, at least, Lorna Sue seemed an abstraction, more icon than human being. Mrs Robert Kooshof, by way of contrast, offered the undeniable bounties of the here and now. Powerful Dutch thighs. Breasts to float a navy. Yet the surprise was not physical. The surprise was this: I was at peace. I was quietly and vastly content.

Afterward, we lounged in the tub with twin glasses of Beaujolais. (Both of us, I must confide, were spent.) 'Talk fast,' said Mrs Kooshof. 'Short and sweet. What happened with you and Lorna Sue?'

I studied her from the far end of the tub. 'The truth, you mean?'

'No long-winded speeches.'

'Well, fine,' I said, 'but I'll have to go back to the beginning.'

'When?'

'Nineteen fifty-two. It'll sound ridiculous.'

'What *doesn't*?' She sighed.

And thus I began as I must always begin, in June 1952, middle-century Minnesota, on that silvery-hot morning when Herbie Zylstra and I nailed two plywood boards together and called it –

'You already *told* me that,' said Mrs Kooshof.

'I didn't tell you about the cat.'

9

Cat

Let us pause over the word *ridiculous*.

It is worth noting – would you not agree? – that our lives are often sculpted by the absurd, the unlikely, the purely fortuitous. Love, for instance. Pay heed to your own pitiful history: that afternoon when you bumped into a certain young man on a sidewalk in downtown Minneapolis, or Sioux City, or Chicago. The time, let us say, was 4:14 P.M. Not twelve seconds earlier, not thirty seconds later. A horn blared. You were startled – you glanced sideways – and in that instant the fateful collision occurred. Your purse dropped to the pavement. Your diaphragm spilled out. The young man smiled. A year later you were married. Five years after that, or twelve, or twenty, the love of your life deserted you and moved to Fiji with a cheap harlot named Sandra.

We marry accidents.

We are betrayed by improbabilities.

The truth, I submit, is that we must *always* begin with the ridiculous, and therefore I said to Mrs Robert Kooshof: 'You recall Earleen's cat?'

'That ugly gray thing?'

'Exactly.' I stretched back in the tub, tested my wine, studied the majestic woman opposite me. (Astonishing, really. Her ample physique, my own good fortune. How it turned out

76

that the two of us had arrived at this singular junction in time and space – *this* house, *this* warm and intoxicating bubble bath – represented its own telling parable about the role of fate in human affairs. Incredible, yes? A tad ridiculous?)

'Now, of course, it wasn't *that* cat,' I told her. 'An ancestor, I assume. Perhaps the great-grandmother, perhaps the great-great-grandmother. I am not up-to-date on my feline generations. In any event, the cat of which I speak – actually a very elderly cat – looked very much like the hideous gray creature you saw today. Identical markings, same stupid face.'

Mrs Robert Kooshof nodded impatiently. 'Cats? Divorce? I don't follow.'

'Pay attention,' I said, and arranged the flats of my feet against her chest.

Mrs Kooshof's intolerance for complexity, for the looping circuitry of a well-told tale, symptomizes an epidemic disease of our modern world. (I see it daily among my students. The short attention span, the appetite limited to linearity. Too much *Melrose Place*.) Ordinarily I am baffled and distressed by this syndrome, yet in the case of Mrs Robert Kooshof I found it almost endearing. She was falling in love. Tumbling, in fact. (Hence her need to plumb my troubles with Lorna Sue. Hence impatience.) To a woman in love, or on the precipice of love, the semantic road between *cat* and *mattress* can seem arduous indeed.

I did my best to reassure her. Charitably, I ran my feet along the slope of her breasts, down to the brownish, outsized, distinctly leathern nipples, which I compressed between my toes.

'Certain detours,' I said firmly, 'can prove rewarding. You have to understand that as children both Herbie and Lorna Sue were fond of animals.'

'Animals? What sort?'

'Oh, all sorts.'

77

I sketched the scene for her: a house filled with wildlife. Ferrets, flies, goldfish, hamsters, pigeons, spiders, earthworms, geese. Most prominently, however, Herbie and Lorna Sue were the proud owners of a snake named Sebastian – a baby python, to be precise – which they housed in a glass cage up in the attic. This serpent, I said, was hardly the most playful pet in the world, and my strongest recollection was of a creature that never moved. ('He's *not* dead,' Lorna Sue used to yell. 'He's *tired*!')

The only fun with Sebastian, I told Mrs Kooshof, occurred at feeding time. Once a week the python required sustenance, which took the form of a live rat, and on Saturday mornings the three of us would troop down to Nell's Pet Shoppe just off Diagonal Road. A compelling experience. To this day, in fact, I could still see Lorna Sue standing before the rat cages, deciding which of the many inhabitants might make the most succulent meal – the plumpest, the juiciest, the most digestible. 'That one,' she'd finally say. 'That one looks delicious.'

Then we'd march home with Sebastian's dinner, which had been placed inside a little pet box with air holes and cotton lining. On the lid of each box was imprinted a poignant epitaph: I'VE FINALLY FOUND A HOME.

'Excuse me,' said Mrs Kooshof. 'Get to the point.'

She made a threatening gesture at the far end of the tub, a hurry-up-or-die motion, her formidable Dutch torso shifting dangerously amid the suds.

I would not be hurried.

'Digressions are digressions,' I declared, 'only to the faint of heart. This next part you will find hypnotic.'

And then at my own pace – slowing down a bit just to tantalize her – I explained how the three of us would troop up into the attic on those long-gone Saturday mornings, how Herbie would remove the cover to Sebastian's cage and grab the rat by its tail and dangle it over the serpent's flat, bored, somewhat puzzled face. 'Soup's on!' Herbie would cry, at which point Lorna Sue would peek out between splayed fingers. (An indelible image: those lustrous brown eyes, the latticework of her tiny fingers. On such occasions I feared my heart might break. Love and death: the drama was unbearable.)

For the rat, of course, it was a different matter: freaky eyeballs, squeaking sounds. Suspended by its tail, the creature clawed at the air as if to seek traction on its own existence. I felt a twinge of revulsion at this, a little knot in my chest, but Herbie seemed oblivious to it all. I do not believe it was a matter of cruelty or malice. I believe he was *curious*. It was in Herbie's nature, I think, to be fascinated – even enchanted – by the biological workings of our world. His round, pasty face positively glowed. 'Come and get it!' he'd chant, and then at the last nerve-snapping instant he would drop the berserk rat to the bottom of Sebastian's cage.

'Okeydokey, that's it,' he'd say, and we would troop downstairs for some Cheetos.

Mrs Robert Kooshof gazed at me. (Flushed cheeks, greenish jowls.)

'You know something?' she said. 'You're a sick human being, Thomas. I mean that from the bottom of my heart. And besides, you're stalling. Snakes and rats – how does it tie in with lying and cheating and divorce?'

'I never cheated,' I said sharply.

'So you *told* me. Everything except the facts – the plain truth.'

Mrs Kooshof sniffed and gave me a belligerent stare. Her churlishness, I instantly understood, was mere camouflage for an immense vulnerability within. The woman had been severely wounded of late: a felon for a husband, a marriage gone stale. Her libido, like her spouse, had been locked away behind steel bars, and I dare say that in different ways, to different degrees, we shared a common hurt.

'Give it a chance,' I said quietly. 'The snake connects to the rats, the rats connect to the mattress.'

'Rats?'

'Of course.'

Mrs Kooshof sighed. 'Well, for Pete's sake. I thought you said *cat*.'

'And so I did. I was just about to –'

'Christ help me,' said Mrs Kooshof.

What happened, I told her, was that on a sunny morning in 1952 – in June, to be exact, barely a week before Herbie and I constructed our plywood airplane – an event occurred that created a chain reaction leading to marital cataclysm half a lifetime later. Innocently enough, this disastrous sequence began with our usual feeding program: the purchase of a fresh rat, the hike back to Herbie's house, the climb up to the attic. All perfectly routine, I explained. Herbie went through his standard pre-feeding ritual, dangling the rat by its tail over Sebastian's cage, chanting 'Dinner, dinner,' partly teasing, partly whetting Sebastian's appetite. On this occasion, however, the rodent was a particularly lively specimen, large and black and brawny, and with a great squeak it suddenly jerked free and dropped to the windowsill behind Sebastian's cage. Instantly, it darted outside and scrambled down to a narrow ledge four or five feet below the window. It crouched there, just out of reach.

Herbie's face creased up. The rat had cost him seventy-five cents – a fortune back then.

Anyone but Herbie, I believe, would have given up. The ledge was at most ten inches wide – thirty or forty feet above a cement driveway – but after a second he made a decisive grunting sound and said, 'Stay here. I'll be right back.' He disappeared down the attic stairs, returning after a few minutes with a length of rope and a large gray cat.

He grinned and flicked his eyebrows and marched over to the open window. Almost immediately, I recognized the logic at work.

Herbie secured one end of his rope to the cat's hind paws, lifted the animal to the sill, grasped the rope, and began lowering the cat head down toward the half-crazed, half-paralyzed rat. Here, I thought, was genius. Insensitive, yes, but Herbie Zylstra had a firm understanding of the laws of nature: Ours is essentially a cat-eat-rat world.

Mrs Kooshof blanched. 'You mean . . . ?'

'I do, indeed. A fishing expedition. Live bait.'

'You're *both* sick.'

I leaned back in the tub, polished off my wine, rearranged my feet against their fleshy cushions.

'Sickness,' I said gravely, 'is beside the point.'

'There isn't any point!' she snapped. 'And get those *feet* off me.'

I responded as a gentleman, with a tolerant, forgiving, wholly benevolent smile. My feet, however, remained in place.

'All in good time,' I said briskly, then reviewed the circumstances for her: how Herbie had tied the cat to a rope – a fairly *large* cat, I added – and began lowering it toward the trembling rat. (This dizzying operation, I will admit, soon nauseated me.) And the cat, too, seemed out of sorts – eyes glazed, hissing, pawing at the air with its front legs. 'Hey, be careful,' Lorna Sue murmured, 'you'll hurt my *cat*,' but Herbie shook his head and told her it was like a carnival ride, lots of fun.

Lorna Sue frowned. 'Well, it doesn't *look* like fun,' she said. 'Topsy-turvy and upside down and everything.'

Herbie paid no attention.

Carefully, muttering to himself, he kept inching his baited

81

rope down toward the cornered rat. The idea, of course, was for the cat to seize the rat in its mouth, at which point Herbie would instantly yank both creatures back into the attic. An elegant concept, but one complicated by issues of geometry and discomfort. Three stories high, suspended by its hind paws, the terror-crazed feline had no stomach for lunch. 'Fetch!' Herbie cried, and swung the animal like a pendulum, working the rope with quick, encouraging jerks. 'Come on, girl, come on!' he chanted. 'Yummy!'

Lorna Sue and I leaned out the window for a better view. I remember our arms touching, a shiver running up my shoulder blades. (Even then, as a child, my passions were high.) I remember, too, the tension in her face, how her tongue curled seductively against her upper front teeth. 'Listen, I don't think this is working,' she said. 'You're almost *hanging* her.'

This seemed a valid point.

Three feet below, the cat was quite literally at the end of its rope, thrashing in raw cat-terror. Somehow its neck had gotten tangled in a large loop, which tightened each time Herbie tugged. Asphyxiation seemed imminent, and with a loud, desperate hiss – a screech, actually – the cat made a sudden corkscrew motion, twisting violently.

Herbie lost his grip on the rope.

The cat dropped to the ledge below, landed heavily, and then peered up at us.

'Okay, smartie, so now what?' said Lorna Sue. 'I *told* you it wouldn't work.'

Herbie's jaw made an audible pop.

'Well, piss,' he said, and climbed out the window.

Herbie Zylstra was not the sort of person to call it quits, not ever. He grasped the sill, turned his back to us, and lowered himself down toward the ledge. For a few seconds he dangled there. (Like a circus act, I thought, except no net.) He stared straight at me, almost defiantly, then let go and dropped the final few inches.

A miracle, really.

He wobbled briefly and then found his balance. 'Moron crappy idiot fuckhead *cat*,' he said.

Quickly, then, Herbie grabbed the cat by the scruff of its neck, gave it a scolding shake, and passed it up to me.

Next he retrieved the rat.

And right then – in what would prove a pivotal intersection in my life – the unwinding reel of our universe clicked into a kind of jerky slow motion. A set of snapshots, in fact.

I remember Herbie uttering the word 'Catch.'

I remember how he gripped the rat like a baseball. How he turned and tossed it up to me.

I remember reaching out with my left hand.

I remember the rat's glittery left eye, a high squealing sound, Lorna Sue's gusty breath against my shoulder.

Two unfortunate variables were at work. Number one, I was still cradling the cat – Vanilla, by name. Number two, I had never been blessed with athletic prowess.

The rat bounced off my fingertips.

I also dropped Vanilla. (More accurately, I juggled the cat for a split second, almost recaptured her, then watched her plummet like a furry rock to the cement driveway.) Contrary to cat mythology, Vanilla did not alight nimbly on her feet. She landed like a heavy foot stepping into a puddle.

'Killer!' Lorna Sue screamed.

Killer? Not only was the charge inaccurate; it was also grossly inconsistent – the purest double standard. Bear in mind that just minutes earlier Lorna Sue had been happily feeding a live, innocent, utterly defenseless rat to her fucking python.

'Killer!' she screamed – absurdly – and I defended myself as best I could. I took the wise course. I sucked up my courage and lied.

'Your stupid cat!' I yelled back. 'It *bit* me.'

Lorna Sue hesitated. I could see the uncertainty in her eyes, those microscopic droplets of remorse and guilt that accompany a convincing piece of deception.

'Bit you?' she said. 'Does it hurt?'

'Like crazy,' I said. 'I need a *rabies* shot.'

And then effortlessly, out of the blue, I summoned the evidence of tears. Real tears, real anguish. (One could argue, perhaps, that I am a born liar. But one could also argue that I had no alternative. I was in love with Lorna Sue Zylstra – madly in love, heroically in love – and simply could not bear the burden of her ill will.)

It was an instructive moment. In matters of the heart, with love on the line, what can be the harm of an innocent lie or two?

'Rabies,' I repeated.

I winced and grabbed my thumb, removing it from view, but already Lorna Sue had performed a rapid medical survey. The concern in her eyes turned to skepticism, then faded into something for which there is no adequate piece of language – something sad and weary and resigned and knowledgeable. A child, yes. But she looked at me with exactly the same expression I would encounter four decades later, on a Tuesday afternoon, the ninth day of July, when she turned her back and walked out on me forever.

As an adult, she said: 'Don't be an eighteen-year-old.'

As a child, in the attic that day, she said: 'You're a liar, Tommy.'

Mrs Robert Kooshof removed my feet from her breasts, stepped out of the tub, and began drying herself with a large monogrammed towel.

'What a jerk,' she muttered. 'I was totally patient with you – I sat there like some idiot psychiatrist – and what's the upshot? You told her a dumb fib. So what? I mean, you could've explained *that* in ten seconds.'

'I'm a wordsmith,' I said. 'It takes time.'

Mrs Kooshof wrapped the towel around her splendidly proportioned upper torso. With a distinct growl, she reached down, turned on the cold water, and left me to the pneumonia bugs.

Dumb fib?

Mrs Robert Kooshof had missed the point.

A pattern was established on that Saturday morning. Issues of trust, issues of faith.

If necessary, we will lie to win love. We will lie to keep love.

(Cat becomes *mattress.)*

Granted, Vanilla had not bitten me – my own fault – but why should a mere accident jeopardize the world's greatest romance? Why should I (or anyone) be condemned by a fleeting lapse of concentration? Why should I (or you) be judged by a piece of bad luck, a fluke of physics, a momentary miscalculation? Under such circumstances, is it truly a crime to rescue oneself with a modest little lie?

Apparently so.

10

Performance

It was not until evening that Mrs Kooshof spoke to me again. I poured on the charm. I followed her around the house in my underwear. Persuasively, like the teacher I am, I insisted that the fate of that poor, crushed cat was entirely relevant to the collapse of my marriage years later. Without such detail, I asked, how could she expect to understand the human being she'd found weeping in her backyard?

None of this helped.

Mrs Kooshof remained incommunicative, silent as stone, and in the end I was compelled to grovel. I did the tear thing, pleaded for a final chance – a first-rate performance – and near dinnertime Mrs Kooshof relented. 'All right,' she said. 'One chance. Divorce. What did you *do* to her?'

I hesitated.

'A long story,' I said.

(The truth, to put it squarely, is that I have always had trouble with the truth. Confession is not to my taste. I fear ridicule; I fear embarrassment.)

Mrs Kooshof may well have suspected my dilemma. The wrinkles along her eyes seemed to soften. 'You stepped out on her?' she said quietly. 'Had a fling?'

'Never.'

'Secret love letters?'

'Hardly,' I said. Then to my surprise I added: 'The betraying little saint wanted me to see a psychiatrist. A counselor! She thought I was – you know – thought I was losing my grip. Thought I was paranoid. Jealous of Herbie, jealous of a hairy goddamn tycoon. Ridiculous! I *told* you, didn't I? Right at the start didn't I tell you point-blank how ridiculous it was? Absurd! You *heard* me, right?'

'Oh, yes,' said Mrs Kooshof.

'Do I *look* paranoid?'

'Well –'

'Totally nuts! Lorna Sue, I mean.' My voice had shuttled up to a high register, quavering. 'Believe me, it was a nightmare. She said she'd leave me if I didn't get help. *Her* phrase – "Get help." What could I do? I faked it. Made up a few stories. So *what*?'

'What sort of stories?'

'Well, you know – the counselor kind. Told her I was busy getting analyzed. Very helpful, I told her. Except one day Lorna Sue picked up the checkbook, asked why I wasn't paying the cocksucker. I was trapped. So I started writing these phony checks to make her feel better. Hid them under the mattress.'

'You invented a shrink?'

'Right.'

'And wrote checks to this . . . this made-up psychiatrist?'

'Right.'

Mrs Kooshof's face lost some of its wholesome Aryan radiance. She seemed to slide down inside herself, quiet and thoughtful. 'Well, God,' she finally said, 'I don't know how you could even sleep at night.'

'Fitfully,' I admitted. 'Poorly, indeed.'

She turned and faced me. 'This whole thing, it's just so incredibly convoluted. You're sure there wasn't something else?'

'Such as?'

'You tell *me*. Girls. Affairs.'

'Certainly not,' I said firmly. 'Out of the question.'

In truth, however, I felt a twinge of guilt. Along with the checks, I had stashed several other embarrassing items beneath my marital mattress, most prominently a certain leather-bound love ledger. It was a diary of sorts, a carefully quantified record of my life as a man of the world. (Names. Dates. Body types. Hair color. Other such vital statistical data.) Perhaps at that instant I should have mentioned the ledger – who knows? – but under the circumstances I saw no point in overwhelming my consort with excessive data. Instead I shrugged and said, 'No affairs.'

Mrs Kooshof sighed.

'Well, sorry, but I don't understand. You could've just – I don't know – just junked the phony checks. Tossed them out. Burned them.'

'An oversight,' I said. 'Major error. I forgot.'

'Forgot?'

'I lead a hectic life.'

My companion pushed to her feet, carried her half-eaten dinner to the kitchen sink, then turned and gazed directly at me for several seconds, her lips moving as if she were at work on a problem of trigonometry. The dear woman had never looked more ravishing: an improbable blend of Great Plains housewife and sturdy strumpet. (Rayon blouse. Black stretch pants. Alpine breasts. Bewitching blue eyes.) In short, to be completely frank, the laws of hydraulics had come into play, and it was with a playful tingle of joy that I rose up, joined her at the sink, arranged my hands at her hips, and suggested an impromptu excursion to the bedroom.

Mrs Kooshof shook her head. 'Zip it shut,' she said. 'You're still not telling me the whole truth. I can *feel* it. What happened next?'

I made a silky, sensuous sound with the tip of my tongue. 'Nothing, really. Pronounced myself cured. Told her Dr Constantine did a bang-up job.'

'Dr Who?'

'Constantine. Ralph. Fictitious, but a good man.'

Mrs Kooshof grunted. 'But what if your wife had gone to a phone book? Tried to find the guy?'

'Unlisted,' I said. 'Exclusive shrink.'

'You told her that?'

'More or less.'

Again, I tried to divert her attention, toying boisterously with a button on her blouse, but Mrs Kooshof pushed me back and said, 'You're right, it's ridiculous. In fact, I don't think you even know what truth *is*. Not a clue.'

She strode out of the kitchen.

For the next hour, if not longer, she busied herself in the bathroom, behind a locked door, and eventually, in a condition of intense discomfort, I found myself attempting to converse through the tiny crack between floor and door. There was no longer any point in holding back. Flat on my belly, lips low, I completed the dismal record – how Herbie gave every indication of being in love with his own sister, how he had spied on me, how he had located incriminating evidence under my mattress and ruthlessly displayed it to Lorna Sue. My performance, I judged, was soulful. I pressed my heart to the door. I wept copiously.

(The word *performance*, I must insist, should in no way imply dissimulation on my part. The exact reverse: I was engaged in heartfelt truth telling. I was throwing an actor's light on the human spirit. Survey, for a moment, your own linguistic performances. When your husband deserted you. When you learned about that cheap redhead named Sandra. Did you not feel as if you were on a stage, or before a movie camera, and did you not play your role with gusto? Perhaps ham

89

it up on occasion? Manufacture a wail or two, exaggerate a groan, embellish your own invective? In one way or another, it seems to me, virtually every human utterance represents a performance of sorts, and I, too, have been known to lay on the flourishes. I enjoy the decorative adjective, the animating adverb. I use words, in other words, as a fireman uses water.)

Hence no apologies.

I wept and emoted and sprayed language through the crack beneath Mrs Kooshof's bathroom door. I fell asleep at the end. (Emotion of any sort exhausts me.)

When I awoke, Mrs Robert Kooshof lay at my side. Her breath came in loud gusts. At first I felt certain she was sleeping, but after a moment it occurred to me that this sweet woman was shedding tears of her own. She shuddered and moved up against me. I held her. She held me. And then for some time we gave way to our grief, a pair of middle-aged love losers, two desperate souls.

Deep in the night, Mrs Kooshof said, 'Thomas, could you ever love me?'

Later she said, 'I suppose not.'

And then near morning, she put her head on my shoulder and said, 'You're a scoundrel, right? All the lies. Just a hopeless, unreliable old tomcat – that was the whole point of your stupid story. And I'll never trust you. A promise – I won't *let* myself.'

But this, too, was a performance.

At daybreak I woke to find her sound asleep, thumb at her mouth, curled up like a little girl.

I was on the road to Minneapolis by seven o'clock. The skies were clear, the air was balmy. At the halfway mark I stopped at a restaurant, consumed a hearty breakfast, and placed a collect call to the Kooshof residence in Owago. No answer, so I tried again when I reached my apartment, then twice every hour until dark. Inexplicably, I felt a flutter of disappointment. Almost terror, almost sadness. I went out for an early supper – called her once more between courses – then took a long, leaden stroll across campus before making my way home.

She stood waiting at the door to my apartment building. Inevitable, I suppose. Yet oddly touching.

I helped with her suitcases, of which there were four, and kissed her in the elevator. She wore high heels, a black blouse, glass earrings, carmine lipstick. She'd had her hair cut.

'Tampa,' she said. 'I'm still invited?'

'Yes, of course,' I told her, then hesitated. 'You realize that we don't leave for two more weeks?'

'I'll wait,' she said. 'Right here.'

'Certainly.'

'And I should warn you, Thomas. I get what I want.'

'Do you, indeed?'

For a few seconds Mrs Kooshof watched the elevator's floor indicator. 'Tampa – it's so boring. Why not Mexico or Guadeloupe? Forget all this revenge business.'

'Not likely,' I said.

She shrugged and unbuttoned her black blouse. 'You care for me, though. You *do*, don't you? I'll bet you're almost in love.'

'Ah,' said I.

11

Goof

The next morning, as I strolled to class, I spotted Goof a half block ahead of me, his face partially obscured by a stop sign. The old terror hit me like a hammer. I stopped, turned into a doorway, waited a few moments. When I looked back again, he was gone.

Granted, it had been thirty-some years since we last crossed paths.

But still.

Coincidence? Mistaken identity? My own failing eyesight? Not a chance. It was Goof.

Over dinner that evening, when I mentioned the incident to Mrs Robert Kooshof, she squinted at me without comprehension. 'Goof?' she said.

'Ghost from the past,' I informed her. 'And a very dangerous ghost at that.'

'Some woman you messed with?'

'Female, no. Messed with, yes.'

For my own reasons, which will become apparent in due time, I was not at liberty to elaborate on the matter, and the best I could manage was an oblique, somewhat evasive reference to certain wartime experiences.

Mrs Kooshof laughed. (Frothy laughter. Bits of broccoli.)

'Soldier?' she said. '*You?*'

'Precisely so.'

'You're not serious?'

I regarded her with pique. 'Not only that,' I said stiffly, 'but a hero to boot. Have I shown you my Silver Star?'

'I don't even know what –'

'Combat decoration. With a V-device, I might add. V as in valor. Very rare.'

Again, the woman burst out in pointless laughter, showering me with the remains of her meal, and in a huff I pushed to my feet, strode into the den, retrieved the medal, marched back to the table, and dropped it on her plate with a sharp clatter.

'Do not,' I said, 'make the mistake of underestimating me. A common blunder. One which Goof himself came to repent. Tulip too.'

'Tulip?'

'And Wildfire. And Death Chant. And Bonnie Prince Charming.'

Mrs Kooshof eyed my Silver Star, a flush spilling out across her cheeks and forehead. (It was apparent that her estimate of Thomas H Chippering was in the process of rapid revision. Bedroom thoughts. Adulation. The usual.)

'But, Thomas,' she said, 'you're not making sense. This wildfire business . . . tulips and medals . . . I just don't follow.'

I fished the Silver Star from her plate, cleansed it with a cloth napkin, pinned it to my lapel.

'Be that as it may,' I said cryptically, 'you may take my word that certain combat traumas are not easily forgotten. I am in point of fact being pursued like some wounded moose, and there is absolutely no doubt – none at all – that we must watch our collective steps.'

My companion squinted again, skeptically, her lovely blue eyes locked to the twinkling Silver Star at my chest. 'You're not imagining this, Thomas? I mean, after all these years?'

'It was a pledge,' I said. 'A threat. They swore they'd come after me.'

'But why, though?'

I shook my head. 'That part remains classified. Let us simply say that I more than earned this decoration. In point of fact, I was *too* brave.'

'Thomas, for crying out loud, I can't see –'

'Believe me,' I said, 'even gallantry can be taken to an extreme. I repeat: *too* brave, *too* heroic, and the consequences have been dogging me ever since.' I looked at her solemnly. 'Imagine, if you will, Lord Jim in reverse.'

Mrs Kooshof sighed and began clearing the table. Plainly, she was baffled by it all, yet at the same time the dear woman could not resist taking several furtive peeks at the Silver Star upon my breast. (Storm clouds, yes, but also the standard silver lining.) After washing the dishes, and after carefully chaining the door of my apartment, I squired my overheated mistress bedward.

I need not dwell on the end product. She was my jockey, I was her explosive young charger.

Still, as we lathered down, I could not rid myself of that chased sensation. The ghosts were real. And for some time I lay sleepless, listening for footsteps, watching headlights sweep across the drawn bedroom shades.

Two mornings later I spotted Death Chant on the steps outside my classroom building.

Delusions?

Again, not a chance: I *told* you I was being chased.

12

Predator

That term I was teaching a pet course entitled 'It's Your Thick Tongue,' in which I placed special emphasis on pronunciation, grammar, and vocabulary. In part, the course was designed to augment a student's word base by one or two percent, a lowly enough goal but one with merit in this age of linguistic neglect. Near the end of each session I would circulate a list of ten common and reasonably useful words: e.g., *debilitate, substance, prevaricate, conjugal, apostasy, turncoat, infidelity, treason, cuckold, tycoon.* As homework, my students were required to spend time with their dictionaries, researching such matters as meaning, etymology, cognates, pronunciation, synonymy, and usage. (It is my well-informed view, I should add, that the dictionary stands as our supreme book of books, an embodiment of both civilization and the very idea of civilization. I tend toward zealotry on this subject. In the evenings, over a cup of Sanka, I read aloud from my *Webster's* just as certain Baptists recite from their Bibles.) In any event, to begin a class, I typically deliver an elegant little lecture organized around the terms listed during our previous session, employing each in context, finally incorporating all ten in a single efficient paragraph.

An illustration might be helpful. Consider, for example, the words listed above. At our first class meeting after spring break, freshened and revitalized by Mrs Robert Kooshof, I concluded my minilecture with these vivid, solidly constructed sentences: 'There is substance to the notion that infidelity, as practiced by turncoats and tycoons, represents our most debilitating form of modern apostasy. I do not prevaricate; I bear witness as a cuckold, a victim of conjugal treason.'

One of my students applauded. A young woman, as it turned out. A brunette. Narrow hips. Trim.

After class, as a matter of good form, I was obligated to flag down my raven admirer. Lively chitchat ensued – invigorating, I thought – and naturally I inquired as to her name, which was Toni with an *i*, short for Antonia with a pair of firmly bracketing *a*'s. To our mutual pleasure, the conversation ran on for a full twenty-two minutes, Toni's eyes appropriately aglow, each tick of the clock chiming with innuendo and possibility. The girl was smitten. It happens: I could not fault her. Near the end of our dialogue we scheduled an appointment to discuss her honors thesis, exchanged hugs, then parted ways with sprightly steps.

Am I a rake? A predator?

Certainly not.

Lorna Sue was mistaken on both charges.

I mention my encounter with Toni for two reasons. First, the episode offers incontestable evidence regarding my stature both as a teacher and as a man of the world. Though far from flawless, I am not without virtues. Among them, I sincerely believe, you would soon discover a rigorous intelligence, manly charm, playfulness, and a rather dangerous sensuality.

I am a war hero. I stand just over six-six. I do my sit-ups. Women notice.

('Predator!' Lorna Sue once yelled, but where was the crime? A closed office door? A Do Not Disturb sign? I touched no one. No one touched me. We live in a world increasingly populated by know-it-alls and backbiters and conclusion-jumpers and ignorant moral watchdogs. My ex-wife, I fear, was one.)

Second, and much more important, I bring up the comely Toni for strictly narrative reasons. Every dark cloud may well have its silver lining, but I have come to learn that every silver lining has its dark consequences. That same evening, during the dinner hour, my slim-hipped coed made the mistake of calling me at home. Worse yet, I committed my own callow error, allowing Mrs Robert Kooshof the privilege of answering the telephone.

When she returned to the table, Mrs Kooshof's complexion had turned splotchy. Instantly, with not a word of warning, she raised her voice to me in a manner that was completely unjustified. I sat stunned. A moment earlier we had been happily discussing our travel plans, daydreaming aloud about Tampa, and now she was bellowing such words as *predator* and *deviant* and *cradle robber*. It was a sonic replay, you might say, of my most unfortunate experiences with Lorna Sue. I felt my own anger rising. Very forcefully, with the outrage of the innocent, I responded by making it clear that I had just met the silly young candy cane, that I had done nothing improper, that I was not lord and master of the city's telephone lines.

Mrs Kooshof seemed taken aback. 'She called you Lucky Duckie.'

'Perfectly explicable,' said I.

'*How?*'

I did not have the stamina to explain. I rose to my feet, moved away from the table, and spent the remainder of the evening in an injured sulk. The hurt was real. In virtually every detail, the evening's incident had haunting antecedents in my defunct marriage, in my whole hideous history with Herbie and Lorna Sue: the rush to judgment, the maligning of character. Even the telephone.

Late in the night, as Mrs Kooshof slept, I found a screwdriver and proceeded into the den. A pity, I thought. Silver linings and so on. How quickly the fair bud of romance fades into trickery.

I took apart the telephone, deactivated its ringer, snapped off the red wire that connects to my answering machine.

A familiar routine. Through several tense years of marriage, the screwdriver had served as a first and final line of defense. (Have I yet mentioned my troubles with the telephone? How Lorna Sue kept asking why the damned thing never rang? How one afternoon she came home with a brand-new Southwestern Bell Freedom model? How I spent half the night prying off its plastic base plate, struggling to decipher its internal workings? A tense few hours, believe me. I have since invested only in the most unsophisticated telephones – rotary style, basic black, no gadgets.)

With my engineering complete, I retired to bed, where I slept peacefully but alone. Mrs Kooshof took her slumber behind the locked door of my bathroom.

13

Pontiac

My apartment was far from spacious. A galley kitchen, a modest bath, two bedrooms (one of which I had converted to a den), and a living room that could be navigated in three or four untaxing strides. Cramped quarters, in other words, especially for two mature adults. Despite all her marvelous qualities, which were legion, Mrs Robert Kooshof cannot be faithfully described as petite, and as a consequence our twelve days of cohabitation proved stressful at times. Agility was required. Patience, too, and geometrical compromise. We were quite literally stuck with each other. Moreover, though it's depressing to admit, I had become accustomed to the bachelor's life since Lorna Sue's departure, setting my own hours, adhering to certain tidy routines, and it was only natural that I encountered a number of purely psychological difficulties in adjusting to Mrs Kooshof's overwhelming presence.

The telephone represented one such problem. Basic courtesy another. The woman took keen interest in my personal affairs – a chronic snoop, in my opinion. A suspicious, shameless busybody. More than once I returned from class to find my underwear refolded, my checkbook updated, my social calendar stained with coffee and large Dutch fingerprints.

Much as I enjoyed Mrs Kooshof's company, it soon became apparent that precautions were in order. Within a week I had my mail held for pickup. I disconnected the door buzzer. (For truly vital communications, I passed out my unlisted phone number to certain favored students, among them the ebony-haired Toni.)

Not that I had anything to hide.

Rather, after my experience with Lorna Sue, I lived in fear of even the slightest misapprehension. Mrs Kooshof, for instance, might well have found cause for worry in those ten or twelve occasions when young Toni required after-hours assistance with her thesis. On my own part it was an open-and-shut case of professional responsibility. I had personally suggested the girl's topic (a close textual study of Western matrimonial vows), and it therefore seemed reasonable that I should be on call for emergencies.

Even so, I was careful. Toni and I rendezvoused at her dormitory, in a cozy sitting room to which she had the only key, and over many productive midafternoon hours the two of us pored through documents both modern and ancient. We put our heads together decoding the Latin, Gallic, and Germanic wedding vows; we rejoiced in our discovery that fidelity, in one form or another, stands as an unvarying multicultural pledge of nuptial union (i.e., 'to love, honor, and obey'); we recited the Greek vows aloud, working on syntax and inflection; we stumbled across astounding parallels between the English admonition 'to have and to hold,' et cetera – with its conspicuously carnal overtones – and the German analogue, '*und ehren und ihn in Freud und Leid treu bleiben, bis der Tot euch scheidet . . .*'

Altogether, I must say, here was a genuinely refreshing academic experience. Rarely does joint scholarship generate such sparks, such red-hot fire, and in all respects my trim Toni positively blistered as a model student. Never tardy. Worshipful. Erotic. The girl dressed well, favoring silks and linens, and plainly appreciated my wit. On one occasion, I recall, the little marshmallow fell into convulsions at some clever barb of mine, her tender brown knee brushing my own, the tips of her fingers alighting on my arm.

I could not help myself. I stiffened. (Affection is one thing, respect another.) I saw no reason to reject the poor girl, whose heart and soul were engaged; thus I settled on the tact of feigning nervousness, adjusting my tie, gently quoting a few lines from Shakespeare: 'Then come kiss me, sweet and twenty/Youth's a stuff will not endure.' The idea was to defuse things. To objectify our master-student paradigm.

Toni misunderstood. She jerked her hand away and said, 'The fuck does *that* mean?'

Instantly, I recanted.

The quotation, I insisted, was simply a case in point. No offense, no harm.

Toni gave me an insolent stare. 'I should turn you in,' she said fiercely. 'Bring you up on charges or something. No joke, I should.'

'Now, please,' I said. 'I was merely citing –'

'What a manipulator,' said Toni.

Manipulator: another word that ices my soul. *Turtle, engine, Pontiac, yellow, cornfield, rose, substance, mattress, manipulator.* Lorna Sue used the term often, violently, with a sadist's relish, knifing me with each cool syllable.

My resolve hardened.

'You're in the presence of a war hero,' I said sternly, 'so be careful. Let's talk this out quietly. Like a pair of grown adults.'

'Bullshit,' said Toni. 'I'm *not* an adult.'

I nodded and said, 'Fine, then. We'll start there.'

It took a good portion of the afternoon, a greater portion of my spiritual resources, but in the end I succeeded in mollifying my hypersensitive young chippie. Flattery, I have learned, is the key. I extolled Toni's intelligence, her work habits, the fact that she would be receiving a unique A-plus in 'It's Your Thick Tongue.' My dark maiden raised a questioning eyebrow. She sat down, crossed her long and shapely legs, brushed her hair back, lit a Virginia Slim without permission. Her expression was ripe with greed. Slowly at first, then rapidly, the girl's anger ebbed as I discussed my wholehearted support for her honors thesis, my willingness to provide help in any way possible.

'Yeah? Well, how so?' said Toni.

I smiled and held up the palms of my hands. 'Whatever strikes your fancy.'

'Write it,' she said.

'Write it?'

'The thesis,' she said. 'I want you to write it.'

We parted on amiable terms. A close call, obviously, but wisdom won the day.

That evening, after one of Mrs Kooshof's sumptuous suppers, I retired to my den and began composing the first chapter of a thesis that would later bear the title 'To You, Betrothed.' In a number of ways I enjoyed the task. I am deft with language; I take pleasure in the wax and wane of ideas. Still, my attitude toward young Toni had been altered irretrievably for the worse, and as I typed well into the night, page after numbing page, I paused frequently to intone the word *manipulator*.*

The two weeks prior to our departure for Tampa were among the most grueling of my life. On top of a full course load, with

---

* Where, one might legitimately ask, was Toni's conscience? Did the girl lose even a wink of sleep over the fact that the fluid sentences and paragraphs of her thesis had been composed by a foreign hand? Apparently not. Several weeks later, when I probed for moral misgivings, the luscious little fraud giggled and said, 'Well, heck, *I* don't mind.'

the usual crush of exams and papers, I was under pressure to sort through my wardrobe, purchase film and suntan lotion, prepare a game plan for revenge, attend to Mrs Kooshof's needs, and complete the final six chapters of Toni's honors thesis. The girl proved a demanding taskmistress. Several times she sent me back to do rewrites, or to the library for additional research. She would scan my hard-won pages, frowning, chewing on a pencil, scrawling comments and suggestions in the margins. 'Too dense,' she'd write. 'Too stiff. Too wooden. *Fix it!*'

All in all: a most nerve-racking experience. I felt dizzy at times. I snapped at assistant professors. At one point I temporarily misplaced my sex drive, which was always just short of rapacious.

In the evenings, as I frantically composed on my old black Royal, Mrs Kooshof would sit with me in the den, sometimes with a book in her lap, other times just scowling and watching the pages accumulate. Her displeasure was palpable.* On one late-night occasion she issued a huffy, exasperated sigh. 'You never *talk* to me,' she said, completely out of the blue. 'You never ask questions or anything.'

I glanced up from my typewriter. 'Questions? About what?'

'Just me, Thomas. Who I am.'

'Ah, yes,' said I. 'In that case, you pique my curiosity. Who are you?'

The woman assaulted me with a stare. 'Don't condescend. At least you could show a little interest in my life. Everything I've gone through.' She was thoughtful for a time, surveying her own history. 'I mean, you could ask about Doc.'

---

* My paramour was under the misapprehension that I was at work on a commissioned essay for the journal *Critique*, a firm deadline rapidly approaching. Still, being female, she felt neglected. (Every man in America will surely sympathize.)

'Doc?'

'Doc. My *husband*.'

'Thought the man's name was Robert.'

Mrs Kooshof snorted. 'Right there, that's condescension. You don't give a hoot about anything except your egotistical, self-centered self. Come on, ask me something. Anything. I dare you.'

I rolled a fresh sheet of paper into my Royal. The distraction was irritating, but I made a demonstration of putting my mind to the matter.

'All right,' I said, and struck back with my own rigid, ravaging stare. 'Where, exactly, did you first have sex?'

'Where?'

'The venue. Where?'

'That's juvenile,' said Mrs Kooshof. 'Ask something important. Ask why I don't have children.'

'Well, I'm sorry,' I told her, 'but take it or leave it. And I wouldn't call the question "juvenile" by any means. *Where* matters. Profoundly.'

I removed a flask from my pocket, treated myself to a droplet of schnapps. It could not hurt, I reckoned, to take a brief break.

'In my own case,' I informed her, 'it was a cornfield. Just off Highway 16. Very memorable.'

'Well,' said Mrs Kooshof, 'I don't know if I should tell you the whole –'

'A cornfield in autumn. Chilly night. Windy. A light frost, actually.'

'But *I'm* the one who –'

'One moment,' I said. 'I'm not finished.'

Autumn, I told her.

October of 1961.

Lorna Sue and I were juniors in high school, inexperienced

but very much in love,* and for months we had been debating the pros and cons of testing our romance against the high standards of sexuality. I took the affirmative, Lorna Sue the negative. Parked in her dark driveway, she sometimes allowed me access to her thighs and breasts, which I gratefully accepted, but the results were less than satisfying. In large part the problem was mechanical. To wit: Lorna Sue's hair. Throughout high school and for a good part of our marriage, she wore her black tresses long – very, very long. Not only that, but this river of sinuous, gorgeous, Spanish-noir hair was most often arranged in two loosely flowing braids, each of which she decorated with whatever odds and ends struck her fancy: bells, bows, poinsettia leaves, Hershey's Kisses. One can imagine, therefore, my troubles in the driveway. The gropings of an apprentice Don Juan are always clumsy enough, but my own difficulties were compounded by episodes of bondage and rope burn and entanglements of the most unlikely variety. (To this day, I confess, the word *hair* spooks me.)

Beyond all that, and more tellingly, Lorna Sue used her hair as a transparent excuse to avoid the climatic moment. 'You're mussing me!' she'd yell. Or she'd yell: 'I can't *move*!' In point of fact, however, I am almost certain that Lorna Sue's reluctance had to do with her brother, his ferocious jealousy, the eerie sensation that Herbie was always there *with* us. It was Herbie, in fact, who finally pushed us into that windy cornfield. We had tried the traditional make-out spots in Owago – Perkins Park, the Rock Cornish Drive-in Theater – but neither of us could shed that constant watched-over feeling. Headlights appeared at critical moments. Odd noises, too, and suspicious movements in the dark.

* At least on my own part. For Lorna Sue, I fear, the word *love* was as treacherous as the Mississippi in late April. A wiser man than I would have purchased flood insurance.

Near the end of September, after some point-blank begging on my part, Lorna Sue more or less agreed to consummate things. Even then, however, she stipulated a number of conditions. Absolute privacy. A new wristwatch. No bragging.

'Wristwatch?' I said.

'A good one. No crummy Timex.'

(*Timex:* still another word that signifies one thing to the world at large, something entirely different to me.)

'Right,' I said judiciously. 'A good one.'

'With a gold band,' she said. 'Real gold. Not fake. And it better be brand-new.'

Lorna Sue's requirements brought about a short postponement in our plans. I scouted out sites, did my bargain hunting, took a job bagging groceries after school. It was not until late October that I was able to present her with a new Lady Whitman. Lorna Sue examined it skeptically. She tried it on, held it to her ear, then sighed and said, 'So where do we *do* it?'

I had come up with four or five options – splendid ones, I thought – and we spent the afternoon cruising from venue to venue in my father's green Pontiac. Nothing struck Lorna Sue as appropriate. She found the Owago municipal dump (my own first choice) far too dismal. The church pews too irreverent. The courthouse garage too public. The whole while she kept peering down at her new Lady Whitman, impatient and distracted, as if late for a much more pressing engagement – a habit that would drive me loony during our years of marriage – and I finally braked in the middle of Main Street and asked her to hand over the timepiece.

'It's mine,' Lorna Sue said.

'Not for long. Make up your mind.'

She frowned. 'I need *nature*.'

'You need nature?'

'Stuff like . . . alive. Stuff that grows.'

'Let's have it,' I said. 'The Whitman.'

'Someplace green,' said Lorna Sue. Swiftly, and rather defensively, she tied one of her braids to the armrest. 'I mean, Tommy, that shouldn't be so hard. I thought you *loved* me.'

I growled and drove straight north out of town.

That part of southern Minnesota was farm country, flat and monotonous, almost entirely without trees. There *was* no nature.

After seven miles, I pulled onto a gravel road and stopped the car. It was a cold, sullen afternoon, a brisk wind rattling up against the windows.

We sat listening for a time.

'Pretty natural,' I finally said. 'Good enough?'

'I don't know,' said Lorna Sue. 'It's sort of . . . What if somebody drives by?'

'They'll think we're part of nature.'

'Don't be a smart-aleck, Tommy. I can still say no.'

'Well, sorry,' I said, 'but it's a farm road, no traffic at all.'

Lorna Sue scanned the bleak horizon.

Plainly, a moral tug-of-war was in progress. She glanced wistfully at her new wristwatch, at the endless prairie, then closed her eyes. 'Okay, I suppose,' she said, 'but it's sure not what I wanted.'

'Very healthful,' I said brightly.

I turned up the heater and began taking off my shirt. Lorna Sue watched for a second with puzzled eyes.

'What's going on?' she said.

'Sex.'

'It's *daylight*.'

'Daylight's natural. Pure as all get-out.'

Lorna Sue folded her arms stiffly. 'No chance. Not *that* natural. I want bubbling brooks and stuff.'

'Bubbling brooks?'

'Right.'

'Well, fine,' I told her. 'Pass over the wristwatch. I'll trade it in for a bubbling brook.'

'You're being nasty.'

Something tightened inside me. I reached out and seized her by the braids, one of which remained knotted to the armrest. 'Listen, there *aren't* any goddamn bubbling brooks. You've got corn. You've got soy-beans. Take your pick.'

Lorna Sue shook her head. 'I need the dark. And a movie first. Next Saturday night, I promise.'

'That's almost a *week*.'

'Six days,' she said. 'And count your blessings. You aren't getting the watch back.'

Mrs Robert Kooshof gazed at a spot in the vicinity of my coiled manhood. Her expression was menacing.

'Problem?' I said.

She tossed her shoulders. 'Not at all, Thomas. I mean, honestly, it's a relief to talk things out. Thanks for listening.'

My companion pushed to her feet, left the den, and returned after five minutes with a glass of my best malt liquor. She had changed into a midnight-blue negligée that nicely set off her Dutch ancestry, all those nourishing cheeses. (I could not disguise my interest in her expansive, very bouncy décolletage. One evening back in Owago I had taken her to the tape: just over thirty-nine standard inches.) There were numerous occasions, not excluding this one, when she seemed positively ripe with estrogen, part starlet, part mother figure.

She caught me looking.

'Don't even think it,' she said coldly. 'I'm just curious. Where do you get the – I don't know – the incredible stinking nerve? We were supposed to be talking about *me*.'

I forced my eyes to the typewriter. 'Well, of course, and we were almost there. You didn't let me finish.'

'You didn't let me *start*.'

'Just helping out,' I replied. 'A pertinent example sometimes makes it easier.'

'In bed,' she muttered.

'I beg your pardon?'

'I did it in bed, Thomas! The first time. I don't *need* an example.'

I nodded. 'In bed. Unique.'

'You bet it is,' said Mrs Kooshof, 'and I don't see why you can't just shut up and listen. The world doesn't revolve around Abe Chippering.'

'That is not my name. And I must request that you –'

'My *own* bed. *Twice*. With my *third* boyfriend.'

'I see.'

'It was fun! He had brown hair!'

Mrs Kooshof's voice had skittered up to a pitch that endangered my fragile hearing. She trembled, sat down, and quickly consumed her drink.

'Brown hair,' I said. 'Is there more?'

Mrs Kooshof did not respond.

More than a full minute passed by – I gave her ample opportunity.

'In that case,' I said, 'perhaps you'd be interested in how things turned out with Lorna Sue? As I mentioned, the *where* matters.'

The wait for Saturday night still ranks among the major tribulations of my eventful sojourn on this planet. Exciting, yes, but so much tension I could barely function. I skipped two days of school; homework was out of the question. Each evening, I practiced in my room, imagining how Lorna Sue and I would comport ourselves in the backseat of my father's

Pontiac. Details consumed me. I borrowed a blanket from my mother's linen closet, dosed it with Old Spice, and stashed it the trunk.

By Saturday evening I had reached a state of premature exhaustion. If not for all the labor, I would have canceled, and it required the last of my willpower to shave* and get dressed.

At seven o'clock sharp I rang the Zylstra doorbell.

Ned and Velva stood waiting in the hallway, flanked by Earleen and a half-dozen aunts and uncles. The family had arranged itself in two rows along the hallway, like an honor guard, and as Lorna Sue approached they stood grinning and gaping at me. Ned flicked his eyebrows. Earleen shot me a sly, flirtatious wink from her wheelchair.

Lorna Sue, I must say, looked delightful that evening, though perhaps a speck sacrificial: white skirt, white blouse, white stockings, white shoes. Her hair had been freshly braided, each long plait decorated with such items as tie tacks, feathers, and what appeared to be Cracker Jack prizes.

Altogether, in any event, I had the impression that our appointment with destiny was no secret.

Outside, I glared at her.

'You blabbed,' I said. 'You told everything.'

'Not exactly. They sort of guessed.'

'Guessed? It's not something you *guess*.' Instantly, a sequence of hard truths struck me. 'What about Herbie? I suppose he guessed too?'

'Maybe. He didn't look happy.'

I slid into the Pontiac, started the engine, glanced up at the yellow house. 'How could they just guess?'

---

* Not only my face but my chest and arms and portions of my upper thighs. I prefer the sleek look, and all my life, as part of my morning toilet, I have ridded myself of unnecessary body hair. Thomas H. Chippering, à la buff, is a sight not soon forgotten.

'I'm a girl,' she said briskly. 'I needed advice.'

The drive down to the movie theater was stiff with acrimony. Apparently Lorna Sue had confided in her mother, which was like confiding in the Pony Express, and for several days the entire family had been preparing for this night. Ludicrous, I thought. The whole idea had been to escape Herbie, to give our relationship a boost of intimacy and solitude. Now I faced the specter of disembowelment. Herbie Zylstra was not someone you wanted to upset. Under any circumstances. Ever. Standing in line at the movie theater, I kept my eyes open for sudden movement. 'This advice,' I said, 'you could've asked *me*. I'm good with advice.'

'Not this kind,' said Lorna Sue.

'Like what?'

'Stuff. Female stuff.'

'At which point I nearly marched off into the night. (Certainly my life would have taken a far different trajectory.) Instead I shook my head. 'What about the honor guard – where does that fit in? Most families, they'd get out the shotguns and start –'

'We're Zylstras,' Lorna Sue said primly. 'We're not *most* families.'

About that, if little else, she was absolutely right, and in all our years together, which were numbered from the start, Lorna Sue would never speak truer words.

For the next ninety-eight minutes we sat in the back row of the Rock Cornish Theater, Lorna Sue's eyes pinned to the screen, my own scanning the crowd. The film, I believe, was a Western, though I remember very little about it – periodic gunfire, people falling off horses. When it ended, we exited by a side door, circled around to the Pontiac, took a discreet route out to Highway 16.

Hormonal issues were no longer paramount. I was suddenly terrified, full of doubts, weakened by a strange biological fuzziness. (*Perform:* the word loomed before me like a locked door.) Thus, as I turned up the gravel farm road, I took a deep swallow of pride and informed Lorna Sue that we were calling it off. 'It's just a bad time,' I said. 'I'm not ready.'

She tilted her head back and chuckled.

'Too late, Tommy. Everybody knows. No matter what happens – either way – they'll think we did it. Besides, you're not getting the watch back.'

'Keep it,' I said.

'Oh, you know I will,' said Lorna Sue. 'It's mine. Whether we do anything or not.'

Her voice had a mocking, singsong quality that compelled me to strike back. 'All right,' I said. 'You *asked* for it.'

Immediately, I turned onto a tractor path, thence into the dense, crunchy folds of an autumn cornfield. I pulled the emergency brake, listened for a moment, then got out and retrieved the blanket from the trunk. When I returned, Lorna Sue had moved to the backseat and was busy unbuttoning her blouse. 'You can't just watch,' she said. 'Close your eyes, wait till I'm ready.'

I sat there with folded hands, rigid, more apprehensive than aroused.

The mood was wrong. (Plus nasal pains.) Events seemed to have conspired against my receiving the slightest pleasure from all this.

'Look, I don't want to force you,' I said. 'We could always try later. Maybe after we're married awhile.'

Lorna Sue shrugged. 'Just make it fast.'

She seemed relaxed, not in the least fearful, and as she spread out the blanket I found myself wondering about her family's reproductive history. Images of Herbie flashed through my thoughts. I peeked out the window, then turned back toward Lorna Sue. Bare to the waist, she was wearing mesh stockings hooked to a wire belt of some sort. Lower, at hip level, I discovered a number of wires and metallic flaps and what seemed to be a curtain of Christmas tree tinsel.

'What's this?' I asked.

Lorna Sue smiled. 'Sexy, don't you think? My mother made it.'

'Velva?'

'Mostly. Earleen helped with the tinsel.'

I peered down with interest.

'A special treat,' said Lorna Sue. Her eyes clouded. 'You don't like it?'

Stupidly, I shrugged.

'Then hop to it,' she said.

An impossible assignment, of course, but for the next several minutes I did my best to remove the contraption. One needed the dexterity of a juggler and the eyesight of a jeweler, but more than anything I was troubled by an image of Earleen and Velva rigging up this unlikely garment.

Eventually Lorna Sue sat up and lent a hand. She loosened a metal flap, lay back, and opened her arms to me.

'There,' she sighed. 'Do the rest yourself.'

With no foreplay whatsoever, Lorna Sue yanked me down, clamped my head to her breasts, and began humming a soft, mostly indecipherable chant in my ear.

'Amen!' she squealed at one point.

Here, I reasoned, was a very complex young woman. I started to pull away, but then, to my relief, I felt an unmistakable hydraulic surge. I fumbled with my shoes and jeans and shirt, kicked off my underwear, and for the next few minutes succeeded in blocking out the world – prayers, bribery, blackmail, honor guards, Herbie, the whole dysfunctional Zylstra clan. I was powerful. I was the burglar at the door. Altogether, things went beautifully until the instant of entry, at which point Lorna Sue tugged at my ears and cried, 'Stop it! My *hair*, for God's sake! There's no room!'

I kept lunging. 'Plenty of room,' I assured her. 'A good fit.'
'I don't mean *there*!'

She squeezed her legs shut, gripped my shoulders, and muscled me down into the foot well. We were roped together by three feet of braided black hair.

'It's just too dern crowded,' said Lorna Sue. 'I'll get a cramp. I can't even move.' Her tongue moved across her upper teeth as she pondered the mechanics. 'We'll have to go outside.'

'Like where?'

'Anywhere. Let's go.'

I glanced out at the windy cornfield. 'You're kidding. It's almost *winter*.'

'Hurry it up,' she said. 'Take the blanket.'

Which brought us at last – inevitably – to the icy hood of my father's Pontiac.

It often amazes me how little we retain of the critical events in our lives. A snapshot here. An echo there. The details of my first conquest were largely swept away by a frigid October wind. I remember the critical gaze of an Indian-head ornament. I remember frost on the hood, the car shaking, Lorna Sue crying, 'It hurts!'

Was there gratification in this? Delight? The most fleeting bliss?

Perhaps so. But I do not recall.

Lorna Sue hogged the blanket. She made whining noises. She yelled at me. She issued stern commands. Slower, she insisted. Faster. Gentler. Rougher. More romantic. She snaked an arm around my neck, yanked me down. She bit my throat. At one key juncture, when I began to falter, she emboldened me with the palm of her hand, levered me in again, beat on my buttocks.

All that I remember vividly. Along with the cold and the ferocious wind. We had left the engine running, with the idea it might warm us, but the elements that night were beyond the capabilities of my father's Pontiac. In hindsight, I now marvel at my youthful performance. I was valiant. Inexpert, no doubt, and outright shoddy by later standards, but I remain convinced that under the circumstances even a polar bear would have called it a night.

Afterward, there was no pillow talk.

We dressed quickly and drove back to town. I dropped her off a block from her house.

'Well, I hope you're happy,' she said glumly. 'I suppose now you'll just dump me.'

I smiled. The notion had not yet occurred to me.

'All depends,' I said thoughtfully. 'You'll tell Herbie I backed off? Too much respect for his sister?'

Lorna Sue's eyes narrowed. 'Anything else?'

'The whole family,' I said. 'Nobody hears a word.'

'What else?'

'Tomorrow night. Someplace warm. Cute new costume.'

She rolled her eyes and waited a moment. She knew what was coming.

'What else?'

'An expensive one,' I said. 'No crummy Timex.'

Mrs Kooshof was gone by the time I had finished telling my story, and the schnapps too.

For a considerable time I sat motionless at my desk, trolling through memory, all the good things. Lorna Sue's brown eyes. Her smell. Her laughter. How she purred and hummed and finally bared her teeth as we made love. How at the end she squealed, 'I'm coming! I'm coming!' How the wind howled. How she wanted to do it again. How the word *Pontiac* would never again mean Pontiac.

Granted, there were bad things too. But the bad wasn't always so bad.

'Fucking cornfield,' I murmured, but sweetly – a rare instance of Chippering profanity. Then I laughed, switched to cognac, and resumed my labors on young Toni's thesis.

Much later, in bed, Mrs Kooshof said, 'You actually married this crazy bitch? She married *you*?'

'Of course.'

'But why?'

'A beautiful love,' I said. 'Greatest ever.'

14

Virtue

It strikes me that by accident, or out of anger and pain, I may well have painted an unflattering portrait of my former wife. Such was never my intent. I loved Lorna Sue desperately, even obsessively, and more than anyone on this earth, including her brother Herbie, I can appreciate those glittering gems at the center of her soul. As a corrective, therefore, I offer this short sampler of Lorna Sue's innumerable charms:

– On not a single occasion, so far as I know, did Lorna Sue feign orgasm. She was brutally honest in this regard and kept me well informed.

– Though by no means expert in the kitchen, she was more than willing to try her hand at preparing a random meal. I remember, in particular, a heap of noodles seasoned with onion powder.

– I will tell the simple truth: I was in awe of her. As a twelve-year-old, and as a thirty-year-old, I dreamed Lorna Sue dreams. I lived inside her name. I was terrified of losing her even before she was mine to lose.

– I proposed to her at a New Year's Eve party, in a ballroom at the university's faculty club. I was a green, gangly graduate student; she was Lorna Sue, and beautiful. But we were in love. And for both of us it was a hard, happy, electric love, full of the past, full of the future. I had not planned on proposing that night, nor was marriage a topic we had ever talked about in any depth, but something in that festive ballroom: the temperature, the voices, the New Year's Eve nostalgia – *something*, I do not know what – something magical and terrifying and glorious, something radiant, seemed to wrap itself around us and lift us up and carry us off to another region of our universe. I looked at her. Lorna Sue looked at me. (How do I convey this without sounding like an eighteen-year-old?) I loved her so much, and she loved me, and I tried to speak, tried to say *Marry me* but could not – I said nothing, no words at all – and her face went bright and she said, 'Yes, I will, yes.'

– From the start, Lorna Sue and I had trouble sleeping in the same bed, a problem for which I was entirely to blame. I talked in my sleep. I twitched and moaned, flailed at demons, shouted the most vile obscenities. (Vietnam was still a fresh memory.) With the aid of earplugs, Lorna Sue did her best to endure all this, but in the end, after two or three weeks, she began spending nights in the spare bedroom. To this, of course, I vocally objected. 'We're husband and wife,' I reminded her. 'I'll call a doctor. I'll find a cure.'

Lorna Sue shook her head.

'Too expensive,' she said. 'The spare bedroom will be fine.'

She was thrifty.

– In our fourth year of marriage, Lorna Sue and I attended a convention of the Modern Language Association in downtown Las Vegas, where I delivered to no small acclaim a scholarly paper entitled 'The Verbs of Erotica.' On our final evening, to cap a happy time, we indulged in some gaming at a blackjack table in the hotel's noisy casino. All night I handed her twenty-dollar bills. I won, she lost. But then, near midnight, our luck abruptly changed – a complete reversal of fortune – and Lorna Sue's stack of chips grew like a skyscraper, while mine dwindled to nothing. Without thinking, I reached over and helped myself to a handful of green chips, at which point Lorna Sue snatched my wrist and yelled, 'They're mine!'

She was *very* thrifty.

– I do not mean to mock her. She was my sweetheart, the love of my life, the girl of my dreams. And I have lost her forever. Who, then, can blame me for some periodic vitriol? Look into your *own* broken heart.*

– A devout Roman Catholic, Lorna Sue missed only a single Sunday Mass in our many years together. She believed in the blood of Christ, its real presence, and accepted without question the doctrines of corporeal resurrection and immaculate conception. Even in bed, making love, she radiated piety the way lesser spirits radiate passion or good cheer. Artificial birth control was forbidden. At the instant before climax, as I beat my biweekly retreat, Lorna Sue would reach down to make certain that our uncoupling was complete. 'It's sad,' she'd say, 'how men are so ... *so messy*.' Clean of mind, clean of body, she would produce a wad of Kleenex. (Do I exaggerate? I do not. And I can guarantee that over the years,

---

* Over the past empty months, as your ex-husband combs the far-off beaches of Fiji, have you not felt exactly what I feel? A contradictory mix of despair and hope, longing and regret, ferocious hatred and barbaric love? Be truthful. Did you not conceive, if only briefly, your own plan of revenge? Did you not imagine hurting him just as he hurt you? Did you not picture him on his knees, begging forgiveness, and did you not covet that moment when you would shrug and turn your back and walk into the arms of a handsome young lover of your own?

no unwholesome substances gained entry into the pristine, well-vacuumed chapel of her soul.)

– I have already discussed her long, black, braided hair. But I have not explained how her flesh – the tissue itself – smelled of chlorophyll and coconut oil. (Like the mountains of Vietnam, I thought.) She favored a bath gel called Youth, a perfume called Forever, expensive skin products from the laboratories of France and Switzerland. She made regular use of a sunlamp. Eternal vigilance and a set of tweezers had for the most part eliminated unsightly chin hair.

– We honeymooned in northern Minnesota, at a resort called Portage Pines, where we spent seven days in the company of Lorna Sue's family. The whole clan was there – Earleen, Ned, Velva, aunts and uncles, a jovial priest from Duluth, two cousins, the ever watchful Herbie. En masse, honeymooning as a family unit, we played charades, watched the sunsets, slept in the same communal loft each night. Awkward, yes. At times frustrating. Yet how could anyone fail to applaud Lorna Sue's devotion to kin, her filial piety? 'I'm a Zylstra,' she said. 'This is how we do things.'

– She had a way with words. Often pithy. Always eloquent. 'Don't be an eighteen-year-old,' she once said.

– She was independent. She took several vacations alone, several others with Herbie. There were times when she would vanish entirely, for days on end, without warning and without subsequent explanation. She had secrets. She knew how to keep them.

– How does one do justice to things aesthetic? Her pouty lips? Those puppy-brown eyes flecked with orange and violet?

The smooth, sloping transition from hip to waist? Physically, Lorna Sue was a marvel of anatomical engineering, expertly tooled, made for the long haul. (On the day she walked out on me, her hair remained a lustrous coal black, her figure trim and dangerous.) Throughout our years of marriage, she had taken justifiable pride in her body, carefully attending to its needs, sometimes addressing it in the regal second person. She ran six miles a day. She avoided fats. She chewed vitamins like candy. At dinner one evening, when I suggested that we begin thinking about children, Lorna Sue put down her fork and hurried to a hallway mirror. 'Ruin *this*?' she said.

– In strictly sexual terms, Lorna Sue's most attractive feature, far and away, had to be that mysterious, purply-pink scar on the palm of her left hand. Call me macabre, or call me Catholic, but I found it arousing to moisten that awesome cicatrix with the tip of my tongue, to close my eyes and envision the instant of penetration – iron nail, pliant flesh – the sudden pain, the release from pain, the little cry rising from her throat. How could my tongue go elsewhere? For whatever reason that wrinkly red scar had a powerful, hypnotic effect on me, like a piece of pornography.

Not so for Lorna Sue.

'God, you're such a sap,' she told me. 'It's just a worthless little scar. Nothing else.'

She was a realist, not a sentimental bone in her body, yet at the same time something rang false in her voice. Too flat. Too pat. At times I suspected that her entire being, her sense of Lorna Sueness, was purely a function of that small jagged scar. She hated it and adored it. (As perhaps she hated and adored herself.)

One evening I found her sitting on the lip of our bathtub, bleeding from the palm of her hand, using a nail file to gouge open the old wound.

She was crying.

She was a little girl again.

'For Pete's sake,' she said, 'give me some goddamn privacy.'

She was a mystery.

– How can I overlook the virtue of fidelity? During my long, dangerous year in Vietnam, Lorna Sue never once stepped out on me. I know for a fact that she lived with her brother in Minneapolis. They shared a bedroom. She was chaperoned at all times.

– Sometimes at night I liked to relax in front of a good crime drama on TV. To her credit, no doubt, Lorna Sue found this sort of escapist fare beneath her. 'How can you *watch* such garbage?' she'd mutter, often marching out of the room, sulking until I finally switched to a program of her choice. Lorna Sue had taste. She discriminated. Her eyes positively glowed through the full sixty minutes of *Melrose Place*.*

– Intelligent and well educated, with a bachelor's degree in art history, Lorna Sue was determined from the start to make something of her life. 'I need a real career,' she informed me on the eve of our wedding. 'I mean, what if I divorce you or something? What if you get sick and die?' Thus, in our first year of marriage, she entered medical school at the University of Minnesota, then switched to law, then quickly

---

* An episodic American television program of the 1990s, the primary action of which, so far as I could tell, revolved around the premise that everyone betrays everyone else. In such cruelties Lorna Sue took unabashed delight. She squealed. She squirmed in her chair. She spoke aloud to the various characters, offering advice and encouragement, sagely egging them on.

back to medicine. In year two, she opened a dance studio in Saint Paul; in year three, in the wake of financial disaster, she received her calling as an actress, which led to a local television commercial featuring Lorna Sue's exquisite calves and a pair of no run panty hose. Although none of these career alternatives panned out, Lorna Sue doggedly pursued her dreams, traveling widely, exploring professional options in California and New Jersey, always faithful to her original pledge.

She was no housewife. Indeed, she was barely a wife at all.*

– She was a published author. Local church press. A cookbook. Her own kitchen-tested recipes. (This from a woman who only rarely set foot in a kitchen.) The pulses of our mother tongue, of course, were well beyond her, and in my role as ghostwriter I spent weeks translating the silly book into English, a chore for which I received the special thanks of a home-cooked dinner. (Noodles! Onion powder! Delicious!) She was tone deaf, to be sure, but determined to make the very best of herself.

– Unclouded by sentiment, guided by the ethics of realpolitik, Lorna Sue made her decisions with clearheaded pragmatism. She willed our love dead. She shot it through the heart. She divorced me. She did not look back. She removed herself to a new life, a new city, a new bed. She remarried almost instantly – a tycoon to boot. No time wasted. No decent burial, no mourning period.

I was never sacred to her.

* Lorna Sue, of course, would furiously defend herself. To one and all, in that scolding, sanctimonious tone of hers, she would proclaim that she had done nothing but shower me with love; that our problems were entirely of my own manufacture; that she had endured for as long as possible my jealousies and suspicions and petty paranoia.

– It would be instructive, finally, to explain how Lorna Sue came to lose her long black tresses. The place: my den. The time: a late evening midway through our marriage. The cause: a silly argument. (I was in the midst of rewriting her cookbook; Lorna Sue could not understand why all the 'stupid commas' were necessary.) One thing led to another, and I made the mistake of suggesting that she find some other disciple to do her goddamn ghostwriting. It was the word *disciple*,* of course, that set her off. (The ghostwriting was no problem.) 'What's that supposed to mean?' she snapped, to which I responded with a churlish and very unfortunate remark about her 'Jesus hair.' She paled. She backed away. Then without a word she spun around and rushed to the bathroom. By the time I caught up with her she had already succeeded in hacking off a good twenty-four inches of hair, at least a pound's worth, and was in the process of plunging the scissors into the palm of her hand.

She did it twice. Hard.

The blood was copious – I nearly fainted – but Lorna Sue displayed not a sign of pain. She pulled out the scissors, held the bloody hand up to me.

'Jesus hair,' she said, not softly, not loudly either, just that flat, cold, neutral voice with which she would later tell me not to be an eighteen-year-old. 'You don't *know* me, Tom. Not at all. Comments like that one . . . I don't think you ever will.'

She was a seer.

She could read the stars.

---

* Alas, the awesome power of words. They start wars, they kill love. In my own case, I once paid dearly for using the term *cooze* at a black-tie faculty party. (It cost me, in point of fact, my fifth straight Hubert H. Humphrey Prize.) And over what? Two consonants, three vowels. What if the *z* and the *c* had been transposed? Would I have been blackballed for describing President Pillsbury's wife as a 'dumb zooce'?

15

No/Yes

My literary endeavors demanded long hours, late nights, but I completed Toni's thesis three days before departing for Tampa. She had given it her tentative approval on a Wednesday afternoon. ('A few tiny changes,' she'd said, 'and you're home free.') By Friday morning I had finished the required thirty-eight pages of rewrites, plus footnotes and a bibliography, and at noon that day, only an hour behind schedule, I carried a hefty manuscript up the front steps of her dormitory. My raven beauty stood fidgeting in the sitting room. 'You're *late*,' she snapped, 'and if I get docked for this, Tommy Boy, you're in for a shitload of motherfucking shit.'

There can be nothing more stunning, I thought, than angry eyes in perfect union with polished brown skin. I passed over the thesis, proud of a job well done.

'Hey, the *copies*,' she said. 'What about the motherfucking copies?'

Forty-five minutes later I was back with six freshly minted Xeroxes. Apparently Toni had prior appointments, but she had left behind a note with precise delivery instructions. (The note, I must point out, was signed with a bold and highly suggestive X. Youth's bawdy ways! My heart ticked fast!) I spent a buoyant three hours strolling from office to office, dropping off copies, and then in midafternoon, chores complete, I paused to celebrate at a nearby campus bar. The place had long been among my favorites. At all hours, without a single exception in my experience, one encountered a bounty of exquisite Nordic-blooded sweeties – a positive surfeit – not one of them beyond the prime age of twenty-two. It was here, as my marriage collapsed, that I first conversed with Little Red Rhonda, who was succeeded a month afterward by the luscious Signe. Both girls eased my days. Both would later perform superbly in my seminar on the etymology of gender. Both would graduate with full honors.

On this occasion, feeling carefree, I ordered a rare martini and joined a likely covey at the rear of the establishment, where until closing time a number of us drank and discussed spring fashions. Karen and Deborah escorted me home.

The hour was late. Mrs Kooshof had already turned in, and when I tried to awaken her, she blearily declined my invitation to join us for a frisky game of Scrabble. It was somewhat later – close to daylight – when my Dutch consort finally made her appearance, in a pair of fuzzy pink slippers, black panties, and little else. 'I *live* here,' she said, inaccurately. 'I don't *have* to be dressed. They do. Get them out of here.'

Karen was asleep, Deborah was not.

It took only a few minutes to clear the place, but it required the remainder of the day to calm Mrs Robert Kooshof. I outlined for her the sociology at work. Modern mores, modern methods. I had to wing it, as my sophomores say, at several key transitions.

Mrs Kooshof took a more combative approach. 'You screwed them,' she said. 'I'm in the next room, Thomas, and you're out here making goo-goo. With kids. Babies.'

'They were plainly of age,' I told her. 'And I screwed no one. Scrabble.'

'Oh, stop it! They barely had clothes on. What *was* it – strip Scrabble?'

I did not rise to this bait, though in truth Mrs Kooshof was uncannily on the scent. (In my defense, I must point out that none of it had been my idea. Nor had I participated. Nor was it my place to enforce morality. I was a teacher, not a vice officer.)

'What a creep,' said Mrs Kooshof.

She left the room. Not only that, but over the next several hours she came close to leaving altogether. Eventually, in the bedroom, I indulged her need for a tearful *mea culpa*. Too much drink, I said. Impaired judgment. Couldn't live without her.

'Oh, face it,' she muttered. 'You like girls.'

I blinked at this.

'True,' I said. 'I like girls.'

'And I'm a woman.'

'You are, indeed.'

Mrs Kooshof sat stiffly on the edge of the bed. We were both silent for a time, appraising each other. When Mrs Kooshof spoke, her voice was much softer than I had anticipated, almost wistful.

'Thomas, listen,' she said. 'I wish you'd level with me. Is that so hard? All this elaborate nonsense about checks and mattresses, it's just a cover for the real problem.'

'Which would be precisely what?' I asked.

'You know.'

'I don't. Tell me.'

She shook her head sadly. 'It's like you're a rabbit or something – jumping from woman to woman. Can't ever get enough. One more victim, aren't I? A fresh scalp?'

'Mixed metaphor,' I said. 'And you're wrong.'

'Am I?'

'You are,' I said. 'You're wrong.'

I was operating on zero sleep and excessive ardent spirits, a combination that produced a peculiar melting sensation in my chest and stomach. Something collapsed inside. I was not intending it, but after a second I heard myself rambling on about certain private items that I had always preferred to keep locked away. Certain insecurities. Misfit. Loner. How I sometimes felt empty inside. How I would do almost anything to fill up that hole inside me. A craving, I said – a love hunger. Always terrified of losing the few scraps that were thrown my way.

When I finished, Mrs Kooshof looked at me gravely.

'Well, Thomas, I'm sorry,' she said. 'But it doesn't excuse last night. How can you hurt me like that?'

'Stupid,' I told her. 'Not thinking.'

She got up and moved to a window. In the long silence I could hear my future clicking like the tumblers of a rusty lock.

'Well, listen,' she said. 'If you really want that hole filled up, here I am. And not such a bad catch. Darn wonderful person.'

'Yes,' I said.

'I'm smart. I'm pretty.'

'You are.'

'I'm *nice*. Nice isn't something you laugh at.'

'Right. I'm not laughing.'

Mrs Kooshof stared out the window. It was a warm spring morning, flooded with sunshine, and her face struck me as uncommonly attractive. Not girlish by any means. Better, I thought.

'This business you have in Tampa,' she finally said. 'I don't understand it – revenge, I mean – but I was willing to tag along. I thought we'd have time together. Thought maybe you'd fall for me. Hard, I mean. I guess I'm still hoping.'

'Good,' I said. 'Don't stop.'

She turned toward me. 'No more Scrabble?'

'Hate the game. Words.'

'And no girls?'

'Not a chance,' I said. 'All I need is a smart, pretty woman. A nice one.'

Which was exactly the thing to say.

We left for Tampa on a rainy Monday evening.

I had canceled my classes for the week, rescheduled three committee meetings, and the only complication was a small party I had arranged to celebrate the acceptance of Toni's honors thesis. The gathering took place in my office two hours before departure. I had invited five or six favorite coeds, all charming, and together we raised a number of toasts to Toni's accomplishment. The reviews had been remarkable – highest honors the university could confer. ('A gifted if somewhat verbose student,' one of her committee members had commented. 'An astonishing scholarly debut.')

Toni was radiant.

Bubbly, in fact. She could not stop smiling. She wore high heels, a white blouse, a black skirt cut high over waxy brown legs. For me, the high point came when she called for quiet and delivered a short, heartwarming speech. She was thoroughly gracious, almost to the point of modesty, as she thanked her friends and family and me for our succor and encouragement. (Direct quote: 'Succor and encouragement.' Imagine my joy! The blush at my cheeks!)

Near the end Toni got a bit tipsy. We were alone by then. The hour was late, the champagne low. She had arranged herself in a provocative pose on my desk. 'Without you,' Toni said, 'I probably couldn't have done it.'

'Nonsense,' I said.

She shook her thick brunette tresses. 'No, I mean it. You're a total jerk, Tommy Boy – I can't lie – but at least you came through on *one* count.'

Once more, I pooh-poohed the notion. I told her she had a first-rate academic career in front of her; I wished her well at

Kansas State or wherever else she ended up.

'You think so?' she said.

'I certainly do. A born scholar.'

Toni toyed with the hem of her skirt. 'Well, I guess we could do it *once*.'

'We could?'

'I guess.'

Several contradictory thoughts intersected in time and space. A recent conversation with Mrs Kooshof. A plane to catch. Toni's firm, brown, muscular thighs.

I nearly wept.

Such opportunities do not present themselves every day. And it therefore seemed monstrously cruel, monstrously unfair, that only a day or two earlier I had so impetuously pledged my allegiance and my chastity to Mrs Robert Kooshof. It was fate's ugly face.

'Rain check?' I said.

'You're saying no?'

'Well, no.'

Toni frowned. 'No? Plain no? Or you're *not* saying no?'

'One or the other,' I said.

I made my flight with six minutes to spare. There had been a delay, fortunately, due to heavy rains, and I found Mrs Robert Kooshof seated in the back row of a Boeing 727. The weather had brought on one of her foul moods; she was not interested in my complaints about the city's taxi service.

'You smell like a winery,' she said.

'I do?'

'And something else.'

I did not ask further questions. There was no need: I had requested a rain check, after all, and the irony of her accusation astounded me. Act honorably, one still absorbs the consequences. Why, in other words, should I stand convicted of a crime I had so painfully declined to commit? However tentatively, however provisionally, I had looked into Toni's thighs and uttered the word *no*.

What a world.

After takeoff, I ordered a bone-dry martini, which led to another, and I was soon pondering the subtleties of that innocent-seeming syllable – *no*. How incredibly perilous! How fragile! Its meanings and usages encompass such fundamental human phenomena as denial, impatience, disgust, disagreement, surprise, refusal, uncertainty, despair, and grief. ('No!' I wailed on the afternoon Lorna Sue left me. 'No!' I still scream in my sleep. 'No,' I told Toni.) High over Tennessee, it occurred to me that the fluidity of *no* has its precise analogue in the fluidity of emotion itself. Denial leads to disgust. Refusal leads to uncertainty. 'Do you love me?' a woman asks, to which you respond, 'No.' But after losing her, after six months of celibacy, you might well be squealing, 'No! No!' at the sight of her passing car.

It was raining, too, in Tampa. We checked into our hotel, unpacked in silence, showered, slipped into bed, then lay in the droning dark without touching. Barely a moment elapsed before I felt the strike of a terrible premonition. I jerked up, but Mrs Robert Kooshof was already sighing. 'Tom, do you love me?' she whispered. 'Even a little?'

I am convinced it was not a coincidence. Fate again: the conjunction of weather and a misled life.

'Well,' I murmured, 'it's interesting you should ask,' then I went on to discuss the nature of love, the physics of infinity. I did everything in my power to avoid the word *no*.

'Yes or no?' she said.

And so, for the second time that day, I heard myself requesting a rain check.

'I guess that means no.'

'No,' I said. 'Even *no* doesn't mean no.'

'What on God's earth are you *talking* about?'

I rolled onto my side and feigned sleep. The day had been a long one, full of almost intolerable strife, but exhaustion now translated into a flow of images that kept me awake for several hours. Lorna Sue drifted by. Then Herbie. Then Toni and Deborah and Karen and Carla and June and Little Red Rhonda and Mrs Robert Kooshof.

'Well, if you don't love me,' Mrs Kooshof said near dawn, 'I can't see any point.'

I glared at Satan's teasing face.

'All right,' I said. 'Yes.'

'Yes?'

'Right.'

Her eyes dissolved into a pair of warm blue puddles.* 'You mean it?' she said. 'I mean, does *yes* really *mean* yes?'

'Got me,' I said. 'Let's have breakfast.'

In the dining room downstairs, while I devoured my ham and eggs, Mrs Robert Kooshof positively beamed at hers.

The word *yes*, unlike its antonym, apparently carries magical restorative qualities, for my companion's face had shed a good ten years' worth of romantic blight. I was reminded, curiously enough, of young Toni's honors thesis, in one section of which she had compared the standard English and Germanic marital vows. Where in America we would dully intone the words 'I do,' our German friends respond with the much more telling phrase '*Ja, und Gott helfe mir.*' Translated, it reads, 'Yes, and God help me,' which approximated my own emotions on that early Tampa morning.

* Improbable, perhaps, but true. Even the feminists of our world, in whose ranks I have long and proudly marched, must concede that love is both blind and blinding. Mrs Kooshof was human. She was no stick figure. She was ample in all respects.

'Yes,' I'd said, but was this a promise?

Was this duplicity?

Mrs Kooshof's question, remember, had come in two parts. Did I love her? Even a little? My eventual response – which was pried out of me like a wisdom tooth – had addressed the interrogatory as a whole, not merely its unqualified first component. Yet I doubt Mrs Kooshof took it that way. She was a woman; she was in love; she had forgotten her own botched utterance. And it *was* one question. Not two. Otherwise, I would have responded, 'Yes, yes,' or, more probably, 'No, yes,' or, possibly, 'Yes, no.'

In any event, my malfeasance – if there was any – had to do with an understandable reluctance to remind her of this intricate linguistic sequence.

I purchased peace with the coin of silence.

I let well enough alone.

We spent the remainder of the morning, and most of the afternoon, enjoying the fruits of our confused and misapprehended truce. Mrs Kooshof was shameless in her joy. She smiled during the act of love, then smiled in her sleep afterward. A lovely thing to witness, in part, but also frightening. For some time I lay very still, attuned to her breathing, and to the steady rain, and to the alternating buzz of yes and no.

In late afternoon I slipped out of bed, took a shower, then used the bathroom telephone to call Lorna Sue. (Her number, I must confess, was committed to memory. Over the past several months, I had often dialed those heartless digits for no purpose but to hear her voice.) There was no answer on this occasion, but I knew instantly where to find her. When I called Herbie's residence, Lorna Sue picked up on the first ring. I listened briefly, then disconnected.

Now, I thought.

It starts.

All the scheming, all the waiting, and it was hard to contain myself as I placed my next call, which was to a certain downtown real-estate firm. (The word *glee* may be taking it too far, yet I have come to discover that acts of vengeance are often accompanied by a swollen bladder, an airy tickle at the tip of the urethra.)

After two or three telephonic miscues, I succeeded in reaching the tycoon's secretary, who rudely put me on hold, and it was a good four minutes before the tycoon himself deigned to receive my call. The man's voice was more cultivated than I remembered, low-pitched and sugary. He made the word *Yes?* sound like a donation to the mentally impoverished.

I almost giggled.

Instead, according to plan, I informed the wife-rustling monster that Lorna Sue wished to be picked up at her brother's house.

'Picked up?' he said. 'Who *is* this?'

I could not help myself – at this point I did giggle. (Lightly, of course. Covering it with a cough.) 'An emergency,' I said. 'If I were you, sir, I would waste not a moment.'

'But what –?'

'Incest,' I said.

Wickedly, then, I hung up.

I waited a moment, dialed 911, and reported a domestic dispute in progress.

There was no need to awaken Mrs Kooshof.

I dressed quickly, hurried outside, and hailed a taxi. Weeks earlier, on a previous visit, I had taken care to scout out the terrain at Herbie's place – vantage points, angles of vision – and upon arrival, thirteen minutes later, I instructed the cabbie to park under a pair of shaggy trees diagonally across the street. The wait was short. In two or three minutes a blue Mercedes pulled up. The tycoon emerged, trotted to Herbie's front door, rang the bell, shifted from foot to foot in the steady drizzle. Clockwork, I thought. Despite myself, I could not resist a self-congratulatory chuckle.

'Watch closely,' I told the cabbie. 'You may well profit from this.'

My view was obstructed by the tycoon's ridiculously wide shoulders, but even so I could make out the surprise on Herbie's face when he opened the door. He had the appearance, if I may say so, of an ostrich attempting to swallow a toaster. His tongue fluttered. A hand jerked up. He took a stride backward, almost gawking, clearly on the defensive, and then a moment later Lorna Sue stepped into view. To my disappointment, she was fully clothed.

What was said, precisely, I could not tell, but the conversation did not appear to me tranquil. The decibels multiplied: indignant gestures, theatrical poses, histrionic queries and responses. The word *incest* was surely in the wind.* After a moment Lorna Sue shouted something, disappeared inside, and returned with her purse.

It was at that instant, somewhat tardily, that the Tampa police force put in its appearance. Two squad cars. Four stern officers of the law.

Again, I could make out not a single syllable, yet my imagination filled in the gaps. (Accusations and denials and disbelief.) The officers stood awkwardly on the front doorstep, hats under their arms, and judging by the tycoon's well-flushed face, I felt confident that issues of embarrassment were now exceeded only by those of marital suspicion. (A question for philosophers: Do we ever truly *know* our husbands and wives, our lovers, our friends, our brothers and sisters? What do we

---

* One should not underestimate the power of suggestion. For the remainder of his life, I most fervently pray, the tycoon will be massaging the word *incest*. Like me, he will always wonder.

believe? How do we believe? Where is your husband at this instant? In a Hilton? Or, at a downtown travel agency, where he has just purchased a pair of one-way tickets to Fiji?) It was gratifying, in any case, to watch the epistemology unfold. The seeds of doubt, so recently planted, were now germinating in the steady Tampa rain, and I could not help but be reminded that human relationship hang by the most fragile of threads. How easily we are mutilated by life's random intrusions: a frivolous lawsuit, a gossipy neighbor, a malicious midday phone call.

All good things must end.

In short order the tycoon escorted Lorna Sue to his flashy blue Mercedes. They stood talking for a moment, eyeball-to-eyeball, then Lorna Sue slipped into the car and slammed the door. The tycoon slammed his too – much harder – and as they sped off, I caught a glimpse of the gentleman's unhappy face. Not so handsome now. Puffy and bright red. His lips, I impishly noted, seemed to be curled in a snarl.

'Not bad,' the cabbie said.

Back at the hotel, I found Mrs Kooshof waiting in the bar. One quick glance: she seemed to know.

'Lorna Sue?' she said.

I nodded.

'And?'

For the first time in months I grinned the old Chippering grin. 'It's hard to be sure,' I said, 'but I believe her marriage may be on the rocks.'

16

Shell

Curiously, as I lay abed that night, I found myself feeling a (bare) modicum of sympathy for Lorna Sue's doomed and exceedingly hairy tycoon. It was all so wretchedly familiar, suspicion and countersuspicion.

Who can explain the wee-hour workings of the mind?

Perhaps it had to do with the sweet stress of revenge, but for several hours my thoughts kept looping back to an incident that occurred on the occasion of my seventh wedding anniversary. Half elated, half melancholy, I lay on the tiny patch of bed left to me by Mrs Robert Kooshof, attuned to the endless rain, picking at the scab of that seventh anniversary. (*Anniversary*: the word reaches out to embrace a set of meanings that can be described only as painfully conditional. *Anniversary* means: 'I love you if.' *Anniversary* means: 'Maybe.')

In the weeks leading up to our day of marital celebration, Lorna Sue had been disappearing for extended periods, sometimes with prior warning, sometimes without. The excuses were multitudinous, but it invariably turned out that she had been in the squalid, incestuous company of Herbie. In virtually any other circumstance, I would have been justified in calling a divorce lawyer – obvious adultery, yes? – except the accusation left me open to an equally obvious rebuttal. ('Christ, he's my *brother*!' Lorna Sue snapped whenever I summoned the courage to complain.*

Short of discovery *in flagrante delicto*, there was little I could do. 'Your loving brother,' I'd murmur, which would open the door to Lorna Sue's anger: 'So *say* it, Tom. What exactly are you suggesting?'

She knew full well that I was helpless, that I could never broach the subject openly.

Yet there was plenty to 'suggest.' Her disappearances. The way Herbie looked at her – obliquely, penitently. I will never know, I suppose, if anything physical occurred between them, but in a sense it no longer mattered. Their bond transcended sexuality – more enigmatic than simple incest – and though I doubt it was ever conscious, ever fully formed, I could see the trappings of a bizarre love cult all around me, something unworldly.

Case in point: our seventh anniversary.

I had come home early from class that day, put on a fresh suit and tie, and sat waiting for her with a dozen roses and high hopes. Nine hours elapsed. Near midnight she finally called from Herbie's house: music in the background, people laughing. Lorna Sue's voice betrayed not a trace of remorse. A surprise party, she informed me. Herbie had picked her up at noon. Lots of fun, lots of friends. Did I wish to come over? When I ventured the notion that someone might have thought to invite me, Lorna Sue seemed genuinely surprised. 'I'm inviting you *now*,' she snapped. 'And don't spoil things.'

'Fine, then,' I said. 'I'll be there.'

---

* Language itself offers clues to my predicament. The phrase 'Christ, he's my brother!' can be taken two ways. ('My brother is Christ.') And just as easily, with the same passion, Herbie might well have screamed, 'Christ, she's my *sister*!' He was Catholic. He had nailed her to a cross.

There was a short, brittle silence before Lorna Sue said, 'Well, you don't *have* to come.'

'Ten minutes,' I told her. 'Stay put.'

When I rang Herbie's doorbell, the celebration was already on its downslope. Five or six strangers lingered in the living room – friends of the family, I supposed, none of whom displayed pleasure at my appearance. I took Lorna Sue by the arm, squeezed hard, and announced that we were departing.

Herbie gave me a bemused smile. 'Good old Tommy,' he said softly. 'Glad you could make it.'

The ride home was all fury. I cannot in good conscience repeat Lorna Sue's language, which was tasteless, but in general terms she insisted that I shape up fast. I was paranoid. I had ruined her party. Yet not a word about Herbie. And not a word about her own warped psychology, or the stench of depravity, or the fact that I had just played a tuneless second fiddle on my wedding anniversary.

Which of us, therefore, needed to shape up? Which of us had ducked out on marriage?

My own emotions broke loose.

I was hurt and bewildered, full of rage, and I told her so at a pitch that made my throat raw.

I remember pulling off the road, stopping in front of a busy gasoline station. Directly ahead, a large neon sign cast a yellow sheen across the windshield, lewd and bright, the S of the word SHELL flickering on and off through some technical malfunction. (SHELL/HELL: another linguistic butcher knife.)

'Fucking anniversary,' I said. 'You could've included me.'

And then I said other things too. Partly accusing, partly pleading.

Did she love me, or did she not?

Where did Herbie fit in?

To whom was she truly married?

Lorna Sue's face went pensive in the gaudy yellow light. She made a little gasping sound – like a tin can popping open – and blinked into the yellow haze. Several seconds went by before she looked at me.

'All right, I'll try to be clear,' she said. 'I'm married to you. For now. But I'm not a piece of property. Not yours. Not his.'

'Certainly,' I said, 'but that's –'

'I belong to *me*.'

I was amazed. And angry. 'Hey, *you're* the one who left *me* waiting for nine hours. Did I imagine it?'

'No, but –'

'What's going *on*? Tell me. Brotherly love?'

Lorna Sue closed her eyes, clenched her jaw, as if deciding something. 'Okay, I'll say this one time. You're right – Herbie loves me. Maybe too much. Too possessive. But that goes for both of you.'

'Possessive? I'm your *husband*.'

'Except you don't know me,' she said. 'It's hard to explain – I won't even try – but Herbie takes care of me when . . . when things are bad, when I want to hurt myself. Or hurt you. Or the whole world.'

I was at sea.

I wagged my head and said, 'You damn well hurt me tonight. Nine hours' worth.'

'I'm sorry. But you don't know what hurt *is*.'

'I think I do.'

Lorna Sue shrugged.

A few seconds slipped by, both of us silent, just the on-and-off buzz of that Shell/Hell sign. Then she reached into her purse, pulled out a fountain pen, uncapped it, held up her forearm, glanced at me, and swiftly thrust the point into the flesh just below her elbow. She did it twice, fast. She licked the blood away.

She said, '*Do* you?'

Then she said, 'Sometimes I want to hurt *you* that way, Tom. And Herbie. Everybody.'

She jabbed the pen into her bare thigh.

Into her arm again.

Into her hip.

Into the palm of her left hand.

She murmured something, laughed, held the pen to my nose.

'My whole life, Tommy – ever since we were kids – it's like I've been squeezed from two sides, these two walls pushing in. You and Herbie. And sometimes I just want to run away from both of you. Or else hurt you. That's the other alternative.' She looked at me without emotion, then returned the fountain pen to her purse. 'Anyhow, I don't know where you get these sick, disgusting ideas of yours. But it has to stop.'

I was stunned, a little woozy, yet I finished the thought for her. 'Or else?' I said.

'That's right. Exactly right.'

'Leave? Walk out?'

Lorna Sue shrugged. 'If, Tom. Just if.'

'If,' I murmured.

Anniversary. Shell. Hurt. If.

17

Tampa

The next morning, a Wednesday, Mrs Robert Kooshof and I spent three invigorating hours on the beach behind our hotel. The rain had let up only a little. 'It's my vacation,' she said staunchly, 'and I won't waste it indoors.'

Ever dutiful, I bundled up in a pair of heavy woolen sweaters, plus a nylon jacket, and accompanied her down to a cabana-style bar at water's edge, where we took shelter under a roof of artificial bamboo. The day was cold and sodden, not at all improved by lightning to the west. Mrs Kooshof slipped on a pair of sunglasses. The frames were a fluorescent purple, the lenses molded in the shape of twin hearts.

'Romantic, isn't it?' she said. 'The rain and everything. I think it's cozy.'

'Toasty,' I said. 'Snug as a porpoise.'

I ordered a trio of hot toddies, Mrs Kooshof a tropical drink involving canned pineapples. The booze helped, and after a time I began to find merit in our nippy outing. A pert young waitress attended to our needs, keeping the drinks stiff, refilling the peanut bowl, and even the rain had a nice medicinal effect, steady and lulling. Not cozy, by any means, but tolerable. On her part, Mrs Kooshof seemed in high spirits, chatting amiably about life in Owago, her likes and dislikes, her plans for the future. The word *yes* had done wonders for her disposition.

Perched (as she was) on a barstool, legs crossed, my Dutch mistress had never looked so thoroughly feminine. She wore a terry-cloth jacket, white sandals, the purple sunglasses, a pink one-piece swimsuit. Statuesque to begin with – six feet of unfurled womanhood – Mrs Kooshof looked larger than life in that bright swimsuit, her long, closely shaven legs unwinding before me like twin roads to eternity. Erotic, to say the least, and as we conversed, I ran my fingertips along her inner thighs, nodding occasionally, paying heed to that no-man's-land where goose bumps gave way to silken secrets.

I was on my third toddy. Mrs Kooshof's voice seemed to come from the clouds. 'For me,' she was saying, 'it's all or nothing. No in-between.'

An uncommon languor in her tone made me raise my eyebrows.

'Us,' she said. 'You and me.' She recrossed her legs and gazed out at the merciless rain. 'Don't think I'm not serious. Soon as we get back – right away – I'm filing for divorce. Sell the house, that's the first step. Then put Doc's stuff in storage. Get things rolling.'

'Divorce?' said I.

'Naturally. We're in love, aren't we?'

'In love. Ah.'

A little muscle moved at Mrs Kooshof's jaw. She pulled down her sunglasses and looked at me with skeptical, challenging eyes. 'I've made up my mind,' she said crisply. 'I plan to fight for you, Thomas. For both of us. Whatever it takes.'

I nodded.

The innocuous word *yes* – like its antonym – apparently had the power of an earthquake. The morning seemed chillier now, the clouds more ominous.

'In love,' I said thoughtfully. 'That's us. But at the same time –'

'Don't back off, Thomas.'

'Certainly not. Merely clarifying.' I hesitated and glanced up at her. 'As one example, there's this unfinished business with Lorna Sue. Herbie too. I believe I've been extremely clear about it, extremely forthright.'

'Obsession,' she said. 'Let it go.'

'I fear life is not that simple.'

Mrs Kooshof issued an unladylike clatter through her nostrils. 'It *is* simple. I love you, Thomas. She doesn't.'

'Now, that's –'

'And this revenge nonsense,' she said in a rush. 'It's not healthy, it's not normal. It can't go anywhere *good*.'

There was thunder to the west, and for some time we sat watching the stormy sea. Our young waitress, I noted, had slipped on a parka vest and a pair of mittens.

'What I should do,' Mrs Kooshof said quietly, 'is pack my bags. Call it quits. Maybe then you'd come crawling.' She sighed again and reached down for her beach bag. 'But it wouldn't work, would it? You'd end up bedding down with the hot little slut over there.'

'Who?'

'The tramp. The one with the pocketful of tips.'

'Oh, *that* one,' said I.

Mrs Kooshof pulled a towel from the beach bag, removed her terry-cloth jacket, stood up and straightened her shoulders. The pink swimsuit was cut low, highlighting two of her most admirable character traits.

She caught me in midstare.

'Take your time,' she said. 'Thirty-six years old, but not all that bad. We could hoist them out, Thomas. Compare them with hers. Apples and oranges.'

'Many thanks,' I said graciously. 'It won't be necessary.'

'All right, then.' Her voice mellowed only slightly. 'But you see what I'm getting at? I'm a warrior. I'll fight.'

Odd thing, but then she kissed me. A gentle kiss, actually, and affectionate.

'Just so you know,' she said.

'I do. I know.'

She nodded. 'Quick swim?'

I looked out at the turbulent waters. The thought occurred to me that I was already immersed quite deep enough; I shook my head in the negative.

'Your choice,' she said breezily, and handed me her purple sunglasses.

She turned, made her way down to the water, and waded in up to the knees. Her stride, I noted, was determined. I slipped on the sunglasses and watched through a filter of glowing violet as she waved at me, struck a competitive pose, spun around, dived under, and came up swimming hard. For a second I considered joining her. And why not? A gorgeous, loving woman. She had sticking power; she was a knockout in that pink swimsuit. For the first time, really, it struck me that I could simply give up the whole enterprise with Lorna Sue. Start fresh. Be alive.

It was risky, though – far too risky – and common sense soon won the day.

I beckoned the young waitress.

It is my experience that life will occasionally offer us the opportunity to make good on our most cherished dreams, to realize those glittering hopes and ambitions that are at the core of our ideal selves. To my amazed delight, one such opportunity presented itself as I sat scanning a local newspaper on that cold, dismal morning.

The item appeared on page two: Three more church fires. Confirmed arson. Investigation stalled.

Call it coincidence. Call it good fortune.

Herbie was at it again. Plainly, my letter to the authorities had gone unheeded, or had led nowhere. And thus, without a moment's hesitation, I rose from my chair, made my way into the hotel lobby, and used a public telephone to dial 911. Within seconds I was in conversation with a representative of the Tampa police force.

I named names.

I listed dates and places.

Anonymously, to be sure, yet with the forcefulness of one who knows, I supplied information regarding a set of virtually identical incidents that had unfolded in the small prairie town of Owago, Minnesota. I mentioned the crucifixion episode, Herbie's stay with the reforming Jesuits of Minneapolis. I gave the police everything, in short, but the smoking gun. Even so, to my displeasure, the officer on the other end of the line seemed more interested in my own name than in Herbie's.

'Irrelevant,' I said testily. 'I have just handed you a surefire conviction. Take advantage of it.'

'Yes, sir,' the man said, 'but if we could interview you –'

'Certainly not,' I snapped. 'I am not a stool pigeon.'

There can be little on this earth more fundamentally satisfying than a piece of impeccably executed vengeance.

How easy it is, I thought, to meddle in another human life. I had learned the hard way that truth is immaterial, that accusation alone is more than sufficient. (Gossip becomes fact; speculation becomes certainty; arraignment becomes its own life sentence.) Consider how simple it would be, for instance, to charge your former husband with – who knows? – zoophilia, let us say. Not a wisp of hard evidence. A word here, a word there, and for the rest of his life your betraying ex-hubby would scurry past pet stores. Even in Fiji, where he now dwells with that poaching young redhead, he would feel his heart flutter at the sight of a cute cocker spaniel.

*   *   *

Mrs Robert Kooshof and I had a delicious lunch via room service – fresh pears, seared Gulf grouper, Key lime pie. At my request, she dined in her swimsuit, which clung beautifully, and midway through dessert we discovered new and more compelling appetites. In short order, we closed the drapes, pulled back the bedspread, and commenced a lusty frolic that proved memorable in all respects. Mrs Kooshof used her teeth and fingernails. I used mine.

Near the end we slipped to the floor. 'I *am* a battler,' she whispered. 'And I won't quit.'

'Uncle,' said I.

An hour later Mrs Kooshof departed for the hotel's tanning salon, and right away, somewhat deviously, I seized the opportunity to place three brief phone calls.

I made dinner reservations for Herbie and Lorna Sue at our hotel.

Then a room reservation – in Herbie's name, of course.

Then I dialed the tycoon's office number and left a short, titillating message with his secretary.

My own cunning astonished me.

When Mrs Kooshof returned, I enlisted her assistance in placing two final calls. She was reluctant at first, but I explained that it was in our mutual interest to speed things along. A female voice, I said, would add a spicy touch.

She moved in slow-motion to the telephone.

'I'm no idiot,' she said, her voice resigned and sad. 'It's in *your* interest. Period.'

Things went more smoothly than I had any right to expect.

Neither Lorna Sue nor Herbie answered, which was a piece of good luck, and in short order Mrs Kooshof left nearly identical messages on their machines. (Weeks earlier, I had carefully scripted this phase of the operation, the central idea of which was to lure Lorna Sue and Herbie into the hotel. Simplicity itself: a command.)

'Your brother *needs* you there,' said Mrs Kooshof.

Then a moment later: 'Your sister *needs* you there.'

No explanations.

Mrs Kooshof disconnected, sat silent for a second, then rose up and went out to the balcony. She stood in the rain, with her back to me.

I let some time pass before I joined her.

'You did well,' I said.

She laughed without laughing. 'Wonderful. But from now on, I stay out of it. Manipulating people – I'm not made that way.' Her voice was camouflaged by the rain, almost inaudible. 'Anyway, it's all a fantasy. You can't trick somebody into loving you. It won't work.'

'It'll work.'

'Not in the long run.'

I shrugged and said, 'This is the short run. The long run takes longer.'

Mrs Kooshof studied me for a time. There were little wrinkles at her eyes, a bruised darkness just beneath the skin. She was not a young woman. Nor was I a young man. Briefly, as if gazing into a mirror, I saw my own decaying shadow, my coming corpse, and it occurred to me that both Mrs Robert Kooshof and I were on the back slope of our bungled lives, skidding fast, two lost and lonely souls.

She looked away.

'Just tell me one thing,' she said softly. 'What do you *want* out of it?'

'Hurt them,' I replied.

'You mean that?'

'I do. Yes. Make them burn.'

'But what's the point? She doesn't *love* you.'

Inexplicably, I felt something tear loose in my stomach.

Maybe it was the rain. Or a fuse inside me. Or months of sorrow, or bewilderment, or the rage of rejection.

Whatever the cause, I could not help myself. I took her by the shoulders, hard, and pinned her against the balcony railing, pressed her backward, lifted her up, heard myself whining and growling – animal noises – and then came a sudden rupture in the physics of time, a great clock-stopped silence, yet even then I kept lifting and pushing and bending her backward over the railing.

Again, I have no idea what came over me, or why I took out my rage on Mrs Kooshof, but I felt dangerous.

I *was* dangerous – a powerful, aching, dizzy feeling.

Then, dumbly, I smiled. I released her and stepped back.

Mrs Kooshof edged sideways. She looked at me, then looked away, then looked back again. Her lips seemed to form a question – *Why?* – but I had no ready answer.* I smiled my senseless smile.

After a moment she slipped around me. She went inside and began stuffing her belongings into a suitcase.

I could think of nothing worth saying. I stood there in the rain, empty and stupid, the word *balcony* blinking on and off in my head.

In ten minutes Mrs Kooshof went to the door with her suitcase.

'God knows what happened out there,' she said. 'Something frightening. Something terrible.'

She closed her eyes. She opened them. She turned. She walked away. She did not trouble to close the door behind her.

*   *   *

* One clue may be embodied in the word *balcony*. Bad memories. Later in this narrative, if I am up to it, I will do my best to elaborate. For now, however, it is an act of courage merely to peck out the word *balcony* on this trusty old Royal.

Abandoned again, and it was hard to take much pleasure when Lorna Sue and Herbie wandered into the hotel lobby that evening. I had stationed myself up in the mezzanine, in a leather armchair, which provided a clear view of the registration desk and a small, glass-enclosed restaurant. Herbie arrived first, precisely on time; Lorna Sue appeared fifteen minutes later. They spoke briefly, looking puzzled, then strolled into the restaurant and took seats at a corner table. Oddly, I felt no great emotion. A brittle coldness. Mild curiosity. My thoughts kept jerking back to Mrs Robert Kooshof, like a gear that would not engage.

Part of me, I suppose, was still out on that balcony. Another part of me was void. No resolution, no clarity, and in a peculiar way Lorna Sue now struck me as a virtual stranger. Still beautiful, yes, but it was like looking at a mannequin. Expensive jewelry. Thick black hair and brown eyes and summer skin. All I could feel, though, was a hollowed-out version of the old love. In the end, I thought, that's what betrayal does. It sucks away the passion. The delight, too, and the hope, and the faith in your own future.

Hard to accept, but Lorna Sue had never been mine. Not wholly. And it was never love.

Again, the image of Mrs Robert Kooshof took shape before me, so big and blond, so full of promise.

Interesting fact: I missed her.

After five minutes, when the tycoon sauntered in, I had come close to calling off the whole venture. My dreams of sabotage now had a sterile, antiseptic feel, and I had trouble summoning even the most listless curiosity as the tycoon approached Herbie and Lorna Sue. Not that I was disappointed. It all worked beautifully, in fact, and in any other frame of mind I would have chortled at the way my little trap snapped shut: first surprise, then confusion.

Hard to absorb it all.

Hard to care.

The tycoon made a slight jerking motion, as if tugged backward by invisible wires. A reddish flush slid across his face, followed by darkness. His jaw flexed. From the mezzanine, of course, I could not make out any words, but it was evident that he was having trouble wrapping his tongue around the English language. Like me, almost surely, the man had been plagued by unwholesome suspicions – Lorna Sue's disappearances, her silences – and the hotel now added a touch of the illicit, an aura of sleaziness and secrecy. (There was also the message I had left with the tycoon's secretary. A suggestion that he stop by the hotel. The word *incest*.)

He had come expecting the worst. He had found it.

Lorna Sue took him by the arm, settled him into a chair, spoke to him with sweaty animation. (Denials, of course. Declarations of innocence.) From experience, however, I knew how lame such excuses sounded, how empty language can be, how appearance is everything. I almost smiled. This was justice. Perhaps it was my own imagination, or wishful thinking, but for a moment I could almost read the poor bastard's lips: *Your own brother*.

I sighed and called over a bellhop.

Swiftly, almost sadly, I issued a few curt instructions and handed over a twenty-dollar tip.

The bellhop saluted.

He made his way down to the registration desk, picked up a pair of keys, then entered the restaurant to inform Herbie and Lorna Sue that their room was ready.

18

Lost

Lost: that was the feeling. Or, more properly, a mix of many feelings.

It could be said, for instance, that I was lost without Mrs Robert Kooshof. That I was at a loss. That I had lost her. That I had lost myself. It would be accurate, too, to say that I had been thrown for a loss, implying depression, distress, and exhaustion, or that I had lost a rare and magnificent opportunity for happiness, implying waste and forfeiture. Or that I was a lost soul. Or lost in space. Or lost in dreary, rainy Tampa – condemned, marooned, alone, helpless.

Twice that evening, with no luck, I called Mrs Kooshof's number in Owago. The ring of a telephone had never sounded so forlorn and far away.

Around nine o'clock, to occupy myself, I took a wet and very chilly stroll along the beach, under a leaky umbrella, then afterward, on a whim, stopped in for solace at the hotel bar. My pert young waitress from the cabana (whose name, I recalled, was Peg) happened to be on duty; I happened to sit at her table. And over the course of the evening, which turned out to be a long one, we happened to fall into a double-edged conversation. Chitchat, at first. The rain was cutting into the girl's tips. Her musician boyfriend – a drummer – had recently hit the road, as it were, without a word. (At this, I nodded. 'Pity,' I purred. 'No boyfriend.')

By midnight, the place was deserted except for Peg and the bartender and me. (The bartender's name, I soon discovered, was Patty. Chestnut hair. Walnut eyes. Maple-red freckles trickling down into the lacy black bucket of her cleavage.) My mood was dismal, yet Peg and Patty did their best to pep up the evening.* They danced for me. They treated me to tiny sausages on toothpicks. At one point, I remember, Peg inquired about my 'lady friend,' who had also hit the road, to which I responded with a shudder and the word *lost*. Peg took my hand; Patty took both our hands. I felt like a Girl Scout. And then later, well after closing time, we huddled on the floor behind the bar, as at a campfire, eating sausages and exchanging stories about lostness, its forms and essences, its horrors.

'I lost my mother,' Patty said. 'I mean, like, she died. *That's* lost. But one time before that, I lost her in this department store. Looked all over the place, like eight floors or something, then finally I end up in the toy department. And I see this big stuffed panda bear. I mean, I'm eight years old, I lose my fucking *mother*, but this huge panda bear sits there smiling at me – a real goofy, happy smile – and I'm not lost anymore. I'm *found*. About a week later I got that stupid panda for Christmas. And then my mother dies. So at night I cuddle the panda bear, I pretend it's my mother, I take it to school with me. I talk to it. I love it. But what happens? One day at school I lose the goddamn panda bear. Gone – just disappears. See?'

I did not. I nodded.

'Must've been a *male* panda bear,' Peg said. 'I'll bet the furry fucker walked on you.'

'Probably,' Patty said.

---

* I supplied champagne and tips. One cannot buy love, perhaps, but one can almost always secure a credit line on companionship.

Peg sighed. 'Guilt trip. Traded in your mother for some big-dick panda bear, then the creep walks out the door. Right?'

'Right,' Patty said.

'Who the heck can you *trust*?' Peg said.

'Not panda bears,' said Patty.

'Not men,' said Peg.

The time had come to nudge the conversation toward some sensible topic. I removed my necktie, my sports coat, my shoes. I rolled up my sleeves. 'If you want lost,' I said, 'I'll *give* you lost. Try the mountains. Try Vietnam.'

Patty giggled and hooked my arm. 'God bless you, I dig Vietnam types. I really do.'

'Studs,' said Peg.

'Stallions!' said Patty.

Lost, I told them. Lost as lost gets. Abandoned in those mountains, no compass, no north or south, just the dense green jungle blurring into deeper jungle, and for two days I followed a narrow dirt trail that led nowhere. Here was a place where even *lost* gets lost. Everything was a mirror to everything else. And none of it seemed real. A joke, maybe: My six comrades would not have left me to perish out here. Except the joke was now two days old and getting stale.

I spent the second night wrapped in my poncho along the trail, listening to ghosts out in the fog, then in the morning I saddled up and headed eastward. The fog became rain. The sun vanished. At times my little trail turned to ooze; other times it gave out entirely, blocked by the face of an implacable rain forest. Unreal, I kept thinking. It could not be happening. Not to me. I was civilized; I *believed* in civilization. There was a reason, after all, that mankind had invented indoor plumbing, chimneys, brass beds, cotton sheets. It was in man's nature to defy nature. Why else the Industrial Revolution?

Why else four-wheel drive and mosquito repellent? Why else language?

To name it is to tame it.

House, I thought. And as I struggled through the rain, through the dripping underbrush, I murmured the word aloud – *house* – and then other such words.

I was an indoor person, caught now in an outdoor world, and my disorientation far exceeded the physical. I felt wronged and forsaken, double-crossed by my own comrades. At one point, during a rest break, I wondered if they might simply have forgotten about me.

The thought made me laugh. A moment later I was snarling. Betrayal – as usual.

'Real fascinating,' Peg said. 'I had this crazy boyfriend once – a Vietnam type too. I go for that shit. Grunt groupie, that's what he always called me. Turn-on, you know?'

'Danger,' Patty said.

'Death,' Peg said.

Patty giggled and said, 'Same difference.' She pulled off her bartender's apron, her bow tie, her blouse. 'You mind?'

I shook my head. Here was something new.

'Me too,' Peg said. 'Hot!'

'Hot!' said Patty.

Ordinarily I would have enjoyed such sportive interplay, but given the solemnity of my topic, I felt abused and ignored, like a teacher whose classroom had collapsed into inexplicable chaos. Granted, the hour was late, and we had imbibed beyond the limits of prudence, yet I suspected that my two youthful pussycats were intentionally missing the point.

Somewhat irritably, I refilled our glasses.

'These six so-called comrades of mine,' I said, 'they left me to rot. Walked away. Deserted me.'

'Like my panda bear,' said Patty.

155

'Except this was war.'

Peg nodded. She was playfully wrapping her black bow tie around my wrists. 'So you greased them, right? Shot off their nuts?'

'Now, please,' I said.

'You had a gun, right?'

'A gun? Yes indeed.'

'Well, jeez,' Peg said. She cinched the bow tie, fashioned a snug knot at my wrists. Patty was busy securing my ankles. 'Then you should've offed them. Like Rambo or somebody.'

'I was *lost* – that's our *topic* – and I would very much like to continue.'

My tone of voice was a trifle brusque, and I rapidly backtracked with a smile. Bizarre creatures, I decided, yet undeniably fetching in their stripped-down slumber-party costumes.

Peg glanced at Patty, Patty at Peg.

'Go ahead, then,' Peg said. 'But talk fast, Professor. Before we put the gag on.'

I did not 'talk fast.' I will *never* talk fast. Lucidly, in well-measured paragraphs, I described for them the soul-killing dimension of true lostness. Or, more accurately, the utter absence of dimension. Without up, I asked, where is down? Without hereness, how does one locate thereness? And so on.

By my third day in the mountains, lost had become a state of mind. I was not myself. I was an infant – a lostling – part of the rain forest, part of the sky, and at times the very notion of singularity dissolved all around me. This fuzzed into that: one waterfall became every other waterfall, this tree became that tree. Eventually the rain let up, which made the march easier, but the mountains remained webbed in a great silver mist.

In midafternoon I descended into a deep, grassy valley, and for more than an hour I was able to hold a bearing straight eastward.

No problem, I told myself.

Sooner or later, no matter what, I would run dead-on into the South China Sea.

But then, abruptly, the valley began to rise again, and soon the jungle closed in tight, and within minutes I was more lost than ever – pure greenery, no trails at all. I blundered along, once on my hands and knees, snagged up in vines and deep brush and hopelessness. I was no longer aiming at anything. Not even survival. Except for an occasional whimper, I had lost my capacity for language, the underlying grammar of human reason; I had lost the *me* of me – my name, its meaning – those particularities of spirit and personality that separate one from all, each from other. I was a grubworm among grubworms. One more fly in God's inky ointment.

Near dusk, therefore, it came as no shock to look up and behold a mahogany billiard table before me.

Well, I thought.

After which I thought: Am I thinking?

The old billiard table stood on a stone patio. Adjoining the patio was a dilapidated stucco house – a villa, it seemed, or what I imagined a villa must be, with blue shutters and blue trim and a rolled tile roof. Beside the villa was a swimming pool, and beyond the swimming pool was a well-barbered lawn dotted with fountains and gardens. I remained still for a time, waiting for this mirage to vanish, then I ventured a slow breath and approached the mahogany billiard table. It seemed solid to the touch.

Twice, cautiously, I circled the villa. Maybe an old rubber plantation. More likely a product of my own imagination.

The front door stood ajar. I hesitated there, almost knocking, then stepped into a cool hallway. Instantly, the notion of civilization reasserted itself. At the end of the hallway, I came upon a large sitting room furnished with cane chairs and cane sofas. Gauzy white curtains fluttered in an open window. The room had a lived-in feel, no dust or dirt, things neatly in their places. I made my way through a teak-paneled dining room, down another hallway, thence into a sunny, well-equipped kitchen. There was a gas stove, a GE toaster, crates of C rations, a refrigerator stocked with beer and fresh vegetables and packets of frozen meat. Somewhere nearby, I realized, a generator had to be running, which meant the place was inhabited, but for the moment I put these thoughts aside and sat down to my first meal in days.

Afterward, I explored the remainder of the villa.

On the second level I found three bedrooms, each furnished with cots and blankets and mosquito netting. Nothing fancy, but still miraculous. I selected one of the bedrooms, closed the curtains, stripped down, and soon fell into a deep and civilized sleep.

Patty laughed. 'Like that old fairy tale, right? Goldilocks and the three bears?'

'Pandas!' said Peg.

Awkwardly, I tried to sit up, a feat that was made difficult by the bow ties secured to my wrists and ankles – also an apron snug around my knees – and by the fact that Patty was now tugging my shirt down around my elbows. I struggled briefly, then tipped onto my side.

My two mates lifted me by the hips.

'Upsa-daisy,' said Peg.

Patty slipped my trousers down; Peg bundled them tightly around my thighs.

'And when you woke up,' Patty was saying, 'I bet those three nasty bears were there. Mama bear, papa bear, itty-bitty baby bear.'

Peg growled and reached for my belt. 'Who's sleeping in *my* bed?'

'Very funny,' I snapped. 'Are we finished?'

'Not hardly,' said Patty.

Peg pulled off my belt and looped it around my neck like a dog collar. She winked and gave the belt a little jerk.

'Now, *please*,' I said, 'I believe it's time to –'

'What a lech,' said Peg.

'A sickie,' Patty said. 'Tie him tight.'

I looked up helplessly as Peg folded a wet washcloth. Again, the thought crossed my mind that I was dealing with two very special young ladies, unique beyond measure. Their antics struck me as decidedly unfeminine, and after a moment, in austere tones, I informed them that these bondage antics had gone a step too far. Entirely inappropriate, I told them.

'You're a pig,' said Peg.

'Nonsense,' said I, and blinked. 'What did I *do*?'

Patty laughed. 'It's not what you did, man, it's who you are. Your whole sleazy personality. How you talk, how you walk. How you put the scam on every poor woman who walked through here tonight. Us included. Talk about an ogler.'

'I was taught,' I said primly, 'to look people in the eye.'

'You *don't* look them in the eye. You look them in the tits.'

I nodded cagily. 'That may sometimes be so. God forbid that a gentleman should happen to make eye contact with the weaker sex.

'Weaker sex?' Peg growled. 'That's why you're *in* this fix.'

I ignored the semantic smoke screen. 'And, moreover,' I said firmly, 'it was not I who stripped off his shirt this evening.'

'That was to make a *point*,' Patty said.

'Which you did. Four.'

Patty looked down at me with an expression that conveyed roughly equal measures of disgust and pity. 'That comment sums it up – thanks for helping. Peg and me, we've had it up to here with ridiculous old fogies on the make.'

'On their behalf, I apologize,' said I. 'But a fogy I am not. And what about my story? *Lost* – that was our subject.'

'We're making up a new story,' Peg said.

'The lost lech,' said Patty.

'Open wide,' Peg said. 'Say *ah.*'

I smiled uncertainly. 'I know we're having fun, but I'd very much appreciate –'

'Fun, my ass,' Patty said. 'Be a good boy. Nice and wide.'

Peg bent down, pried me open, and stuffed in the washcloth. Patty tightened the belt.

'That should do it,' said Peg.

'I *hope*,' said Patty.

The lights went off. There was giggly laughter, then a shuffling sound, then more laughter. A moment later Patty knelt down beside me. I could not really see the wicked lass, just sense her.

'A word to the wise,' she said, very gently, almost compassionately. 'Pick on women your own age. This is a brand-new world.'

She patted my shoulder.

Briefly, a door swung open, then swung shut again, and for the remainder of the night I lay trussed up in the humid Tampa dark. What was it in my nature, I wondered, that so attracted and so repelled the women of this world? No answer was forthcoming, only a flurry of interwoven questions: whom to trust, what to trust, when to trust, how to trust?

As dawn broke, I counted up my losses. A wife. A marriage. A mind. Mrs Robert Kooshof.

19

Found

Just after 8:00 A.M. I was released by a kindhearted janitor by the name of Delbert, an elderly gentleman with white hair and glossy black skin. He seemed amused at my predicament. 'It appears to me,' the man said, slyly and unnecessarily, 'like you went and tied one on last night.' He chuckled at this. '*Tied* – get it?'

I scowled, worked the blood into my wrists, helped myself to the hotel's whiskey – a double.

'Got it,' I said. 'Quite clever.'

Delbert nodded. 'Peg and Patty, I figure. Count yourself lucky they didn't use handcuffs.' The janitor flicked his bushy white eyebrows at me. 'And now you're fit to be tied, so to speak.'

I looked up with mild curiosity.

Lingually, the old man was by no means sophisticated, hardly in my league, but it seemed apparent that we shared a common interest in the subtleties and textures of the English language. I also noted a challenge in his eyes, one to which I could not help but respond.

'Tie the knot,' I said grimly.

'Tie-up,' said Delbert. 'Like with traffic.'

'Tied down,' I said. 'As in busy, occupied.'

'Railroad tie,' he said.

'Ties of marriage,' I said.

'Tie tack,' he said.

'Tycoon,' said I.

Delbert frowned. 'No way, man. That one doesn't count.'

'Spoilsport. Very well, then – tied score.'

'Tongue-tied,' he shot back. 'Tie-dye. Tie into. Tie that binds. My hands are tied.'

I shrugged.

'Not bad,' I said, and poured the old gentleman a whiskey. One had to admire his competitive spirit. 'If you're interested, we could try the word *lost*. In fact, there's an excellent story that goes with it.'

'A tie-in?' Delbert said.

'Right,' I said crossly. 'A tie-in. But there's nothing worse than a show-off.'

Thus, in swift narrative strokes, while Delbert mopped the floor, I brought him up-to-date on my current situation, abandoned by one and all, and how my plight had antecedents back during the war – deserted then, deserted now. I told him about the mountains, my six traitorous comrades, the old villa where eventually I found refuge. 'There I was,' I said, 'sound asleep on that cot, and what finally woke me up were these –'

'Voices,' said Delbert.

'Voices. Yes.'

'Your buddies,' the old man said. He leaned on his mop. 'I figure it was your buddies, right? The ones that dumped you?'

I glared at him.

'Sorry, sir. Just trying to speed things up.'

'Speed,' I said curtly, 'is irrelevant.'

The old man glanced at a clock behind the bar. 'But it *was* your buddies, right? And I figure they were using the place to hide out – like a base or something.'

I took time refilling my glass.

For a professional teacher – perhaps for all of us – there is little more irritating than to be cut short by incompetent guesswork.

'On the most simplistic level,' I said, 'I suppose you're right. My comrades, yes. A base of operations. But that's hardly the point.' For a few seconds I rebuked him with silence. 'Now, if you don't mind, I'd be happy to fill you in. The subject is *lost*.'

The old man fidgeted. 'Well, sir, it sounds interesting, but I've got toilets to clean.'

'Fine. I'll join you.'

'Sir, I don't think –'

'Lead the way,' I said resolutely. 'The labor may help you concentrate.'

Until that early Tampa morning, I had no idea how many public rest rooms the typical hotel contains. More than a score, in point of fact. At least two for each bar, each restaurant, each ballroom, each swimming pool, each sauna and fitness room and major corridor. Plus the lobby. Plus recreation and utility rooms. It was an arduous morning, in other words, both for myself and for my new friend, Delbert. (I was going on no sleep; Delbert was going on seventy-five years.) We divided up the labor, more or less – I handled the talking, Delbert the brushwork – but I dare say that by noon both of us were approaching the end of our respective tethers.

My behavior, I must confess, had become a trifle erratic. Compulsively jabbering. Easily distracted.

In general, I do not respond well to physical fatigue, or to tension, but I now felt positively overwhelmed by the loose ends in my life – Lorna Sue and Herbie and the tycoon and Mrs Robert Kooshof. On top of this, each hour seemed to bring still other distractions and complications: first Toni, then Peg and

Patty, and now I found myself plodding dizzily from commode to commode in the company of a smart-ass old janitor.

My entire life, it seemed, had become a great looping digression.

Nonetheless, though groggy and exhausted, I was determined to complete my tale. 'To be honest,' I told Delbert, 'you were pretty much on target. My so-called buddies, it seems they were Green Beret types. Using the old villa to stage all kinds of nasty business. Covert, of course.'

'Covert?' the old man said.

'You know. Secret.'

Delbert leaned over a toilet bowl and gave it a vigorous workout with his scrub brush. 'I know what *covert* is. But what's the point?'

'Betrayal,' I told him. 'Betrayal and loss.'

He looked up with moderate interest. 'Famous old tag team,' he said. 'Betrayal and loss. But if you ask me, sir, you should get yourself some sleep.'

'Soon,' I said. 'First the story.'

The old man handed me his brush. 'All right, I'll listen,' he said wearily. 'Finish up that toilet for me. Those other ones too.'

'You don't mean . . . ?'

'Good and sterile.'

Delbert lit up a pipe and took a seat in the adjoining stall. Fleetingly, though not for the first time, I felt the squeeze of dislocation – that blurred, random sensation.

I sighed and rolled up my sleeves. Sanitation was not my cup of tea and never would be, yet there comes a time when one must pay a price for human sympathy.

I dipped in with my brush.

'You awake?' I said.

'Absolutely,' said Delbert. 'Nasty business. Covert.'

*   *   *

My six comrades – if 'comrades' is the proper term – did not seem in the least surprised to see me. On the contrary, they scarcely looked up when I marched down the stairs that morning. There were no apologies, no explanations.

The old villa, as it turned out, was situated barely a half mile from our original ambush site, and over the past several days I had been wandering mostly in circles, recrossing my own path several times. Apparently, too, my comrades had been keeping tabs on me the whole while, watching me traipse along – no doubt snickering at my ineptitude – and in at least one important sense, it could be said that I had never been lost at all. (A curious bit of relativism. *Lost* can be viewed as both a state of mind and a state of being, and the two conditions are not always in harmony. One can *feel* lost without *being* lost. One can *be* lost without *feeling* lost. Very tricky.)

Even so, I protested. I accused them of deserting me, leaving me to the mosquitoes, yet this outrage seemed not to register. 'No sweat,' one of them said, a wiry little youth with the nickname Spider. 'We had you totally covered, man. Like a blanket.'

'*Wet* fuckin' blanket,' someone else said, and the others laughed.

The general mood, however, was mirthless.

'What I recommend you do,' said Spider, 'is consider yourself blessed. You once was lost, now you're found. Let it go at that.'

'Amen,' said Tulip.

There was no point in pursuing the matter. Clearly, these six sadists had their own agenda, which did not include the care and feeding of orphans like myself, and I swiftly opted for a course of caution. I was alive, after all – freshly found – and my goal was to stay that way.

Over the next several days, a predictable routine set in. I was assigned a cot, a footlocker, regular chores around the villa.

By daylight, I spent most of my time on KP, preparing meals, cleaning up after the others, and then at night, most often with Spider, I pulled four or five hours of guard duty. None of this was pleasant, to be sure, but on the whole I preferred it to the jungle. I kept my mouth shut, my ears open, and gradually a few salient facts began to surface.

The villa was part of an old French tea plantation, long abandoned, and for months my comrades had been using the place as a base of operations. They were all Special Forces – 'Greenies,' in their own self-congratulatory parlance. When they spoke to me, which was not often, it was in a brusque, clandestine code, to which I had no key. Everything was hush-hush. Their voices, their style, even their mission. In the late afternoons, just before dusk, two or three of them would sometimes slip off into the rain forest, gliding away without a word, then returning a day or two later with the same oily stealth. Where they went, or what they did, I never knew in any detail. In many ways, it was like belonging to a bizarre social fraternity, one with secret rituals and secret rules, except no one took the time to explain anything. Even their names were classified. They went by aliases and nothing else – Spider, Goof, Wildfire, Death Chant, Tulip, Bonnie Prince Charming. Not that I cared. My sole concern was staying found.

So I followed orders, stayed silent, bided my time. A week went by, maybe two weeks. Sooner or later, I reasoned, we would be returning to the firebase, and until then it seemed prudent to get along with my six spooky compatriots.

All in all, it was a ticklish period, obviously, but not without occasional delights. Sometimes, in the mellow hours of afternoon, it was easy to forget that we were in the heart of a war zone: drinks on the veranda, a quick dip in the pool, perhaps a leisurely stroll before dinner. Like a resort, I'd think. Very peaceful, no pressures. Twice a week, by some peculiar arrangement, a dozen or so Vietnamese civilians would appear out of the jungle – mostly female – and under a blazing white sun they would spend the day tending the villa's lawn and gardens. When my own chores were finished, I sometimes looked on while they raked and hoed and trimmed. To my mind, at least, there was something decorous about it, something tranquil and reassuring. It was as if the villa had been snagged in a time warp, a dreamy regression to a more exotic era – the tropical heat, the languor, those mysterious, brown-skinned women toiling away in their straw hats and bare feet.

Erotic, I thought. And I liked that too.

One of these young laborers, in fact, had taken a fancy to me, and on occasion I would invite her up to the veranda for a glass of lemonade. Her age was hard to guess: maybe sixteen, maybe twenty. Slender and delicately boned, with bashful black eyes, the girl reminded me of a little gazelle, alert and tentative, ready to bolt. Her name, as she spelled it out for me, was Thuy Ninh, which to my Western ear sounded uncannily like 'Take In.' Who would not be captivated? The very sound thrilled me, and with those two seductive syllables, so crisp and tantalizing, I imagined she was issuing an invitation of sorts, maybe even a promise.

Sometimes we would hold hands. Sometimes she would give me a shy little smile.

'You will love me?' she said.

'You didn't?' said Delbert from the adjoining stall.

'I *had* to.'

'Had to? She was just a kid, I thought.'

'Advanced for her age. Insistent too. She virtually forced me.'

Delbert issued a sharp sound of disapproval, which echoed through the tiled rest room, and the judgmental snap in his voice instantly brought to mind a certain childhood confrontation with Lorna Sue. The same moralistic piety. ('You kissed

Faith Graffenteen's *face*! You kissed her snotty nose!' To which I had responded as I was still responding: 'She forced me.' Incredible, is it not, how our earth revolves in such precise, repetitive circles?)

I scrubbed silently for a time, working on a stubborn stain at the bottom of a commode. 'It may be difficult to believe,' I said, 'but there is something about me – my manner, my essential selfhood – that women seem to relish.'

'Oh, yeah, like Peg and Patty?' said Delbert. The old man snorted. 'So you took advantage of this little Vietnamese gal?'

'Not in the least,' I said. 'Romance. An affair of the heart.'

What happened at the villa, I told him, could best be understood as an extension of my life history up to that point, one more chilling episode in a long pattern of sacrificing common sense to the exhausting demands of love.

Even in a war, I could not shake the curse of romance. It was my destiny. The story of my life.

From childhood on, I had been consumed by an insatiable appetite for affection, hunger without limit, a bottomless hole inside me. I would (and will) do virtually anything to acquire love, virtually anything to keep it. I would (and will) lie for love, cheat for love, beg for love, steal for love, ghostwrite for love, seek revenge for love, swim oceans for love, perhaps even kill for love.

Am I alone in this?

Certainly not.

Each of us, I firmly believe, is propelled through life by a restless, inexhaustible need for affection. Why else do we trudge off to work every morning, or withhold farts, or decorate our bodies with precious gems, or attend church, or smile at strangers, or pluck out body hair, or send valentines, or glance into mirrors, or forgive, or try to forgive, or gnash our teeth at betrayal, or pray, or promise, or any of a trillion large and small behaviors that constitute the totality of the human trial on this planet?

All for love.

All to *be* loved.

In my own case, obviously, this love drive went haywire at a very early stage. Like some horrid cancer, the need for affection multiplied into a voracious, desperate, lifelong craving. The benign became malignant. Desire became compulsion. Hence my hosts of female acquaintances; hence innumerable peccadilloes and compromises and heartaches and broken promises and embarrassments and outright humiliations. In my defense, however, I must quickly declare one other fundamental truth: the motive was never physical. Repeat: *never*! The motive was love. Only love. Thus, over the course of a spotty career, I have enjoyed carnal relations with a paltry four women. (Or three. Depending.) On the other hand, I can boldly credit to my account one hundred twenty-eight near misses, two hundred twelve love letters, fifteen boxes of chocolates, well over five hundred significant flirtations and alliances and dalliances. (I keep books. I do a rigorous monthly tally. The count *counts*.) And yet the quantities never proved sufficient. I had to keep fueling the furnace, refilling the hole, topping off my leaky love tank.

Which brings us to Thuy Ninh.

Nothing coy about it. 'You will love me?' she said.

And so we locked limbs on the billiard table, on my cot, in the swimming pool, in the dusty shade of the rain forest. For me, at least, it was an education, and my learning curve could be judged spectacular. Thuy Ninh would chant her name to me. (*Take in! Take in!*) I would gamely oblige. Slim-hipped and girlish, with a libido built on box springs, my vigorous young beauty was plainly well tutored in the ways of joy. Her appetite was healthy, her standards were high. 'Like *this*!' she would demand. Occasionally, I found myself wondering where she had acquired such skills, at once so technical and so bawdy, but in my naive way, blinded by romance, I chalked it up to precociousness and the influence of the jungle.

One afternoon, I recall, we lay entwined at the lip of a deep gorge behind the villa. (Cool and shaded, the place was among our favorite love venues. A narrow river descended from the mountains, passed through the gorge, then plummeted ten or fifteen feet in a magnificent little waterfall.) We had already made love twice that afternoon; we were now embarking on session three. In the speckled sunlight, Thuy Ninh's eyes had become moon slices, the irises in high orbit, tiny slivers of black sailing sideways beneath her upper lids. The soles of her feet were thrust skyward. She did a squeezing trick with her thighs, rolled me onto my back, screamed at the sky.

All this was memorable in its own right. (Chiseled into my chromosomes, in fact.) But adding to the frenzy was an impressive B-52 strike in the mountains to the west. The planes themselves were invisible. The consequences were not. Over Thuy Ninh's bare shoulders, I could see the distant jungle take fire – bright orange, bright violet, bright black. An entire mountainside collapsed. Seconds later a heated wind swept down the gorge, soon followed by several rapid concussions. Thuy Ninh seemed not to notice. She arched her back and exploded. There were secondary explosions too, plus aftershocks, and then I closed my eyes and unloaded my own devastating tonnage.*

Afterward, Thuy Ninh laughed. 'Sergeant Superman,' she said.

---

* Where in my affections, one might reasonably ask, was my beloved Lorna Sue during all this? The short answer: She was in Minneapolis. It is true, I suppose, that in this one instance I was unfaithful to her. Yet no marital vows had been uttered, no promises made. It was wartime, et cetera. Moreover, consider this: What if the girl of your dreams – your one and only, the woman you were meant for – happens to be on permanent holiday in La-La Land?

170

But it was not just sex.

The girl had snagged my affections; she filled up that part of me that needed filling. For once, it seemed, I had found something unimpeachable and pure. Granted, the physical pleasures were wondrous, but so, too, were all the simple things. Curling around her at night. Holding hands – that perfect fit.

On the veranda one evening, as my comrades looked on, I taught Thuy Ninh the waltz, humming in her ear, and for the moment we could have been actors in some silver-screen musical. At the finale, my six comrades offered tepid applause.

'Heartwarming,' Death Chant said.

'The cockles,' said Bonnie Prince Charming.

Goof yawned. 'This dude's heart,' he said wearily, 'is where his dick should be.'

Not much later, the six of them trooped inside. When they were gone, Thuy Ninh and I sat alone on the veranda.

'What was all that?' I said.

'That?'

'You heard them.'

The girl looked at me for a moment, almost in tears. 'Must go,' she said, then stood up, kissed me, and hurried off into the shadows of the rain forest.

Something odd had just occurred – a secret commentary, a secret reproach – and although it was a mystery to me, I had trouble sleeping that night. The unease stayed with me over the next several days. At times I caught Thuy Ninh studying me with a kind of apprehension; other times I had the feeling that my comrades were enjoying a droll, slightly macabre insight into the world.

'This tale,' said Delbert from the adjoining stall, 'seems told by an idiot. Doesn't signify jack-*any*thing.'

'It soon will,' I assured him.

'Sound and fury?'

'You bet,' I said.

A strange, tense time, I told him.

Late at night, invisible Phantoms and B-52s pounded the mountains to the west. One evening, jolted from sleep, I found Thuy Ninh crying in the dark. The girl pushed up against me, clamped her hands to her ears. 'Bad,' she whimpered. 'Shitty bad war.' There was nothing I could say. I held her until she fell asleep, then went to the window. Down below, on the veranda, my six comrades sat huddled around a large map, their faces lighted by a pair of candles. Their voices were indistinct, but after a moment I heard the squawk of a military radio – a buzzing sound, a pilot's voice – and then it hit me that my six pals were busy orchestrating this whole nighttime extravaganza. Wildfire relayed grid coordinates over the radio; the others scanned the mountains through field glasses.

There was no mystery now about their mission: search and scald.

And they enjoyed it.

Three or four of them had painted up their faces and torsos – bright colors, weird designs, like savages around a campfire. As I backed away from the window, Death Chant looked up and raised a hand to me.

'Love bombs!' he cried. 'Try a little tenderness!'

These men, I realized, were beyond gone. They were lost the way lunatics are lost.

For another hour I lay listening to mayhem – the thunderous bombing, the howls outside my window – and then I dozed off. When I awakened, Thuy Ninh was gone.

Immediately, I got dressed, went downstairs, and slipped out a side door.

The whole countryside was burning – everything – rocks and trees and earth. To the northwest, a mile-long silhouette of stone flared up in brilliant reds and violets. The sky was on fire, and the moon, too, and the nighttime clouds. A powdery white ash fluttered down like snow.

I moved along the side of the villa, edged up close to the veranda, stopped there and stood watching as Spider and Wildfire coordinated another air strike over their radio. In the dark, at the far end of the veranda, the others seemed to be performing a dance of some sort. I could not make out much, just wriggling shapes here and there, the phosphorescent paint on their bodies.

At one point an invisible jet passed low overhead – a shrill whining sound; a metallic hiss; a sequence of tremors rolling upward from the center of the earth; a brilliant orange flash to the east and then the faint, fleshy stench of napalm.

How long I stood there I am not sure. At least a full minute.

The night had gone to bedlam.

'Love bombs!' someone squealed, and someone else screamed, 'Love, love, love!'

There was a rushing noise, another jet, another orange flash, and in the flowery glow I spotted Thuy Ninh at the end of the veranda.

I took a single step forward. I took no more.

It was not the act of sex – not yet, not quite. Thuy Ninh stood swaying in the night, rapt and lovely, unclothed, painted up in blues and greens, presenting herself like a peacock to my dancing comrades. Instantly, I understood the source of her expertise in the art of love. She was slick with treason.

I am not an incapable man. (My IQ has tested out at well over 175.) But I am also human. I have psychological limits: That balcony sensation. That clock-stopped silence in my soul.

At first light I packed my rucksack.

I went out to the veranda, unfolded the map, switched on the radio, quietly called in my coordinates. I requested the whole tasty menu. Yes, I *did* – high explosives, napalm – and then I walked across the lawn and out into the rain forest.

And I felt not the slightest guilt.

(Anything for love.)

I did not wait to measure the results. There was no need. I could see it in my head. The object, of course, was not to kill, merely to terrify, and to this end I took satisfaction in the vision of my six betraying comrades cringing under a rain of Chippering wrath.*

So, yes, I simply walked away. East through the mountains. Across two muddy rivers.

By nightfall I was back at the firebase, at my desk in the adjutant's office, where I popped open a Coca-Cola, smiled to myself, flexed my new moral muscle, rolled the appropriate form into my typewriter, and awarded myself the Silver Star for valor.

'I'm a war hero,' I told Delbert.

I am Fury.

Do not fuck with me.

---

* Even at the time, I realized full well that there would be a penalty to pay. They would be displeased. They would come looking for me. Still, for once in my life, I felt the sweet glow of vindication.

20

Ledger

I was in sad shape when Delbert escorted me to my room that afternoon.

Agitated and weepy, confused as to my emotional whereabouts, I allowed the old janitor to tuck me in and draw the shades and leave me to a well-earned rest.

I slept for eighteen hours. Alone, as usual. Where, in time of distress, were Peg and Patty? Where was Toni? Where was my beloved Mrs Robert Kooshof? Even in deep slumber I missed her. Once, in the middle of the night, I jerked awake and dialed her number in Owago, with no results, and then for a long while afterward I lay paralyzed by the suspicion that my tempestuous companion was no longer fully committed to our relationship. (*Commitment* – surely among the most suspect words in our language. After an act of betrayal, can one truthfully say, in the past tense, 'Well, I *was* committed,' and if so, what fuzzy function does the word serve in our intricate, ongoing web of promises and expectations? If commitment comes undone, was such commitment *ever* commitment? By what slippery standard? What small print? What fickle sliding scale? The betrayal of love, in other words, seems also to entail a fundamental betrayal of language and logic and human reason, a subversion of meaning, a practical joke directed against the very meaning of meaning.*

My mood, in any case, was far from peppy. The next morning, even after the refreshment of sleep, it was all I could do to lumber through the motions of shaving and showering and getting on with the chores at hand. My heart was not fully engaged. It was a labor, as they say, without love, but at this point there was no going back.

I spent a final day in Tampa, wrapping things up, spreading a last coat of icing on my poisonous cake. By telephone, I sent flowers to various parties, under various names, with various messages. In late morning, after a cocktail or two, I visited a travel agent near the hotel, spent a studious half hour browsing through several colorful brochures, then booked Lorna Sue and Herbie on a seven-night honeymooners' cruise through the Gulf of Mexico. (At no additional charge, the travel agent very graciously agreed to hand-deliver the tickets to a certain real-estate office in downtown Tampa.)

Outside, buoyed by accomplishment, I strolled across the

---

* Certainly you, if anyone, can understand this. After all, you devoted more than twenty years of your life to a man who now dwells with another woman in the tropical isles of Fiji. He had sworn to love you until death did you part. And you remember this, don't you? Late at night, in particular, you lie thinking of your wedding day, in mid-July, an outdoor wedding beside a lake in a piney woods, and how the two of you stood side by side on an old wooden dock, and how it was there that he had solemnly murmured all those splendid pledges. You wore a white satin dress. The day was hot. You were happy – you believed. But now even the past is corrupt. You cannot think of that lake, or that dock, without also thinking of Fiji. *Forever* no longer means forever. *Forever* means for a while. *Forever* means until a pretty young redhead comes along. And so you cry yourself to sleep. You have been betrayed not only by a man but by your mother tongue.

street to do some honeymoon shopping. The perky young salesgirls in Victoria's Secret were more than helpful as I picked out a new wardrobe for Lorna Sue – peekaboo bras, panties, negligées, camisoles, garters, chaps, teddies, pigskin leggings – all of which the gals enthusiastically packed up for me and dispatched by courier to the tycoon's downtown real-estate office, along with an accompanying note signed 'Herbie.' (The sales-girls, in ascending order of mystery, were Katrina, Caroline, Deb, and Tulsa. 'Why Tulsa?' I inquired, which caused the lanky lass to lick her lips and whisper, 'Oil rigs, darling.' I asked no more.)

My fortunes, in any case, appeared to be picking up. A sense of progress; modest new control over my life.

I had a late lunch with the gals, collected four emergency phone numbers, then returned to the hotel and again tried calling Mrs Robert Kooshof. (There is little on this earth more dispiriting than the repetitive, one-note drone of an unanswered telephone.) Over the next hour, I called twelve more times, still without response, then I packed my bags and prepared to check out. I was only moments from departure, in fact, when there came a sharp rapping at my door.

Instantly, in my bones, I knew it had to be Mrs Robert Kooshof, an estimate that was at least partially confirmed when I opened the door. What I could not have predicted was that a smirking Herbie would amble in behind her.

Uninvited, this unlikely duo strode into the room and took seats upon my bed.

In Mrs Kooshof's lap, I could not help but notice, was my old leather-bound love ledger.

'What a scuz,' she said.

In my experience, it is a commonplace but still remarkable truth that the raw materials of one's life – objects, people, places, words – have a way of converging in time and space, coalescing like the elements of a dream, drawn together by a powerful but altogether mysterious force of nature.

Here again, I realized, was fate's cunning hand at work.

How did I respond?

Alarm, of course. A moment of panic.

Who, after all, would not be discomposed by the sight of one's arch-enemy sitting so casually at the side of a beloved consort? Dressed in crisp chinos and a blue polo shirt, the complacent prick radiated a bright, prosperous, upscale masculinity. Physically, as always, he was in superb condition: narrow waist, impressive chest and biceps. His dark hair was slicked straight back in what I believe is called the 'wet look'; his smile was glossy white, his aftershave crisp and pungent. This was no longer the snot-nosed delinquent of childhood. A total makeover – a latter-day smoothie.

Herbie's presence, I confess, was sufficiently unnerving in its own right. Yet even more so was the leather-bound ledger in Mrs Kooshof's lap: an embarrassing and easily misunderstood document. So embarrassing, in fact, that I may have thus far failed to underscore its altogether critical role in the collapse of my marriage. (Self-criticism is not my strong suit; I have avoided the confessional for two guiltless decades.) But, yes, the ledger was without doubt a volatile artifact, one that I had last seen on the night Herbie reached under my marital mattress and proceeded to ruin my life forever.

I looked at Mrs Kooshof, then at Herbie, and said, 'Fancy this,' somewhat nervously, with the knowledge that several jigs were on the rise.

Another moment elapsed before I was able to add, 'Burn down any churches lately?'

Herbie grinned. 'Have a seat,' he said, 'and forget the bullshit. You're in no position.'

I glanced again at my ledger, hesitated, then selected an upholstered armchair situated a safe six feet from Mrs Kooshof.

My consort sat turning pages. 'Sleaze,' she muttered. 'Scum.'
Herbie laughed at this.

There was considerable electricity in the room, considerable
ill will, enough of both to suggest that our very universe had
been organized around the single teleological principle of
heaping upon me piles of grief and anguish. Fate again – a
conspiracy. And what could I do but endure it?

'Stinking liar too,' said Mrs Kooshof. Her voice was listless.
She did not so much as look up at me. 'All that crap about
checks under a mattress. You don't know what truth *is*.'

'Nor do the philosophers,' said I. 'Nor do you.'

'Lies.'

I wagged my head. 'Not at all. I happen to be a half-truth
teller. Fluent, as a matter of fact.'

'Liar,' she said. 'Nothing else.'

Again, Herbie laughed. He crossed his legs and appraised
me with a small, composed smile. Very silky, very self-satisfied.
Months earlier, I had done some rudimentary detective work,
turning up the essential facts of his life in Tampa: he ran a
successful import firm specializing in electronic toys from the
Orient; he traveled extensively and dated even more extensively
– no commitments, no entanglements; he lived alone; he paid
his taxes in quarterly installments; he attended Mass at Our
Lady of the Sacred Heart; he dined out five nights a week;
he was in love with my former wife, his own sister, once the
girl of my dreams.

Forewarned is forearmed.

I did not blink. (Remember: a war hero.)

For the present, however, the more problematic issue was
Mrs Robert Kooshof, who turned the pages of my ledger with
quiet fury.

There was little to be lost by flashing her a sexy smile. 'So,
then, here we are,' I said gaily. 'And may I ask how this cozy
rendezvous came about?'

She made an apathetic motion with her shoulders. 'I needed to find things out for myself. Showed up on Herbie's doorstep.'

'So you've been staying –'

'Right here,' she said. 'In the hotel. Under your nose, as usual.'

'You might've let me know.'

'I might've.'

Even then, she refused to look up at me. Grimly, without pity, she kept flipping through the ledger, scanning my neat rows and columns.

Herbie watched with obvious amusement. 'Fascinating two days, Tommy. Comparing notes and so on. Very informative.'

'An education,' said Mrs Kooshof.

I eyed my ledger.*

'Whatever's happening here,' I said severely, 'you should understand that you're in possession of stolen property. Herbie burgled my bedroom – my marital mattress. He has no right to it.'

'A matter of opinion,' Herbie said.

'It's *mine*. It's *private*.'

Mrs Kooshof snorted and turned a page. 'Private's not the word. I mean, listen to this. "Hand-holdings: 421. Nuzzlings: 233. Valentines: 98. Marriages: 1. Meaningful gazes: 1,788. Home runs: 4. Near misses: 128."' She gave a little toss to her hair. 'The whole thing, Thomas, it's revolting. All these ridiculous subcategories. Telephone numbers. Body types. Hair color. Names and dates. It doesn't *stop*.'

'Well,' I admitted, 'I do think of myself as meticulous.'

Herbie beamed.

---

* I did not inquire as to why the ledger was still in Herbie's possession. I already *knew*: to threaten me, to keep me at bay, to use against me in circumstances just like these.

'Sick,' Mrs Kooshof muttered. 'It's like you're – I don't know – some perverted public accountant. Inflow, outflow. Assets and debits. Except you're counting up human *beings*.' She paused, squinted at the ledger, then held it up toward me. 'What's *this* mean?'

'Where?'

'Right here.'

I leaned forward. 'That would be the young lady's state of origin. I believe I'm missing Delaware.'

For a few moments we sat in silence, then Mrs Robert Kooshof closed the ledger and looked directly at me for the first time.

'The thing is,' she said, 'I can't pretend to be shocked. Not even surprised. That story about the checks – so weird, so convoluted – but the whole time it was the most common thing on earth. A little black book.'

'Not so "little,"' I sniffed, 'and far from "common."'

'No wonder she left you.'

I stiffened. 'Rubbish.'

'Lists of women? Under the mattress?'

'But I didn't *do* anything.'

Mrs Kooshof laughed without mirth. 'How noble. You didn't sleep with them – so what? Keeping these ridiculous statistics. It's obsessive and demeaning and . . . You can't file people away like a bunch of index cards.'

'They liked me,' I said. 'They paid attention.'

'Liked you?'

'Well, yes. It matters.'

Tiny wrinkles formed across her forehead. She hesitated. 'So where would you file *me*? Under "Dutch"? Under "doormat"?'

I stayed silent. (There was little to be gained by informing her that I had recently inaugurated a new and much improved ledger.)

After a second Herbie chuckled.

'Honest Abe,' he sighed. 'Compulsive liar. Compulsive ladies' man.'

'But not a pyromaniac,' I said tartly. 'I don't burn down churches.'

'You, then? You sicced the cops on me?'

'Concerned citizen,' I replied.

He looked at me without speaking for a moment, a blue vein twitching near his left eye. 'Just don't try it again,' he said. 'You're pushing where you shouldn't push.'

'I gather they asked some difficult questions?'

'What a baby,' he said, and glared at me. 'Christ, if you understood the first thing about –' He stopped and shook his head hard. The vein was still twitching. 'I swear to God, you'd better leave it alone. You're ignorant. Keep the fuck out of it.'

For a second I wondered if he might resort to his old crucifying tricks. Clearly, I had struck a nerve, but his reaction seemed to go well beyond anger; something else was happening behind his eyes – indecisiveness, a tug-of-war.

I waited a moment.

'Well, perhaps I *am* ignorant,' I said. 'But I didn't destroy any marriages.'

'It was your life, Tommy. Your blunders. Not mine.'

'But you didn't have to –'

'She's my sister,' Herbie said softly. 'I *did* have to.'

At that instant the old rage rose up inside me. I wanted to push needles through those complacent, pious, self-righteous eyeballs. So smug. So certain of his own virtue.

I was trembling.

'Sister,' I said. 'And that's all?'

'All?'

'You know.'

Something changed in Herbie's expression. 'I don't know. Tell me.'

'Think dirty,' I said.

'Tommy –'

'Sisterly love. That old rugged cross.'

Herbie folded his arms, studied me with a patented Zylstra stare. A muscle moved at his jaw.

'Tell you what,' he said slowly. 'I'll ignore that.'

'That's not an answer.'

'Don't press it.'

Gracefully, smiling again, Herbie picked up the ledger and cradled it in his lap. He seemed thoughtful.

'I'll try to be diplomatic,' he said. 'I do care for my sister. But whatever you think, whoever you blame, Lorna Sue has a brand-new life now, a pretty good life, and all these juvenile pranks you've been pulling . . . I recommend you cut it out.' He gave me another of his irritating smiles. 'We're not kids anymore. Things change, people change. No more make-believe. Fantasies suck.'

'Fantasies?' I said.

'You're divorced, Tommy. End of story.'

I knitted my fingers together. 'And what about you? Living here in Tampa? Following her around like a puppy dog? Do the fantasies suck?'

'Out of bounds.'

'Seriously,' I said. 'Still dreaming sister dreams?'

He went rigid, his whole body coiling up, and it occurred to me that the sleek new Herbie, so controlled and polished, was still struggling to hold back an explosive eight-year-old still inside him.

He rose to his feet, tossed the ledger to me. (Which I fumbled. Same old problem: dead cats.) 'Some things, man, you'll never understand,' he said quietly. 'No more pranks – stay away from us.'

'*Us*,' I said.

'I mean it, Tommy. Be careful. You're way out of your league.'

I nodded and said, 'No doubt,' but it gave me secret pleasure to imagine that Lorna Sue's handsome tycoon was at that very moment examining a pair of pigskin leggings and a packet of cruise tickets.

'Happy honeymoon,' I said cheerfully.

Mrs Robert Kooshof and I caught an early-evening flight back to the Twin Cities. It was not, of course, a full-scale reconciliation. Nor quarter-scale. The flight had been booked well in advance – both fares paid by none other than yours truly – and our joint journey was the doing not of Eros but of standard Dutch parsimony. My bewitching vixen, needless to say, sulked through much of the flight, at times staring out the window, at others browsing restlessly through my ledger.

Explanations were out of the question. Mrs Kooshof was in no mood to pay heed, nor was I in condition to sketch out the intricate psychology at work. Even in the most banal circumstances, human love is a subtle and enigmatic phenomenon, almost beyond analysis, but in my own particular case, which was nothing if not unique, the ordinary complexities seemed to have been multiplied by a factor verging on the infinite. On the one hand I had loved Lorna Sue completely and absolutely. On the other hand there was the reality of my ledger. Between these two poles lay the force field of my individuality, that ceaseless internal warfare we call 'character.' (I was no simple Lothario; I was *complicated*.) I yearned for steadfast, eternal love, as represented by the lasting fidelity of one woman, but at the same time I wanted to be *wanted*. Universally. Without exception – by one and all. I wanted my cake, to be sure, but I coveted the occasional cupcake too.

On this hazy principle, I had inaugurated my love ledger as a precocious twelve-year-old. (Faith Graffenteen, Linda Baumgard, Pam and Ruthie Bell, Corinne Vander Kellen, Beth Dean, Lorna Sue Zylstra – these budding, unseasoned kitty-cats were among my earliest entries.) By the time I reached high school, Lorna Sue had been firmly installed as the love of my life, yet I saw no harm in continuing to chart those minor flirtations that occur by the dozens in the flow of a typical school day: a shy smile in the cafeteria, a lingering bit of eye contact in biology lab. Who could fault me? Life is awash in such incidents, a confusing erotic flood, and to keep myself afloat I had no choice but to maintain an accurate running tally. It was a hobby of sorts, a benign and often amusing diversion that I pursued during four lonely years at the University of Minnesota, then through five years of restless bachelorhood, then with increasing regularity during my two decades of marriage to Lorna Sue. An ego booster, one might say.

All this and more I would have explained to Mrs Robert Kooshof, but instead we sat in silence for most of the journey, attuned to the sound and sway of our aircraft. The tension was funereal – sad and final. At one point, after a drink or two, Mrs Kooshof blotted a poetic tear from her cheek.

'You could've told me,' she said, no anger in her voice, only resignation. 'We were starting fresh. You didn't need to lie.'

'Pride,' I said.

'Oh, I'm sure. But I thought we *had* something.'

I nodded and closed my eyes. 'And now it's too late?'

'Probably,' she said. 'Yes.'

Then silence again. The jet's engines had the effect of a dreary lullaby.

Had I been able to summon the energy, I would have pointed out to her the substantial difference between lying and withholding inessential elements of the truth. Granted, the ledger had been a primary cause of my final separation from Lorna Sue; granted, too, it had been unwise to stash the document beneath our mattress. Still, despite appearances, I had been absurdly faithful to my wife, enduring much along the way, and the ledger amounted to nothing more than a statistical daily diary, a record not of misdeed but of a tidy mind collating life's random brushes with the rapacious, completely opposite sex. Are we not all entitled to our idiosyncrasies? Our harmless little crotchets and caprices? My only felony, after all, had been to organize the raw materials of experience into a coherent whole. The naughty young Toni, for example, had been duly registered as one of two hundred fifty-five brunettes with whom I had very innocently dallied. Much can be deduced from such data: hidden preferences, erotic probabilities, correlations of pigmentation and temperament. In point of fact, as Socrates himself admonished, I have come to know myself by way of my ledger, just as any corporation eventually finds profit in its spreadsheets.

Such were my thoughts when Mrs Robert Kooshof suddenly jerked upright and turned on me.

'Thomas, for God's sake,' she said forcefully, out of feminine nowhere, 'just this once I wish you'd stop *justifying* everything. Just one time in your wishy-washy life!'

Here was an alarming moment, obviously – my startled reaction was by no means counterfeit. It was as if the woman had read my mind.

'I mean, Jesus, you're like some fickle, randy old alley cat,' Mrs Kooshof was saying, loud enough to attract the attention of a buxom young businesswoman across the aisle. (Jade eyes. Toshiba computer. A come-hither upper carriage that had caught my eye back at the boarding gate in Tampa.) 'I'm serious. You should be neutered – no morals at all. Can't you at least apologize?'

'Of course I can,' I said, and blinked in wonder. 'But for what?'

'*What?*'

'If you mean –'

'I mean your personality,' said Mrs Kooshof. 'And stop ogling Miss Milkshakes.'

'I am definitely not ogling,' said I. 'Plainly not.'

'You are so! Right *now* – this instant!' She sucked in oxygen. 'My God, you're *still* doing it!'

Mortified, I raised an eyebrow at the woman across the aisle, who flashed me a conspiratorial frown before turning away. (It takes two, I believe, to tango. She preened, I took notice. Both of us, in any event, were no doubt yearning for parachutes as Mrs Kooshof went on to list my character deficits in a voice that competed successfully with the jet's twin engines. She was reminding me, in particular, that I had recently uttered the word *yes* in response to certain inquiries regarding my amatory frame of mind. 'I don't care what you say,' she growled. 'Yes *means yes*. I took you at your word. I thought we were in love.'

'Well,' I said, 'time will tell.'

'Time?'

'We've barely –'

Mrs Kooshof emitted a scornful noise from the back of her throat. She glowered at the businesswoman across the aisle, leaned back heavily in her seat. In our many weeks together, I had yet to see my companion so exhausted, so thoroughly drained of spark and color.

After a moment, in the tone of a physician delivering bad news, she sighed and said, 'If it makes you feel better, I'll take part of the blame. Maybe I wanted it too much. Went too fast. Thirty-six years old, biological clock buzzing like crazy, and it looked like my last chance for – you know – for real happiness. Romance. Whatever. So I planned this whole pretty future around you, a brand-new life, but then right away you started backpedaling. Ignored me. Almost pushed me off a balcony. 'And now this sophomoric black book of yours.'

'It is neither black,' said I, 'nor sophomoric. It is a professional's daily log.'

'More split hairs.'

'Yet accurate. Not frizzy.'

Mrs Kooshof yelped in frustration.

'If you ask my opinion, you're a sick, dangerous, compulsive skirt chaser. And a sneak. And a liar.'

'Fortunately,' I said, 'I did not.'

'Not?'

'Ask.'

I glanced sideways at the woman across the aisle. Clearly, she was intrigued. (Moistened lips. A becoming tilt to her head. It was my obligation to offer a wink of apology.)

'Dangerous,' Mrs Kooshof repeated. 'And that's the plain truth. You could hurt people, Thomas. Physically.'

'You're joking, yes?'

'I'm not,' she said. 'I think you're capable of . . . I don't know. Almost anything. That day on the balcony, you could've killed me. I still don't know what happened, exactly, but I'll tell you this much: It scared me. Plus the whole revenge business. And the way you attack me – in bed, I mean. It's too rough, like you're working out some old grudge.'

The businesswoman cleared her throat. (Was it my imagination that she squirmed? That she recrossed her legs, scratched her nose, twisted a ringlet of auburn hair around a trembling pinkie? The signs of estrus were evident.)

'You love women,' Mrs Kooshof concluded, 'enough to hurt them any way you can.' She paged through the ledger. 'Spankings: sixteen. The fuck does *that* mean?' I sat speechless. From across the aisle, however, came an audible groan. 'And the thing is,' said Mrs Kooshof, 'you don't act like I'm really important to you. I mean, you never even use my first name. Maybe you don't *know* it – I'll be you *don't*.'

'Enough,' I said sternly.

'Go ahead, then,' she said. 'What is it?'

'I will not be quizzed.'

'My name! Say it!'

The jet struck an air pocket. I was instantly (and luckily) overcome by nausea – a brackish taste in my throat – and it was with the greatest effort that I unbuckled my seat belt and retreated to a cramped lavatory at the rear of the plane.

Remarkable, is it not? How words truly matter?

Nouns. Names.

For some time I sat racking my memory, amazed at the tidal influence of language in our lives, and when I returned to my seat a half hour later, still shaky, Mrs Robert Kooshof was huddled in neighborly comradeship with my jade-eyed, top-heavy businesswoman. Together, they were feeding on my ledger like a pair of cornfield crows.

'Donna?' I said.

21

Rain

As in war, so, too, in romance.

Knee-deep in hell, amid the smoke and din, we lose our internal bearings. Terrors multiply. Options narrow. Like flotsam, we are caught up in the swirl, no right or wrong, ambiguities everywhere, each of us carried to a puny destiny by the great fateful flood. In times of moral complexity, events have a way of accelerating beyond the reach of human reason.

I had little choice, in other words, but to propose marriage to Mrs Robert Kooshof.

Thus, over prunes and buttered toast on a cool late-April morning, two celibate days after returning from Tampa, I dropped to my knees and popped the imprisoning question. On the sexual weather front, to reach for a metaphor, it had been a rare and very frustrating dry spell, enough to make one dizzy with desire, and on that particular morning Mrs Kooshof happened to be breaking fast in her midnight-blue negligée.

'Will you?' I inquired.

'Will I *what*?'

'Oh, stop it – you know exactly what. Will you have me?'

It was worth a try. Evidently, though, my soon-to-be betrothed had developed a wary, altogether distrustful attitude toward our capricious universe. She insisted on precision.

'Have how, Thomas? What does *have* mean?'

'The obvious,' I said.

She gazed at me without mercy. 'Then say it. The words. I want to hear the *words*.'

My knees, I must remark, were chafed by the time we had completed our transaction. 'Yes, *yes*,' my beloved new fiancée finally cooed, although by that point she had imposed a number of rather stern provisos: I would henceforth be keeping no books. I would shun the city of Tampa. I would renounce revenge. I would kick, cold turkey, my so-called girl habit. I would repair the telephone. I would be present at meals. I would address her by her Christian name.

'Agreed,' I muttered wearily. 'And perhaps a new wristwatch?'

Mrs Kooshof rolled her shoulders. 'Just a ring,' she said.

A most delicate negotiation, all in all, yet I had the foresight to drive my own hard bargains where necessary. Thanks in part to my work on young Toni's thesis, I carefully wrapped our connubial contract in a profusion of syntactic bows and ribbons, inserting key paragraphs of small print, framing certain critical clauses in the obscure, hedging locutions of eighteenth-century diplomacy. I did not, for example, phrase my proposal as a formal question. Rather, I used the clear-cut imperative: 'Marry me!' – a distinction, I believe, that would hold up in any court of law. Moreover, since Mrs Kooshof was already a well-wedded woman, coupled to a felonious jailbird of a husband, I took the precaution of appending a deft bit of language stipulating that she be 'free and unencumbered' prior to any final alliance.

The objective, of course, was to buy time, to smooth Mrs Robert Kooshof's ruffled feathers while preserving room for maneuver.

Loopholes, in short.

Escape hatches. Swiss cheese.

'So what you mean,' she said warily, 'is that I'll have to get divorced first? From Doc?'

'Correct,' I said. 'Brigham Young I am not.'

'But that could take months.'

'Perhaps so,' I nimbly responded. 'Eyes on the prize and imagine the reward.'

Mrs Kooshof made a grinding motion with her jaw. She remained dubious. 'Okay, I guess you're right, but you won't back down afterward? You won't leave me stranded?'

'Don't be silly.'

'That's an evasion,' she said. 'Just answer me. Yes or no?'

Disarmingly, I spread out my hands, palms up. I had learned my lesson in Tampa; no power on planet earth would drag either of those poisonous syllables through my firmly sealed lips. 'We have nothing,' I told her solemnly, 'if not trust. All else is subordinate.'

'That's *no*?'

'Trust,' I repeated cheerfully.

Mrs Kooshof fell into a meditative silence. Clearly, I thought, my prospective partner-for-life had become skittish about matters of the heart, my own in particular, and now her fixed, cool, skeptical stare suggested that I had a great deal still to prove. She consumed her banana without once looking away.

'Well, just don't forget the ring,' she finally said. 'And don't think I'm stupid. You were boxed in – you *had* to propose.'

'Whatever,' I said.

Mrs Kooshof frowned and fidgeted, her defenses not yet fully breached. 'And here's a warning,' she said. 'This is your last chance, Thomas. I'll be watching like a hawk. No trips to Tampa.'

'Banish the thought.'

'And you'd better *be* there for me.'

I flicked my eyes bedroomward. The banana she had just swallowed, in conjunction with her midnight-blue negligée, had already summoned moisture to a dry April morning.

*   *   *

192

The trick with women, I have learned, is to keep upping the ante. Lose a hand, double the stakes. Lose another, redouble. To infinity. Like any gambling junkie, the female animal wants it all – your purse strings, your heart, your spirit, the very breath of your lungs.

The jackpot forever beckons.

Needless to say, Mrs Robert Kooshof was wholly and full-figuratively a woman, plump with passion, engorged with greed, and our bedroom rampage that morning belongs to the ages. She was ferocious; she consumed me wholesale. Her self-absorption, I must say, was at once embarrassing and educational, at times bordering on the scandalous. (In deference to my beloved's privacy, I will not detail modes and methods; at one point, however, I found myself smothered by what can only be described as a pair of astral earmuffs.) It was, to be frank, an experience: a close encounter with eternity.

At the ultimate moment, as I alighted in paradise, Mrs Robert Kooshof chuckled and stroked my forehead and whispered, 'Commitment, Thomas. That's all I ever wanted.'

Afterward, with a little sigh, she got up and moved off to the bathroom, her stride languorous and proud. (Six feet even. Heroic frontal matter. One hundred fifty-three muscular Dutch pounds.) She grinned at me, took a seat on the toilet, relieved herself with the door wide open.

Already the woman was reaping the matrimonial harvest.

A chatterbox on top of it.

'That was fine,' she was telling me, 'but once we're married, I can start to – you know – start to let *go*.' She paused. 'Of course it won't be easy. The divorce, I mean. Doc won't take it lying down.'

I looked up with interest. 'How so?'

'Nothing. Except he can get – what's the word? – he can get

193

nasty. I mean, he's behind bars right now, which helps, but he knows people.'

'People?' I said.

Immodestly, Mrs Kooshof cleansed herself, rose up, and turned on the shower. 'Bone breakers,' she said, rather too casually. 'He'll make trouble, we can almost count on it, but this time I'm not knuckling under. No way, nohow. For once, I know what I *want* in life – you and me – and I won't let anything stop us. Not in a million years. Never.'

I drew a shallow breath.

'Bone breakers?' I said. 'Tell me more.'

'Oh he won't be happy, that's all. Things might get unpleasant.'

'I thought the man was a veterinarian. A puppy doctor.'

Mrs Kooshof opened the shower curtain, beckoned me with a curled finger. 'I'll handle Doc,' she said. 'You handle me. Come here now.'

Reluctantly, I joined her. (Much as I adore a good shower, I have never comprehended the point of sharing lavation fluids. Where is the romance in imitating goldfish?) The tall, bulky Mrs Kooshof completely dominated our limited space, not to mention the hot water, and for some time I stood there soapy and chilled to the core as she shampooed and conditioned her hair.

My cozy bachelor world, I realized, had swiftly come undone.

True enough, I did not want to lose her, hence my hasty proposal, but on the other hand I had been counting on a lengthy engagement – three to five years, minimum. (I was still attached to Lorna Sue; I still required the catharsis of revenge.) Plainly, though, Mrs Robert Kooshof was jumping the matrimonial gun. Humming to herself, eyes like sparklers, she was computing her unhatched chickens with the perky, overconfident impudence of a newlywed.

Stunning, I thought, how quickly the apple rots.

For the present, however, the more urgent issue took the form of Mr Robert Kooshof, alias Doc, and as we stepped out of the shower I went fishing for pertinent facts and figures. None of it was encouraging. According to my beaming bride-to-be, the man had always taken an aggressive approach to problem solving. Not your standard veterinarian, she explained. Ill-tempered and spiteful. A wrestling enthusiast. A prototype bully – precisely the sort of human pestilence I had always despised and feared. 'God knows why I married him,' she said sadly. 'A cruel, cowardly, abusive rat. Sometimes I think he became a vet because he loved putting pets down. Lethal injections, you know? And a born cheat too – amazing he didn't end up in jail years ago.'

She finished drying herself, dropped her towel on the floor, sprinkled talcum powder over a pair of lithe (but unshaven) legs.

I retrieved her towel, returned it to its proper peg on the wall.

'If you don't mind my saying so,' I muttered, 'you might've mentioned all this a bit earlier.'

'Well, God, I tried to,' said Mrs Kooshof. 'You never let me talk about myself. There's a trillion things you don't know.'

'So talk,' I said.

'Maybe now I don't *want* to.'

'Oh, you do,' I purred, and over the next half hour, trolling the troubled Kooshof marital waters, I netted the following facts:

They had been college sweethearts at the University of South Dakota. Married sixteen years. Twice separated. Moved to Owago in the late 1980s. Far as I could gather, Mr Doc Kooshof's tax difficulties had their source in wild, grandiose avarice – hidden income, inflated deductions, altered records, an impressive array of mathematical errors. 'That's the kind of person he is,' said my rosy-bottomed, well-scrubbed fiancée. 'Miserly and arrogant. Mean as a pit bull. You won't believe this, but he actually claimed exemptions for a couple of children. Non-existent, obviously.' She studied her hands for a moment. 'Children. My big dream.'

'And not his?'

'Of course not. Drain on the economy. And he didn't want the mess. The anal type.'

I made an appropriate tsking noise. (Lorna Sue popped to mind – another rabidly antichild spouse.) By that point we were seated at my walnut dining table, sharing a pot of coffee, and I could not help making a quick survey of my once spick-and-span kitchenette, now strewn with smudged glassware and blackened pots and pans. (Not to mention a refrigerator piled with leftovers, wads of soggy blond hair clogging the bathtub drain, bedroom closets that had come to resemble a Laura Ashley fire sale.)

I slipped a coaster under Mrs Kooshof's coffee cup.

'Anal,' I murmured. 'Imagine that.'

She bobbed her head. 'Drove me nuts. And the thing is, Thomas, he'd get violent about it – scary violent. Sometimes I'd have to lock myself in the bathroom just to feel safe. I guess maybe it's a habit now.'

'Perhaps so,' I said.

'Well, now you know where it came from. We're talking about a weird, frightening guy.' She looked across the table at me, her eyes slick with moisture. 'If anything happens . . . I mean, you'd fight for me, wouldn't you? If he got out on parole or something?'

'Parole?' I said.

'Possibly.'

'How possibly?'

'Pretty possibly. In seven or eight months. But that's not the point. Would you *fight* for me?'

I considered the alternatives, none of them appealing, then shrugged and sat back. When in doubt, redouble.

'Tooth and nail,' I said soothingly.

'Honest?'

'No quarter. Lethal injections.'

She gave me a relieved grin. Bad as things were, I still had the knack.

When it rains, it pours.

Now came the torrent.

On that same April morning, as I recuperated from life's latest onslaught, the delicious young Toni put in a long-overdue appearance during my weekly office hours. She was wearing, I happily noted, a pair of yellow bicycling shorts, a copper necklace, no shoes, no underwear, a pink sorority T-shirt that had been neatly snipped off just below glandular level. Without preliminaries, Toni locked the door and perched cross-legged on my desk, facing me straight on – ostentatious female to clear-cut male.

'We got ourselves a problem,' she announced. 'A real piss-ass motherfucker.'

(Teacup kneecaps. Thighs of iron. Foul mouth. Coarse, sable hair suspended in a festive ponytail.)

I lowered the venetian blinds and said, 'Delighted.'

Toni scowled. 'Didn't you *hear*? You and me, Tommy Boy, we're up against it. My roommate's turning us in.'

'One step at a time,' I chirped merrily. 'First the welcome wagon.'

I withdrew a decanter of port from my file cabinet, poured each of us a ritual two and a half inches. Here, I rapidly deduced, was a case of adolescent love fever, pure and obsessive. All else was pretext.

Toni consumed her beverage in three indelicate gulps.

'You don't *get* it,' she snarled. 'My roommate, she knows

197

about the thesis, all the succor and encouragement you gave me. How you pitched in and helped.'

Toni's way with the language, I thought, was unquestionably inventive, though to my taste a speck egotistical. The words *succor* and *encouragement* seemed especially euphemistic, and it occurred to me that the girl would make a splendid squid should her academic career ever falter – a rare ability to squirt ink upon everything but paper. I stretched back in my chair.

'Oh, succor, succor,' I said, and waved a dismissive hand. 'A token. The least I could do.'

Toni nodded savagely. 'Well, *I* know that, *you* know that, but it won't stop Megan. That's her name – my little fuck-pig roomie. She plans to squeal on us.'

'Us?'

'Well, naturally. And she's going to the dean unless we do something fast.'

I issued a small, appreciative chuckle. 'In my experience,' I said calmly, 'a little denial goes a long way. There's no proof, right?'

Tony sighed. 'Well,' she said, far too slowly.

'Well *what*?'

'My stupid diary,' she moaned. 'I wrote down a few things. About the thesis. About you and me. And now that rotten, rat-fucking Megan, she's bringing it to the dean.'

I shut my eyes. The word *diary*, like its close relative *ledger*, immediately took its place in my interior dictionary. (Sticks and stones may break our bones, but words will truly crush us. Do not forget Fiji, where your ex-husband now inhabits a little grass shack by the sea, his nights lighted by a trillion stars and a willowy young redhead named Sandra. Is Fiji still Fiji? Does not the word *redhead* make your tummy turn? So, too, with me, the word *diary*.) I could not be blamed, in any event, for feeling a wave of trepidation; my priggish colleagues would have trouble understanding the joys of a closely supervised tutorial.

'The whole story.' I sighed. 'Start at the start. I'll need every detail.'

'I already *told* you.'

'Everything. Pretend it's life and death.'

It required ten minutes of stern interrogation, but I eventually learned that Toni and her roommate had fallen out over a trivial matter involving the university's hapless football team. The particulars were difficult to follow, but apparently Toni had 'borrowed' a certain young linebacker for an evening, a chap who happened to be Megan's personal chattel. Escalation ensued. Push came to shove.

'What gets me,' Toni whined, 'is they barely even knew each other. It's not like they were married or engaged or anything.'

(*Engaged*: Do I make my point?)

'So you entertained this gentleman?' I inquired. 'Your roommate's boyfriend?'

'Well, yeah. And Jake too.'

'Jake would be . . . ?'

'Megan's backup. He's a wide receiver. It's really childish, if you know what I mean, but she got pretty mad at me. She went out and did Ronny.'

'Did?'

'Did. The usual.' Toni yawned and curled up on my desk. 'Ronny was mine. Cute guy. Naturally I had to get back at her – I *had* to – so I did Sid.'

'You did Sid?'

'Yeah, I did.' She blinked at me, then glared. 'This isn't the time for bullshit. You'd better come up with something fast.'

Briefly, my gaze fell to her thighs.

It was a temptation, I must say, but decency and common sense prevailed. (Betrothed is betrothed.) Fond as I was of this tasty side dish, I could not condone such escapades, or participate, and yet even so I felt a sharp stab of jealousy at Toni's indiscriminate ways. Plainly, I was not the only barracuda in this mermaid's steamy sea.

'The diary,' I said. 'Incriminating?'

'Yeah. Pretty much.'

'And this meddling roommate – where would I find her?'

'At the dorm,' said Toni. 'She's there right now. I mean, if you can fix this, maybe then we'll see about . . .'

Provocatively, she let the sentence slither off into the romantic underbrush.

'Done,' I said.

Not an hour later, I was in face-to-face negotiations with the roommate in question, Miss Megan Rooney, a creature of smallish stature but multiple charms. I was dazzled: a pinup girl for gnomes. This choice little tidbit topped out at four feet eight – barely visible from my lofty elevation – yet each taut, symmetrical, hard-won inch counted at least double on the Chippering erotometer. (Long chestnut hair. Enchanting hindquarters. Amoral gray eyes.)

Fearing refusal, I had not telephoned for an appointment, instead simply announcing myself over the dormitory intercom. After a disgraceful thirty-two-minute delay, the young lady made her appearance, dressed in the fashionable togs of the day: black tights, short pleated skirt, yellow scarf, clashing red shirt. She led me into the very sitting room in which Toni and I had spent so many happy hours communing over Western wedding vows.

Miss Rooney's posture was slack, her attitude insolent.

'So where's my slut roommate?' she mumbled. 'Afraid to face me, I suppose.'

I gave her a severe smile. 'As far as I am able to ascertain,' I replied, 'neither one of you lacks for nerve. This is between you and me.'

I then went straight to the point.

She was in the presence, I explained, of a war hero, a recipient of the Silver Star for valor, and therefore not one to be trifled with. (A rare instance in which a Chippering sentence labored under the weight of a misplaced preposition.) I informed the little tigress that actions carry consequences, that Judas eventually found himself at the end of a rope, that tit will almost inevitably lead to disastrous tat.

The microscopic Miss Rooney seemed less than overwhelmed.

'If that's a threat,' she squeaked, 'you're in even *deeper* shit. You better just watch it.'

'Is that right?' I said. Her tinny voice had distracted me. Like a Saturday-morning cartoon character – a talking flea, perhaps, or an inchworm. Moreover, despite the serious business at hand, I could not help but admire the girl's scaled-down physique. Toothsome, I thought. (An engaged man, yes, but not yet blind to our glorious, ever bountiful world.)

I sat beside her on a sofa, reducing our height differential, and then proceeded to outline several compelling arguments in behalf of discretion.

The simple cliché, I had long ago discovered, is almost always effective with the sophomoric crowd, and I now employed the device in abundance. (No need to rock the boat. Let bygones be bygones. Do unto others. Cast no stones.) My tone remained firm, to be sure, but I tempered these remarks with the occasional gesture of sympathy: a reassuring squeeze of the knee, an avuncular stroke of the hair.

'Believe me, I completely understand the situation,' I said gently, even soothingly. 'And I'm sure it's all very upsetting. Jake and Ronny and Sid. I know how treason feels.'

The diminutive Megan rolled her eyes.

'What about Geoff?' she said. 'I had dibs on him. A punter, and really cute, and he'll be a kabillionaire someday.'

'Punters,' I said stiffly, 'were not mentioned.'

'I just bet they weren't. Or Billy Bob. Or Jumbo Tomilson.' She looked at me with something close to anguish. 'How would *you* feel? I mean, it's like she's hogging the whole stupid team.'

Again, I had not been given all the facts – barely half, as it turned out. It occurred to me, however, that there was something to be said for the brutish sport of football. Although far from successful on the gridiron, these Golden Gophers certainly had no want of offensive punch, and thenceforth I would be following their fortunes with a much keener eye.

I shifted position on the sofa, sliding closer to Miss Rooney.

'You're right, the numbers don't lie,' I said rather smoothly. 'A breathtaking body count by any standard. Your roommate, if I may say so, appears to be – what's the proper term? – perhaps something of a glutton.'

'A porker!' Megan cried. 'A sow!'

I nodded compassionately I put a calming hand to the small of her back.

'Sow, indeed,' I said. 'And clearly you're the victim here. You've been swindled, I dare say – shortchanged in the punter department – but all the same I see no reason to strike back at the blameless. I'm a mere spectator, after all. Consigned to the bleachers.'

I transferred my hand to her stomach.

(Her red shirt had slipped upward a revealing inch or two. Serendipity, of course, yet I found myself examining the tiniest navel I had ever encountered, taut and mysterious, an inverted little thimble that positively beckoned my pinkie.)

'The point,' I said shakily, 'is that you needn't involve me. I'm an innocent in all this – driven snow, et cetera.'

'What a laugh,' Megan muttered. 'Innocent.'

'Precisely.'

'So get your hooks off me.'

I smiled. 'A mere plug of lint. Consider me your chimney sweep.'

'Off!' she piped.

The girl jerked away.

'Toni was right,' Megan said, and tugged down her shirt.
'I mean, Jesus, you really *are* a pompous old jerk. Fucking
desperate too.'

I sniffed at this. 'Incorrect,' I said. 'On all counts.'

'I've got the *diary*! I've got *you*!'

'Perhaps so,' I said. 'And I must insist upon its instantaneous
return.'

Megan laughed her squeaky laugh. 'Get real. It's all there
in black and white, so you'd better start looking for a job in
. . . in the Yukon.'

'Yes?'

'Or Siberia!'

Under the circumstances, to be frank, her suggestion struck
me as tempting. Recent developments had strained my emotional
boundaries, and for a few moments I envisioned life in the cool,
uncomplicated confines of a north-country igloo. No visitors.
Certainly no women. Perhaps a perimeter of land mines to
keep out the riffraff.

It was this image, in part, that brought a quaver to my voice.
Inexplicably, my breath came in quick, raspy gobs.

And then out of the blue, without forethought, I heard myself
issuing the most shameless pleas, nearly sobbing, an altogether
loathsome performance that even at the time shocked and
embarrassed me. Yet I could not stop. (Stress, no doubt. Too
many irons, too hot a fire.) My voice sailed up a full octave,
high-pitched and hollowed out, and for an instant it seemed
that this sudden squeaky condition had been transmitted to
me by way of a terrible new virus.

Disgusting, yes, but my little outburst paid off.

The girl finally sighed. 'Jeez, all *right*,' she said. 'I guess we
can figure something out. Keep your spit off me.'

I sat up straight.

'A solution?' I said.

'Maybe. Let me think.'

Once again, her taut little navel had worked its way into my field of vision. The girl frowned, ran a hand across her stomach, then smiled with pygmy pleasure.

'Okay, here's the deal,' she said. 'I hear you have a way with words.'

'God's gift,' I admitted.

'So let's do business.'

It was a straightforward transaction. The young lady was a junior; her thesis was not due for nearly a year; we had time to burn. On the downside, to be sure, Megan was an art history major, one of the few subjects in which I am less than wholly versed. Still: no problem. For years, through thick and thin, I had been a fervent, even zealous, believer in the value of adult education.

I nearly giggled.

By all rights, I had driven a merciless bargain. Quickly, before she could add to my work load, I shook the girl's hand, turned on my heel, and walked away a victorious and much lightened individual.

Outside, Toni paced the sidewalk.

'Done,' I said happily. 'It's fixed.'

'Nifty. What about my diary?'

I pulled the little volume from my breast pocket, began to hand it to her, then halted.

In an age chilled by purgative sexual politics, feminine extortion has become the bane of all who trod the bleak, arctic halls of academia.

I returned the diary to my pocket.

'Safety first,' I said.

But this was hurricane season. The torrents did not abate.

That evening, at the conclusion of the dinner hour, Mrs

Robert Kooshof leaned back in her chair and announced with devious solemnity that she had acquired the services of an attorney in Owago. She had initiated divorce proceedings; her incarcerated husband-beast had been alerted via certified letter; her house was up for sale; she had begun the tedious labor of assembling a bridal trousseau. That very day, in fact, she had spotted the ideal engagement ring – a trove of diamonds nestled in solid gold – and had taken the liberty of putting down a modest deposit in my behalf.

As I digested these facts, along with Mrs Robert Kooshof's Swiss steak and scantily mashed potatoes, I was startled to hear my telephone awaken from its long slumber.

Mrs Kooshof smiled.

'And a new phone,' she said brightly. 'I hope you don't mind.'

Fiancée or otherwise, she had no right. Already, in our short relationship, the woman had rearranged my furniture, repainted the den, cluttered the bathroom with feminine con-trivances of every stripe, and roundly criticized the remaining decor as 'Bunker Sterile.' (Amazing, is it not, how quickly the conjugal contract takes effect? How the words 'I will' have all the potency of their linguistic kissing cousins 'I do'? Familiarity breeds cheekiness, if not outright contempt.)

Now the telephone.

Sulking, I rose to my feet and plodded down a hallway to the squealing electronic beast, only to be greeted by the unhappy voice of Lorna Sue's tycoon.

'You fucker,' he began.

Beyond that, his language eluded me – a blue streak, a biblical blur – but the essential nut of it seemed reasonably clear. Lorna Sue had left him. She was threatening divorce. He blamed me. (There was a reference, I am quite sure, to certain purple undergarments.) The man's voice was bellicose. And he was not calling from Tampa. He was in a phone booth down the street, in possession of a hockey stick, and wished for an interview.

I begged off with a few choice words, none consolatory, and abruptly replaced the receiver. A moment later, even before I had processed the momentous news, my new telephone once again bawled for attention. 'It's *me*,' Toni said. (I had no time to correct her grammar.) Next came a hooting noise, then young Megan's squeaky voice: 'Yeah, man, and *me*!' Drunkenly, giggling like the silly schoolgirls they were, the duo requested my presence at an evening soirée in progress along fraternity row. 'The whole team's here,' said Toni. 'We need you to run interference.'

I glanced down the hallway.

'Interference,' I said crossly, 'seems right up your own dark alley.'

'Oh, come on!' said Megan. 'Rock 'n' roll, Tommy!'

Tersely, with no further effort at decorum, I explained that I could not make it. I alluded to storm clouds. 'Believe me,' I told them. 'When it rains, it pours.'

'*What* rain?' said Toni.

Megan laughed and said, 'Wear your rubbers, tiger.'

Again I declined.

Again I replaced the receiver.

And again I had taken not three steps when the phone once more injected its venom into my fragile, fast-beating heart. Lorna Sue this time. Her voice sounded shaky, the connection full of static, but I gathered she was calling from a DC-10 winging its way northward from Tampa.

She wanted me back.

She forgave me everything.

'I'll be there,' she said, 'in an hour.'

'An hour?' I said.

'Right. Maybe less.'

My dreams, in a sense, had come true, yet I confess that

it was a bewildering moment for me. Telephonic overload, in part. A gorged sensation. Mrs Kooshof's spicy Swiss steak still lingered on my palate. 'Splendid,' I whispered. 'But let's make it tomorrow.'

There was an intake of breath at the other end of the line. 'What's wrong with right *now*?' said Lorna Sue. 'Is somebody there?'

'Don't be ridiculous.'

'Well, I can't see why –'

'Tomorrow,' I repeated. 'At the office. Be sure to knock.'

As I moved back to the dinner table, reeling, it struck me that my pitiful little life had taken on complications that might test the sturdiest human constitution. A love triangle was one thing; this had assumed the shape of a heptagon.

'So who was it?' said Mrs Kooshof.

I shrugged and thought fast. 'My travel agent. She recommends Siberia.'

There was a brief respite, then another telephonic clap of thunder.

Herbie.

He was calling from the Tampa airport.

His flight departed at midnight.

He would be looking me up in the very near future.

'Home wrecker,' he snarled, which I found nothing if not ironic, but by that point it was hard to pay heed to each drop in the bucket, each cat and dog.

The phone exploded once more as we were preparing for bed. I did not blink an eye. *Sur moi le déluge.*

Wearily, I picked up the receiver and listened for a few moments to the inspired jailhouse invective of Mr Robert (Doc) Kooshof. Large portions of the conversation went over my head, but I was given to understand that I was now a dead man. In one particularly poetic passage, the good doctor referred to me as a 'wife-fucking motherfucker,' a phrase of such inanity that I could not withhold a small chuckle. Which was a tactical error: The gentleman had no sense of humor, nor would he listen to reason when I attempted to explain that I was laughing not at but with him. 'Here's the skinny,' Doc hissed. 'She's my mother-fucking wife. You marry her, I'll make it a funeral. Same flowers. Same church.'

I thanked him and staggered back to bed, where Mrs Kooshof lay waiting in all her immodest Dutch splendor.

I was a dead man.

Why not?

Then again at midnight.

Groggily, now envisioning a retaliatory raid upon the grave of Alexander Graham Bell, I reached for the foul instrument at bedside.

'Hey, jerkoff,' said a voice from my distant past. 'Guess who?'

'Spider,' I sighed.

'Yeah, man, Spider,' said Spider. 'And guess what else?'

'I'm a dead man?'

'Ooooo! Right as rain!'

I nodded at the dark. In the face of this drencher there was little worth saying.

'You there, man?'

'More or less,' I said.

'Ain't that the truth? More or less. Anyhow, this is just a reminder that we got your number, Tommy. And we also got these super-duper, extra-sticky memories.' He laughed at this. In the background, barely audible, were several other familiar voices. 'You want to talk to Tulip? Bonnie Prince Charming?'

'Not though he were the risen Christ,' said I.

'No sweat. Understand completely. But the fact is, man, they think of you often.'

'Do they?'

'Oh, *yeah*. Like almost every hour, every day.' There was a short, icy pause, then he laughed again. 'That air strike you called in on us – I mean, holy cow, we pooped in our panties. Yes, sir, each and every one of us. Naughty, naughty boy.'

I stared stupidly at the telephone. 'You're still upset?'

'Who said "upset"?'

'It sounded –'

'Just keep your eyes peeled, Tommy. And watch your back. Judgment Day.'

I sat up in bed, rubbed my eyes, glanced over at my dead-to-the-world fiancée.

'You've been tailing me?' I whispered. 'All these years – watching?'

'Maybe so, maybe not,' purred Spider. 'Who the fuck knows? Even this call, Tommy – maybe it's your imagination.' His voice was silky and humane, almost comforting. 'On the other hand, a promise is a promise. We *told* you there'd be a price to pay.'

He laughed again.

'Nighty-night,' he said, and hung up.*

As Mrs Robert Kooshof slept on, I spent a laborious half hour with my screwdriver, removing the telephone's base plate,

---

* At the risk of saying 'I told you so,' I think it is well within my rights to point out that I most emphatically told you so. Not once, but often: I *am* being chased. The precise details will unfold at an appropriate moment in this record, but for the present I can truthfully say that I have been a marked man for decades now. In a sense, I suppose, all of us live in the shadow of an approaching Judgment Day, in the knowledge that we are being pursued through history by our mismanaged lives. Yet in my own case the metaphor becomes reality. Spider was correct: *A promise is a promise.* They had vowed to come after me one day, and more than anything, it was the vow itself – the pledge, the threat – that had been chasing me down the decades.

209

disconnecting the ringer, all the while trying to imagine a remedy to the myriad problems at hand. Even for a man of my spiritual dexterity, I had far too many balls in the air, too many bases to cover, too many demands issuing from too many directions.

My instinct was to flee. An early-morning flight to Puerto Rico, perhaps, and then onward to Guadeloupe or Martinique. The notion sorely tempted me – a fresh start, a clean slate – yet when my repairs were complete, I retired to the bedroom and lay at the side of Mrs Robert Kooshof.

Sleep did not come.

For several hours I watched the lighted dial on my alarm clock, hoping for a brainstorm, but my thoughts seemed deformed by desperation. At one point, as dawn approached, I found myself studying the calm, contented face of my fiancée. Truly lovely, I thought. So generous and goodhearted and loyal. Inexplicably, lying there in the dark, I felt a sharp, unfamiliar stab of sentiment. I curled up against her; I nearly broke into tears.

Certain truths were manifest.

I did not want to harm this woman. I did not want to lose her.

By all rights, Mrs Robert Kooshof was the ideal partner for me, yet I also had to face squarely one other looming truth. This was not love. Not yet. Not what I imagined love to be. Right or wrong, my entire life had been devoted to Lorna Sue – the one and only, the girl of my dreams – and there was no relief from the unspeakable pain of betrayal, the grief and horror, those aching ligaments of love that reached all the way back into childhood.

My vision blurred.

I heard myself moan.

I gazed down at Mrs Robert Kooshof, but what I beheld at that instant was Lorna Sue standing against a small plywood cross. And opening her arms to me in an autumn cornfield. And playing blackjack till dawn. And sprinkling onion powder on a heap of noodles. Granted, she could be self-righteous and self-centered. She could be greedy. She could be slothful, imperious, vain, cruel, thoughtless, pious, glacial, sullen, short-tempered, narcissistic, sarcastic, callous, unfaithful, and unloving.

Yet she was Lorna Sue.

Irrational, maybe, but the human heart beats at its own brute pace, obsessive and mindless, mere muscle.

22

Twinkle

The next morning Mrs Kooshof departed for Owago just after breakfast. Earlier, upon awakening, we'd had an unfortunate little tiff over the matter of parole. It was my contention that she ought to have informed me of Doc's pending prospects, while Mrs Kooshof took the position that love conquers all. (Tell it to Romeo. Tell it to Lorna Sue. Tell it to your ex-husband, that unfaithful traitor who now dwells in Fiji.) In any event, after some acrimonious give-and-take, we had more or less agreed to disagree, sealing it with a quickie, after which Mrs Kooshof drove off under the apprehension that the world and we were well.

Her departure gave me operating room.

For my reunion with Lorna Sue, I dressed in a natty red bow tie and my favorite seersucker suit, applied a splash of cologne, armed myself with an umbrella, and motored swiftly across town to the university. I was apprehensive, of course, about a possible encounter with Lorna Sue's jilted tycoon, not to mention the more dangerous Herbie, and therefore took the precaution of ascending a back staircase to our sixth-floor departmental offices.

My heart, I will admit, was beating fast. A day of trial lay ahead.

Quickly, I picked up my mail and messages, pausing only to greet a well-machined new secretary by the name of Sissy Svingen. (Twenty-three years of age. Twenty-two-inch waist. Flared nostrils, sandy brown hair, bowling-pin hips, hearing aid, bulging black sweater, a lamentable dusting of dandruff at the shoulders.) I cleaned the girl up, gave her a welcoming hug, and then listened attentively as she informed me that the university's president had requested that I stop by his office later that afternoon.

The news instantly cheered me.

'Well,' I sighed. 'At last.'

'Sorry, sir?'

Tragically, the girl had difficulty manufacturing her *s*'s – a damp, sputtering hiss that filled my airspace with hard-driven moisture. (The *déluge* continued.)

I edged backward.

'A long, dismal story,' I told her. 'But well worth your while.'

Briefly, then, I informed her that I had been a seven-time nominee for the Hubert H. Humphrey Prize for teaching excellence; that in each instance I had been torpedoed by collegial skulduggery; that over the years I had lodged more than a dozen formal complaints. Given this background, plus an urgent presidential summons, it was safe to assume that I had finally trounced the pathetic competition.

'It's that time of year again,' I confided, 'and I suspect the prize is mine. More than suspect – I am *due*. Overdue.'

To her credit, my frothy new secretary positively glowed at this happy news. Here, as usual, were the signs of hero worship.

'Well, that's swell!' Sissy said, with a spray of sibilance that called out my handkerchief. 'You should celebrate. Kick up your heels! Spread your wings!'

I nodded and stepped out of harm's way.

'And perhaps we shall,' I said, without hesitation. 'A drop of the bubbly after hours? A plate of oysters?'

'We? I and you?'

'Certainly,' I said. 'I and you.'

It occurred to me, if only for an instant, that these events had a troubling historical chime and that I was biting off, as it were, far more than I could reasonably chew. Yet in times of distress there can be no harm in distraction. Misery loves firm company.

'What we'll do,' I instructed, 'is meet at the Ramada. Six-thirty on the dot.'

'Ramada?' said Sissy.

'A short, healthful stroll.'

'I know where it *is*,' she said. 'But I think – you know – I think it's probably a hotel, isn't it?'

'The dining room,' I said sternly.

The poor girl blushed. Furtively, with understandable nervousness, she tucked a lock of hair around her hearing aid. 'Well, gosh, that's super-super sweet. Except – well, you know – we're both university employees. I mean, is it allowed?'

'Oysters?' I said.

'No, silly! Consorting! This is my first job out of sec school, and I sure don't want trouble.' She studied me with a flustered yet unequivocal gaze of admiration. 'You aren't married, are you?'

I blinked.

By coincidence, this was precisely the question I had asked of myself at the very instant I caught sight of this lusciously handicapped chippie. And the answer was a resounding negative. (Mrs Kooshof, of course, would have objected. But on the other hand, to risk an automotive analogy, what possible harm could come from kicking Sissy's well-balanced tires? Or to stretch the analogy to its fulsome extreme: If young Toni had the sleek lines of a Jaguar, my new secretary could be likened to a safe, sturdy, meticulously engineered Volvo. Nothing fancy, but the wipers worked.)

I informed her, in any case, that I was currently on the open market – a free soul – and then raised my eyebrows. 'Do I impress you as the encumbered type?'

'Yeah. Kinda. What about a girlfriend?'

I hesitated only an instant.

'Indeed so,' I said. 'I am blessed with a phalanx of such chums, hundreds upon hundreds.'

'I don't mean that.'

'Well, dear, then I am not sure –'

'I mean a *steady*,' she sputtered. 'Somebody *serious*.'

Reflexively, I gripped my umbrella. With each misty syllable I had the sensation of revisiting my morning toilet.

'Serious is as serious gets,' I said craftily, and perhaps meaninglessly. 'Think it over. No reason for a snap decision, of course, but bear in mind Shakespeare's advice. "What's to come is still unsure/In delay there lies no plenty."'

Sissy stared at me blankly. 'Jeez, I'm not much on Shakespeare. Like I said, I went to sec school.'

'And a most talented graduate,' I assured her. 'Each of us would benefit, I am quite certain, from a rigorous erotic curriculum.'

Her eyes narrowed. 'I said *sec* school.'

'Exactly.'

'Secretarial! Are you making fun of me?'

My confusion was genuine. The time had come to repair to the snug, dry confines of my office. 'Bear in mind the Shakespeare,' I said hurriedly. '"Youth's a stuff will not endure."'

All in all, then, it was an amusing initiation to the workday, and as I marched down the corridor I made a mental note to enter the moist young lady's essential data in my ledger. (This would require, in Sissy's case, the manufacture of brand-new columns and categories, but of course such innovation was in large part the joy of it all: refining the various phyla and biotypes.) In my office, door locked, I immediately set to work on the project, and for more than three hours I was oblivious to the pressures upon me. (For safety's sake, I had stored my new ledger in a well-secured file cabinet, away from prying eyes and burgling brothers.) It was good to be back on the job. For the first time in weeks I felt a professional contentment, safe in my scholarship, and at one point I found myself humming a happy little marching melody from those distant glory days of Vietnam – I *met a girl in Tijuana* . . . (It struck me, just in passing, that I might someday author a monograph on the eerie similarities between wartime combat and peacetime romance. Blood lust. Mortal fear. Shell shock. Despair. Hopelessness. Entrapment. Betrayal.) *She knew how but she didn't wanna.*

At noon there came a knocking at my door. I speedily buried the ledger beneath a pile of ungraded term papers, brushed my hair, buttoned my coat, then pushed to my feet with a bittersweet mixture of anticipation and dread. Lorna Sue's face seemed to balloon before me. (Eternal hope! Eternal joy!)

It was a major letdown, therefore, to unlock the door and find young Sissy waiting.

I had already screeched the word *reptile*.

Twice, in fact.

Naturally enough, poor Sissy was shaken. I sat her down, piled her with port, explained the circumstances. Even so, the girl peered at me with stiff terror, and it was a testament to my salesmanship that she eventually softened. I emoted shamelessly. I told tales of treason. I spoke of tycoons and incipient incest.

Near the end, groundwork complete, I relocked the door,

knelt at her side, and gingerly allowed my head to incline in the direction of her shoulder.

Even then, it was touch and go.

'Well, my gosh,' she said. 'You scared me silly.'

'And for that, my dear, I apologize.'

'*Silly*!' she spat.

Deftly, I drew out my handkerchief.

'That awful scream,' said Sissy. 'You should have *seen* yourself! Like a serial killer or something. Like that guy – that famous murderer – what's his name?'

'I have no idea –'

'Son of Sam!'

This shocked me.

Unconsciously or otherwise, the girl had struck a nerve. I said nothing, and did nothing, but a cold shiver passed through my bones. Sissy must have felt it too, because she moved a hand to my knee.

'Listen, I didn't actually mean it like that,' she said. 'I can see why you're in such sad shape. Her own brother. I mean, that's so . . . so *sick*!'

'And a tycoon too,' said I.

The thaw was complete. She leaned closer, her lips now approaching my right ear. It was an oceangoing experience in many ways, but I braved the salty spray of commiseration. 'Seriously, I'm really, really sorry,' she said. 'Nobody ever told me about this in sec school. I don't even know . . . Gosh, I'm not sure what to *do*.'

I waited only a moment.

'The Ramada,' I said. 'Six-thirty sharp.'

An essential digression: Son of Sam.

The word *serial*, I must now submit, is deceptive in the extreme. It smacks of the abstract, the mathematical and mindlessly repetitive, something cold and bloodless, and we would be wise to bear in mind that on a higher spiritual plane the issue of sequence is wholly irrelevant. What counts is quality. In the case of a serial lover, for instance, is it not possible that he (or she) might find each instance entirely and absolutely unique? Each case a universe in itself? Each nimble 'target' distinctive and memorable and beyond compare? If number sixteen takes the form of a glorious redhead, should that in any way detract from the lusty, acrobatic humanity of number twenty-seven?

Let us not be ridiculous.

Same-same for Son of Sam.

I rest, for the moment, my case.

At two o'clock Lorna Sue phoned from the Mall of America. She was running late. She was in search of a lace tablecloth.

Given the experience of a long marriage, this explanation made a kind of historical sense, yet even so I had trouble disguising the disappointment in my voice.

'Tablecloth,' I murmured. 'No wonder you're delayed.'

'What's *that* supposed to mean?'

The challenge was unmistakable; I did not wish to upset her.

'Tablecloth,' I repeated casually. 'First things first.'

'Well, right,' she said. 'Isn't that the truth?'

Her tone was bouncy and matter-of-fact. Typically selfish, typically inconsiderate, Lorna Sue seemed to care not a whit that matters of the highest import remained on hold while she roamed the Mall of America in search of lace. (Imagine this woman as an air control officer.)

Still, thus was her nature, and I responded with phenomenal restraint. If reconciliation was the goal, I explained to her gently, it would be in everyone's best interest to fuck the fucking tablecloth.

Lorna Sue chuckled.

'Tom, don't get snooty,' she said. 'I'll *be* there.'

'What about the tycoon?'

'Who?'

'Your hairy new husband,' I said. 'The latest love of your life.'

'Oh, right. He's around.'

'Which means what?'

'Around,' she said briskly. 'I'd watch out.'

'And Herbie?'

'Sure, Herbie too. I guess they're both sort of upset.' It was hard to be certain, but she seemed to release a muffled giggle. 'Look, Tom, this is a pay phone. It's costing me money.'

'Could you estimate when . . . ?'

'Soon enough,' she said irritably. 'Maybe an hour. Probably two. Stop thinking about just yourself.'

For each of us, no matter how mentally fit, there comes a point at which the internal wiring begins to smolder. My own such time had now arrived.

I could taste the ions.

The subsequent wait for Lorna Sue was excruciating in itself, enough to cause several hasty excursions to the men's room, but on top of this I had to contend with the possibility of physical violence from at least two different quarters. The wrath of a brother, I realized, could only be exceeded by that of a routed tycoon. Each footstep in the hallway made me freeze. I misspelled the word *impediment* in my ledger.

It was with some anxiety, therefore, that I eventually departed for my popular three o'clock seminar. (Boldly entitled 'Methodologies of Misogyny.')

The old Vietnam instincts had awakened.

I again made use of the back staircase. Outside, alert to ambush, I took a firm grip on my umbrella, scanned the terrain, then grimly set off on the long march across campus.

The afternoon was sunny and warm, deceptively peaceful, yet I proceeded with utmost stealth. (An urban university, one must understand, is not unlike the darkest Asian jungle, dense with peril, and I was in no way fooled by the surface serenity of things.) I watched my back, ignored traffic lights, jaywalked when necessary, sought safety in the bustling afternoon crowds. Only once, as I passed the Chi Omega sorority house, did I pause to take delight in the ripening bounties of springtime. We were late in the school year, final exams barely a week away, and the sorority's lawn had been tastefully decorated with a bevy of swimsuited young coeds, each bronzed and bewitching, each in possession of a Walkman and tanning lotion and a well-thumbed edition of the latest Cliffs Notes. I exchanged greetings with two or three of them; I waved at several others. In virtually any other circumstance I would have responded to their playful salutes and catcalls – my reputation for student-faculty solidarity had clearly preceded me – but with a bittersweet sigh I soon turned and hurried along toward destiny. It occurred to me, however, that even in the most hazardous of moments, with the barbarians at the gate, one can find solace in the timeless repetitions of nature. (Robert Bruce and his spiderweb. Ted Bundy and his watercolors. Brigham Young and his brood.) Despite all odds, the human spirit endures beyond endurance, denying despair, salvaging hope in a rainbow or a birdsong or a simple sunset.

I was contemplating these and related matters as I entered my classroom, amazed at my own capacity for survival, and as a consequence I did not at first take notice of Herbie and the tycoon seated side by side in the third row.

This oversight, I fear, was predictable. While on the job, I like to project a brisk, businesslike, even punctilious image; I eschew small talk; I rarely establish (and never sustain) unnecessary eye contact with my male students, who on the whole seem to be convalescing from the trials of a communal lobotomy – listless, insolent, prelingual. On this particular afternoon, as always, I thus lost myself in the critical minutiae of professorship, logging in absentees, adjusting the fickle lamp on my lectern, shuffling through my notes and papers. (Though 'Methodologies of Misogyny' was billed as a seminar, I had little choice but to run the show in a straightforward lecture format. What can be served, after all, in trading opinions with troglodytes? Professors profess. Gum-chewers chew.) Without looking up, therefore, I sharply rapped the lectern and opened with a few broad remarks about the biological function of language in our rituals of courtship: how the sounds we utter carry meanings far beyond anything to be found in a dictionary. (The love cry of a coyote, the rut blare of a moose, the impassioned croak of a bullfrog.)

At this point I glanced up. A remedial cliché seemed in order.

'It is not always *what* we say,' I declared, 'but *how* we say it.' I paused to let this sink in, gazing in the direction of a perplexed young lady in row one. It was gratifying, I must say, to see the girl slowly nod and scribble down a note or two. We exchanged bashful smiles – again, the *how* matters – then I took a moment to consult my seating chart and placed a tidy asterisk beside her name.

'As an example,' I said, 'let us consider the word *Beverly*.'

I turned to the blackboard, preparing to jot down this tantalizingly improper proper noun, only to notice that I had been preempted by a heavy masculine scrawl. The entire blackboard, in fact, was littered with a host of creatively vulgar phrases, each misanthropic in the extreme.

I took an instinctive step backward. I may well have blushed.

There were giggles, I recall, but for the moment I could only gape at this vicious graffiti, some of which was merely abusive, most of which foretold my doom in graphic detail. I

was threatened with implausible forms of injury and disfigure-
ment; I was offered instruction in the transfer of body parts to
preposterous locations.

The words *hockey stick*, in particular, rang baleful bells.

I turned swiftly, spotted Herbie and the tycoon, steadied
myself against the lectern.

Already they had risen from their seats. They gave the
impression, I thought instantly, of a pair of midcareer Treasury
agents, firm-jawed and incorruptible, each dressed in a dark-
gray business suit, black shoes, and necktie. Herbie carried a
leather briefcase; the tycoon carried what appeared to be a
plastic yardstick.

They proceeded briskly up the center aisle, flanked me left
and right, gripped me by the arms.

All this occurred in but a moment.

Did I attempt escape?

I did not. There was no such possibility. I was told to remain
silent under penalty of fracture. ('Shut the fuck up,' said the
tycoon, 'or you'll be shaking hands with your lips.')

At that instant, I am almost sure, Herbie grinned at me.

His eyes twinkled.

On the surface, at least, it was hard to believe that this was
the Herbie of my youth, or even an adult version of my old
backyard playmate, yet there was no mistaking that impish,
dangerous, Ritalin grin.

He was twinkling.

23

Yes/No

I have reached the moral divide of my narrative: the jumped-off cliff, the burning bridge, the stark and sinister sine qua non. Here, if you will, we approach that fatal intersection at which my life took its turn toward chaos and desperation and what others (dimwits) might call madness.

Such amateur diagnostics, of course, are patently foolish, yet I must concede that in the coming pages I may well be cast in a somewhat less than favorable light. The self-righteous will surely jeer and condemn. The squeamish may shudder. Bear in mind, however, that in times of emergency there are scant few of us, sane or otherwise, who cannot be pressed to an extremity of deed. And remember, too, that I have issued fair warning with respect to my capabilities. (I am a decorated war hero. Why do none but my prey take this seriously?)

So, yes: we perch on the precarious fulcrum of this intriguing testament.

A lovely springtime afternoon.

Herbie on my left, the tycoon on my right.

Much of what occurred over the next horrific minutes never registered, or has since been eradicated by that faithfully protective mechanism called pride. In another sense, however, the details remain fully alive in my memory, embossed there like a garish nightmare. I can still see that twinkle in Herbie's eyes. I can see the tycoon's dental fillings, the spittle at his lips, the whitish-silver beads of sweat on his forehead.

The facts, I believe, speak for themselves.

I was made to kneel before my lectern.

I was made to remove my bow tie and jacket and shirt and trousers. (My jockey shorts, fortunately, were fresh. Pale blue. Floral pattern.)

'Off,' said Herbie.

Immediately, the tycoon struck me across the flank with his plastic ruler.

'The underpants,' said Herbie. 'Pull them down – just the back part. Right now.'

Again: that murderous twinkle in his eyes. And thus – impossibly, monstrously – I was compelled to present my pale hindquarters to an assembly of thirty-eight enthralled undergraduates. (You have come to *know* me in these pages. I am a modest man; the disgrace was beyond words.)

'What we have here,' Herbie announced, 'is a horse's ass.' He paused for effect. He tapped my chilly left haunch. 'Repeat it for the class, Tommy. Horse's ass.'

'Repeat?'

'Loud and clear. Say it. Horse's ass.'

There was no alternative. (Bear in mind, this malicious creature had burned down a church or two; he would have maimed me.) And therefore, in a half whisper, I uttered this vile bit of language.

Herbie clucked his tongue.

'Man, we can't hear you,' he said. 'Volume, Tommy. Turn it up. Wiggle that white ass.'

'I certainly will not –'

'Wiggle!'

Again, viciously, the tycoon struck me with his plastic yard-stick. I gasped, crabbed sideways, and found myself peering up into young Beverly's vacant blue eyes. The girl seemed to nod in encouragement.

I nodded back.

Emboldened, I then executed a subtle rearward sway. More a twitch than a wiggle. Nothing theatrical, nothing flamboyant.

'So,' I said. 'Are we finished?'

'Not even started,' said Herbie.

And indeed all this was but prologue, an overture to the excruciating symphony to follow.

I was brutalized.

I was slandered.

Without hurry, taking turns, Herbie and the tycoon proceeded to deliver lectures of their own, meticulously cataloguing my alleged misdeeds of late – wife stalking, harassment, invasion of privacy, marital meddling. With each unjust charge, the tycoon used his plastic yardstick to administer what can be described only as a painful, altogether sadistic spanking.

My students were spellbound. There was applause at one point.

In all such situations, I suspect, the human mind tends to contract upon itself, focusing on the tiniest, most inconsequential details, and in my own case I am left with a collage of trite sensory data: a wad of moist tissue on the floor before me, a muscle twitching at the corner of my left eye, the frayed hem on young Beverly's plaid skirt. For some ten minutes I was quite literally on my hands and knees, abject and helpless, the object of public castigation and public ridicule. My students, I must report, took positive pleasure in this malignant sideshow. Dull-eyed coeds squealed in delight; farm boys rose from their seats for a better view; all of them urged the sternest possible measures.

My mental processes eventually shut down.

I was dust.

I remember my molars grating. I remember Herbie's twinkling gray eyes, the tycoon's swiftly descending yardstick, Beverly's luscious, elongated tongue as she winced and moistened her lips.

My heart went dry.

I heard myself sob.

In hindsight, it was not so much a question of physical pain, but rather the dark certainty that my entire life, my very *being*, was undergoing a hideous and irreversible mutation. The spanking itself, while it carried a sting, seemed almost irrelevant in comparison to the torment of disgrace. My fall was absolute. All had changed. Permanently.* Never again would I enter a classroom with my head high, my credentials beyond reproach.

At one point I glanced up at Herbie, who smiled and winked at me – a mocking, lordly wink – and in that instant something froze in my heart. Here was the final straw: my bloody and rubescent Rubicon. The alliterative nickname Son of Sam sprang to mind. I now understood Sam's chosen vocation, his special calling, and even with my buttocks bared and bruised I had begun thinking in strictly serial terms. No mercy. No remorse. No going back. I knew my own future. In a sense it was a frightening moment; in another sense it came as a relief. Either way, my star had risen, and the cognate *seriatim* flashed before me like a twinkling Broadway marquee.

Curious, is it not, how the mind works? A wink – that simple – and all was decided.

For the next several minutes I actually took satisfaction in each cruel stroke of the tycoon's yardstick. Near the end I

---

* How could I – or anyone – recover? I had become the impeached Andrew Johnson, the caned Charles Sumner, the branded Hester Prynne, the disgraced Clifford Irving, the red-faced and far-fallen Richard M Nixon.

must have risen to a higher plane, utterly disengaged from the here and now, and when I blinked and looked up, it was no surprise to find Lorna Sue standing at my side.

How it happened I cannot be sure; no doubt she had been hovering nearby all along. She was simply *there*. Icy, beautiful, pitiless.

Incommoded, still on my hands and knees, I hailed my ex-wife with a smile.

Her response was null.

Stiff as concrete, dead silent, Lorna Sue studied me with the same nerveless stare she had summoned up on the day she strolled out of our marriage. 'Don't be an eighteen-year-old,' she had said, and now, with her eyes, she was saying it again: that I had behaved as a juvenile; that she had not been deceived by my pranks down in Tampa; that I was receiving precisely the punishment I deserved – the brisk, heartless paddling one gives a child. She was saying, too, I am quite certain, that this degrading encounter had been a setup from the start; that she had not for an instant planned on returning to me; that I should grow up; that I should accept reality and rise to my feet and square my shoulders and cease being an eighteen-year-old.

(Ironically, here was the gist of my little lecture that day: how language flows not only off the tongue but from the entire human being – eyes, lungs, bones, stomach, heart.)

Nothing was said. Nothing had to be said.

Lorna Sue looped an arm around the tycoon's waist. Quietly, she turned away, and this alone conveyed a simple, awesome truth: the girl of my dreams no longer cared.

Yet I was a man of words. I had to ask.

'Do you *love* me?' I yelled as Lorna Sue walked away with her hairy new husband, and as my students filed out, and as young Beverly bent down to hand me my trousers.

'Yes or no?' I cried.

Then I yelled: 'Say something!'

The subsequent silence was its own answer.

'Come on, man, be real,' said my blue-eyed Beverly, very tenderly. 'She hates you.'

24

Noogies

I am not ignorant. I know what *correct* is. Though out of touch in some respects, I am fully cognizant of the stern and strident politics that sweep through our modern epoch like the very winds of hell. And I realize, therefore, that there are those who will stand and cheer at my humbling comeuppance. Right now, for that matter, I can hear the feminist flies buzzing at my buttocks, those jackbooted squads of Amazon storm troopers denouncing my indefatigable masculinity. Oh, yes, I can *see* the sorry spectacle – thousands of ill-mannered, cement-headed, shrill-voiced, holier-than-thou guardians of ovarian rectitude, each squealing with delight at my public humiliation. They condemn my ardent (and nonpartisan) sensuality; they point accusing fingers at my lifelong parade of scrumptious young lovelies; they find fault in my bluntly animated terms of discourse (the word *lovely*, for instance, when used as a noun).

Inevitable, I suppose.

But to all such demagogues of gender I hereby respond with a phrase borrowed from my very first honors student, a gorgeous, quick-witted bonbon who went on to become Miss Saint Paul in a year of savagely competitive mudslinging.

I quote from memory:

Tough fucking noogies!

('You just don't *get* it,' my feminist critics will carp, to whom I hotly reply, 'I get plenty.')

25

Fire

It had been a day of trial, to be sure, yet also a day of decision, and I felt curiously cleansed – yes, invigorated – as I crossed campus for my final appointment of the afternoon. There was relief, I discovered, in hitting bottom. Where others might dissolve under the strain, I strode forward with a stiffened spine, a level and withering gaze. I was the newborn son of Son of Sam. I was Saint Nicholas gone to steel, making my list, checking it twice.*

A few minutes ahead of schedule, I entered the plush outer offices of President Theodore Wilford Pillsbury, secure in the knowledge that I could fall no farther.

Already, in fact, my ascent had begun.

Upon announcing myself to a pleasantly lanky secretary

---

* Obviously, I could not permit my public humiliation to go unanswered, and as a matter of pride I would be striking back hard at all three of my sadistic tormentors. (No mere pat on the bottom. Massive reprisal – a bolt from the heavens.) Indeed, a vague plan for vengeance had already begun to form, one that would call upon my experience with certain varieties of military ordnance. The precise *hows* and *whens* and *wheres* were not yet clear to me, but take my word that the final chapters of this testament will prove explosive in the extreme.

– flat as Nebraska, limber as the Platte – I was led into a small waiting room, where the two of us engaged in amiable chitchat about that year's Humphrey Award. The young lady's eyes flashed with risqué delight as she presented me with a sheaf of paperwork and instructed me not to peek. (President Pillsbury himself, I deduced, wished to break the news.) Her smile was conspiratorial, her posture just short of idolatrous.

I nodded crisply.

'Fine, then, no peeking,' I said. 'But if I may venture an opinion, I earned this *years* ago. Decades, in fact.'

'So I've heard,' said my rangy hostess.

The wait proved mercifully short.

I was midway into a delicious cup of Nescafé when a pager sounded at the girl's waist. Promptly, with a flirtatious little arch of the eyebrows, my doting Hermes rose to her feet and escorted me into the inner chambers of President Pillsbury. (Agricultural history. No relation.) My nerves were understandably ragged, my pulse was quick, and these border-line medical conditions were in no way relieved by the sight of Miss Megan Rooney seated in a chair alongside the president's large walnut desk.

To Megan's immediate right, also comfortably seated, was the ebony-haired, shamefaced, teary-eyed Toni.

Instantly, with not a word spoken, I understood that once again this was not to be my year for the Humphrey Prize.

I need not elaborate on the defamatory motives behind the presence of these two long-clawed kittens. A sad and ancient story – perfidy of the highest order – and for the sake of concision I shall recount only the highlights of the ensuing half hour.

They squealed.

They betrayed both my confidence and my far too philan-thropic friendship.*

Over the next several minutes I gathered that it was the diminu-tive Megan who first spilled the beans, leaving Toni no choice but to save her skin by transferring all fault to me. (Apparently the two girls had squabbled again over Gopher mating rights; Megan had sought advice from an assistant professor in the Gender Studies department – a blackguard feminist who for years had had me locked in her sights. Within hours the whole spicy story had fallen into the lap of President Pillsbury.)

The writing, in any case, was on the wall – guileful but no less apocalyptic.

With a perfunctory, altogether frosty nod, President Pillsbury suggested that I take a seat, an offer I gingerly accepted, after which the plump little bureaucrat cleared his throat and informed me of the 'serious nature of the occasion.' (The Doughboy's insipid wording, clearly not my own.)

Neither girl met my gaze. In her shrill rusted gate of a voice, Megan summarized the ups and downs of my profes-sional relationship with Toni, placing special emphasis on the deadly issue of a certain suspect honors thesis. I was additionally (and falsely) charged with a variety of killjoy offenses that could be roughly subsumed under the catchall phrase 'sexual harassment': e.g., consorting with students, the use of explicit gender-related language, uninvited romantic overtures, classroom leering, closed office doors, after-hours dormitory visits, et cetera, ad nauseam. 'The guy's famous for

* I was reminded of the medieval encyclopedist Vincent de Beauvais, who describes the female of our species as 'the confusion of man, an insatiable beast, a continuous anxiety, an incessant warfare, a daily ruin, a house of tempest, a hindrance to devotion.' This catalogue, while gently worded and by no means complete, struck me as a point of departure for further investigation in Methodologies of Misogyny.

this shit,' the wretched leprechaunette squeaked. '*Somebody* had to blow the whistle.'

I blushed and began to defend myself, but at that instant Toni herself entered the conversation. The verb *manipulate* echoed like a jackhammer; the noun *predator* reared its monstrous head. (Shades, in both cases, of Lorna Sue.) Here was a flamboyant performance in all respects, an outrageous blend of indictment and tearful confession: the big lie gone berserk. I sat blank and dumbfounded.

Predator?

Manipulator?

What a nightmare! What a joke!

The girl exaggerated without shame; she perjured herself, distorted, snipped quotations out of context. (At the same time, of course, the pathological little racketeer looked nothing short of spectacular. Black suede skirt, black pumps, bulging black sweater.)

President Pillsbury also took notice. The man rubbed his nose, massaged his paunch.

And, yes, if one did not know better, it would have been the most natural thing on earth to open one's heart and soul to the deceitful tart. Halfway into her spiel, in fact, I was nearly sold on my own guilt.

Yet her allegations were *not* so.

Nor did Toni mention her own acts of extortion and outright blackmail.

Instead the gorgeous fraud claimed that I had 'butted in' by offering 'stupid suggestions' regarding her thesis. With a perfectly straight face, she asserted that the research was entirely her own, that I had done little more than 'pick lint' off a piece of accomplished scholarship, that I had 'gummed it up with a bunch of words,' that my overall contribution to the effort could at best be deemed 'no big deal.'

'That's his job,' Toni whined. 'He's *supposed* to help. And if

I didn't let him, the creep probably would've . . . I don't even want to say it.'

President Pillsbury blinked. 'Say what, my dear?'

'You know. It's just too gross. You should fire him right now.'

Megan giggled.

There was, I distinctly recall, a gas-chamber silence in the room – the quiet sizzle of those lethal word pellets. My world had gone to vapor, or to fire, and I saw no point in demeaning myself. I sat unruffled. I said nothing. Like Caryl Chessman before me, I would bow out with silent grace.*

The paperwork, of course, had been prepared. (It lay in my lap at that very moment.) As a matter of good form, however, President Pillsbury thumbed through a stack of affidavits from former students, each signed in a conspicuously female hand, each attesting to the many hours I had spent slaving anonymously over my trusty Royal. (A prodigious professional output by any standard: seventeen polished theses over a career spanning a scant twenty-four years.) It occurred to me, in fact, that a lining of the purest silver had been sewn into the coarse fabric of this day. No more deadlines. No more last-minute journeys to the photocopier. My time would henceforth be my own – time to burn – and there was not a filament of doubt that I would be devoting it almost exclusively to the pursuit of my rigorous and sequential new hobby: Vengeance with a capital-crime V.

I smiled at Toni. I smiled at the miniature Megan. Already I had the Ripper Itch.

---

* Although I had 'harassed' no one, sexually or otherwise, President Pillsbury could hardly be counted upon to judge the case fairly. It was to the Doughboy's idiotic wife, remember, that I had once directed the innovative phrase 'dumb cooze.' (A single adjective, a deft noun: here again was evidence of the devastating power of language.)

The remainder of our interview was devoted entirely to procedural issues. It is essential to emphasize that I was in no way 'fired' that afternoon; rather, for the record, I merely committed my signature to a number of documents resigning tenure, accepting a none too liberal severance solatium, agreeing to vacate my offices within the week. In exchange, the university would forswear public proceedings.

Was I embarrassed at all this? Did I turn scarlet, or sob, or display emotion?

Not in the least.

Signatures affixed, I rose to my feet.

'You'll excuse me,' I said, 'but I have a pressing dinner date.' Then I beamed at fair Toni, gazing with genuine fondness into the girl's cottony brown eyes. 'Perhaps we'll meet again one day.'

'Yeah?' she said. 'And then what?'

I shrugged. 'Hard to predict. But I hope you'll permit me to bury the hatchet.'

I arrived a half hour early at the Ramada bar, where I took immediate double-barreled refreshment and sat reviewing the day's developments. By six-thirty I had wound my way through all seven stages of grief. Like Vietnam, I thought: nothing seemed real. Near the bottom of martini number three, I was struck by the notion that some tiny quirk in my personality might be attracting all this betrayal. A magnetic malfunction. Or dysfunction. It was true, I reasoned, that my general approach to the world could be viewed as a tad out of the ordinary, particularly with respect to certain attitudes regarding the opposite sex. I was simply too generous, too optimistic, too candid, too openhearted. I resolved to repair all that. Without fire walls, I had learned, one ends up in ashes. (*Fire:* another entry in my lexicon of love. At death's very door, if someone were to scream 'Fire!' I would instantly picture neither smoke nor flame, but rather the blazing image of Toni's accusatory visage.) From this point forward, I told myself severely, I would take the most extreme precautions.

For example: the two lonely maidens seated at the end of the bar.

They had been eyeing me – the usual.

Sissy was tardy.

I required companionship.

Still, once burned is once warned, and I approached the pair like a seasoned prizefighter, determined to size up these two very fit opponents.

'Thomas Henry Chippering,' I said warily. 'Professor of Linguistics. Emeritus.'

As it happened, there was no cause for alarm. Virtually without a glance, as if anticipating my company, the two young ladies – Fleurette and Masha – swept their purses from the stool between them, which I ventured to occupy, and for the next twenty minutes this classy Franco-Russian alliance allowed me the pleasure of topping off their tumblers. (Fleurette: a florid little frog. White stretch pants, sheer pink blouse, flagrantly buxom. And the captivating Masha: slender as my Parker pen, Russian as a troika. Red vinyl boots, violet camisole, all appendages present and accounted for.) Call me what you will – distinguished rake, jaunty ladies' man, expert angler of the flesh – but clearly the Chippering charm once again held sway.

Incorrigible? Dogged as the sun?

Perhaps so.

Yet after a day like mine, how could one respond to two such charmers with anything but a guttural *Da* or an effervescent *Oui, oui*? The will to survive cannot be thwarted.

In any case, waiting for the delinquent Sissy, I sat bracketed by Fleurette to my left, Masha to my right, our limbs in frequent and friendly contact. Initially, the conversation took a predictable course:

Masha: 'You remind me of somebody. I can't place it.'

T.H.C.: 'Martin Van Buren.'

Fleurette: 'Who?'

T.H.C. (with a sigh): 'You may call me Abe.'

Masha: 'My God, that's *it*! Tossing shots with a fuckin' statue!'

Pointless chitchat.

Rapidly, therefore, I nudged the dialogue in a more profitable direction, summarizing with only minor exaggeration the ugly events of that afternoon. I could hardly be faulted for seeking sympathy. Fleurette (my favorite of the two) made toadish clucking sounds as I described the disgraceful beating I had absorbed in my own classroom; Masha (a close second, gaining by the moment) fingered the fabric of my trousers as I bemoaned Toni's duplicity and false heart. I told all. How Lorna Sue had deserted me for a rich, hairy, run-of-the-mill Tampa tycoon. How Herbie had driven an incestuous wedge into my marriage.

It was a relief, I must say, to open up. The dim, soothing, walnut-on-chrome bar seemed the ideal spot for such earthy confessions, and in my revitalized mood I made a mental note to fill out an evaluation form at the front desk. (The piped-in show tunes earned my highest rating, as did our basket of crunchy appetizers.)

In short, I decided that there could be nothing more comforting than the whispery wax and wane of a well-tended drinking establishment, with its multiple prospects both upstairs and down.

'Now, then,' I said. 'Let us become fast friends.'

It was well after seven o'clock when Sissy made her belated appearance.

The girl looked nothing short of radiant. A yellow mohair sweater instantly caught my attention, followed in quick order by a pair of tautly woven jeans, a necklace strung with ersatz jade, and a perfume whose primary ingredient I took to be coriander.

Her hearing aid was visible only to the most exacting eye.

Clumsily, but with genuine delight, I rose and made the introductions.

'Nice to meet you folks,' Sissy more or less spat, then shot me a quick, questioning glance. The girl seemed disconcerted by the presence of my two companions. 'Sorry I'm so darn late, but I couldn't –'

'The delay,' I said chivalrously, 'was excruciating, yet worth every instant.'

'Well, jeez!'

'Exactly,' said I, and reached for a pile of nearby napkins. 'Welcome aboard.'

Promptly, then, I guided our party to a booth at the rear of the saloon. I called for the house's premium champagne. 'We were just discussing,' I explained to Sissy, 'the ravages of my day.'

My sibilant secretary nodded with sympathy. 'Yes, sir, it's the big buzz around campus.'

'The buzz?' I said.

'Oh, yeah. Huge.'

I could not help feeling a bubble of pride. 'Is that right? Talk of the town?'

'Pretty much,' said Sissy, 'and you must be – well, jeez – you must be sick to your stomach. That's why I'm here, because I thought you could use some company.' She lowered her eyes as if embarrassed, used a napkin to dab her lips. '*Lots* of people get fired and spanked and stuff, so you shouldn't –'

'I was not "fired,"' I instantly retorted.

'Well, the way I heard it –'

'The man resigned,' said Fleurette.

'As a *protest*,' said Masha. 'Against the stinking *world*!'

I shifted uneasily in my seat. It was true, I confess, that I had put my own spin on events, and with a modest wave of the hand I tried to make light of the matter. Water over the dam, I told them.

'There, you see?' said Fleurette. 'The guy's a martyr.' Sitting back, Fleurette appraised Sissy for a few moments. Then she smiled. 'So listen, sugar, what do you say we form ourselves a little group later on? A barbershop quartet? Sound fun?'

'Quartet?' Sissy said.

'A foursome,' said Fleurette. 'Like in golf.'

Sissy looked at me with obvious alarm. (I was shocked myself. The Ramada, of all places. Here was an item that would most certainly find its way into my forthcoming evaluation.)

I removed Masha's stockinged foot from my lap.

'Golf,' I declared, 'is not our game.' I reassured Sissy with a paternal squeeze of the knee. 'Tell the girls about sec school.'

Both Fleurette and Masha, I was happy to note, displayed instant interest.

Sissy blushed. 'Hey, look,' she said, 'maybe I should just – you know – just take off.'

'Of course you shouldn't,' I said brightly, and again gave the girl's knee a tweak. 'Go ahead now, fill them in on sec school while I visit the gentlemen's room.'

'An actual school?' said Fleurette.

'Not *sex*!' sprayed Sissy.

Masha flinched. 'Do me a favor, cover your mouth or something. It's like talking to a garden hose.'

'Back in a jiff,' I said.

Heedless of Sissy's protests, I slipped out of the booth and made a somewhat wobbly departure toward the lobby.

My spirits were high, my heart buoyant as balsa wood.

The evening had turned out splendidly, full of promise, and I counted myself fortunate to have encountered three such devoted soul mates.

It was a surprise, therefore, to find myself sobbing as I stood at the urinal.

Where it came from I do not know. Moral exhaustion, I suppose. Lorna Sue's face flickered before me, those cold eyes, the utter absence of love, and I was struck by the heinous reality that nothing would ever bring her back to me.

Then an odd thing happened.

I was still trembling as I recrossed the lobby, paying little heed to my surroundings, but purely by chance, as I passed a set of escalators, I found myself in front of a small shop that had been converted to a travelers' wayside chapel. (Airports, yes, but here was something totally arresting in the field of hotel science.) I entered without hesitation. A pair of electric candles cast the only light, which was barely sufficient, and after a moment I edged forward and took a seat on one of three plastic pews. (Though Catholic by birth, I neither knelt nor crossed myself. It had been years – alas, decades – since I'd misplaced my faith on the vast, sterile prairies of my youth.)

For some time I simply sat there: half inebriated, soul-sick.

Dumbly, I murmured the word *faith*, as if the utterance itself might awaken something in me. But nothing much occurred, just an incoherent buzz in my blood.

What was the point? All the points were pointless.

Pity, I thought.

A lifelong quest for love – a ledger full of names and dates – and it all ended here in the sad sanctuary of a Ramada Inn.

I saw nothing blasphemous in removing my shoes and stretching out for a short nap.

Accompanied by a surly security guard, Sissy, Masha, and Fleurette awakened me not an hour later. 'My gosh, I was worried sick,' Sissy said. 'I thought you went out and – I don't know – maybe strangled yourself or something. I mean, it was *scary*. Seriously.'

With my sleeve I wiped away the leftovers of this oration. 'Fit as a fiddle,' I announced, and crisply sat up.

I put on my shoes, straightened my jacket, and led our party back into the restaurant for an overdue supper.

In my absence, the girls had run up a startling liquor tab, a fact that explained why the splashy young Sissy seemed to be getting along so well with Fleurette and Masha. Over a plate of hors d'oeuvres, the girl cheerfully queried them on the nuts and bolts of their trade: hours, wages, working conditions. (In part, it was the alcohol speaking, yet I also detected an apprentice streetwalker in the making.) Thus, as our entrées arrived, I reminded the seductive trio that idle shoptalk would get us nowhere.

'After all,' I said curtly, 'only one of us is without gainful employment.'

Sissy reached for the champagne. 'Okay, but I was curious, that's all. I never met any – you know – any real-life working girls. It's *interesting*.' She licked a trail of stray foam from her hand. 'Besides, you always talk about *you*. Give somebody else a chance.'

'Bravo!' said Fleurette. 'The guy never listens. Not ever.'

'Deaf as a stone,' said Masha, whose foot had once again found my lap. 'Typical male too. Look at him – a pig in heaven.'

'Cock of the roost,' said Fleurette.

'You said it!' Sissy spat.

I was aghast at this, and rightly so. I glared at my plate. Gallantry alone kept me silent.

'See, the thing is,' Sissy was explaining, 'I'm still an unfinished woman, if you catch my drift. Sex and all that, it's pretty hard to picture.' Her lower lip quivered. 'The act, I mean.'

'Act?' said Fleurette.

'*It.*'

'You're kidding? You haven't . . . ?'

'Not yet. I guess I'm looking for the right guy.'

Fleurette patted her hand. 'Well, hey, aren't we all, honey?'

'You too?' said Sissy.

'For sure – Prince Charming.'

Masha offered an assenting click of the tongue. 'But listen: what about sex school? They didn't make you practice or anything?'

'*Sec* school,' Sissy said.

'Right.'

A blush came to Sissy's face. 'Secretarial – like steno and stuff! *Dictation!*'

Masha nodded. 'Well, sure. That one I'm good at.'

At this juncture a number of provoking questions popped to mind. What in God's name, for instance, was I doing here? How did two hookers and a hissing virgin fit into the grand scheme of things?

In frustration I slapped the flat of my hand against the table.

'This is not the Marine Corps,' I barked, 'so call off the recruitment drive. Let the girl follow her dreams.'

Masha batted her eyelashes. 'She asked, we answered. No harm done.'

'Sure, that's right!' Sissy sputtered. 'Anyhow, you've got your stupid *hand* in my crotch.'

'Inadvertent,' I said.

'Then let *go.*'

'Certainly. My mistake.'

'Like pretty *soon!*'

'Yes, yes,' I said briskly, 'but the point is that human love can be neither bought nor sold. Take my word, I was once married to a woman with a cash register bolted to her nightstand. I forked over thousands – tens of thousands – and I'm here to tell you that the return on investment was damned meager.'

Sissy gripped my thumb and twisted hard. 'Big deal,' she said hotly. 'Maybe you're better off divorced. I mean, jeez, with paws like yours.'

The girl gave my thumb another twist, then blushed and arranged a youthful breast against my arm.*

'Anyhow,' she said, 'there's lots of other fishes in the sea.'

'The sea?'

'You bet!'

She nearly yanked off my thumb.

'Be that as it may,' I told her, 'the upshot is that I kept feeding Lorna Sue's kitty, kept trying to prove how much I loved her. Except it was never enough. When she finally walked out on me – for a tycoon, no less – she made me write out a check for twelve thousand dollars. To finance the transition. Had it down to the dime.'

Masha whistled. 'Twelve thousand!'

My little parable had failed to clarify things. Even Sissy, whose breast I was now buttressing, seemed dazzled by the numbers.

I looked her straight in the eye.

'Do not be fooled,' I said. 'One cannot put a value on love; one can't hold fire sales.'

'Yeah, I guess,' Sissy muttered. 'But twelve *thousand*?'

Hopeless, I realized.

With a resigned shrug I called for the bill and remitted to Ramada the sum of $398.87, excluding tip. The irony of this transaction did not escape me. According to my records, I had

---

* You read correctly. Approach/avoidance. Yes/no. It is not only a woman's right to change her mind; it is also her right to own and operate two minds simultaneously, a duality that most often cancels itself out in pristine nullity.

thus far purchased, since the advent of puberty, some 2,200 full-course meals while in active pursuit of the softer sex, plus well over 17,000 beverages, all of which amounted to a financial grand total that by rights should have entitled me to the mating privileges of a stud bull.

Yet what had ever come of this erotic soup kitchen?

Seventeen honors theses.

A failed marriage.

A career in ruins.

The lesson, if there was one, eluded me. I sighed; we adjourned.

26

Ring

Could I descend any lower, incur greater shame, debase myself with any more artistry or élan?

Certainly.

It was Masha, I am quite positive, who suggested a midnight road trip, Fleurette who seconded the motion, sweet Sissy who provided the means of transport. The hour had grown late – well past my curfew – and to the best of my recollection we departed the Twin Cities just after two in the morning. Fleurette did the driving, Masha navigated, a very drowsy Sissy and I occupied the cramped backseat of her 1986 Chevrolet Nova. Our destination was Owago, one hundred eighty miles to the southwest, where I felt confident we would be welcomed with hugs and a hearty breakfast in the home of Mrs Robert Kooshof. (This estimate, sadly enough, was to prove erroneous.)

The long, dreamlike journey has now largely vanished from memory, snatched away like the fence posts and telephone poles that flashed by in the dark, and I recall very little beyond the odd sensation of barreling down a deserted highway in the company of three virtual strangers. At one point, curiously enough, I awoke from a short nap to find myself shaking with sorrow. The radio, the heater, the tires against the road – these variables had combined to create an atmosphere of almost inconceivable sadness. In part, I am sure, my mood was connected to the traumas of the day, but as I watched the dark, vacant prairie pass by, I was also struck by the appalling knowledge that I was returning home an emotional cripple. (Melodramatic, perhaps, but do not forget your own wee-hour pilgrimages into history.) All of us, one way or another, feel an unsettling stew of emotions as we journey backward into the realms of youth, into those haunted environs where the future still breathes as an infant present. Sentiment seizes us. Good Neighbor Time issues his wistful sigh. On such occasions, it seems, we become acutely conscious of the chasm between ambition and reality, all that we once dreamed for ourselves and all that we now are. The very word *nostalgia*, after all, is itself a kind of verbal orphan, a bastard combination of two unrelated terms from the Greek – *nostos* and *algia* – which together translate as 'the pain of returning home,' or, less literally but more accurately, 'the painful yearning for home.'

In my own case, the pain was oddly fuzzy. Riding along, eyes swollen with fatigue, my thumb killing me, I caught random glimpses of my own childhood: Lorna Sue playing with her dollhouse, Herbie straddling a green plywood airplane, a turtle called Toby. But none of it cohered. Who *was* I back then? (Have I yet mentioned that my father died of heart failure in 1957?* That my mother passed away during my freshman year in college? That loss and abandonment were always my most faithful companions?)

Bad memories, one could say, each of which was stored in a tidy little word bundle. (You too. *Fiji. Hilton.*) In the humming dark, Sissy's head soft upon my shoulder, I thumbed

---

* The details are irrelevant. He dropped dead in the gutter. He deserted me. At his funeral, I yelled, 'Why a goddamn *turtle*?' No use. He was dead.

through my own unhappy dictionary: *Engine. Cat. Cross. Eighteen. Tycoon. Tampa. Cornfield. Pontiac. Angel. Church. Fire.** My heart hurt. My head, too, and my spirit, and my useless thumb. Later, a few miles outside Owago, I realized with a sudden, sickening force that my life's course had been set years and years before, in the silvery-hot summer of 1952, and that the afterburn of childhood still gripped me in a dizzying downward spiral. A convergence was now in progress – the sordid past penetrating an even more sordid present – and I was struck by an almost tactile sense of foreboding. Like the first soft slip of an avalanche, like that puff of smoke from the doomed *Challenger*, events seemed to be approaching the point of cataclysm. Terrible things were about to happen.

An hour before dawn, Mrs Robert Kooshof opened her door to our weary party. Breakfast was not forthcoming. Almost immediately, in the midst of what can only be called chaos, I bade a hurried farewell to my trio of traveling companions. To Fleurette and Masha, who required professional recompense, I presented a pair of generous checks. (An expensive proposition, to be sure, yet the combined total still amounted to far less than Lorna Sue's old hourly rate.) Young Sissy, too, rather brashly requested payment, but to her I offered only a swat on the rump and the advice that she stick with her secretarial strong suit.

Instantly, I regretted the phrase.

* I did *not* set the famous 1957 fire that ravaged the sanctuary of St Paul's Catholic Church in Owago, or the more minor blaze that was extinguished in the church basement a year later. I did *not* scribble graffiti on the church steps; I did *not* cut to shreds any priestly vestments; I did *not* add the large, cartoonish breasts that were discovered on the statue of Christ in the nave of St Paul's. Why I was considered a suspect is beyond me.

'Strong suit!' Sissy sprayed.

The girl gave me a warm parting hug, as did Fleurette and Masha, and with the car's engine running, we exchanged addresses and phone numbers. (I had little choice, obviously, but to hand over falsified data. My erotic calendar was full, and for once in my life, to my own wistful amazement, enough was finally too much.)

Next came the problem of attending to Mrs Robert Kooshof. Bruised feelings, et cetera.

I trudged back into the house, paid a quick visit to the liquor cabinet, then sought out my sulking fiancée, whom I found locked away in her traditional refuge behind the bathroom door.

Agitated in the extreme.

Three of them!' she snarled, as if the number itself were troublesome.

I flopped down, closed my eyes, put my lips to the crack beneath the door. I need not offer a verbatim account of the ensuing conversation. Drearily predictable. The standard pejoratives: 'inconsiderate,' 'shallow,' 'debauched,' 'irresponsible,' 'fickle,' 'juvenile,' 'untrustworthy,' 'hopeless,' 'unstable,' and 'fucking crazy.'*

I was stung, yes. Exhausted too.

Merely to bob and weave proved difficult. The three young ladies, I explained, were but partners in transit. Nothing indecorous had occurred. Wearily, I outlined the horrors that had been visited upon me over the past twenty-four hours – my classroom abasement, Toni's unfounded accusations, my resignation from the services of the university.

I wept a little.

---

* What is it about Thomas Henry Chippering, I often wonder, that so chafes the female sensibility? My doggedness? My refusal to kowtow? I want the truth.

I dozed off.

In late afternoon I sat up, rubbed my eyes, tapped on the bathroom door. 'Say, listen,' I said cheerfully. 'I'm famished. What would you say to a short stack of pancakes?'

Mrs Robert Kooshof snorted.

'Pancakes?' she said viciously. 'You're nuts. What's in it for *me*?'

I sighed.

'Well,' I said, and expelled the bitter breath of defeat. 'An engagement ring?'

The bathroom door swung open.

I have discovered through trial and error that there are numerous routes to a woman's heart – high roads, low roads, and roads in between – but that sooner or later, at the end of each well-beaten path, one inevitably encounters the blinding red lights of a tollbooth.

The ring cost me $1,645.76, tax included.

The tollbooth, in this case, took the form of a cash register at the rear of Hanson's Fine Jewelry in downtown Owago; the tolltaker was embodied – ripely, wondrously – in the person of a young salesgirl by the name of Oriel.

Strapped for cash, newly unemployed, I found myself scribbling out a promissory note to Mrs Robert Kooshof, who in turn handed our juicy jeweler a platinum credit card to formalize the purchase. Inexplicably, both of them seemed to consider me a cheapskate. No matter that I was now committed to a seventy-two-month repayment plan. No matter that I had become co-owner, as the famous slogan suggests, of a very considerable piece of the rock.

'It's your *engagement*,' said our meddling salesgirl. 'You shouldn't be such a miser.'

'To the contrary,' I replied, 'I was merely remarking that glass has a long and very honorable history.'

'Skinflint,' the saucy tart muttered. (Fresh out of Owago Community College. Business major. Eyes like an anaconda.) 'See, here's the deal,' she said, 'you have to look at it as an investment. Diamonds are forever. Just like you two lovebirds – forever and ever and ever and ever and ever!'

The luscious little busybody beamed a smile in my direction: a teasing, salacious, you-could-have-had-*me*-but-now-you're-doomed-for-life grin.

'Forever,' she repeated, and then winked to rub it in. 'We're talking about *infinity*. Like when you get married, right? It just goes on and on and on. And that's exactly what diamonds do. They never, never stop. I mean, like, not *ever*.'

I nodded briskly, requested a business card, and made a mental note to revisit the shop one day soon. With a dentist's drill, perhaps. The cheeky scamp had much to learn about the meaning of forever.

Mrs Kooshof's mood had brightened as we sat down for breakfast in the cramped, bustling quarters of Owago's sparkling new Burger King. Immediately, in a touching little ceremony, she stripped off her tarnished wedding ring and replaced it with our heart-stoppingly expensive acquisition. The woman's face had gone phosphorescent. To my alarm, in fact, the surface of her skin seemed to emit the garish, explosive fireworks of a digital scoreboard.

She ate like a horse. She could not stop beaming at me, giddy and teary-eyed.

I hated to dampen her day. Such unqualified joy is a rare phenomenon, especially in this cynical age of ours, but it seemed necessary to remind my well-lighted fiancée of the circumstances in which I now found myself: a career in wreckage, not a prospect in sight.

Mrs Kooshof scarcely listened. She gazed at her new ring with the astute, calculating squint of an appraiser. 'Well, nothing's insoluble,' she said. 'You can move in with me for a while, find work here in Owago.'

I laughed bitterly. 'Impossible. I'm a trained scholar, not a J. C. Penney clerk.'

'I didn't mean –'

'And I might add,' I said, 'that this burg is hardly brimming with good memories. Think about it – I grew up here. Same house, same backyard. I'm a professor of linguistics, for God's sake, a man of the world.'

Mrs Kooshof nodded. 'But couldn't you – I don't know – couldn't you find something temporary? Some odd job to tide you over?'

'I cannot imagine *what*. Farm machinery is not my forte.'

I sighed and leaned back.

Abruptly, as if struck by a sledgehammer, I felt the full weight of the past twenty-four hours. A defeated sensation. In the course of one vertiginous spin around the earth's axis, I had been stripped as if by a centrifuge of the last elements of my old identity, the man I once was, those few remaining sources of personal pride and self-esteem. Everything had come to nothing. Everything signified nothing. Even my grandiose plans for revenge, which had kept me going in the absence of all else, now seemed sterile and pitiful and forlorn. Yes, even a speck ridiculous.*

There was nothing to hope for. And without hope, our chief bulwark against madness, the human spirit becomes upredictable and sometimes dangerous.

I was hurt.

* *Ridiculous*: Do not forget your own silly antics in the months after your husband departed for the shores of Fiji. You scolded him as if he were still in the room. You fingered his old sweaters, cuddled his tennis racket, composed long, convoluted letters full of venom and hurt. Ridiculous, obviously, but you could not stop yourself, could you?

And I wanted to hurt back. No longer for revenge – just to hurt and keep hurting.

'Maybe you're right,' I told Mrs Kooshof. 'Find a job teaching gender studies. Wait for opportunity to strike.'

27

You

And you?

Do you have a name?

Better without. Unique as you are – and do not for a moment think otherwise – you also represent every brokenhearted lover on this planet, every stood-up date, every single mother, every bride left weeping at the altar, every widow, every orphan, every divorcée, every abandoned child, every slave sold down the river. You are the unmailed valentine. You are the forgotten birthday, the broken promise, the lapsed Catholic, the thirty pieces of silver, the abiding question of the ages: 'Why hast thou forsaken me?'

All this, yes.

But you are also, admit it or not, Thomas H Chippering. Granted, your ex-husband dwells in Fiji, and your heart aches, but like me, you are not entirely without blame. Because you, too, have had your secret love ledgers, your flights of fancy, your delusions, your checks under the mattress, your flirtations and unplugged telephones and petty betrayals of the flesh and spirit.

You are forty-nine years old. (Or thirty-nine, or twenty-nine.) You live alone. You cook for one.

But you have done your best, haven't you?

You drive to work each weekday morning. You pretend to

be what you are not, chatting with your friends, attending dinner parties, visiting relatives. You've thrown away his tennis racket. Scrubbed his cigarette smoke from your carpets and upholstery. But still, at odd hours of the night, you find yourself paging through the memory books, just as I do. (Your lakeside wedding. Your white satin dress. How much you loved him – all that faith.)

At times you second-guess yourself. Too dependent, you think. Took him for granted.

But then later, like me, you feel the sorrow come crushing down again. You realize that it was he who quit, he who abandoned you, he who flew off to Fiji in the company of a statuesque redhead named Sandra. (The word *Sandra*: you hear it on the radio, you come across it in a book, and it slices through your ribs just as surely as any lance or bullet. You hate the name, don't you? You loathe its harmonics, each bitter vowel and consonant.)

And so, yes: One frantic afternoon you left work early, drove to the airport, dashed inside, and without batting an eye purchased a two-thousand-dollar ticket to Fiji.

An impulse, wasn't it?

No reservations, not even a suitcase, and after seventeen sleepless hours you found yourself checking into a resort hotel only four or five miles from his cute little house by the sea. You dined alone, as always. You felt forlorn – a little crazy, a little lost. (I'm on the right track, am I not? I *know* you. And I know what betrayal is.) You had no real plan in mind, just a craving to witness a fragment of your husband's new life, or to validate your own nightmares. And yet for a day or two you did not once leave the hotel. You sat by the pool. Ordered from room service. Hated yourself, hated him. Loved him. Cried. Hated him. Kept your eyes open for redheads.

Then finally, half terrified, half blind with anguish, you rented a car and drove south along the coast toward Suva.

The road was narrow and treacherous – remember? It turned to gravel, then to dirt. Hot day. Flower smells. (You were drenched in Fiji.) Eventually you found his new house, but like some lovelorn teenager you circled and drove by again, then again, several times, both hoping and not hoping that you might catch sight of him.

What was it you wanted here? Confrontation? Apology? Reparations? Face it: like me, you did not have the slightest idea. You heard yourself cursing at one point – foul, goatish, God-hating language – words you never knew you knew. You told him off good, didn't you? Yes, you did. But then you collapsed against the steering wheel. You bawled at the sky, just as I had, for this was Fiji – lush and horried – and nothing you could say or see or do would ever change anything. (What hurt most, I am sure, was the sudden certainty that romance would never again be romance, that you had nothing left to believe in, that the word *Fiji* would forever call to mind this golden, shimmering, love-forsaken paradise.)

You drove straight to the airport. (Left behind that new sundress you had put on hold.)

On the flight eastward you watched a movie with a happy ending, one that would not be yours. You drank martinis. You skimmed an advice column in *Cosmo*. ('We cannot commit to the future,' wrote this well-meaning nitwit, 'unless we come to terms with the past.' Nice symmetry, nice sentiment. But you now understand, as I do, that the phrase 'come to terms with' means 'to assent' or 'to agree.' And you do not agree. The terms are intolerable – you reject them – in particular the term *Fiji*.)

But realize this: Fiji is not Fiji.

Fiji is Pittsburgh. Fiji is Boston or London or Santa Fe or wherever else your faith has gone.

So close your eyes, my sweet, those lovely blue-green eyes, and remember standing on a dock upon a lake in a piney woods, in your white satin dress. Let me hear you take your vows again, alone this time, or with me beside you, two eccentrics, two lost and foolish souls. We know what sacred is, don't we?*

* So there. I have a sensitive side.

28

Spot

I did not descend to teaching gender studies. I did, however, accept a part-time appointment as an instructor at the Owago Community Day Care Center. Frying pan to fire? Perhaps so. The remuneration was abysmal, the pedagogic chores beneath my station, yet in virtually every regard my twelve attentive students proved far superior to those I had shepherded through our state university system. They were obedient in the main, open to new ideas, far less interruptive of my home life. Two or three of my toddling charges, in fact, showed clear signs of lingual promise, or at the very least had not yet developed the bone-chilling habit of misusing the word *hopefully* in every other god-damned sentence. (Pay attention, America! Do not say: 'Hopefully she will sleep with me.' *She* isn't hoping. *You* are. Do say: 'I ogled her hopefully.')

So, yes, the part-time job was fine.

But at this point I must come clean: I was on very shaky spiritual ground. Public humiliation. A lost wife, a lost career.

My return to Owago, to put it bluntly, was fueled by a single thermonuclear motive, namely to strike back at the Zylstra clan with every kilowatt of energy I could muster. I was seething. Day and night, night and day, I had that Son of Sam tick in my heart. How could one forget, or forgive, the sting of a public spanking? How could one overlook the unspeakable facts of cuckoldry and conjugal treason and perverse brotherly love?

It was all too much for me. I could feel the walls cracking in my soul, the seams splitting.

No more silly pranks.

Late one afternoon, after completing my day care duties, I was drawn by a sort of horizontal gravity into a hardware store off Main Street, where (in what can only be described as a sleepwalker's silver haze) I purchased a large, bright-red, ten-gallon gasoline container. Ten minutes later I arrived at the local Texaco station. I do not recall how I made my way home – I remember only the pungent smell of high octane – but within the hour I found myself in Mrs Kooshof's garage, chuckling to myself, stashing the gasoline behind a pile of hoses and garden implements.

That same night, as Mrs Kooshof slept, I raided her pantry – seven big mason jars.

I crept out to the garage in my pajamas.

Bombs, I was thinking, except the thinking was not thinking. Wild pictures in my head: Herbie straddling our plywood airplane; Herbie yelling 'Die!' as he banked into a make-believe bombing run toward his yellow house.

I filled the seven mason jars.

Rag fuses.

And then for some time I squatted there in the chilly dark, rocking on my heels, full of rage, full of hurt, quite literally beside myself. There were two Thomas Chipperings. A lonely seven-year-old and a man of shipwrecked, terrified middle age.

My teeth chattered. Something was happening to me.

I do not mean to suggest that I was 'crazy,' or 'sick,' or 'off balance' – nothing of the sort. I got by. I survived. On the surface I was my suave old self.

Still, the next several weeks amounted to an almost intolerable holding pattern. I had the explosive *how*; I needed the *where* and *when*. And while it would be nice to report that events followed a straight line toward apocalyptic showdown – that I instantly retaliated – the world does not operate by such linear principles. The world meanders. So I watched and waited. I kept my eyes open for opportunity. Sooner or later, I reasoned, the contemptible Tampa crew would show up in Owago, and on that fine day I would be throwing a welcome-home party of unforgettable magnitude.

Meanwhile, to pass the days, I had Mrs Robert Kooshof – often – and I had my new day care responsibilities, both of which helped to bolster those cracking walls inside me.

Back to basics, in other words.

Language.

Partly to bide time, partly because I am a born teacher, I threw myself body and soul into the linguistic education of my toddling charges. (I had taken the job reluctantly, at the command of Mrs Kooshof, yet soon found it among the more profitable experiences of my academic life.) Even at ages three and four, my exuberant tutees seemed captivated by my lectures on the etymology of such key terms as *spot* and *jump* and *Dick* and *Jane*. Where any other instructor might have focused on a moth-eaten mongrel named Spot, I proceeded to the heart of the matter, forming a circle of chairs and discussing with my pupils the overarching nature of spottedness in general. Together, we rubbed our eyes and spotted spots. We spotted one another points at marbles, spot-checked our pronunciation, examined spot rot on an apple – spotlighted, in short, that innocuous yet wondrously polytypic word *spot*. (I did not, as was later charged, discuss with my three- and four-year-olds the infamous G-spot, nor did I allude to 'spotting' in the cyclical or menstrual sense. Otherwise, our lessons were comprehensive.)

This is not to say that things went smoothly at all times. On one occasion, I recall, a sprightly go-getter by the name of Evelyn complained about a 'sore spot' in her tummy. 'I'm *sick*,' she kept moaning, to which I responded with my trademark asperity. 'We are not playing games here,' I informed the little troublemaker. 'A sore spot where, exactly?'

'My tummy!' Evelyn snarled. 'Sick!'

'A spot of the flu, perhaps?'

'Sick!'

A war of the wills ensued, concluding with a decidedly high-pitched tantrum on young Evelyn's part, and it was not long before the center's chief administrator (a somewhat overripened melon by the name of Miss Askold Wick) arrived to separate us. We were ordered into our corners, as it were, after which it was suggested to me that I stick to the textual canon.

I raised an eyebrow. 'You're referring, I imagine, to that infantile "See Spot jump" nonsense?'

'Right,' said Miss Askold Wick. 'And we don't permit spitting brawls.'

'*I* did not spit. *She* spat.'

So, yes: moments of strain. But by and large the day care job kept me on an even keel.

Less satisfactory was my domestic situation. Financial considerations had compelled me to give up my apartment in Minneapolis; by mid-May I had more or less moved in with Mrs Robert Kooshof. The tensions, I must say, were severe. First and foremost, I had forfeited the independence of bachelorhood; I was no longer sovereign in my own domain. Her palace. Her rules. Like some callow teenager, I was made to carry out the garbage, mop floors, change storm windows – all in exchange for a paltry weekly allowance. True enough, Mrs Robert Kooshof paid the bills. And true, too, she offered solace in the wake of my abrupt departure from academia.

Nonetheless, life in small-town Owago seemed a terribly stiff price to pay. (The local night life, as one example, consisted of a shopping mall, a few seedy taverns, an aluminum-sided polka hall called The Coliseum.) For all of us, no doubt, a return to the environs of youth will prove difficult at best, but in my own case it had a very distinct tail-between-the-legs quality. I had outgrown the place; I cared little for accordion music.

So then. Given a temperament like mine, how does one survive in such drear circumstances?

One takes to drink.

One watches *Melrose Place*.

One builds bombs.

I did not wish to kill. Only to rock the complacent Zylstra world, alert them to the consequences of tampering with the spiritual well-being of Thomas H Chippering.

To this end, on an early Saturday morning in late May, I strolled the three blocks down to Perkins Park, placed one of my rigged mason jars on an old sliding board, checked for bystanders, struck a match, lighted the rag fuse, and then rapidly scrambled for cover.

Six times I attempted the test. Six times the rag fuse fizzled.

One can only imagine my gloom. Still, I was nothing if not determined – enterprising too – and at 9:00 A.M. sharp I entered the Ben Franklin store on Main Street.

'Firecrackers,' I said to the young lady behind the cash register. 'Two packs, if you will. Deluxe. Price is no object.'

The vacuous (though soignée) young chippie stared at me with eyes as dusty and barren as Tunisia.

'Firecrackers?' she mumbled. 'They're illegal.'

'But surely you must –'

'We don't.'

I gestured at a large, self-congratulatory sign above the front door. 'What about your motto?' I said severely. 'Right there in black and white – 'You want it, we got it.' That's what it *says*. You can read, can you not?'

'Not firecrackers, though.'

'I *want* firecrackers.'

'Try South Dakota,' she said, 'or wait till the Fourth.'

'The Fourth?'

'Of July. You can *count*, can't you?' The insolent young Popsicle thrust four stiff fingers at me. 'Cruise the neighborhoods. Any kid in town can fix you up.'

I nodded.

'The Fourth,' I said, and turned away. 'Meanwhile, you will be hearing from the chamber of commerce.'

Frayed nerves, obviously.

On a certain level, however, those days in Owago had a flat, repetitive tranquillity, which my spirit, if not my intelligence, found recuperative. I fattened on Mrs Kooshof's Midwestern cuisine. I had my teaching duties, my evening strolls up and down North Fourth Street, my nightly romps with Mrs Robert Kooshof. (Our engagement had brought out the animal in her.) In a sense, one could realistically say, this fallow period amounted to a trial marriage – nuptial routines, nuptial responsibilities.

Grueling, yes, but I learned a few surprising facts along the way:

Mrs Robert Kooshof was not of Dutch ancestry. (Maiden name O'Neill. Imagine my shock.) Her father had been a Democratic governor of South Dakota, later a two-term United States senator. Her brother, Jeffrey, was a movie actor whose name you might recognize. (I did not.) She had twice been pregnant. (Abortion at age twenty-three, miscarriage at age thirty-three.) She had anchored a victorious women's relay at the 1981 US Collegiate Swimming

Championships, the gold medal now at rest beneath a stack of scented silk underwear. (I sniffed around, yes.) She was addicted to over-the-counter sleep aids. She was an heiress. She was filthy rich. (Her grandfather had patented the machine that puts down those repetitive white stripes on every highway in America.) My beloved's bank account, I was stunned to learn, contained in excess of nine hundred thousand dollars, with God knows how much more squirreled away in stocks and bonds.

None of these facts had been brought to my attention, most crucially her wealth, and I remember marching into the living room one evening with a four-page bank statement in hand. (Nuptial rights: I had been snooping.)

'And what is *this*?' I demanded.

Mrs Kooshof glanced up from her knitting. 'Oh, yes. I tried to –'

'We are increasing my allowance,' I said. 'Retroactively. With interest. You might have *said* something.'

She stared at me for an uncomfortable length of time, her expression weary. 'God knows I tried. Ten trillion times.'

'You tried?'

'Sure, but I can never get a word in edge –'

'Totally inaccurate,' I snapped, and with a flourish dropped the bank statement in her lap. 'I trust you have no other such shocks in store.'

'Well, if you really want to discuss the –'

'Is it all yours?'

'What?'

'In your lap. Those statements. The cash.'

My well-heeled companion rolled her shoulders. 'I guess the divorce will cost me, but after that . . . I mean, it's mine, yes. Ours.'

'Oh, yes?'

She smiled. 'We're engaged, aren't we?'

We were indeed.

'Call me Donna,' she said.

Over the rest of the evening the two of us reviewed her holdings with an eye on our shared future. The grand total remained in doubt, but as we retired for our nightly frolics I found myself tooling merrily down the golden-brick road of life, measuring the miles, counting up the infinite white stripes.

'There *is* something I should mention,' Mrs Kooshof said at breakfast the next morning. 'Once we're married, I'll want to try my hand at –'

'Not now,' I told her. 'The kiddies await.'

'I want –'

'We're covering the word *cat* today. I thought I might try out a few derivatives like . . . *catty, cat-and-mouse. Cathouse* might be a bit much.'

I polished off my coffee and began to rise, but Mrs Kooshof pinned me to my seat with a glare.

'Just listen for once,' she said. 'You were complaining that I don't tell you things, so now I'm telling you. I want to get into a business of some sort. Do something productive. I have my own goals, you know.'

I looked at the kitchen clock. 'Very well,' I said, 'but let us be brief. Business? What sort?'

'I'm not sure. Selling pots, maybe.'

'Pots?'

'Flowerpots. You know, like that one I made for you last week. The one I stenciled with little roses.' She paused. 'You remember, don't you?'

'Of course I remember.'

'You *don't*.'

(She was correct. My short-term memory had been dulled by domesticity.)

I covered with a yawn. 'Pots sound splendid,' I told her. 'And I'm sure you will add to your fortune one hard-earned nickel at a time.'

'So you think –'

'Turnover may be slow.'

Mrs Kooshof thought about it for a time. 'Well, I could sell other stuff too. Scarves. Jewelry.'

'Oh, indeed?' I said, then quickly reminded her that the town was already equipped with a satisfactory jewelry outlet, the very establishment in which we had not long ago purchased an absurdly overpriced engagement ring. 'Which brings up another subject,' I continued briskly. 'You can tear up that IOU. What incredible nerve.'

'But you're the male, Thomas. You're supposed to –'

'Male?' I snorted. 'Do I call you Dutch?'

'I'm *not* Dutch. Besides, I don't see –'

'Dutch or no Dutch,' I said, 'we go dutch. Engagements rings and all.'

Mrs Kooshof made an inscrutable sound in the back of her throat. 'Either way,' she said, 'I still need to *do* something with myself. And it has to be – I don't know – something meaningful.'

'Selling pots?'

'I'd *make* them, Thomas.'

'And then what?'

She shrugged. 'Open a shop. Rent space.'

'Fine. But the last I heard ... Surely you don't plan on staying in Owago?'

She rotated her jaw defiantly. 'All I know is this: I won't be one more miserable housewife. I've been down that road. Never again.'

At that point I pushed to my feet.

'Do what you must,' I said, and stood looking down at her. 'For what it's worth, however, I do not intend to squander the remainder of my life in this little one-hen town. I'm here to settle a few scores, nothing else.'

'Scores? What are you up to?'

'That's my affair. But I suggest you consider selling pots in some other part of the world.'

'Such as where?'

'Fiji,' I said, and departed.

Dead town, dead time.

Example one: A night out at The Coliseum. Turquoise tie clasps.

Example two: A 'sauerkraut feed' at the National Guard Armory off Windom Street.

Example three: An operetta staged by the League of Women Voters, complete with . . .

Why bother?

The town of Owago amounted to a sanitarium of sorts, a dull and altogether dulling magic mountain of the prairie (minus any hint of elevation). Now and then, through Ned and Velva Zylstra, I would hear word of Lorna Sue, who was doing well in her new life, and of Herbie, who by all reports was also thriving in the carcinogenic Florida sunshine. Plainly, my efforts at subversion had produced no lasting results. (Hence the need for more explosive methods.) The tycoon still bounced along in Lorna Sue's well-worn leather saddle; Herbie remained the brother-in-waiting, biding his time, no doubt preparing for that moment when he would do unto the tycoon that which the tycoon had once done so maliciously unto me. (Why else follow her to Tampa? Why else lie panting at her feet like an orphaned puppy?)

So let me be very clear. I had not recovered from Lorna Sue. I still grieved. I raged. At times I found myself talking aloud to her, responding to criticisms, reasoning with her, asking such fundamental questions as these: Who quit and who did not? Who slipped instantly into a new bed, new arms, new everything? Who remarried? Who shifted loyalties? Who lives in Tampa? Who lives in limbo? Who cannot forget? Who, in fact, loved whom?

She will never answer me, not directly.

Instead, in my addled thoughts, she will whisper, 'Tom, I showered you with love.'

She will whisper, 'You *made* me leave.'

As if she had no volition of her own.

As if she were innocent by reason of sloth.

On certain sleepless occasions, in the dead of night, I would slide out of bed and get dressed and stroll the hundred yards to Lorna Sue's old yellow house. The purpose of these wee-hour pilgrimages eluded me. Reconnaissance, of course – that was how I justified it – but it also involved some sort of obeisance to history, a reknotting of certain long-loosened ties of the heart. Stupidly, not really sad, not really anything, I would peer up at the darkened attic windows, behind which Lorna Sue used to play with her dolls, and soon I would find myself wondering how love itself could vanish like last month's joke. Along the east side of the house, in shadows, I would stop before a small, gnarled apple tree, never very productive, almost barren, in whose limbs I had once been cradled as a little boy, sometimes with Herbie, sometimes with Lorna Sue, doing whatever it is children do in the branches of an apple tree. Amazing ourselves. Making believe. (It was up in that tree, on a summer afternoon in 1952, that Herbie had first proposed manufacturing bombs out of mason jars and gasoline.) For all three of us there had been a sense of safety up there, a kind of coziness; we felt hidden from the world, and above it. The Magic Tree, Lorna Sue had called it, and somehow I had believed this.

Peculiar, is it not, how the mind works?

Over the years that twisted old apple tree had kept growing in my memory, magnifying itself as the objects of youth often do. And yet, now, in the graying bleakness of my middle age, the tree struck me as scrawny and forlorn and laughable. It held no magic. It meant nothing. It was a tree.

Only two incidents stand out during those empty days in Owago. I bumped into Faith Graffenteen. I became Captain Nineteen.

Faith comes first.

I had last seen her at my high school graduation ceremony, or in that approximate period, but in memory I had carried her through the years as a skinny, hawk-faced, horny little twelve-year-old. Unlike the old apple tree, Faith's growth had been stunted in my head, fast-frozen at that moment when she approached me in my front yard, bent back my thumb, and demanded that I kiss her. (How could I forget? The consequences vis-à-vis Lorna Sue had been considerable. Beyond that, the incident had established a fundamental pattern of my life: i.e., confusion of the romantic and the martial arts.)

All considered, Faith had changed very little – still slim, still tough, still predatory. Predictably enough, she had married a solid, stout-hearted, and extremely well-off physician, who had provided her with three children and a fancy glass-sided house on Lake Owago. Among her kids, as it turned out, was none other than the precocious young Evelyn, and it was this happenstance that brought about our reunion. Little Evelyn, it seems, had taken to muttering a phrase or two from Shakespeare at the dinner table; her mother could not wholly appreciate the fact that her talented, well-schooled four-year-old had mastered portions of Lady Macbeth's famous 'Out, damned spot' soliloquy.

Things began, in other words, on a sour note. I cannot report that Faith actually 'stormed' into my classroom on that blustery Monday morning, but it is certainly true that her demeanor was far from friendly.

A few seconds elapsed before we recognized each other.

'You,' she grunted. 'It figures.'

The subsequent conversation need not be transcribed in all its minutiae. Suffice it to say that Faith stuck to her guns, I to mine, and that the dispute eventually reached arbitration in the offices of Miss Askold Wick.

I took the high ground.

'In *this* classroom,' I declared vehemently, 'there will be no tampering with art, certainly no butchery at the whim of a tone-deaf housewife.' I gave Faith a contemptuous stare. 'What would you prefer – "Out, yucky spot"?'

'Let's not get rude,' said Miss Wick, who nonetheless eyed me with a shy hint of admiration. (Sterling woman. Paunchy. Wart trouble.) 'Anyway, we're talking about four-year-olds.'

'Indeed so,' I rallied. 'All the more reason to set an example.'

'Oh, come on,' said Faith. 'Just change one tiny word.' She frowned. 'Darn spot? Darn, stupid spot?'

'Ha!' I said.

'Ha yourself. This is a *day* care center, not some theater for foulmouths.'

I smiled menacingly. 'Profanity is hardly the issue. You don't hear *me* suggesting "Out, cocksucking spot."'

The debate thus ebbed and flowed.

Acrimony at times. Barbarism up against enlightenment, censorship versus tutorial liberty. In the end, however, we hammered out a covenant by which I agreed to locate less formidable texts for my students. The compromise, I admit, left a painful splinter in my soul – give away Shakespeare, you give away the crown jewels – yet I had managed to salvage, at least to a degree, the principle of academic self-determination. This alone seemed a victory worth celebrating, and as Faith and I exited Miss Wick's office, I issued a cheerful invitation to seal our truce over a drink or two.

Faith begged off.

'Not in a million years,' she said, and drilled me with antipathy. 'Don't think I've forgotten how you sucked on my nose that day.'

'I did no such thing.'

'Oh, you *did*. Disgusting then, disgusting now. Just stay away from my Evelyn.'*

Not a week later I debuted as Captain Nineteen.

This was occasioned, as such things often are, by a series of complex and coincidental circumstances, one of those unpredictable chain reactions that, for want of inspiration, Thomas Jefferson once referred to – altogether feebly – as 'the course of human events.' (Spades are spades. I do not kowtow to celebrity.) Fittingly enough, it began with the precocious young Evelyn. A day or so after my encounter with Faith, near the end of our morning rest period, the tot crawled up on my lap, tugged at my ear, and said, 'He's dead.'

'Dead?' I said.

'Captain Nineteen. And it makes me pretty sad.'

The name did not ring a bell. I did my best, therefore, to redirect our conversation toward more elevated topics, but young Evelyn, being the independent woman-in-the-making that she was, refused to take the rein. 'A spaceship wreck,' she said. 'Captain Nineteen got squashed and he's dead like a bug and I don't *like* it. I almost cried once.' She eyed me. 'Maybe I will now.'

'Please don't,' I said.

'I *feel* like it.'

'Yes, I'm sure,' I said. 'I am pleading with you.' I rearranged

* I am forever astonished at the longevity of childhood. How it never ends. How we are what we were. How turtles and engines and stolen kisses leave their jet trail across our gaping lives.

271

her on my lap, pried her stubby, tenacious fingers from my ear. 'Very well. Who is this unfortunate captain?'

'Nineteen!' she said. 'Captain Nineteen!'

'Yes?'

My bereft little tutee looked at me as if I had been born only yesterday. She had the knack, like most of her gender, for underscoring my inadequacies. (Where do women pick up these tactics? The genetic code? A secret pamphlet?)

'He just *is* who he *is*,' Evelyn said brusquely. 'His spaceship crashed. And he's dead. And I want him *back*.'

'Well, I'm very sure we all do,' I told her. 'But if the man is no longer –'

'You.'

'Me?'

The tot's posture stiffened.

'Once in every century,' she intoned slowly, 'there is born into this universe a special man. With the strength of Atlas. The wisdom of Solomon. The courage of a lion.' She eyed me, then saluted. 'You are that man. *You* are Captain Nineteen. Today's man of the future.'

I could not help but marvel.

The girl's diction and tone of voice had taken on the properties of a movie preview.

At the noon hour that day I happened to mention the incident to Miss Askold Wick, headmistress and chief administrator, who brought me up to date on the comings and goings of Captain Nineteen, alias Hans Hanson. The man had perished not in a spaceship but in a 1996 Lincoln Town Car: a head-on collision along Highway 16. For many years, Miss Wick informed me, the now defunct Mr Hanson – a local jeweler by trade – had hosted an afternoon television program for children, a mishmash medley of cartoons and live talent and ancient Hopalong Cassidy films. The program was broadcast over Owago's community access channel, number nineteen on

272

the dial, hence the dead captain's seemingly random moniker. 'A tragedy,' said Miss Askold Wick. 'Hans was a real . . . He was someone special.'

I looked up with interest. 'Handsome, was he?'

'Maybe. I suppose.'

'Dashing? Debonair?'

'Well, he did have –'

'Your lover, perhaps?'

Miss Wick blushed. 'The man was *married*!'

'Ah,' I murmured, and seized her hand. 'Unhappily, I am sure.'

Privately, though, my thoughts had now locked upon Captain Nineteen. A kindred spirit, I realized instantly. Who on this earth might have guessed that my doppelgänger, my spiritual twin, would take the form of a small-town jeweler and weary space traveler? (A small world, obviously, for it was in Mr Hanson's downtown store that I had recently purchased an engagement ring that weighed as heavily upon my mind as on my depleted pocketbook.)

After work that day, I made a point of switching on Mrs Kooshof's twenty-five-inch RCA, fluffing up a pillow, and sitting back to enjoy a rerun of *The Captain Nineteen Show*. Impressive. Very. The late Mr Hanson, not unlike myself, was a man of conspicuous command presence, rugged and flinty, exceptionally well groomed, with a piercing military gaze that both disciplined and mesmerized his rowdy studio audience (aptly dubbed 'the crew' – children of age six and under). The man had plainly seen much of the world; he ran a tight ship; he did not once abuse the word *hopefully*. On the downside, of course, the show's production values fell far below network standard: an obsolete, altogether seedy spaceship set; a control panel in dire need of updating from analog to digital; a uniform that brought to mind the apparel of a refrigerator repairman, hardly that of a seasoned mariner to the stars.

Still, this was community access television, and I gave credit where credit was due. Rarely boring. Riveting in spots.* During the first few seconds, in a pretaped introductory segment, I soon discovered the source of young Evelyn's oddly portentous oration that morning. As Captain Nineteen gazed resolutely toward the outer galaxies, a beautifully modulated male voice (Hans himself, I assumed) intoned more or less the words that Evelyn had used with me: 'Once in every century,' et cetera. Granted, the girl had botched the language in spots"† – which is par from the ladies' tee†† – but at the same time Evelyn had rather eerily captured the gist of it. I felt a chill, in fact, as the introductory footage rose to its climax: '*You* are that chosen individual. [Orchestral punctuation.] *You* are Captain Nineteen – today's man of the future.'

I felt called to duty.

It struck me – forcefully, in fact – that Captain Nineteen was just the sort of person who could comprehend the military implications of vengeance, a man who might very well stash a bomb or two in his garage. I turned up the volume.

A half hour later Mrs Robert Kooshof trudged in with a crate of clay flowerpots. Much to my irritation, she ignored

---

* *Spot*. Words, I've noticed, have a way of following us around like a nagging old melody. We try to stop humming the damned tune, we bite our tongues, but ten minutes later we are at it again: 'In short, there's simply not/a more congenial spot . . .'

† '. . . for happy-ever-aftering/than here in Camelot.'

†† With women, I have learned, the fundamental function of language is rarely to impart intellectual content, or to share objective meaning; it is rather to give vent to some murky-headed sense of 'emotion.' The delicious young Toni, for instance, could not have composed a precise, readable, well-crafted sentence if her very life were at stake. Upon her deathbed – beside which I fervently hope to kneel one gorgeous day – Toni will no doubt request that I ghostwrite her own last words. (Which, even in the afterworld, she will righteously claim as her own.)

the televised proceedings, prattling on about her new business venture.

Eventually I was compelled to wave a hand.

'If you don't mind,' I said sharply, 'I'm assessing my *own* career prospects. I would very much appreciate your silent support.'

Mrs Kooshof glanced at the screen, upon which Captain Nineteen's steely visage had only that moment reappeared.

'Hans?' she said. 'I don't follow. He's dead.'

'Dead, indeed. Which is precisely the point. I have been asked to replace him.'

'You?'

'None other,' said I.

'But I don't . . . You mean somebody down at the station . . . ?'

'Not quite. The possibility was suggested by a member of his crew. The shaveling Evelyn.'

Mrs Kooshof's laughter was loud and prolonged, a sequence of outrageous squeals that totally eclipsed Captain Nineteen's brief interview with a member of his crew.

'I see no humor in this,' I said acidly.

'*You?* Captain Nineteen?'

'Just an option,' I told her, although in truth I had already cooled on the idea. (The one thing Thomas Chippering cannot abide is ridicule.)

Wistfully, I sighed and switched off the television set.

Pity, I thought.

Thus I dismissed the whole notion.

Gave up, in other words.

Over the next day or two I brushed aside Evelyn's inquiries regarding my future as Captain Nineteen. Out of the question, I told her.

In my heart, however, I felt like a dupe to orthodoxy. I trudged through my day care duties, limped home in midafternoon, collapsed on the sofa, lay watching Captain Nineteen reruns with dull eyes and dull spirit. Today's man of the future, I would think, and then I would laugh aloud at my own cowardice.

In retrospect, I now realize, these were symptoms of a larger, more dangerous malaise. The events of recent months were clawing at me, compressing my heart with the relentless G-forces of sorrow. Late one night I found myself sitting in the garage, holding a lighted match, talking to my bombs as if they were living creatures. Lorna Sue's face seemed to bob before me. 'I *loved* you!' I yelled.

Later I yelled, 'Where *are* you?'

I smiled and swallowed the match.

In the end, it was one of those random, unexpected incidents of life that gusted up out of the blue to rescue me from the spiritual doldrums. One moment my ship was becalmed, the next I was unleashing the lifeboats.

And if not for the sly, persistent Evelyn, a whole fascinating chapter of my life would have surely been stillborn. (I have discovered through trial and error, primarily the latter, that none of us stands at the helm of life's great ocean liner; control is an illusion; destination itself is a pitiful chimera; we are at best mere passengers aboard a drifting vessel, some of us in steerage, some in first class, all at the whim of a ghostly crew and passing icebergs.)

The initial circumstances were hardly extraordinary. As was her custom, the affectionate little Evelyn had crawled up on my lap at the beginning of rest period one Wednesday morning, squirming and tugging at my hair and otherwise misbehaving in the most outrageous ways. Eventually I was compelled to insist that she join her classmates on the floor. (Each student was required to have a bath towel on hand for just this daily ritual.) Young Evelyn, however took poorly to discipline. Fists clenched, her tonsils suddenly in plain view, the little hellcat responded with what can only be called a classic temper tantrum. The decibels were astonishing.

Through all this commotion, and much more, I stood my ground. Even with Evelyn adhering to me like a vicious she-crab, I pushed to my feet and managed to unroll her lavender bath towel.

'I won't *do* it!' she cried, and took a firm new grip on my hair. 'I don't *like* the floor!'

'You *will* do it!' I roared back.

And so on.

Oddly, if only for a passing moment, I found myself revisiting two or three identical struggles with Lorna Sue, in particular those occasions when I had attempted to affirm my connubial rights and privileges. Lorna Sue, for better or worse, was never one for spontaneity. 'I don't *like* the floor!' et cetera.

Call it post-traumatic stress syndrome: Something snapped inside me.

I swatted young Evelyn.

On the backside. Hard.

Curiously, though, the girl neither yelped nor cried – nothing of the sort. She gazed at the center of my forehead as if shopping for a casket.

'You hit me,' she finally said, her voice flat, betraying nothing.

'"Hit" is incorrect,' I told her. '"Hit" is absolutely not the word.'

'It was a *hit*.'

'A tap,' I insisted.

The girl looked at me steadily. 'It *felt* like a real hit. And it hurt.' There was a pause as she allowed this information to work its way through my circuitry. 'You're not supposed to hit children.'

'Well, true, but on the other hand –'

'My mom won't like it, I bet.'

'No. Probably not.'

There was little point, I realized, in debating the issue. After a moment Evelyn sighed and curled up on her bath towel.

'Okay, I'll lie down,' she said, 'except you have to lie here *with* me.'

'With you?' I said.

'Beside me. On my towel.'

I shook my head. 'I doubt that's a good idea. If you wish, I could sit for a moment.'

'No, I want you to lie down,' Evelyn said. She appraised me with cunning blue eyes. 'And you better *do* it. Or else I'll tell my mom how you hit me. Don't think I won't tell her.'

'Of course you will.'

'So come *on*. Right now.'

Slowly, with all the obvious reservations, I removed my navy-blue sports coat, loosened my tie, kicked off my shoes, and rather awkwardly began to arrange my large, gangly frame on Evelyn's lavender towel. The word *manipulator* had come to mind, and as I lay back, I could not help but be reminded of Toni's honors thesis, those late nights at the typewriter, a memory that then blurred into a thousand other such incidents of feminine blackmail.

So, yes. Another jolt of déjà vu. But at the same time, as punishments go, this seemed a fairly modest one. (Evelyn was correct. It had, in fact, been a full-fledged 'hit.') I drew a few sleepy breaths and counted my blessings.

Not so bad, I decided.

Perhaps I dozed off. Perhaps I was merely lost in fluid reverie. Either way, when I surfaced a few minutes later, young Evelyn lay curled up on my chest, appraising me with solemn blue eyes.

'You know something else?' she said quietly.

'What's that?'

The girl wagged her head with genuine compassion. 'I don't think my mom will like *this* either.'

29

Nineteen

There was no room for maneuver. Evelyn made her demands, I bit the bullet, and by this circuitous route, paved with treachery, I found myself auditioning two days later for the role of Captain Nineteen. In part, of course, I felt gulled and used – at the noose end of my emotional rope – yet there was no denying the electric sizzle along my spine as I entered the studios of Channel Nineteen on a cloudy Friday afternoon. I was accompanied by Mrs Robert Kooshof, whose smirking skepticism bothered me not at all.

'He who hoots last,' I declared, which sent my good-humored fiancée into a spasm of inexplicable giggles.

I ignored her.

The arc of my life had bent to its natural end. You, I thought, are Captain Nineteen.

After a short, nerve-racking wait, we were escorted onto the set by a pretty little stagehand named Jessie, short for Jessica, short for mouth-watering. (Strawberry hair. Eyes of cinnamon. Assorted fruits, vegetables, and Virginia baked hams.) Even with Mrs Kooshof at my side, this daring scamp went out of her way to flash me the whole appetizing menu. (If life is a banquet, I thought ruefully, it seemed fiendish that I should now be limited to a single course of Dutch gruel.) Bedazzled, still flirting with her eyes, the outrageous Jessie introduced me to my two outclassed competitors for the job: the first, our local Buick-Oldsmobile dealer – an unctuous, beady-eyed sharpie; the other, a plodding and decidedly heavyset plumbing contractor. Neither struck me as officer material.

The three of us shook hands, wished one another well, then drew lots to establish the order in which we would perform our screen tests. (Plumber first, car dealer second, myself last.) The audition, Jessie explained, would be a straightforward affair. Twenty minutes each. No retakes. A 'crew' of twelve children had been summoned to select the new Captain Nineteen.

Lastly, much to my surprise, we were informed that the whole business would be broadcast live over the channel's three-county cable network.

I cleared my throat.

'Live?' I said.

'Well, sure,' said Jessie. 'Ad lib and all that. With little kids you have to be on your toes.'

I was taken aback. 'In that case,' I said, 'what about costuming?'

'Sorry?'

'The space suit. I'll need a uniform.'

Jessie shrugged. 'Well, that's a problem. We've only got the one – it was Hans's.' She gazed up at me with fawning admiration. 'Hans, he was sort of slender – not as tall as you. I guess you could give it a try.'

I winked at Mrs Kooshof, excused myself, and followed my adoring Jessie into a cramped and categorically sub-par dressing chamber. The room, I noted immediately, was aswirl with ghosts of the slain Captain Nineteen. Memorabilia of all sorts cluttered the walls. Primarily photographs: Hans Hanson tattooing his name to a young woman's bared left scapula; Hans with an arm around the tiny, fluted waist of the 1991 Miss Minnesota; Hans sharing an ice cream cone with a youthful Eydie Gorme.

Here, I recognized, was a man after my own heart. And Jessie, too, seemed spellbound by the photographs. She stood perfectly still for a time, as if at a funeral, then sighed and hugged herself. 'Hans, he was something else,' she murmured. 'Great with kids.'

'Oh, I can see that,' I said comfortingly. 'I'm sure the man was wonderful to work with. I trust that you and I will soon establish the same close relationship.'

The girl squinted at me. 'And what is *that* supposed to mean?'

'Only that I care.'

'Yeah, well,' she said. 'Far as I'm concerned, there's only one Captain Nineteen. The uniform's in the closet there. I'll wait outside.'

'Righto,' I said.

The next several minutes were a struggle. Hans's space trousers barely reached my ankles, the gold-braided jacket bunched up at the shoulders, and as Jessie and I marched back to the soundstage I felt rather like a can of moist and densely packed Spam.

'Gorgeous,' said Mrs Kooshof. 'Those epaulets, I just love, love, love them.'

I blushed.

'My fly boy,' she cooed.

There was a short delay as Jessie moved to a waiting room and led in our youthful crew, all ages six and under. (The extortionist Evelyn, I noted, was among them, and I went out of my way to give the girl a stern, behave-yourself salute as she was strapped into the special 'crew module' at stage left.) Things then rapidly accelerated. Waivers were signed, two cameramen strolled in, lights went up to illuminate the familiar Captain Nineteen spaceship set – a flimsy, stopgap, depressingly out-of-date affair constructed entirely of plywood and painted cardboard. All this, I promised myself, would soon change. Modern electronics. Refitted control panel. Air bags for the children.

'Thirty seconds!' cried one of the cameramen.

Stiffly, with considerable back strain, I lowered myself into a seat beside Mrs Robert Kooshof. The obese plumber had already moved to his mark in front of the control panel. 'This,' I whispered to Mrs Kooshof, 'should prove fascinating. A sewage specialist, for God's sake.'

'He's cute,' she said. 'A big panda bear.'

I snorted. The reference brought back a number of unhappy memories, in particular a long, trussed-up night in Tampa.*

'Panda,' I muttered. 'Perhaps so, but he's hardly a corporal, much less a captain. I give him two minutes before he mangles the word *hopefully*.'

The poor man's performance, as it turned out, was substantially worse than predicted. In the interest of brevity, I need only summarize his blunders. (1) An utter absence of soldierly bearing. Horrid posture. Slothful gaze. (2) No command authority whatsoever. On his ship, the *crew* was in charge. He toadied; he pampered; he flattered and swooned. At one disgraceful point, which shocked even Jessie, the man virtually resigned his commission – allowing a vote, of all things, on the crucial issue of whether to 'scope in' a Roy Rogers episode. (I had learned years earlier, in the classroom, that democracy has its wartime limits.) (3) To my astonishment, the man forfeited all pedagogic pretense. He juggled a set of plumber's tools, bounced little Evelyn on his knee, guffawed like Santa Claus, and said – I quote verbatim – 'Hopefully we're all having a great space ride.' (4) Most alarmingly, by far, the egotistical bumbler was a thief. He exceeded his time limit by a full thirty-seven seconds.

---

* To repeat: Language is an organism that evolves separately inside each of us. It kicks like a baby in the womb. It whispers secrets to our blood.

It was this final aggravation that compelled me to rise from my seat and stalk across the studio toward the trim-figured Jessie. 'You are the stagehand here,' I hissed, 'and I suggest you bring out the hook. Fair is fair. I will not be robbed.'

'Stagehand?' said Jessie. 'I'm the producer.'

I shrugged and aimed a defiant finger at the loquacious, audition-hogging plumber. 'Fine, then – producer – but this is no time for job descriptions. Right now, in case you haven't noticed, that self-centered bozo is stealing my allotted –'

'What a sexist,' she snarled. 'Just because I happen to be a woman.'

'Yes, yes,' I said. 'Believe me, I've taught whole courses on the subject. I can spot misogyny in a flash – the man is a plumber, after all.'

'Not *him*. You.'

The clock was ticking; I paid no attention. 'A pig, indeed,' I said briskly, 'but the issue now is thievery. I must insist that someone pull the plug.'

'You!' she yelled.

'Me? *I'm* not the stagehand.'

I blinked at her. Behind us, in a control booth, some sensitive engineer called for quiet.

'Just back off,' Jessie snapped. 'Put a gag on and wait your turn like everybody else.'

Fuming, I returned to my seat.

A cartoon was played, the Buick dealer took over, and for twenty agonizing minutes I sat glaring at a monitor. I need not detail the car sharpie's errors. He stunk. He fouled his own nest. He maimed the word *nuclear* – 'nu-cul-er,' he pronounced it – and systematically tortured the innocent little adjective *real*. (As in: 'We got ourselves a real swell crew today.') A travesty, in short. Unmitigated barbarism. Furthermore, I would not have purchased so much as a wheelbarrow from this transparent scam artist, much less the loaded Riviera he so brazenly pitched during his interview segment.

I had had enough.

During a commercial break, I hurried out to the car, opened the trunk, and carefully placed one of my bombs in a leather briefcase.

My own audition, if I dare say so, went beautifully.

Jessie beamed at me throughout. She blushed at points; she clawed at her skin.

Immediately, with a vengeance, I seized control of the ship.* Call me Bligh, if you wish, but I restrapped my crew in their seats, delivered a two-minute lecture on comportment, canceled the Road Runner cartoon, and then ran my charges through a rigorous drill of their ABCs. I permitted no referenda. No back talk, no second-guessing. This was not, I informed the crew, a popularity contest. During the standard interview segment, as one example, I insisted upon strictly martial forms of discourse: 'Yes, sir' and 'No, sir' and 'No excuse, sir.' Not a syllable more.

All in all, the crew responded well. There were teary-eyed complaints, of course, when I found it fitting to conduct a spelling bee in place of the usual Three Stooges tripe and when it became my duty to inform one inquisitive toddler that Mr Ed had long ago been rendered into nine hundred pounds of extremely useful glue and fertilizer. (Telephones began jingling offstage. One weak-kneed youngster abandoned ship.) Still, despite these difficulties, all other hands soon shaped up. Certainly no more giggling. I now commanded a reduced crew of eleven very solemn space travelers.

---

* Lest we forget, I have military experience. I know a thing or two about the chain of command, and if required, I am perfectly capable of calling in napalm on my own position.

How could I not feel pride?

From that point onward I could not have shanghaied a more compliant crew. It was a joy to serve with them.

At the same time, however, something ominous was happening inside my space suit. Months of pain and sorrow came pressing down on me. Intense heat, intense pressure – that G-force sensation.

During the storytelling segment, ordinarily devoted to beanstalks and ugly ducklings, I took a seat in the crew module and began recounting the much more realistic tale of my recent divorce. 'Even Captain Nineteen,' I said weakly, 'is defenseless in the face of treachery,' then, with a heavy sigh, I hoisted Evelyn onto my lap, gathered myself, and laid out the sobering details. (A dizzy feeling – I was out of control. I held back nothing.) Gritty material for youngsters, no question about it, and once again I heard the interruptive bleat of offstage telephones. Yet it was no easy matter for me either. I shuddered. I could barely bring myself to describe Lorna Sue's final departure, how she gave me that flat, opaque, reptilian stare and said, 'Don't be an eighteen-year-old.'

In retrospect, weighing the pros and cons, I might have toned down some of my coarser references to the tycoon's villainy – 'a maggot-munching vulture,' 'a rabid, devil-souled shark,' 'a love-killing, wife-stealing, spirit-sucking alien.' Perhaps too, I might have used a somewhat lighter touch in describing Herbie's role in the collapse of my marriage; I could easily have avoided the word *incest*; I probably ought not to have referred to him over the airwaves as 'a fallen Jesuit' or 'a church-burning antichrist.' For all this, however, I will never regret a single ill-tempered syllable.

'What you must understand,' I told my crew, 'is that Lorna Sue was sacred to me. And I to her.' I shifted Evelyn in my lap. 'You know what sacred is? Sacred is forever. Sacred is for better and for worse, in sickness and in health.' I swallowed and looked down at my empty-eyed Evelyn. 'Can you comprehend any of this?'

'Sort of,' she said. 'What's incest?'

I glanced off-camera at Mrs Kooshof, who studied the linoleum, then at Jessie, whose face had gone phosphorescent with hero worship.

Inexplicably, then, the studio went upside down.

An impossible thing to describe. It was as if something had broken loose inside me, a cracking-crumbling sensation. My knees buckled. How long this lasted I cannot be sure, perhaps only seconds, but it was as if the last several months of my life had suddenly given way under the pressure of time and gravity. A psychic avalanche . . . I felt buried. Claustrophobic darkness descended upon me, succeeded by boiling heat, succeeded by a sharp popping sensation at the top of my skull.

A brain plug came loose.

Slowly, in something of a haze, I moved off-camera, retrieved my briefcase, returned to the crew module.

The next few moments are lost to me.

I do not remember pulling out the bomb, or striking a match, or hoisting little Evelyn onto my lap.

I was weeping – that I do remember.

At one point I heard myself issuing a public appeal to Lorna Sue. I begged her to reconsider. I threatened suicide. 'Please!' I screeched, and other such drivel, then surrendered to a surf of tears. One of the cameramen, I recall, was gracious enough to escort me off the set.

What more need be said?

If only once – if only for those few sparkling minutes – I *was* Captain Nineteen.

The world will never know, I suppose, if the crew had been bought off, or if Jessie tampered with the ballot box, or if the final few moments of my audition somehow alienated a sponsor or two. My protests, in any event, went unheeded. The vote had been unanimous – even Evelyn deserted me – and as the inept, silver-tongued car sharpie accepted his commission as Captain Nineteen, Mrs Kooshof seized my arm and swiftly hustled me out of the studio. Our engagement, it seemed, had been called off.

I recall nothing of the ride home. In fact, to be wholly honest, only a few blurred snapshots remain of the next several days.

I did not *need* to be hospitalized.

I did not need the medications, or the snoopy nurses, or the idiotic, simpering, language-crushing pseudopsychiatrists. It was all Mrs Kooshof's doing – the revenge instinct – and I played along only because I had temporarily misplaced my capacity for speech.

30

Nerves

In total, I squandered six perfectly useful days in the Owago Community Hospital, another six in Mrs Robert Kooshof's queen-size bed. Most of this time I devoted to slumber. Sluggish hours, sluggish dreams.*

Granted, I needed the sleep, but in no way could my collapse be characterized as a 'nervous breakdown,' as the purveyors of Prozac so quaintly phrased it. (I am unsympathetic to such mawkish, soft-headed excuses for our minor setbacks in life.) The truth was mundane: I had overextended myself. The divorce alone had completely drained me. And then add to that the frenetic travel, the spying and scheming and marital sabotage, my troubles with Toni, the composition of a brilliant honors thesis, a public spanking, my recent career change, my day care duties, a television debut, my tumultuous, not to mention tenuous, engagement to Mrs Robert Kooshof. For any other man, all this would have constituted a full life's journey; for me, it had been compressed into less than a year.

As a governing axiom, therefore, I must insist that my condition bore no similarity whatsoever to so-called mental dysfunction. I will concede that my muteness – my steadfast refusal to converse

---

* Occasionally, of course, my interior night life proved anything but sluggish. Pursuit dreams. Wildfire hot on my heels, Death Chant howling at my door, a venomous Spider inching up the backside of my soul.

– may suggest certain psychological short circuits. Yet even this self-imposed silence was part and parcel of an overall need for repose. (I *could* have spoken; I was resting my larynx.)

Mentally ill, in other words, I was not. Nor 'clinically depressed.' Nor in the least 'delusional.' Anyone who has enjoyed even a few luxurious moments in my presence would sneer at such shoddy diagnostics.

Beyond that, I need not comment on my hospitalization, except to say that the food was abysmal, the medications were potent and the nurses were far inferior to their collective carnal reputation. Rebecca, for example: forty-six if she was a day. (Forbidding as a lunar landscape, hippy as the Iron Curtain.) While the poor woman clearly entertained robust fantasies about me, she was devoid of those social graces that lead to productive intergender commerce. She mistook the most casual physicality for 'freshness'; she appeared genuinely shocked that a brisk midmorning sponge bath might prove hydraulically bracing. A hopeless case, in short, of menopausal ill temper. (Whatever my shortcomings, I remain wholly sensitive to Woman's fallow fate.) For my dear, dismal, out-to-pasture Rebecca, alas, the great romantic pageant was something abstract and mechanical, ultimately barren. I patted her thigh. I tried to assist. I failed.

Be that as it may, those twelve days in hospital were no doubt good for me, a well-earned R&R, a chance if nothing else to rearm and regroup. I had the time, finally, to update my ledger;* I luxuriated in Mrs Kooshof's wary, somewhat

---

* Twenty-four new entries, in total, including such familiar names as Toni and Megan and Carla and Fleurette and Masha and Peg and Patty and Sissy and Oriel and Deborah and Karen and Beverly and Jessie and Evelyn and Rebecca. (What a harvest!) Each encounter, of course, had to be subfiled under myriad statistical headings; new data had to be entered under 'Body Type,' 'Hair Coloring,' 'City of Origin,' et cetera. Moreover, in the case of little Evelyn, I was compelled to generate brand-new categories altogether: 'Bed Wetters,' 'Thumb Suckers,' and so on.

begrudging solicitude; and most important, I began sketching out plans for the future – refined modes and methods of vengeance. Hospital or no hospital, there was still that loud, persistent tick in my heart. It kept me awake at night. *Tick*, in fact, is the wrong word: an endless siren, an air raid warning.

Surprisingly – shockingly – I found myself looking forward to my daily sessions with the hospital's in-house psychiatrist, one Dr Harold Schultz, a man of smallish stature, neurotic eyes, and long, dark, inscrutable silences that very nearly rivaled my own. The man had been trained to sit speechless; for me, it was a matter of choice. For fifty engrossing minutes each day, we mutely appraised each other from opposite sides of a small conference table, stone silent, locked like two stags in a ferocious contest of wills. Neither of us yielded a hiccup. (Had my health insurance not been adequate, I would have sued this unabashed quack for both mal- and nonpractice.)

Disconcerting, to say the least. Yet how could I not take up the challenge?

A typical session began with an exchange of pleasant-ries – handshakes and smiles, nothing verbal – after which Schultz would pick up his yellow notepad, jot down a key word or two, then pass the pad over to me. The man's tactics were transparent: fighting silence with silence. Third-grade Freud. On my part, immune to such gimmicks, I would respond in kind, scribbling out my own crisp one- or two-word missive, at which point we would lean back and study each other for five, or ten, or fifteen dueling minutes.

To illustrate:

In our very first session Schultz passed me the words *Captain Nineteen*, followed by a large blue question mark. I furrowed my brow, considered the possibilities, then jotted down the words *C'est moi.*

A cruel Germanic smile appeared at the doctor's lips. *Fantasies*, he wrote.

May I help? I responded.

There ensued seven minutes of silence, each of us shrewdly examining the other for signs of tensile failure. I offered the man nothing – not a syllable. It was apparent, after all, that Schultz had already jumped to certain half-baked conclusions: that I had lost contact with the here and now, that I was somehow less than mentally airworthy.

Eventually the grim Nazi glanced at his wristwatch. With a sigh, and with a worrisomely shaky hand, he scrawled something on his yellow notepad and passed it across to me.

Death Chant? he had written.

Chased! I scribbled.

Lorna Sue? he wrote.

Judas, I wrote.

Tycoon? he wrote.

Hairy, I wrote.

Suicide? he wrote.

Avoid, I wrote.

Which broke him. He tossed the notepad aside and leaned menacingly across the table. 'Don't get smart with me,' he snapped. 'I saw the audition tape – making threats, gasoline bombs. You were dead serious, my friend.'

I retrieved the pad.

Theatrics, I wrote.

'Nonsense,' said Schultz. His animosity – his undiluted hatred – had now bobbed to the psychotic surface. 'You've got problems, Chippering – *big* problems – so try communicating like a normal fucking adult. Am I understood?'

I reached for the notepad, but Schultz selfishly clasped it to his belly.

292

'Forget it,' he said stiffly. 'Talk to me. I refuse, starting right now, to read another word.'

I raised my eyebrows at this.

'I *mean* it,' yelled Schultz. '*Try* me!'

From my pocket, therefore, I withdrew a scrap of paper – some long-forgotten damsel's phone number – upon which I composed my reply. I folded the communiqué once and placed it on the table between us. Schultz shrugged. For some time, then, we remained at an impasse, a classic psychiatric standoff, both of us occasionally eyeing the scrap of paper.

It was a question of self-discipline. I had it. Schultz did not.

A twitch came to the corner of his lips. He folded his arms, refolded them, glanced down at my missive, then again stared at me with undisguised hatred. (God knows why, but I have discovered that the male fraction of our species responds poorly to my persona. Distrust at best. Raw loathing at worst. It should be noted, for instance, that I have no 'buddies.' No chums or pals – at least not of the masculine variety. Except for the case of Herbie, and then only in childhood, I have been the lifelong victim of the most ferocious male jealousies and insecurities, a state of affairs with which I can wholly sympathize but that nonetheless remains a source of bitter regret. Only women, alas, seem to appreciate my quirky virtues. Thank heavens for the gentler sex. Politics and physique aside, I could cochair a NOW convention or take my seat at any midafternoon kaffeeklatsch.)

No surprise, in any case, that Schultz should display the usual masculine rancor.

The man glared at me.

'Asshole,' he muttered. (A healer, no less. A physician of the soul.) With an audible moan, he then snatched up the piece of paper upon which I had impulsively printed the word *Peek-a-boo*.

*   *   *

One other fascinating development:

On an otherwise peaceful Tuesday afternoon, in the midst of my nap period, I was visited in hospital by Earleen and Velva Zylstra. They had stopped by for no apparent purpose but to celebrate my incapacitation. I was aghast; I could neither speak nor run. (For safety's sake, I had been strapped to my mattress.) One moment I was happily dreaming of vengeance, the next I was confronted by these two time-pitted monuments to imbecility – Earleen in her wheelchair, Velva in all her distinctive flatulence. For some time they simply peered at me.

'Well, Jesus H Christ,' Earleen finally said, 'I guess it figures. You was long, long overdue for this.' She flicked her eyebrows. 'Seen you on the teleconfusion – too bad you didn't just blow yourself sky-high, save everybody a lot of trouble.'

Velva tittered. 'Captain Stupid,' she chirped.

I sighed and faced the wall. On this wide and various earth there could be nothing so depressing, so cruelly debilitating, as the stench of two such subhuman creatures. My recovery was already in much jeopardy.

This encounter itself, of course, is barely worth recording – they gaped, they taunted, they studied me as if I were a zoo animal – and I mention the incident for only one reason. But a very crucial reason. After five or ten minutes, as the pair made their way toward the door, Velva stopped and turned. 'Look, I got to tell you this straight out,' she said. 'I heard that crap on TV, all that begging of yours, and I don't want no trouble when Lorna Sue comes home this summer. Keep your sick self *away* from her, like miles and miles away. The same goes for Herbie and her husband and our whole family.'

Swiftly, I snatched up a pencil and a scrap of paper.

Summer? I wrote.

'Fourth of July,' said Velva. 'So what? Just don't come nowhere near.'

Imagine the flutter in my breast. For the first time in weeks, perhaps months, a genuine smile crossed my lips. (*Happy holidays*, I wrote, but by then they were gone.) Still, that newfound smile stayed with me for the remainder of the day, then for most of the night.

Fireworks, I kept thinking.

In mid-June, with little fanfare, I received my honorable discharge from the Owago Community Hospital, after which I was brusquely transferred to the care of Mrs Robert Kooshof. The meals instantly improved. As did the mattress. In all other respects, however, I soon found myself looking back with keen nostalgia at my period of hospitalization. Mrs Kooshof was no nurse. Her bedside manner was gruff, her response time inadequate in the extreme. (On numerous occasions, often for up to twenty minutes, I would lie in need of attendance, helpless as a baby, my wrists numb from swinging the tiny copper bell she had placed on the nightstand.) The woman had no patience for my decision to remain mute. Cavalierly, and with what I can only surmise was malice aforethought, she went out of her way to ignore my written communications – even ridiculed them – which forced me into primitive (and humiliating) sign language. Not only that; she professed to misunderstand my perfectly legible menu memoranda. She groused at mealtime. She refused to assist with my morning toilet.

Lastly, worst of all, my paramour stole a page from Dr Schultz's therapeutic manual, inexcusably refusing to utter so much as a polite 'Good morning' or 'Good night' or 'What can I do for you?'

Her silence became absolute. No exceptions.

Apparently the woman remained miffed over the concluding

moments of my audition. (Begging for Lorna Sue's return, I confess, represented a tactical misjudgment on my part.) Yet the punishment far exceeded the misdemeanor. Hypersensitivity is one thing, holding a grudge another.

On my own part, I pretended not to notice that she had removed her engagement ring. I kept my complaints to a minimum, observed the proprieties of a standard patient-nurse relationship. But my on-again, off-again fiancée stonewalled it. (Refused to sleep with me. Refused to smile. Refused to participate in my required midmorning sponge bath.) In short, it was as if she had given up – as if she no longer cared, or *cared* to care.

The latter indignity broke my heart.

At best, this was malfeasance of office.

At worst – hard to face – it was love treason.

In essence, then, I lay alone and incommunicado through those hot days of June, all but abandoned, my hours passing in a silky narcotic fog.

Lithium, Xanax, Thorazine, Restoril – these were my only true and faithful companions.

It is important to reemphasize, however, that my mental health was in no way at risk. I sometimes wept, true. I sometimes spoke sharply to the television. (Again, in sign language: my own inventive variant.) And, yes, I admit that I crept out to the garage on one or two late-night occasions, cradled my bombs, chuckled, cursed, cried my eyes out, imagined a big yellow house in flames. But bear in mind that I had been drugged to the gills. And remember too, that for almost a year I had held up beautifully under stresses that would have incapacitated a rhinoceros. Who among mortals would *not* have indulged in an occasional bout of tears? I had earned each salty droplet.

As indicated earlier, the hapless Dr Schultz had (mis)diagnosed my condition as delusional, depressive, and suicidal. Yet the hard realities suggest otherwise.

Let me briefly address the charges one by one:

1. Delusional. No way on earth. Quackery. To be sure, there were times when I simply could not shut off the ugly pictures in my head. Hour after hour, flat on my back, I watched obscene, graphic, X-rated images of Lorna Sue and her tycoon rippling across Mrs Kooshof's bedroom ceiling. I watched the love of my life take her pleasure under the weight of another man. I saw the pupils of her eyes roll back. I saw the sweat at her loins. I read her lips as she whispered, 'I love you.' And other pictures too. Lorna Sue's face on the day she left me forever. The bleak, neutral, deep-winter landscape in her eyes. ('Let's not have a scene,' she had said. 'Put your pants on,' she had said. 'It's finished,' she had said. 'Don't be an eighteen-year-old,' she had said.) Delusions? I think not. Here was a creative imagination working in syncopation with a rock-solid memory.

2. Depressive. Reread the lines above. (At Auschwitz, as the condemned marched to their showers, some nervy shrink no doubt pronounced the whole lot clinically glum.)

3. Suicidal. Here, finally, we encounter a scrap of truth. I will not dispute the fact that recent events had worn me down. Like an exhausted swimmer, I had reached that point at which the struggle for buoyancy no longer seemed profitable. The depths beckoned. In many respects, I must concede, the past several months could be seen as a headlong plunge into oblivion, a leap overboard, the flailings of a man about to go under. Suicidal? I had every goddamn *right*. For instance: On the day Lorna Sue left me, after the door snapped shut behind her, I stood there in my underwear for some immeasurable length of time – outside of time, outside myself – just looking at that curious white door,

waiting for it to swing open again, knowing it would not. I did not weep. Not then. I remember the word *eighteen* shaping itself on my tongue. I remember the sound of a radio in another room. I remember a male announcer pushing a product called Lexus. Oddly, however, I have no recollection at all of making my way across the living room, or of opening up the drapes, or of stepping out onto the narrow balcony that overlooked University Avenue.* I was simply there, in my white socks and white undershorts, wondering if this was what an eighteen-year-old would do, and wondering what a Lexus might be, and wondering if I should perhaps remove my white socks. It struck me, even as I hooked a leg over the balcony railing, that the world of thought is nothing but a world of words. The very word *world*, for instance, had taken on a radioactive glow at the instant of my thinking it – there it was, gleaming, the world! – and the word *balcony*, and the word *socks*. *Socks*, I thought, and from that moment onward, for the rest of my life, socks would never again be socks. I straddled the railing. *Eighteen*, I thought. *Socks*, I thought. *Turtle*, I thought. *Tampa*, I thought. *Lexus*, I thought. I did not think *suicide*. I thought *pavement*, for there was a sidewalk below, and I thought *I'm thinking*. I did not think *Lorna Sue*. The railing was a high one, four feet or so, and I temporarily found myself off balance, unable to launch the remainder of my lanky frame into its short journey through space. I could scarcely move at all. One leg was still draped over the railing, the other tenuously rooted to the balcony floor, and for some time I hopped up and down in a struggle not of life and

---

* It will be recalled that earlier in this narrative I promised to elaborate upon the grief-laden word *balcony*. Here, then, is indisputable evidence – Lorna Sue's complaints notwithstanding – that I am a man who goes out of his way to honor a pledge.

death but only for some final dignity. Those uncomfortable moments no doubt saved me. Ridiculous, one might think, but even in my awkward pose high above University Avenue I could not help feeling distinctly irritated at the word *Lexus*, which buzzed at my ears like a pesky fly. There are very few nouns in our lexicon, proper or otherwise, that I do not instantly recognize. Lexus: its etymological source was plainly Greek. And of course I was fully aware of its homophonic connections to the word *nexus*, with all the attendant linkages of meaning and morphology. Still, I was puzzled enough to disengage my left leg from the balcony railing. I pulled up my socks, waved to a gathering of upturned heads below, then hurried inside to seek out my *Webster's Third New International*. It was a professional relief, I must say, to find the word *Lexus* unlisted. (Proper noun, it turns out.)

In summary, then, the facts overwhelmingly indicate that mine was not a 'nervous' but rather an 'existential' condition. Again and again, the important personages of my life had betrayed me: Herbie and Lorna Sue and Toni and Megan and Evelyn and Carla and Little Red Rhonda and Peg and Patty and President Pillsbury and even my bizarre excomrades in Vietnam.

Now, to my considerable alarm, it appeared that Mrs Robert Kooshof had joined the Judas list. (The disappearance of an engagement ring. Her slothful, indifferent ministrations. Her refusal to speak to me or to grace my bed.) Such provocations were troubling enough in their own right, but on June 22 our relationship took an ugly turn for the worse. On that morning I had thrice requested, via well-worded memoranda, that the air-conditioning be turned up, with absolutely no result. Bed bound, awash in my own sweat, I lay ringing my tiny copper bell for what seemed a lifetime. Not a creature stirred. The whole house, it seemed, had been abandoned, and myself along with it.

In the end I had no recourse but to rise from my sickbed, don my pink satin robe, and on weakened legs make my way out to the kitchen. Mrs Kooshof sat comfortably in front of an electric fan, sipping from a glass of iced tea. A number of travel brochures lay spread out before her.

My own voice took me by surprise.

'This,' I declared, 'is a disgrace.'

Mrs Kooshof shrugged indifferently; she seemed unimpressed by my recovery.

For a few seconds I stood absorbing the scene. Her pile of pamphlets encompassed such exotic locales as Guadeloupe, Cozumel, Martinique, the Canary Islands, Crete, Grand Cayman, and Fiji. Intriguing, yes, but the woman plainly should have consulted me.

'I must caution you,' I said gravely, 'that I am not yet well enough for extensive touring. Nerves and so on. Bedsores.'

This elicited a grunt. 'It's *my* trip,' said Mrs Kooshof. 'Solo. I'm done being a wet noodle.'

'Solo?'

'You heard me. No more doormat.'

Her voice was a monotone, perfectly flat. Very determined, I thought. Concrete-hard. And over the next moment or two other such transformations caught my eye: her fingernails were freshly polished; her blond hair – noteworthy to begin with – had been frosted to a soft, silvery sheen; she had lost a pound or two at the waist, just enough to cinch up the hourglass. In a nutshell, Mrs Robert Kooshof gave every appearance of a woman baiting the hook, preparing to troll.

I waited a moment, stopped by a rush of fear, then shook it off and occupied a stool at the counter. 'On the other hand,'

I said casually, 'I *have* found my voice. A sea cruise, I was thinking. Or Venice.'

My fickle, newly renovated companion rolled her shoulders. 'Have fun. I'll expect a postcard.'

'Which means?'

'Nothing,' she said. 'It means nothing.'

Suddenly, for no apparent reason, the woman then flung an arm out, swiveling on her stool, a gesture that caused her iced tea to go sailing into my exposed, overheated lap. I was clothed in a robe. The tea was iced. There was no buffer.

I yelped and stood up smartly, but Mrs Kooshof seemed not to notice.

'I'll *help* you understand!' she said fiercely. 'You're out of here.'

'Out?'

'Yes – *out!*'

My satin dressing gown was all but ruined.

I disrobed on the spot, moved to the sink, attempted to rescue the garment under a stream of cold water. (Mock me, if you wish, but it is a well-known fact that individuals under intense spiritual stress will often focus upon the most incidental details. Eichmann counted paper clips. Nixon redecorated. I rinsed. And if such examples do not suffice, I could well inquire as to the petty behaviors that *you* pursued in the weeks after your husband deserted you in favor of a cunning redhead named Sandra. Did you not shampoo the rug? Did you not clip coupons and rearrange the furniture? A piece of advice: Cast no stones.)

My efforts, in any event, were fruitless. (It is another well-established fact that Ceylonese green tea, iced or otherwise, has long been the mortal enemy of satin.) After a moment I tossed the robe aside and stood naked, as Mrs Kooshof continued to flog me with epithets.

Her language I cannot repeat. The gist of it, however, had to do with claims that I was still 'pining' for Lorna Sue, that I had made 'a fool' of her (i.e., Mrs Kooshof herself) over the public airwaves, that I treated her like 'some substitute leading lady,' that I could not stop 'hemming and hawing,' that I refused to 'commit,'* that I was little more than a 'sponging, freeloading, ungrateful, oversexed tomcat.'

At that juncture I stopped her.

'This has degenerated,' I said crossly, 'into tautology.' I gave the woman my harshest stare. 'Sponging? Freeloading? Repetition gets us nowhere.'

Mrs Kooshof made a shrill scoffing sound. 'Fuck you, Tom, I'm not one of your cow-eyed coeds!' She threw a dish towel at me. 'Put that *on*. Right now. You look ridiculous.'

Her tone took me aback. I wrapped the towel around my middle, secured it with a convenient clothespin, stood awaiting the next onslaught.

A tiny muscle moved at the corner of her right eye.

'Listen very closely,' she said. 'I've done everything under the sun to please you, to make you *want* me. Coddled you. Filed for divorce, followed you down to Tampa, put the goddamned house up for sale. What a moron I've been! Stupid, stupid me – I even tolerated your whining about shithead Lorna Sue. A bitch, by the way. Not half the woman I am. Not a *zillionth*.'

She shook her head as if stumped by the mathematics, as if nothing added up.

'I mean, seriously, it's like you can't even *see* me. Men think I'm dynamite. Heads pop up. I'm sexy and smart and . . . You don't care, do you? You don't. All this time together, you can't even call me by my first fucking name. I think you're *afraid* of

* See Chapter 20 for an inspired and rigorous analysis of that much abused word *commitment*.

302

it.' She bit down on her lower lip and studied me for several seconds. 'You *are*, aren't you? Afraid.'

I examined the puddle of iced tea at her feet. No sensible reply came to mind.

'Do it,' she said. 'Start a sentence with *Donna*. Donna, I'm sorry. Donna, I wish I'd done better. Donna, we could've had a good life. Try it. Anything.'

I nodded – I did try – but my vocal cords went lax.* The word *Donna* would not form itself. Whatever the cause, spiritual or biological, I could only gape.†

Mrs Kooshof shut her eyes.

'Well,' she said.

Then a minute later she opened her eyes, smiled, and said, 'Once you're on your feet, Thomas, I just want . . .' She held up a hand. 'Don't say a word to me. Please. Just go.'

Her smile, of course, was not a smile. And the word *go* settled between us like a fog.

'You're sure?' I said. 'You really want it to end like this?'

'I never wanted *any* endings. I wanted good things.' She picked up her brochures, smiled brightly again – falsely. 'That night you showed up here, I was so . . . Crummy town, crummy husband. Then I find this wacky guy lying there by the birdbath. Like out of a spaceship or something.'

'Captain Nineteen.'

'Captain Nineteen. And right away – *almost* right away – it

---

* At that instant it occurred to me, as it must now be occurring to you, that my earlier muteness may not have been entirely volitional.

† All my life, for as far back as I could remember, I had been prefacing my thoughts with the words *Lorna Sue*. I would be taking a bubble bath, say, and out of nowhere I might think – or say aloud – *Lorna Sue, I need a bar of soap* or *Lorna Sue, where are you?* or *Lorna Sue, how the hell could you ever do this to me?* Second nature. Nature itself. And to substitute the name *Donna* – to address myself with such intimacy to another being – seemed a violation of something hallowed and divine.

felt like somebody gave me a chance. That's all. A chance.' She closed her eyes, stepped backward, lifted her travel brochures as if to shield herself. 'I mean, you're not what I'd always dreamed about, not even close, but it felt . . . This incredible perfect rightness. The funny things you say, the way . . . Look at yourself – that stupid dish towel. You can be cute, and you've got this good heart, and you're intelligent and screwy and . . . If you could just stop trying so hard.'

'I'll remember that. 'Try not to try."'

She started to smile again, but the smile failed. 'Some things you *should've* tried. You should've tried me.'

'Right. No nerve.'

'You should've.'

She turned away. She left me there in the kitchen, alone, with a ruined robe and something sour in my throat.

'Donna!' I almost yelled.

I almost yelled: 'Please!'

31

Visitation

On the second day of July, Herbie and Lorna Sue and her pretty-boy tycoon arrived in Owago for the holiday weekend. By chance – or more accurately, I believe, by a gift of fate – I was out for a stroll that afternoon, alone, and happened to see the big blue Mercedes pull up just before dusk: tycoon at the wheel, Herbie beside him, Lorna Sue hogging the commodious backseat.

I did not, of course, literally gasp.* But I must say that the word instantly popped to mind, as if my brain had somehow done the gasping for me. My heart raced. I immediately sat down on a neighbor's ill-tended lawn. It was one of those moments when the world comes into stark focus, when all the emotional horrors of a lifetime are squeezed into a single amazing instant.

For weeks, of course, I had known they would be arriving, yet the prospect had always seemed an impossible fantasy, a pipe dream. Bear in mind, I had not laid eyes on these three blackguards since the day of my public spanking. The passage

---

* I may have slightly misstated the above facts. My presence that evening was not altogether by chance. I had been on stakeout for three straight days – more or less around the clock. My feet were killing me.

of time, however, had done nothing to eradicate that brutal incident from my memory. Night after night, hour upon hour, I had been picking at it like a scab: my bared haunches, the disgrace, the sting, the twinkle in Herbie's eyes, the tycoon's swiftly descending yardstick, Lorna Sue's indifference, the whole multiplicity of injustices and fifth-column betrayals.

Now, at last, here they were. Delivered to me like cattle for slaughter.

I had been ordered to depart Owago that very evening, and it was therefore necessary to inform my balky host that I would be extending my stay by at least two full days.

On the surface, Mrs Robert Kooshof did not take the news well. She strode in the direction of the telephone, threatening eviction, at which point I hastily rose up and unplugged the whole works. I looped the cord around my neck. I pulled it tight. 'Two additional days,' I declared, 'will harm no one.' (Strictly speaking, this was not the case. Immense harm, in fact, would surely be the lot of a certain triad of perfidious love villains. Last gasps, et cetera.)

'Two days,' I said, and winked. 'I'm sure we can find ways to make the time fly.'

Mrs Kooshof took the cord from my neck.

'All right, I can't evict you,' she said. 'But it won't change anything. I really do want you to leave.' Then she paused and squinted. 'What's *happening*, Thomas? I can tell by that silly smirk of yours that something –'

'It is not a smirk,' I said crisply. 'It is a Fourth of July twinkle.'

Well into the night, as Mrs Robert Kooshof slept the sleep of the spent, I moved in stealth to the garage. Pulled out my seven mason jars. Topped them off with an inch or so of fresh gasoline.

Fuses, I reminded myself, remained a problem.

First thing in the morning, I would put my mind to the matter. A solution would be found.

For now: a bit of reconnaissance.

A trial run, if you will.

My plan, as hinted at earlier, was to issue a loud, fiery, unmistakable wake-up call – not to hurt but to scare, to vaporize that private bubble of theirs, to let them know I was a human being and not some game piece on the checkerboard of treachery. (Childish, you think? I think not. Keep in mind your impulsive, somewhat less than mature trip to Fiji: how you contemplated your own ferocious wake-up call. Except you backed off. You went chicken. And you regret it, don't you?)

So, yes, a trial run, and it was with fluttery glee that I advanced in my ruined robe and corduroy slippers to the big yellow house on the corner.

No surprise to find the front door unlocked. Small town. Slovenly household.

Easy.

Down a hallway, up a flight of stairs. Little had changed: the scent of mildew and boiled cabbage. The same old clutter, the same icons and crucifixes and ceramic figurines of the Virgin Mary. I bit down on my lower lip, paused briefly in the second-floor corridor, then slipped into the first of three darkened bedrooms. Door number one: degenerate old Earleen asleep in her wheelchair, Ned and Velva in the moonlit bed beside her. Door number two: Herbie in his underwear. Door number three: imagine my grief.

Obsessed?

Time heals all wounds?

Look on the bright side?

Wish them well?

Get on with my puny little life?

Bygones be bygones?

You do not know what I know. You did not see what I saw. Lorna Sue slept with her left arm hooked around the tanned, narrow, naked waist of a male individual whose name I have vowed never again to utter, a faceless nonentity whom you have come to know (from afar) as 'the tycoon.'

Face reality?

I certainly did.

I squatted down, in fact, and inspected the vile tycoon from a distance of eight or nine inches. Handsome, yes. Yet hardly flawless. Even in the pale, curtain-filtered moonlight I could make out his graying nostril hairs, a vast crop of winter wheat swaying with each lucky breath. An incipient blackhead upon the nose. A bulbous, crunchy-looking Adam's apple. Sadistic lips. The telltale stains of hair dye. A chipped incisor.

And beside him lay Lorna Sue – those dark eyelashes, that smooth, summer-brown skin.

My state of mind, like my heartbeat, was irregular.

Indeed, yes: I faced reality.

Much too real.

I looked away. Drew a breath. Looked back again. It was this odious conjugal scene that I had been envisioning for so many months, a slow torture of the imagination, but now the undeniable facts took on a much more banal, vulgar, and lasting substance.* The girl of my dreams – my Juliet, my eternal Magdalene, my Lorna Sue – lay aboard a mattress† with this hirsute, interloping primate. (Surely, in your own tortured daydreams, you must have pictured your ex-husband snoring in the arms of his cheap new redhead? And with sufficient courage, would you not do as I did? Creep into their little

---

* As the thread becomes the cloth, so do words weave themselves through the coarse, tattered fabric of our lives. *Substance*. See Chapter 6.

† *Mattress*. The horror! Can you feel what I feel?

thatched hut by the sea? Crouch at bedside? Stare into the love grave? Pay heed to each pornographic detail?)

Live vicariously, then:

The house was far from silent. Echoes of history. Childhood voices. Creaking sounds. The incessant racket of my own thoughts.

I should have strangled the son of a bitch.

Obsessed?

What is love, for God's sake, if not the most distilled obsession?

Yes, I should have plucked off his pistil, crushed his purply parts with the sleek volume of summer fiction splayed open on the nightstand. Instead – who knows why? – I gently covered him with a sheet, wiped a trickle of sweat from his forehead.

A stream of empty time went by, perhaps minutes, perhaps seconds. Then I sighed and stood up and moved to Lorna Sue's side of the bed.

Even in the humid dark I could not help shivering.

Tentatively, I reached down and placed the flat of my hand upon Lorna Sue's bared left hip, holding it there to absorb her warmth. She did not stir. (How things change. In the old days the slightest touch would have awakened her.) She slept like an angel. No bad dreams, no second thoughts.

Reality?

Of course.

Yet none of it felt real. A breach of nature. Even the flesh at her hip had the texture of plastic, as if this were a facsimile of the real Lorna Sue, grotesque and artificial, and with a little shudder of revulsion I yanked my hand away.

I may have moaned.

I know for a fact that my spleen was not functioning properly, that it was necessary to kneel beside the bed and wait for the biles to abate. Again, there was some dead time. I noted the digital clock at bedside – 3:33 A.M. Later it read 3:55.

Then 4:18. Briefly, I drifted off. Memories. Visitations. (It was a product of my imagination, perhaps, but at one point Lorna Sue seemed to sit up and take me in her arms. She repented. She promised a happy ending.) Thus, in such singular ways, I found it calming to while away those wee hours in the presence of my beloved ex-wife and her tycoon, to breathe their air, to appropriate their heartbeats, to share with them the fluid movements of the unconscious.

At the first sign of dawn I slipped into the bed of Mrs Robert Kooshof.

'You've been gone,' she said.

'Just a walk.'

'A walk where?'

'Nowhere.'

'Bad night, then?'

I shrugged and said, 'Not terrible, not good. Go to sleep now.'

'Down the street, I'll bet. Sweet memories. Sweet Lorna Sue.'

I said nothing. For ten or fifteen minutes Mrs Kooshof lay very still, her eyes fixed on a patch of pinkish light spreading out across the ceiling.

'Thomas?'

'Here.'

'Maybe I haven't been totally clear. I do love you. Very much. All I can.'

'It's clear.'

'But you still won't . . . ?'

The question dangled there – incomplete, unanswered – then she turned onto her side, facing away from me. Her crying was scarcely noticeable.

After an hour, when her breathing evened out, I curled up against her and shut my eyes, trying for sleep, but something in Mrs Kooshof's scent – her shampoo, I am almost certain – made me begin reviewing our months together. Simple things: meals, baths, bed. How she had taken me in, given me exactly what I needed. How loyal she was. How she never quit. (Her vital data – all those manifest and uncommon virutes – filled nearly three pages in my ledger.)

But what did I feel for her? What did I truly want? The human heart, I fear, is nothing if not ambiguous, and no definitive answers came to mind. It occurred to me, obviously, that the sensible thing would be to make amends as rapidly as possible: beg forgiveness, let the past be the past, marry her, fly off to Guadeloupe or Mexico City. For months now I had been living like a maniac, out of control, chasing my own diseased history, and in the marrow of my bones I knew that nothing good could ever come of it.

Even so, I was helpless – pulled along by the undertow of my own obsession, a need to finish things. Explosions in the attic. Windows cracking. Lorna Sue screaming the word *sacred* through eternity.

I could almost hear it.

'Sacred!' she'd wail – that pious, God-infected, betraying little sweetie pie. 'Sacred!'

32

Velocity

Wednesday, July 3.

Summer hot, small-town quiet, but the entire day had a choppy, accelerating, out-of-control feel. After breakfast I checked on my seven bombs, bade *adieu* to Mrs Robert Kooshof, then set off at a brisk pace for the Owago County Library to pursue some background reading on the subject of explosives. For all my military experience, I had little technical expertise in such arcana, and it was therefore with considerable gratitude that I was guided by my helpful young librarian (one Miss Laurel Swanson) to a dusty volume entitled *Demolitions: A Handbook*. The girl stood well within nose-shot as I perused the title's index. (Her cologne, for the record, was generic Walgreen. Her toothpaste Gleem. Her mouthwash fruity – pineapples, I reckoned – but of indeterminate trademark. Other vitals: Viking-blue eyes, slim haunches, boarding-ramp pelvis, elfin ears, a bust of telescopic grandeur, all professionally fitted on six sleek feet of high-grade Swedish soapstone.) I was pleased, of course, to detect the usual seeds of infatuation in her eyes.

I snapped the book shut, squared my shoulders. 'Just the ticket,' I told her. 'I am in your debt, young lady, and can only hope to return the favor. Very soon, I trust.'

'No favor,' said Laurel. 'I'm a Christian. A librarian too, so it's my job.'

'Which you perform most exquisitely. A saint of the stacks.'

The girl shrugged, frowned, stepped back, squinted at the hefty volume in my hands. 'Well, good luck,' she said. 'I guess you're making fireworks.'

'Fireworks?'

'Cherry bombs and stuff. That book there.'

'Ah, yes,' said I. 'Fireworks.'

She bobbed her pretty Nordic head. 'The Fourth of July, it's my favorite almost, except for the holy days, Easter and Christmas. And don't forget Lent – that's probably the best of all. Sacrifice and everything.' Her voice was alarmingly nasal, her eyes aglow with a very tempting evangelism. She tilted toward me in a chummy, confidential pose. 'I'm Church of Jehovah,' she said seductively. 'What are you?'

'I?'

'Come on! Don't be a shy goose. Your *religious* affiliation.'

'Oh, that,' I said. 'Up for grabs.'

I eyed the girl's twin telescopes, imagining the rewards and punishments of a quick look-see. (Yes/No. No/Yes.) A sad thing to admit, but I could not resist sinking my teeth into this tempting Swedish apple. A noon luncheon appointment was proposed; Miss Laurel Swanson greedily accepted. (Again, the world pays little heed to linearity; our lives wander to and fro, sometimes along scenic Scandinavian byways. A 'tomcat,' Mrs Kooshof called me – who would not take secret pride? – and even now, at the bitter end, I remained true to my essential self.

Miss Swanson and I settled on a venue – the Rock Cornish Café – smiled our farewells, then parted ways with the mutual expectation that our noon hour would prove well and deliciously spent. (Cherry bombs, indeed!)

Thus booked, I retired to a quiet reading room and devoted the next hour to a study of detonators and primers and related technical topics. Fascinating material, to be sure, yet I found it hard to concentrate. A fuzzy feeling. No cohesion to the world. Even my immediate plans were less than fully formed: the problem of fuses still stumped me.

In midmorning, on a whim, I left the library, crossed the street to the Ben Franklin store, and once again inquired about the availability of firecrackers.

Same snippy salesgirl, same response. 'I already told you,' she said, 'they're illegal. You can *hear*, can't you? Try the playgrounds.'

I nodded dismally.

Odd thing: Not a single retaliatory barb popped to mind – in fact, no language at all – and as I turned away it struck me that my mental dexterity was rapidly deteriorating.

For the remainder of the morning, at times drifting outside myself, I wandered from park to park, with not a whit of luck. Blank faces. No explosives. The internal brain winds blew violent, chaotic snapshots here and there. A plywood airplane went pinwheeling by, then a turtle named Toby, then Herbie and the tycoon and Lorna Sue. At one point, in Perkins Park, a young tyke aboard a teeter-totter stared at me for several long seconds, his eyes fluent with pity.

'Firecrackers?' he said quietly. 'Shit, man. You're a grown-up, aren't you?'

At noon, now thoroughly depressed, I arrived on schedule at the Rock Cornish Café. I waited in a back booth for thirty-eight minutes before Miss Laurel Swanson called to beg off. A sick colleague, she said. Couldn't break away. Would it be satisfactory if she stopped by my home that evening?

As I put the phone down, a number of related thoughts swept in all at once.

First: Why had I not uttered the word *No*?

Second: What on earth was happening to me?

Third: Would Mrs Robert Kooshof be willing to throw together a coffee cake?

The rest of the day is largely lost to me. More brain winds. Fuzziness at the moral periphery of things.

I do remember sitting on the brick steps of St Paul's, where I had a vantage on both Lorna Sue's house and my own.

I watched Herbie mow the lawn.

Watched the tycoon supervise.

Watched Lorna Sue bring out two bottles of beer. (She laughed at something. She swatted the tycoon's rear end. She had no appreciation for the word *sacred*.)

My reaction to this, whatever it was, has now faded. Wistful memories, I suppose – good things and bad.

How much I had loved her.

How much I had lost.

Later in the afternoon, around four or five, I was surprised to discover myself standing at an ironing board in Mrs Kooshof's living room, pressing the wrinkles out of my old military uniform.

My erstwhile fiancée watched from the sofa.

'Tom, please,' she finally said.

'Please *what*?'

'Please tell me. What are you *doing*?'

I grinned. I held the uniform up. I showed her my twinkling Silver Star with its V-device for valor.

'A war hero,' I said. 'Have I told you about it?'

The doorbell rang at 7:24 P.M. I had completely overlooked my invitation of hours earlier, and it was necessary to feign surprise as I escorted young Laurel into the living room.

'A guest!' I cried. 'And what a delight!'

Even with Doomsday around the corner – my head crackling

315

with short circuits – I could not shed the trappings of civility. I made the introductions, offered Laurel a seat on the sofa beside Mrs Kooshof, selected for myself an upholstered easy chair directly opposite my two north-country beauties. (Scenic vista, safe distance.) It goes without saying that both of these succulent, high-spirited creatures were initially ill at ease; thus I took it as my first duty to assure them that this was purely a social visit, not a mating competition.

I outlined for Mrs Kooshof the spiritual background of the occasion; I explained to Laurel that (contrary to earlier appearances) I was not at present living completely alone.

Both gals nodded their appreciation.

'So then,' I said jovially, and clapped my hands. 'Off to bed. Hope the two of you enjoy your little séance.'

To this, Mrs Kooshof responded with scant enthusiasm. She riddled me, in fact, with eye bullets as Laurel rummaged through her handbag and plucked out a booklet chronicling the origins and history of the United Church of Jehovah. The girl placed it on Mrs Kooshof's lap.

'Must run,' I murmured, beginning to rise.

'Must stay,' said Mrs Kooshof.

I sat back. 'Well, fine – for a few moments, perhaps.'

Laurel seemed perplexed. The girl giggled prettily, gestured at the booklet in Mrs Kooshof's lap. 'I wasn't expecting . . . I mean, I sort of thought this would be a one-on-one witness.' She paused and tugged at her skirt. 'Anyway, maybe you can tell me something about your religious targets.'

'Religious what?' said Mrs Kooshof.

'What the Lord wants for us,' said Laurel. 'Spiritual goals and all that. It's awful darn important to have good targets to aim for.' She clasped a hand to her daunting left breast. 'Salvation – that's one of my own biggies. And to lose four pounds.'

My surly housemate glowered at me. 'William Tell's mistress,' she muttered.

'Pardon?' said Laurel.

'Lose four pounds. And what exactly do you weigh, my friend?'

'Gee, I don't know. One twenty-six, probably.'

'And how *old* are you?'

Laurel blinked. (To keep smiling in the face of such inquisitorial pressure, I thought happily, had to rank supreme among the girl's long list of credits.) 'Twenty-three,' she said, 'but I don't see why –'

'That's *my* target,' said Mrs Kooshof. 'To be twenty-three. To weigh one twenty-six. Apparently it's what you need to impress the men of this world.'

There was a moment of starchy silence.

'Well, honestly,' Laurel said, 'I don't mean to make trouble or anything. I'm just here to witness and recruit, if you know what I mean.'

'Oh, I do,' said Mrs Kooshof. 'Target practice.'

It was high time, I decided, to retire for the evening. I pushed to my feet. 'You really must excuse me' – I yawned – 'but tomorrow is a busy, busy day.'

With an exhausted wave, I adjourned to the bedroom.

Soon I was without troubles. Dreamland: the windy beaches of Fiji. (I spotted your ex-husband at one point. Or was he I? In which case, who would you be?)

Not until after midnight did I awaken, alone beneath the sheets, disoriented and very, very thirsty.

Strolling into the kitchen – most fortunately garbed in my ruined satin robe – I found Laurel and Mrs Kooshof enjoying the spirituous manufacture of Mr James Beam. Neither bothered to glance up as I filled a tumbler with ice water. 'So why do you *stay* with him?' Laurel was asking, as if I were some nocturnal repairman, to which Mrs Kooshof wearily replied, 'Love, love, love – God, how I hate the word! But it *was* love.

It is. Every woman on earth, they'd all say, "Dump him, just get away." Everybody except that one blind bitch who's actually *in* it. In love.'

Refreshed, I sallied back to dreamland.

33

The Fourth
(Morning, Early Afternoon)

Thursday, July 4.

Up at the first thunderous crack of dawn.

Bracing shower. Pat dry. New blade for my razor. Caution required. Close shave. Clean white undershorts, clean white socks, tan chinos, green polo shirt. (Green as in *Go*.) Then out to the kitchen for a breakfast of toast and coffee.

And what a splendid summer morning! Barely a cloud. Heat to come. No traffic. No pedestrians. Serene as the soybeans. July the Fourth – a day of rocketry and reckoning.

I carried my coffee to the big picture window in Mrs Kooshof's living room, also the living room of my youth, where for some time I conducted a nostalgic survey of the small-town scenery before me. Swept sidewalks. Trimmed hedges. Tidy patios. July butterflies. St Paul's kitty-corner across the street. (Brooding brick edifice. God help me, I am forever the quaking Catholic.) A stop sign still dented from the expulsions of Herbie's old Roy Rogers BB gun. The gutter in which my father dropped dead. (Unrepentant. Still no airplane engine.) Mrs Catchitt's barn-red house, flag flying, miniature windmill, the environs smothered under a great summer-burst of flowering botany.

From my glassy vantage I had no angle on the Zylstra homestead, but with little effort I envisioned the tycoon's insolent Mercedes bragging about itself in the driveway.

Simple jealousy?

Yes.

Fury?

Yes.

But.

But something more, as well. Namely this: my pain now had a sweet, distinctly exhilarating aspect. I had shed my professor's skin, and it was time now for simple, unsophisticated vengeance, as in the glory days of Rome.

Payback, as in Nam.

Mrs Kooshof rose at 7:35 A.M. (Foggy-minded I may have become, yet to the end I remained a cut or two above the average inexact historian. I could be trusted with detail.) It was 7:35 on the dot. She sat down to breakfast in her midnight-blue negligée, my favorite.

'Love, love, love,' I said.

'That was the bourbon talking.'

'Nonetheless?'

She did not look up from her oatmeal. 'Nonetheless, I want you out of here. Not a joke.'

'But we haven't –'

'There isn't any *we*. I know you can't believe this, Thomas, or even hear it, but I need you to walk away.'

'I am not,' I told her, 'a walker-outer.'

'Ride. Run.'

'Donna, I can't –'

'Donna?'

'Well, certainly.'

She sighed. 'Nice try. What a manipulator.'

'It was not a "try."'

'Oh, well.'

'Oh, well, *what*?'

'Just oh, well,' she said. 'I loved you, Tom, but love isn't everything. There's that wonderful thing called peace of mind. I need some.'

Velocity again.

Just before noon I managed to 'score,' as they say, a packet of Joker's Wild firecrackers from an enterprising young arms trafficker in the playground at Perkins Park. Ten years old, tops, the freckled little felon played dumb as I mentioned a series of escalating dollar amounts.

The boy vetted me with cool suspicion. 'Depends on what you're after,' he said softly, as if our conversation might be bugged. 'What do you want?'

About this I was uncertain. I rolled my shoulders and said, 'Killer junk, the usual.'

'Real money?'

'If you insist.'

The sinister towhead appraised me for a moment, then muttered an improbable and completely gratuitous expletive that made me pine for a bar of soap. 'I seen you on TV. Captain Nineteen, he isn't some stupid old crybaby.'

'Who cried?'

'You did.'

'I plainly did *not*,' I said, and glared down upon him. 'Let's see the goods.'

'Let's see your wallet.'

I obliged – there was no alternative – after which the avaricious hoodlum led me across the playground to a sliding board. He looked over his shoulder, bent down, and opened up a cardboard caisson stuffed with the latest high-tech munitions. One had to be impressed; here, in tidy bundles, was sufficient firepower to bring down Baghdad: cherry bombs, sparklers,

321

skyrockets, snake coils, numerous bundles of factory-fresh Joker's Wild firecrackers.

The little delinquent grinned at me with contempt. 'You aren't gonna cry, are you?'

'Certainly not. Joker's Wild, if you please.'

The deal was thus done. He handed me the ordnance, I handed him a sum of funds sufficient to keep Lorna Sue in noodles for life. When I turned away, the boy laughed.

'Captain Crybaby,' he said.

'Listen, you malicious little prick –'

'Right on TV, man. You bawled and bawled.'

'Didn't.'

'Did!'

'Absolutely did fucking *not*,' I growled, then rapidly exited the playground, proud of myself, armed to the teeth, stalwartly whistling an old Vietnam marching ditty as I headed for the wars. July the Fourth. Call me patriotic.

In the garage, doors safely barred, I removed the makeshift rag fuses on my mason jars, replaced them with the costly but much more up-to-date Joker's Wild firecrackers.

Then blank time: I recall nothing of the next hour or so. I was told, well after the fact, that I had left a somewhat garbled message on the answering machine of Dr Harold Schultz, MD, Quack. That I was spotted by a nosy neighbor – the antiquated Mrs Catchitt, I am almost certain – climbing the apple tree alongside the Zylstra house. That my face was smeared with what appeared to be charcoal. That I was dressed in military fatigues. That I carried binoculars. That I looked 'deviant.' Nonsense, most of it.

I do recall returning on foot to Perkins Park for an explosives test. My old combat fatigues, yes. Charcoal, yes. But far from deviant.

It was now 3:10 P.M.

My arrogant, nouveau riche arms dealer looked on from the top of his sliding board as I placed one of the rigged mason jars in the huge communal sandbox. New respect blossomed in the boy's eyes.

I lighted the fuse, moved away in haste, threw myself to the ground at the foot of the sliding board.

A few lifetimes passed.

It was 3:12 P.M. when my mason jar blew a hole in the Fourth of July.

I sneered at the cringing young crimemaster.

(Talk about crybabies.)

'You have been *fucking*,' I yelled, 'with a fucking war hero!'

34

Spider

Once more, for the final time, I digress. One or two loose (and hair-raising) ends require knotting, in particular those stemming from my wartime adventures in the verdant mountains of Southeast Asia.

(1) I did not, as may have been incorrectly surmised, actually dispatch anyone during my brief combat sojourn of 1969. Close but not quite. My ex-comrades Spider, Death Chant, Wildfire et al., in fact survived my wee-hour retaliatory air strike, as they were meant to, for I had called in grid coordinates a good two hundred meters from the mountain villa. Scorched their minds, yes – shrank their supersoldier testicles – which for a batch of betraying Greenies was revenge aplenty.

(2) There was, of course, a price to pay. Somewhat peeved, the boys returned from the bush and looked me up not two nights later. Hoisted me from my cot. Poncho over my head. Hands bound. Led me out to the base perimeter. Made a show of a firing squad: leveled weapons, last requests, ritual commands. Yet not for an instant did I take any of it seriously, nor would I grovel or apologize or emit so much as an entreating whine.

'Dead white meat,' said Goof.

'For the flies,' said Bonnie Prince Charming.

But it was ridiculous – like the war itself, like the bulk of human experience as I have rather cynically come to know it. A pitiful, unfunny joke. Little boys playing war. (Or a little boy, in my case, playing love.) For the record, however, it is important to note that I comported myself with dignity throughout the entire incident, not once flinching, standing my incredulous, disbelieving ground in the face of an inane eternity. I shocked myself. (If only Herbie had been there to witness it. For once – with style – I was his equal in matters macho. What had gotten *into* me? How and why such unexpected mettle? I will never know, I suppose, and I can only guess that my short-lived gallantry had its roots in simple statistical probability. Sooner or later even the cowardly mouse will roar.)

Afterward, the boys treated me to a beer.

'Bravo,' said Wildfire.

'Huzzah,' said Goof. 'Our ballsy bud.'

'Yeah, and that bombing stunt of yours,' said Spider, 'it was just pure outfuckingstanding, right up to snuff, evil as the stars. We shat monkeys, man. All of us, we pooped zee wet icky poop.' He clapped my back. He smiled. 'You realize, of course, that now we'll have to kill you for real?'

'Not right this instant,' said Tulip.

'No way,' said Bonnie Prince Charming. 'Right this instant we're toasting your brave ass.'

'We'll kill you later,' said Goof.

'Mucho, mucho later,' said Spider, who had adopted the cartoon lilt of gay San Juan. 'After zee war. The years flit by, maybe you forget, maybe you *almost* forget, but then – poof – in zee dark of daylight . . .' He smiled again. 'The cost of courage. You were supposed to scare.'

'I can still do it,' I said. 'I'm capable.'

Spider nodded. 'No question about it. But too bad. Your golden opportunity, tiger, and you blew it – couldn't just chicken out like the world-class chickenfuckingshit you truly are.' He popped open a fresh beer, took a swallow, and generously passed it over to me. We were seated in a crowded NCO club. The music was drums, the clientele post-weary weird. 'And for us, you see, there is now zee great big *problema* of honor. We pooped fat monkeys. Goof here, the guy's got busted eardrums. You almost on-fucking-purpose *killed* us.'

'One more chance. I'll scare.'

Spider clucked his tongue. 'Sensible, but so, so sorry. A tough turn of events, but you've come up against the burden of the brave. Irony, I guess. It's like a law or something. Chicken out, you're fine. Act the hero, man – even once – and you just fucking *know* you'll have to do it all over again.' He sighed. 'What a universe.'

'This Bud's for the brave,' said Bonnie Prince Charming.

'Watch your back,' said Goof.

'Forever,' said Spider.

(3) Over all these decades, in other words, I have had to live with the consequences of a single, senseless act of valor. (It was an accident, for Christ sake! It was a virus!)

(4) I am not, of course, a simpleminded determinist, and I do not wish to blame the war for my subsequent emotional troubles, or try to make more of this business than it was. Yet it was *something*. The 'burden of the brave,' as Spider aptly called it. (Recall, if you will, the issue of unplugged telephones. Obscenities in my sleep. Separate marital bedrooms. A certain subtle frenzy to my life.)

Who knows, in the end, how much this episode contributed to my eventual difficulties?

Some. Probably more than some. But this much for certain. There has been a Spider crawling through my thoughts for the past quarter century, a Death Chant buzzing in my ears.

*　　*　　*

It was no coincidence, therefore, that on that hot, hazardous Fourth of July, in late afternoon, a somewhat portly Spider strolled into Mrs Kooshof's garage and stood watching me stow my six remaining bombs in a cardboard box. How long he had been there I cannot be sure.

'Tommy, Tommy,' he murmured, then chuckled. 'Up to old tricks.'

Well, I thought.

Zee dark of daylight.

A startling development, of course, yet hardly a surprise. I had been dreading this for years now, well over two decades, and plainly he had taken care to select the right occasion: this fatal afternoon, and none other. Still, as I looked up at him, I could not withhold a little moan. Nor could I help wondering if his presence was a product of my imagination, those feverish brain winds now gusting at hurricane velocity. Framed by the garage door, a sheen of bright summer sunlight behind him, he seemed to float toward me without ordinary means of locomotion.

I stood up, wiped my forehead, shook his hand. 'You're here to kill me?'

Spider laughed and flicked his eyebrows. 'Well, hey, that would spoil the fun, wouldn't it?' He glanced at my bombs. 'Come on, Captain Nineteen, let's you and me take a space walk.'

'At the moment I'm –'

'Oh, I know, I know. We've been keeping tabs.'

He wrapped a chubby arm around my shoulder, led me out of the garage and down the sidewalk. (A gliding sensation – what a sleepwalker must feel.) The world, I realized once again, has a way of derailing our lives, taking odd twists and turns, and a distinct faintness overcame me as we made our way to a tavern just off Main Street. I ordered a pair of vodka tonics, Spider the pretzels-and-a-pitcher special.

I blinked and looked straight at him. 'Keeping tabs? What, exactly, does that mean?'

He laughed.

'A hobby, you could call it – checking in now and then. And I'll say one thing, it's been a deluxe education watching you wreck your sorry little life.' He lifted his glass. 'Cheers.'

I waited a moment. 'What about killing me?'

'Oh, that.'

'That,' I said.

'For crying out loud, man.' His eyes glistened. 'Took it to heart, did you?'

'I did. You haven't answered me.'

He seemed to be enjoying himself, sitting back, slowly destroying a mouthful of pretzels. 'The thing is, I can't be real definitive here. Maybe we'll kill you, maybe we won't. If I go ahead and tell you it's all a joke – a big goof – well, jeez, that'll take something real special out of your life. Suspense, you know? That over-the-shoulder feeling.' He smiled widely. 'Best to leave it vague, keep you on your tippy-toes.'

'What about the others?'

'Oh, you know – mainstream America. Tulip coaches basketball, Death Chant runs this nifty boutique. Me, I'm fat. I sell pianos. War's over.'

'That's it?'

'More or less. Peace on earth.'

I looked at him hard. 'What about the burden of the brave? It was a question of honor, I thought.'

Spider shrugged. 'Yeah, well.'

'Yeah, *well?*'

'Right, don't lose sleep. Anyhow, Tommy, it looks to me like you got enough problems as it is. Mental distress. Bombs. That's why I'm here, in fact – to add to your problems. Rev up the pressure.'

He gave me a chilly, unnerving stare, then stood up and moved off toward the men's room. It was five minutes before he returned. 'Fucking prostate, Tommy. Getting old.' He laughed. 'Where were we?'

'Pressure,' I said. 'Whether to kill me or not.'

'Right, right.'

'And where do we stand on that?'

Spider frowned. 'Like I say, the whole point is to keep it kind of vague. Makes life interesting.'

'Interesting?' I said.

'Well, yeah, here's the thing,' said Spider. 'For the rest of us, Tommy, the war's history – gonzo – but in this really nifty way you've kept it going. That life-and-death edge, man, it gives *meaning* to everything. Keeps you in contact with your own sinnin' self.' He chuckled again. 'Thanks to me, you're still in the Nam, still up in those creepy mountains. Seriously, I *miss* all that.'

He removed a length of piano wire from his pocket, uncoiled it, formed it into a noose.

'Lucky Tom,' he murmured. 'It's like this gift we gave you. Judgment Day. Most of us forget it's on the calendar.'

I nodded and watched him test the piano wire.

In a sense, I realized, he was right. For better or worse, the whole terrifying business had given definition to the past couple decades of my life. That pursued feeling – it was something to believe in, a replacement for Easter.

Spider reached out and looped the wire around my neck.

'You're in a special position, Tommy. Among the elect, so to speak.'

'Elect,' I said. 'That would be I.'

'That sure as fuck would be. And the rest of us poor yo-yos, we're the Walking Numb, totally blind to our own pitiful mortality.' He looked me in the eye, tightened up the noose. 'In the civilian world, man, it's just so doggone easy to forget that we don't live forever. I guess that's why we get off on war so much, because it's like this . . . well, you know, this nifty reminder.'

'Good point,' I said. 'My neck.'

'Your neck, your neck,' he cooed. He was the old Spider again. 'You really want me to call it off? Lose this Closer-God-to-Thee-ness?'

'Up to you. Completely.'

Spider stared. 'It is, isn't it?'

After a few seconds he sighed, removed the wire, coiled it up, and returned it to his pocket. Again, very powerfully, I was struck by that sleepwalking sensation.

'Tell you what, let's drop this whole subject,' he said quietly, his voice pleasant again. 'Go on just like before, keep it a mystery. Maybe I'll be back someday, maybe I won't.' He reached for the pitcher, refilled his glass. 'Anyhow, Tommy, the way I look at it, you'll be awful fortunate not to blow yourself sky-high tonight. Easy does it, my man. Don't hurt yourself.'

'You mean that?'

'Hey, sure I do,' he said, then laughed lightly. 'Tulip and the rest of the boys, they'd be super-duper pissed if you ended up in pieces.'

'They would?'

'Absolutely. Spoil the fun of killing you.'

We parted ways a half hour later.

Afternoon shadows were falling as we trudged through the hot, silent, small-town Fourth of July. At the corner of Main and Diagonal, he stopped in front of the bus station.

'This is where I get off, pal.' He clapped my shoulder. 'Seriously, watch yourself tonight. Weird thought, but you make my world hum. Wouldn't want to lose my reason for living.'

I shrugged and began to walk away, then turned back.

'One last question,' I said. 'I *was* brave, right? At least that once?'

Spider nodded. 'Once is all it takes,' he said gently. 'War hero, man.'

35

The Fourth
(Late Afternoon, Evening)

My world had gone G-force hazy, warped and somewhat suspect, yet I plodded onward up Main Street, past the Ben Franklin store, past the Rock Cornish Café and the Farmers Union State Bank. The time was 4:40 P.M., the temperature ninety-two sizzling degrees. Quiet as the cornfields, peaceful as Pluto. Closed-down shops, no traffic, barbecue smells, flags hanging limp on their front-yard poles. Somewhere a dog barked. Somewhere a lawn mower buzzed. There can be nothing on our planet, I decided, quite so tranquil as small-town America decked out in its Fourth of July sleepwear.

Back at the house, after bracing myself with two fingers of iced bourbon, I moved out to the living room and found Mrs Kooshof napping away the afternoon on her leather sofa. Pity, I thought. Lovely human being. Warm heart, decent instincts. Much to offer a man.

I will admit it: my frontal lobe had cracked.

It struck me that I was about to lose her forever, exactly as I had lost everything else in my life. And I was powerless to prevent it.

Disjointedly, as if wading through quicksand, I wandered out to the backyard, sank down into Mrs Kooshof's old hemp hammock, and spent the next hour or so in a languorous summer daze. Not asleep, exactly, but not awake either. Silky air, silky thoughts. I was exhausted from the day's uncommon events – a trifle nauseated, a soft buzzing in my ears. At one point, I am almost sure, I heard Mrs Kooshof calling to me from an upstairs window; later, less definitely, I heard a noise coming from the garage to my immediate left. What its source may have been I cannot say: a rustling, raspy sound. Perhaps laughter. Perhaps of human origin, perhaps not.

Just before 6:00 P.M. Mrs Robert Kooshof joined me in the backyard. She looked tired, a little upset. 'I want the truth,' she said, and her lower lip trembled. 'What's going on?'

'In what sense?' I inquired.

'Don't do this. Tell me.'

'I have no idea what –'

'Velva and Ned – I just *talked* to them. Peeking in windows, snooping, breaking and entering . . . God knows what. People *saw* you.'

'Be that as it may.'

'Binoculars? Up in a tree?'

I dismissed this with a snort. 'Surveillance, yes. Snooper, no.'

'Thomas, this is all getting too weird. I'm scared.'

'Of what, may I ask?'

'That's not . . . I don't even *know* yet.' She blinked into the early-evening glare. Briefly, then, but forcefully, it occurred to me that the past several months had visibly worn her down. A dark, purply puffiness had come into the sockets of her eyes. 'Something's wrong, Thomas. I can just feel it. Something bad is coming. Can't we –?'

'We?' I said.

She looked away for a second. 'We could leave. Right away. Tonight.'

333

'I presumed the "we" was dead.'

'But if you could just try to . . . People change. People start over, they turn a new leaf.'

'Meaning?'

There was a hesitation before she shook her head. 'Meaning nothing, obviously. Except I'm an idiot. So much for last chances.'

She turned and disappeared into the house.

Then for a long while I lay incubating in the July heat, gathering strength, hatching plans, listening to a soft, persistent hum that seemed to bubble up from the center of our violent universe.

We dined separately that evening, Mrs Kooshof behind a locked bedroom door, I at the kitchen counter.

It was clear what she wanted from me: absolute surrender, the forfeiture of heroism, a return to the pathetic norm. In theory, perhaps, this was little to ask, but as much as I cared for her – which was a great, great deal – I could no more give up the thirst for vengeance than stroll down to a convenience store and purchase a new personality.

At dusk I changed back into my old combat uniform.

A pair of jungle boots too, and a bush hat, and my polished Silver Star with its V-device for valor.

Firecrackers. A book of matches.

Velocity again.

It was full dark when I slipped out to the garage. After the strain of recent months, I now felt an electric sizzle in my bones, partly anticipation, partly dread. I was capable of anything. For a few seconds I stood there in the dark garage, envisioning a big yellow house afire, an exploding Mercedes, a family of turncoats running for their lives. The image made me snicker.

I dipped into a sack of briquettes, charcoaled up, then went over to the cardboard box where I had stashed my remaining bombs.

Which were gone.

All six of them – not a trace.

Immediately, I recognized Herbie's thieving hand at work.

Something seemed to ignite inside me. At great speed, in one indignant motion, I hustled down the sidewalk, rapped on the Zylstra front door, formed a pair of fists, stiffened myself for the fray.

Herbie himself greeted me.

'No small talk,' I said savagely. 'I want my *bombs* back.'

My old chum's eyebrows bunched up. He stood casually in the doorway, lean and handsome, neatly barbered, like one of those slick male models in a J Crew catalogue. (White slacks, white golf shirt, gold necklace, shiny brown loafers.) It astonished me, as always, to think that this was the Herbie of my childhood. He was a stranger to me; I simply did not know him.

'Surprise,' he murmured, and smiled. He surveyed my uniform, my charcoaled face. 'Looking natty.'

'The *bombs*,' I repeated. 'Let's have them.'

'Bombs? Come on in.'

He frowned slightly and escorted me into the musty, cabbage-scented inner sanctum of the Zylstra household. An uncomfortable moment passed by, or perhaps several moments, during which Herbie caught me staring at a photograph of the tycoon and Lorna Sue.

'They're out back,' he said. 'Family picnic. You're welcome to join in.'

I shook my head. 'The bombs,' I told him, 'and I'll be on my way.'

'You're sure?'

'Bombs. Now.'

Herbie stood with his hands in his pockets, perfectly at ease, appraising me with the smug, commanding superiority that had driven me crazy since we were kids – as if he had some God-given sovereignty over me. 'Well, look, I heard you've fallen on hard times,' he said cheerfully. There was a short pause. 'Unemployed, right? Hospitals?'

'Not so bad,' I sniffed. 'A sea change.'

Involuntarily, I found myself scanning the living room for signs of Lorna Sue. My legs felt wobbly. 'If you don't mind,' I said, 'let's stick to the subject, which happens to be burglary. You stole my bombs.'

'Bombs?'

'Precisely. Mason jars.'

Herbie laughed and grasped my arm. 'Just like the old days, Tommy? Still in your time warp?'

'Where I am,' I said archly, 'is none of your concern.' I glanced down. 'My arm.'

'I was –'

'Release it.'

For a few seconds he looked at me with an expression that in any other human being might have been considered wistful. It lasted only an instant, and then he moved away, took a seat on the couch, crossed his legs, and gazed up at me. There was something peculiar in his eyes. 'No offense, Tom, but don't you think it's time to end all this? I know you blame me for everything, but I've never felt anything except . . . just compassion for you. That's the truth.'

I glared at him. 'Compassion. Broke up my marriage. Took her away from me.'

'You know better than that. She was *always* away. From day one.'

'What does that mean?'

He seemed to drift off for a time. His voice, when he finally spoke, had a resigned, listless quality. 'Tom, you can't go on like this forever. At some point, someday, you have to cut out all the crap. Prowling around, interfering with other people's lives. It's not healthy.' He motioned at my sooty face, my jungle boots and fatigues. 'I mean, look at yourself.'

'I look fine,' I said. 'Perfectly respectable.'

'Climbing trees?'

'Exercise. An outing.'

He made a dismissive motion with his head. 'Walking into the house, man – into her bedroom. That's illegal. I was wide. awake, Tommy. I was right there.'

'Oh, were you?'

'I was.'

'So why didn't . . . ?'

'Compassion.' He leaned forward, folded his hands. For a moment I recognized the old Herbie: the ghost of friendship. 'And maybe something else too,' he said. 'I admire how you've stuck in there, Tommy. Kept trying, kept battling. Loyal in your own quirky way.' He chuckled to himself. 'A little like me.'

'Like you?'

Herbie nodded. 'We both love her. Different ways, different reasons.'

He rubbed his eyes, blinked, stood up, and moved to a window overlooking the backyard.

Beyond him, on the lawn, I could make out the glow of a barbecue grill, smudgy silhouettes moving in the dark: Earleen in her wheelchair, Ned and Velva, the tycoon, Lorna Sue, two or three others.

I watched Lorna Sue light a sparkler and wave it overhead.

Herbie, too, was watching.

'Some advice,' he said, very quietly. 'Get away from all this. Permanently. Her. Me. Stop *caring*.'

'I don't –'

'That's how you get revenge. Stop caring.' His voice was quiet, below a whisper, but there was also a ripple of anger in it. 'Face the truth about her, Tom. This one time, right now, try to get your head out of those love clouds. Lorna Sue, she lives only for herself. Classic narcissist. Can't help it, I guess. That fucking cross – that nail – it *did* something to her: it made her into – I don't know what – some fake little goddess. She doesn't want a real life. She wants worship.' He shook his head violently. 'I'm not saying you should stop loving her – that's impossible – but you can walk away.'

'Like you did?'

'No, Tommy. Not like me.'

Even in the frail silence that followed, it seemed he was trying to tell me something, or to warn me.

I moved closer to the window, looked out at the nighttime lawn party. The clan was busy lighting Roman candles, shooting the sky full of color, but in a curious way it was like watching someone else's dream. Lorna Sue's dream. And I was no longer part of it.

Herbie stepped up beside me. Together, almost touching, we watched the fireworks.

'So what's your point?' I said.

Herbie made a short, ragged sound – maybe laughter, maybe not.

'The point . . .' He swept a hand across the window as if to wipe it clean. 'Think about it, for Christ sake. I've never gotten married – never got close. Never had a life of my own, not one day, not a single hour.' There was that ragged sound again. 'Take a look, man. Out there. That's why.'

'Lorna Sue?'

'She's not some innocent lamb. This whole family . . . sometimes I think I'm the only –' He cut himself off, shook his head bitterly. Outside, the Roman candles were opening up like great orchids, greens and yellows. Herbie's skin seemed to absorb some of the color. He looked ill, his face carved up and careworn.

'The only *what*?' I said. 'The only sane one?'

'Maybe. They are who they are. Not bad people, really, except it was like growing up in an old monastery. Dark Ages. Pearly gates and harps.'

'I thought you were part of all that.'

'I was. Maybe I am. Who the fuck knows?' He took my arm again. 'Drink?'

'Of course,' I said. 'Big one.'

He smiled again and nodded. 'Like old times, right? You were the only solid thing I had. Halfway normal.'

'Halfway, yes.'

'That airplane of ours – remember that?'

'I do,' I said.

Peculiar, is it not, how moods come and go? How they collide? How in the midst of rage we will sometimes break out in capricious laughter, or collapse in tears, or both at once? And how a moment later the rage comes rushing back all the stronger?

So it was for me.

After Herbie moved off toward the kitchen, five or six minutes ticked by, most of which has evaporated from memory. My only firm recollection is of standing at that filthy window, watching both the fireworks and my own eerie reflection. I realized with bone-deep certainty that my old life was now finished and unsalvageable. Who knows how the mood struck? That house, maybe. Fireworks. Lorna Sue. At one point the word *ridiculous* came to mind – the charcoal on my face, my ill-fitting uniform. In the window a gaunt, piteous, broken-down Thomas H Chippering was superimposed upon Lorna Sue and her tycoon. Curiously, this made me yearn for a hot, sudsy bath. Wash away the charcoal. Take Mrs Kooshof out to dinner – a steak, perhaps, or a pair of succulent Rock Cornish hens.

That mood swirl: I wanted to hug Lorna Sue. I wanted to wish her well.

I also wanted to blow her to smithereens.*

I was studying myself in the window when Herbie returned with two large, frosty glasses of essential refreshment. 'You okay?' he said. 'You don't look –'

'I'm fine. To plywood airplanes.'

'Sure. And engines.'

'Turtles,' I said.

Herbie grinned. 'Turtles. Almost forgot. What the hell did turtles have to do with anything?'

'Life mystery. Turtles and tycoons.'

There was a clumsy silence.

'Yeah, well. The man has a name.'

'Not for me,' I said. 'A nonentity.'

'Right, but maybe she needs somebody like that. Room to shine.' He glanced at me as if to test my reaction. 'A cipher, you know? Somebody she can turn upside down and . . . I'm sorry.'

'You didn't have to mess with my marriage.'

'Shit, I just . . . It seemed necessary.'

* Should you question any of this, I recommend a perusal of your own volatile history. In those weeks after your husband departed for Fiji, accompanied by a tall young redhead, did you not one evening open up an old album of photographs? Did you not caress your husband's image? Did you not whisper to him? (You said, 'Come home.' You said, 'Please.') But in the next instant you screeched his name and rose to your feet and flung the album into your fireplace. (You did. You yelled, 'Burn in hell!') And then barely a moment later, giddy with sorrow, did you not scorch your fingers in the act of rescuing that tattered old album? Did you not clutch it to your breast? And did you not wonder, if only briefly, about your own ferocious contradictions, your own capacity to love and to loathe with the same blistering force?

'To wreck my life?'

Herbie stared out at the backyard fireworks. 'Don't take this the wrong way, Tom, but some things you're totally blind to. You just don't know. Never did.'

'She was my wife.'

'True. But still. That fucking cross.' Outside, the sky went fuzzy with reds and golds. 'I didn't mean to hurt her, you know. It was like an experiment or something, like research. I was just so goddamned *curious*. Wanted to see if she'd go to heaven. If I'd go to hell. If the skies would open up. *Curious*.'

The booze, I could tell, was having an effect on him. He lifted his glass.

'Here's to curiosity,' he said, far too brightly. 'The sacred mysteries. And now everybody's messed up. Me too.'

'You were a boy,' I said.

'And now I'm not.' He finished his drink, reached out, and took my glass. 'One more won't hurt, will it? The Fourth. Big celebration.'

He turned and left the room.

I heard a toilet flush, water running. When he returned, his eyes had taken on a red puffiness. He strained for a smile, which seemed to snap in half, and handed me my glass.

His own drink was already mostly gone.

'This whole mess, Tom. My own fault, I know that, but all the guilt – tons, I mean – it's not easy lugging that around your whole life. Can't ever put it down. Catholic, right? Doing my penance, looking after her, making sure she doesn't –' He stopped abruptly, moistened his lips. His expression was occluded, his eyes once again pinned on the shadowy backyard. 'Like I said, it had an effect on her. Made her different.'

'Different?'

Herbie rolled his shoulders. 'Unique. Complicated.'

Outside, another skyrocket exploded – brilliant red.

'She *wanted* me to do it,' he said quietly. 'The cross, I mean.

She kept pestering. I'm not absolving myself – I don't mean it like that – but it wasn't like I forced her. She was part of it.' He stopped and gave me that plaintive look again. 'We were *both* curious. Both kids. I end up in reform school.'

'I cannot see the relevance of –'

'Let me finish this. I go to reform school, I come home, I'm nine fucking years old, packed to the gills with guilt. Bad shape, you could say. And Lorna Sue wasn't exactly the same person either. Superpious. Superreligious. Hanging out in the church basement, playing nun, talking with God. Delusions almost, except there was this incredible hatred too. Lots of it. I mean, you can't blame her – blame *me* – but it seemed like she despised the whole world. Everything. Even God. Especially God.' Herbie turned and looked at me. 'Those fires, remember? In the church.'

'That was you,' I said.

'No.'

'Don't try to –'

'Tommy, wake up. She's sick.'

Instinctively, I looked out at the lawn. The fireworks had died out; the backyard was sheathed in a flat, impervious dark. Something twitched at the back of my thoughts. The word *sick*. Disbelief, at first. Then certainty.

'The bombs,' I said sharply.

I swung away from the window. Five or six items occurred to me in rapid succession. A Shell/Hell sign. A fountain pen. A summer day in 1952, the three of us sitting in a withered apple tree, Lorna Sue urging us to fill our jars with gasoline. ('It's a dare,' she'd said. 'You aren't scared, are you?') And the interrogation in Father Dern's office after the fire back in 1957, how Herbie had withheld things, so mute and evasive. Other items too: the girlish graffiti on the church steps, the defiled statue of Christ on his cross – lipstick and mascara and breasts. And Herbie's constant watchfulness over the years.

Headlights in the dark. (That night back in high school, parked in her driveway, those smudgy faces at the window. 'They're *watching*,' Lorna Sue had said. '*He's* watching.') Old facts, new spin.

I turned toward Herbie.

'It seems feasible,' I said, 'that I've misjudged you a little. I always thought –'

'I know what you thought, Tommy.'

We looked at each other. The next several moments, I realized, would prove difficult.

'A blunder,' I said. 'Incorrect call.'

'But *incest*, for God's sake?'

'I'm human.' I glanced out at the backyard again, where an explosive finale was in progress. 'Those bombs,' I said. 'I think she might have them.'

'Come on, you aren't serious?'

'Mason jars, gasoline. They were in the garage, now they're gone.'

A web of wrinkles formed along Herbie's eyes and forehead – a puzzled expression, then anger. He pushed to his feet, crossed over to me, roughly seized my elbow. 'Let's hear it. Fast.'

Over the next several minutes, under a measure of physical compulsion, I outlined my activities of recent date. Near the end Herbie grasped my shoulders, shook me hard. 'For Christ sake, *why*? What the fuck were you thinking?'

'Thinking?' I said.

'The purpose, Tommy. Bombs – what were they *for*?'

I pulled free.

This was not the proper moment to call attention to his inelegantly suspended preposition.

I made a choking sound.

'Some noise, some thunder,' I said fiercely. 'I wanted her to *notice* me, that I'm alive, that we used to –'

Sadly, my voice box was not functioning properly, nor my

343

sense of self. (Like Herbie's preposition, my spiritual health dangled from the most tenuous of threads.) I managed to blurt out a few words more, but these were largely lost amid what had become a wailing noise, a childish blubbering that mortified me even as it rushed from my throat. I sank to the floor. I hugged myself and rocked on my knees and tried to explain that the whole idea was to make her care, to make her remember. 'I was her prince!' I yelled. 'She used to love me – that's fact! She did!' I took a breath. '*Didn't* she?'

Herbie hoisted me to my feet. 'Sure,' he said.

'There, you see? Real love.'

I sobbed again, then laughed.

Because I knew otherwise. A Lady Whitman had come to mind, and separate bedrooms, and noodles with onion powder, and a greedy night in Vegas, and the word *if*, and that cold, opaque, practical look in her eyes when she finally instructed me not to be an eighteen-year-old. Yo-yo, I thought.

Herbie led me down the hallway to the front door.

'Go on home, Tommy,' he said. 'Sit tight, don't budge. I'll handle this.'

Which in a sense, I now understood, was exactly what he had been saying to me all his life.

But then he did an odd thing.

He took my hand. He pressed it to his cheek, held it there for a moment.

'Lock your doors,' he said.

I did not immediately rejoin Mrs Robert Kooshof. Rather, minutes later, I found myself standing at the old white birdbath in the backyard. For some time I simply existed in the summer dark. A great fatigue pressed down upon me, a surrendering sensation, the weariness that a lost hiker must feel after a long, circular journey that has taken him back to the embers of last night's campfire.

I stripped naked, dipped my hands into the birdbath, rinsed the charcoal away, lay in the grass to dry.

Lovely night, I thought. Stars.

A squandered life.

All those years of willful ignorance. Hiding from the truth. Fooling myself. The girl of my dreams – my one and only – but like the summer stars she was beyond reach, utterly unknown, a bright and very distant mystery.

I stood up, naked as a baby, and let the Fourth of July bathe me.

Each of us, I suppose, needs his illusions. Life after death. A maker of planets. A woman to love, a man to hate. Something sacred.

But what a waste.

36

The Fourth
(Late Night)

I showered, shaved, slipped into my unlaundered robe, prepared two cups of tea, moved to the bedroom door, knocked, stepped inside, and begged Mrs Robert Kooshof to marry me. I made promises the saints could not keep. I meant virtually every word.

An hour later, near 10:00 P.M., her eyes betrayed her. She was a woman; she adored me. Her better judgment, I reckoned, was good for another two hours, tops.

At midnight, on schedule, she said, 'Well, maybe it's possible, but you need help, Thomas. The professional kind.' (Uncanny echoes of the past, obviously, but nonetheless I nodded and slid beneath the covers.)

'Done,' I said.

'No phony shrinks. I'll be watching. I'll check under the mattress.'

'Indubitably. Who could blame you?'

'I *mean* it,' she said.

And I am very sure she did mean it, insofar as words can ever carry firm meaning. (Note the vaporous flexibility of the following: 'I love you.' 'I do.' '*Ja, und Gott helfe mir.*' 'Sacred.') Much more significantly, Mrs Kooshof then looked at me, rolled her eyes, and laughed – loud, husky laughter. At

346

what, or why, I cannot be certain. Granted, there was a patently mirthful aspect – even, dare I repeat, a ridiculous aspect – to our beleaguered relationship, yet on this occasion I saw no cause for such foolish sniggering. I felt cuddly; I felt safe. (In short, I can be as sentimental as the next man.)

After a second Mrs Kooshof snapped off her bedside lamp. We lay in the dark for a time, silent, thinking our thoughts. Even with my ear fast to her bosom, I could barely detect her breathing.

'Your last chance,' she finally said, but then laughed again, as if to resign herself to the mutability of such ultimata, the elasticity of the English language and the human heart.

I held her tight, then tighter.

'Make love to me,' she said.

Fireworks, indeed! A Fourth of July extravaganza! A lusty, withering, half-hour cannonade – the barrels melted; I had to spike my guns – after which I collapsed into the edgy sleep of a survivor.

Then came a wild late-night dream. Bloodcurdling, to say the least.

In one unforgettable episode, an all-female Congress had been convened; hundreds of very angry (hence resplendent) young women milling about the floor of a great convention hall, the place seething with taut buttocks and placards and denunciatory feminist rhetoric. I spotted Toni in a Shriner's hat, Megan in next to nothing. The tattooed Carla was there too, and a buxom little businesswoman with a Toshiba, and Deborah and Karen, and a nurse named Rebecca, and Peg and Patty, and Little Red Rhonda, and the sputtering young Sissy, and Laurel in a red choir robe, and Masha and Fleurette and Jessie and Evelyn and Faith and Signe and Katrina and Caroline and Deb and Tulsa and Oriel and blue-eyed Beverly and many, many, many others, whose names and vital data had long since blurred into the larger panorama of things erotic. Curiously, the crowd seemed displeased with me. Much taunting and fist shaking – pandemonium, in fact. At one horrifying point I tried to make my escape, scampering down a long, narrow aisle, but the throng immediately cornered me near the podium, wrestling me into a wooden chair, roping me in tight and lifting me overhead like some captured beast.

And then, for what seemed an eternity, I was womanhandled in the most unspeakable ways. Here, quite literally, was the nightmare of all red-blooded nightmares. A bad dream, I thought, even while dreaming. Yet it would not end. Teetering aboard my fool's chair, I was assaulted with mucus and spiteful epithets; I was stripped to my lanky essence; I was pawed in private places; I was passed from hand to hand like a rag doll, used like a party toy, gnawed upon like a felled zebra, then rudely hauled up to the speaker's platform by several burly members of my seminar on the Methodologies of Misogyny. What I had done to warrant all this was beyond me. '*Innocent!*' I tried to squeal, but my lips had been stapled shut.

And then what?

Loud, venomous speeches. Bitter invective, outrageous accusations, loudspeakers blaring out old hymns and marching anthems. There were guest lectures. The Indigo Girls performed. And then out of nowhere Lorna Sue was there. She seemed to float up to the platform – or levitate, or fly – alighting beside me with a candle in one hand, my leather-bound love ledger in the other. Her eyes had a metallic, cauterized appearance, like polished aluminum. She wore a black cape, a black bonnet, black tights, black gloves, a diaphanous black veil. What her garb may have signified I had no idea, except that she resembled some sort of renegade mother superior. The hall went silent. Heads bowed – even my own.

Slowly, then, Lorna Sue drifted toward me, hovering there, smiling a vague, cold, sightless smile. Once again I tried to speak, to defend myself, but a pair of unmanicured hands instantly grasped me from behind. Electrodes were attached to my naked limbs, a metal headpiece fitted to my skull. Lorna Sue winked. She was chanting now: an incantatory prayer that was soon taken up by the entire assembly. My fate was sealed, obviously, but even then I could not help but take note of Toni's beckoning brown thighs, Carla's tattoos, Megan's navel, Sissy's moist little tongue, all those firm and fleshy bounties amassed before me like a sumptuous last supper.) The girls' fury bothered me not. Nor their bleats of censure. They were here, obviously, for me. For no other. And had I not been strapped to the chair, I most certainly would have raised a hand in affectionate salute. I did, in fact, manage a forgiving nod, but in the next instant a hooded executioner stepped forward – Miss Jane Fonda, I believe. 'We're people, we're individuals!' she bellowed. To which, through stapled lips, I replied: 'Well, for God's sake, of *course* you are, A to double-D, all shapes and sizes.' This got me nowhere. The executioner – indeed, the above-mentioned Oscar winner – took hold of a large red lever at center stage. (Crass symbolism I leave to the quacks.) I steeled myself for the lethal jolt. Oddly, I felt almost no fear – a tingle of anticipation, if anything – but this changed swiftly when Lorna Sue turned toward the crowd and lifted her candle to my priceless love ledger. I jerked upright. At that instant the executioner did her duty. There was a flash of white light – I was sizzling – and the final image was of Lorna Sue putting the flame to my life's work, my crowning intellectual achievement, my enduring gift to posterity. It all went up in smoke. As I did.

Two stark thoughts had already imprinted themselves on my mind as I awakened. First, fireworks. Second, I had failed to lock the doors.

Mrs Kooshof's bedside clock showed 2:46 A.M.

For a time I lay listening, sniffing the acrid night air, and after a few seconds before the word *smoke* returned to me as if curling out of the dream. I may well have whispered it aloud.

I slipped out of bed, put on my pajama bottoms, toddled to the kitchen. For whatever reason, I felt no great alarm; there was just that wispy smoke at the margins of my thoughts. I poured myself a glass of ice water, stood at the kitchen counter, and not until I had finished drinking and carefully rinsed the tumbler did it occur to me that there was nothing in the least dreamy about the odor in my nose.

Bombs, I thought.

I hurried out to the living room, bolted the front door, checked the den and spare bedroom, returned to the kitchen, stood sniffing again, bolted the back door, then switched on the basement light and made my way down.

(Basements, I add parenthetically, are not to my taste. Cobwebs.)

Yet nothing was amiss.

Briefly, I scanned the furnace and hot-water heater, peeked into a cluttered storage room, then trudged back upstairs. The smoky odor was now quite powerful. I use the word *smoky* advisedly, for this was not *just* smoke. There was also the distinct smell of gasoline.

At that point I knew.

I unlocked the back door and in my bare feet stepped out onto the lawn.

The fire had mostly extinguished itself: tiny tongues of flame, a reddish-orange glow, a charred wooden cross burning against the garage. (Pathetic? Trite? Such is our dismal human journey. We are what we were. We end where we began.) I crossed the yard. At my feet, in the lingering red glow, lay several shards of glass – fragments of a mason jar, I surmised. A large swath of grass had been scorched, the garage itself badly blistered.

What my emotions were I could not be certain. Plainly not surprise.

'Lorna Sue!' I yelled.

I waited a moment, then yelled again. There was no response. Crackling sounds from the plywood. The dark Minnesota prairie.

But she was out there, I was sure.

The second bomb went off at 3:28 A.M., the third only a heartbeat later.

I had just returned my weary bones to the side of Mrs Robert Kooshof when the twin explosions seemed to flare up behind my eyelids. I jackknifed sideways, flailed against the sheets, caught a glimpse of the bomb's silver afterburn over Mrs Kooshof's left shoulder. (She was already at the window: a compelling image by any standard. Profile view. Backlighted breasts. Here, even under wee-hour attack, was the purest evidence of my lifelong philogyny, my rock-solid affection for the more malleable sex.)

I disentangled myself from the bedclothes, sped to Mrs Kooshof's side, took up a defensive stance behind her.

The window still shimmied from the blasts.

For a moment or so I felt my very blood wobble. Though partially blinded, I put a hand to Mrs Kooshof's waist, steadying myself, and peered out at the incontinent night. Not thirty yards away, kitty-corner across the street, a pair of microwave-size fires blazed upon the broad brick steps of St Paul's.

Lorna Sue stood close by, dressed in a long white night-gown, her face oddly childlike, partly solemn, partly ecstatic. Somehow, as if by magic, she seemed to have shed forty-odd years – a kid again, barely of age. After a second she looked up at our window. Perhaps it was my imagination, but she seemed to incline her head slightly. (An acknowledgment of some sort? A farewell? A threat? I will never know.) A few dark moments slipped by, then Lorna Sue giggled and reached down and lifted her nightgown waist high. Once again she looked up at our window, seemed to smile at something, stepped sideways into one of the fires, stood motionless for a time, and then, without the least hurry – without pain, it appeared – stepped out again, lowered her nightgown, and carefully brushed a streak of soot from its hem.

She skipped down the sidewalk toward her house.

Appalling, yes. But what it signified I had no idea.

For a minute or two Mrs Kooshof and I watched the fires die out. 'All right,' she said. 'What was that?'

I began to reply – to tell her about fountain pens and burning churches – but right then, as I exhaled the breath of history, the phone rang. It was Herbie. He needed me.

'Fast,' he said. 'Get over here.'

I threw on a pair of trousers, a fresh cotton shirt, a tie, and carried myself at a trot to the Zylstra home, a half block away. It was now nearly four in the morning, July the fifth. The front door stood ajar. I stepped inside, followed the sound of sobbing into the living room. (A thousand times in my youth I had trodden the same path; I *knew* this place – feared it, loved it – and in odd, indelible ways it was truly my second home, as deeply embedded in my dreams as my own childhood abode: a snake named Sebastian; a cat dangling from a third-story window; an honor guard; Lorna Sue playing with her dollhouse up in the attic.) Now, though, I sensed something new and undefinable. In the cluttered living room I found Velva in hysterics, Ned and Earleen doing what they could to comfort her, the tycoon sprawled virtually comatose on the sofa.

I began to turn, looking for Herbie, when Mrs Robert Kooshof appeared in the hallway to my right. She was clad in her blue negligée, a pair of incongruous spike heels strapped to her feet. Apparently, she had followed only a step or two behind me. (Apparently, too, she had outfitted herself in something of a rush.)

She glanced at Velva, then at the tycoon, and after a hesitation marched to my side, her pretty Dutch face betraying a sort of embarrassed solicitude.

'Don't ask me to leave,' she said. 'You're mine, Thomas.'

'This isn't the occasion for –'

'It *is* the occasion. I belong here.' She regarded me with a calm directness I had never experienced before, a steadiness that Lorna Sue would never have attempted, certainly not equaled. 'New world, Thomas. Understand me?'

'I do. Thank you.'

She nodded. 'So where *is* our little firebomber?'

I raised my hands in a display of ignorance. Velva's sobs had ebbed to a garbled moan, and a restful few moments passed before the woman was able to replenish her lungs.

'My little girl!' she screeched. 'My house!'

(Which, to me, made not the slightest sense.)

Mrs Kooshof assisted Velva to the sofa, depositing her beside Lorna Sue's insensate tycoon. He, too, was weeping. Occasional nuggets of delirium issued from his debauched, wife-purloining lips.* I smiled and folded my arms. A curious peace passed over me at watching the DNA of this family come unknit before my very eyes.

Perhaps another minute went by, each lengthy second chock-full of blather, and then Herbie came into the room. Exactly how, or from where, I did not notice – he had snatched

---

* I was pleased to note that the man's IQ had plummeted like the mercury on a deep-freeze thermometer. Handsome, yes, and tycoon rich, but at the moment he could not have passed first-grade finger painting. All of us, I believe, can take heart in the scene. Things come around. Now and then, given time and patience, the world does in fact dispense a kind of justice.

my arm even before I saw or heard him. (Like Mrs Kooshof, he was dressed more or less for slumber: boxer undershorts, a T-shirt, bare feet.) He hissed something at me, made a meaningless gesture at the ceiling, then tugged me toward an open doorway at the far end of the room.

Mrs Kooshof intervened.

'Slow down,' she said briskly. 'What's happening here?'

'The attic,' Herbie said. 'Lorna Sue, she has those fucking bombs up there – *Tom's* bombs – and we have to . . .' His voice snagged; he was having trouble, like the rest of the clan, pinning language to thought. He blinked at Mrs Kooshof, plaintively tugged at me again. His face was layered with a shiny coat of sweat.

'Where Thomas goes, I go,' said Mrs Kooshof. 'Attic or no attic.'

'You *can't*,' Herbie said.

'No cans, no can'ts. I am.'

'Yes, but listen, you don't really . . . I mean, it's dangerous.'

He was on the edge of panic, his voice ragged, yet even then my newly adhesive fiancée refused to budge.

'It's settled,' she said. 'I tag along.'

Behind us, Velva emitted another lungful of incoherence. Herbie glanced at her, then up at the ceiling, then at Mrs Kooshof. 'I can't explain it now,' he said, 'but you're part of what's going on here. What set her off, I mean.'

Mrs Kooshof laughed. 'She's *jealous?*'

'Not exactly, but she thinks . . . she thinks you've corrupted Tommy. Subverted things.'

There was a rubbery silence before Mrs Kooshof laughed again.

'Jealous!' she said.

Then Mrs Kooshof looked at me. For all her showy courage, I could see she was frightened – of Lorna Sue, of me, of whatever remained between us.

354

'I'm still going,' she said. 'I need to be in on this. Please.'

Herbie shrugged.

Without a word, he turned and led us up to the second floor, then down a corridor to the attic staircase. He motioned for Mrs Kooshof to stop there; together, my old pal and I climbed twelve creaky steps into the loft.

I edged forward, one hand against Herbie's back, the other reaching out for eternity.

The only illumination was supplied by a swath of moonlight streaming in from an open window to my left – the same window, in fact, from which Herbie had once gone rat-fishing with a terrified cat. The smell memories were now sweeping through me. Attic dust, attic mildew.

Directly ahead, in the dark, I heard a short giggle: the giggle of a seven-year-old.

I stopped and squinted. For a second I felt myself sliding off a psychic edge, tumbling backward. Here, in this musty old loft, Herbie and I had first broached the subject of a plywood cross, all the possibilities. ('It'll be neat,' Herbie had said, and Lorna Sue had looked up from her dolls and smiled at me. We were in love. Puppy love, one might say, but it was full and genuine – as real as love can ever be. 'Well, I *guess* so,' she had said, and then giggled.)

Now she giggled again.

I took another step forward, but in the next instant a great white star flared up directly in front of me.

I dropped flat to my stomach, thinking the crisp, elegant thoughts of a dead man. There was a sharp crackling nearby, another girlish giggle. 'Easy now,' Herbie was saying, yet even then I had to will my eyelids open.

The rafters glowed yellow-orange. I rolled sideways and sat up.

Near the window, six feet away, Lorna Sue crouched with her back to the wall, chuckling at my folly, a blazing Fourth of

July sparkler held high overhead. In front of her stood my three remaining bombs. Eerie, yes, but what unsettled me was the flickering image of Lorna Sue herself: both middle-aged and impossibly young. How she managed this I do not pretend to know. An illusion of circumstance, perhaps, or my own misapprehension, or the way she giggled, or her little-girl posture, or the fierce, undulating light of the sparkler, or some mysterious inner spirit that came bubbling to the Tampa-tanned surface of her skin. I shielded my eyes and looked again, not quite believing, but there was still that ghostly double exposure, that sense of beholding the child inside the woman.

Herbie saw it too. I know he did: by the way he put his hand on my shoulder; by the inflection in his voice when he said, 'Don't worry. It happens sometimes.'

Lorna Sue carved a quick, brilliant loop with her sparkler.

'It happens!' she said gleefully.

'Come on, please,' Herbie said. 'Let's just –'

'It happens, though! It happens, Tommy!'

Her voice had a lilting, melodic sound, like some singsong children's chant. She made a face at me, leaned forward, and passed the sparkler over one of my rigged mason jars.

'Boom!' she cried. 'It happens!'

I rose awkwardly to my feet.

In the flaring light I could make out my Joker's Wild firecrackers, their slender white fuses jutting up from the jar lids. And I could also see the contempt in her face. (This is not to suggest that she appeared deluded or deranged. She knew what she was doing; she always had known.) Her gaze was steady. She was in command – quite literally – not only of her emotions but of our very grip on the here and now.

Herbie moved back a step. 'Put it down,' he said. 'Tommy's here.'

'Oh, gee! Tommy!'

'Right, baby – just like I promised.'

'Funny old liar-liar, flirt-bird Tommy?'

'That's the one,' said Herbie. 'Let's go downstairs now. We can talk there.'

Lorna Sue shook her head and grinned at me. 'Scared?' she whispered.

'So it seems,' I said.

'Well, you *should* be. You should be a whole *lot* scared.' She gave her sparkler a quick twirl. 'Just a scared old flirt-bird.'

I bobbed my chin, more or less assenting. (If nothing else, Lorna Sue had a keen eye for my spiritual shortcomings.) I dared an oblique glance at Herbie, who had inched forward a step or two.

Lorna Sue also noticed. 'Hey, Tepee Creeper,' she said. 'I think you better stop right there.'

'Sure,' Herbie said.

'You better.'

'Fine, honey, I've stopped. Let's just –'

'Then *stay* stopped,' she said, almost playfully, and made another threatening sweep with her sparkler.

Herbie squatted down.

'Listen to me, sweetheart. You don't want to hurt anybody, do you? Not really.'

'Maybe I *do* want to.'

'You don't.'

'Well, that's for me to know,' she said. 'Either way, you better stay right there.'

'I will, sweetheart. I am.'

'And Tommy too.'

'Don't worry. He's not budging.'

Herbie's calm impressed me. He spoke in a lulling, liturgical monotone, his movements as slow and practiced as any altar boy's.

Clearly, this was a situation he had encountered more than once. Herbie the suppliant, Lorna Sue the dispenser of grace.

Briefly, then, a number of thoughts came streaming at me in disarray: the whole unnatural bond between them, which I now perceived as a terrible shackling, each of them chained to a single summer day in 1952. She was forever the maimed girl-goddess; Herbie was forever her guardian and caretaker. They were frozen in the great permafrost of history. Stunted. Trapped. Compulsively, like a pair of drug addicts, they could not stop replicating the horrid past – a rusty nail, a plywood cross.* True, there were mysteries I would never fathom, a silent center to it all, but at bottom this was not an erotic relationship; I had been in error on that count.

At the same time, though, as I watched Herbie's frightened, tender face, I could not help thinking that Lorna Sue had always been far more his than mine.

Hard to admit, but I had married a child.

How much time elapsed I cannot accurately estimate. Not long – probably only seconds – yet it seemed as if the three of us had been pressed together in that dark, stuffy attic for a lifetime.

When Lorna Sue's sparkler came close to burning out, she used it to light another.

'Both of you,' she said, 'you're *both* to blame. And this whole smelly, rotten house. I should just blow it all up. Kaboom.'

'You shouldn't,' Herbie said quietly.

---

* A common phenomenon. Little Red Rhonda, for instance, once confided to me that she had been the victim of a sexually abusive father. 'Even so, for some stupid reason,' she told me, 'I keep chasing perverted old fruitcakes like you.' (A sad story. I comforted the girl as best I could.) It also occurs to me, by the way, that I cannot exclude myself from this redundant psychological paradigm. Again and again, over the course of a lifetime, I seem to have repeated certain fundamental mistakes. Witness the word *mattress*. Witness a wellstocked love ledger. Witness my desperate, bumbling, ill-starred attempts to win a hand or two in the rigged poker game of romance.

'Why not?'

'Because you don't want that, princess. Because we all adore you.'

She flicked her eyes at me. 'Even you, Tommy?'

'Even what?'

'Do *you* adore me?'

My gaze shifted to the three mason jars in front of her. 'For the time being,' I said judiciously, 'the issue seems neither here nor there.' I essayed a winning smile. 'Those bombs of mine: how did you happen to . . . ?'

'You spy, I spy, we *all* spy,' she said. 'Answer my question. Do you adore me?'*

'Do I adore you?'

'Right.'

'That calls for a yes or no, I presume?'

'What the heck *else*?' she snapped.

And thus once again, my very existence now in the balance, I was dragged kicking and screaming into a familiar box canyon. The curious thing, however, was that the old, easy response did not leap to my lips. Not so long ago I would have screamed a defiant, ear-splitting *Yes*. Now I was not so sure. Moreover, to complicate matters, I could not help but be aware of Mrs Robert Kooshof on the stairs behind me.

It was necessary to rely on instinct.

'Let's put it this way,' I ventured, testing the elasticity of the

---

* *Adore.* Check your *Webster's Third*, sense number 1: 'to worship with profound reverence: pay divine honors to: honor as a deity or divine: offer worship to.' (At this point I would suggest that you pause to ask yourself a simple binary question: In your heart of hearts, after all is said and done, do you still adore your faithless, unfaithful ex-husband? Does the word *adore* mean what it once meant? Is not language itself as pliable as the human heart? Yes or no?)

past tense. 'You were my one and only. You were the girl of my dreams.'

'*Were?*' she said alertly.

'Why quibble over –'

Lorna Sue cut me off with a caustic laugh. 'Right there,' she said, 'that's why I should blow you to pieces. Always evading. Like when you sucked Faith Graffenteen's nose, you couldn't just admit it.'

'That was a lifetime ago,' I said irritably, 'and I sucked no one's nose. A buss upon the cheek. And she forced me.'

'Forced you?'

'Exactly,' I said, and sighed.

We had plowed this fallow ground before, and it struck me that nothing in our lives ever comes to absolute closure – not love, not betrayal, not the most inane episode of youth. We are surrounded by loose ends; we are awash in whys and maybes. An absence of faith, one might call it.

Lorna Sue instantly proved the point.

'I suppose all the *rest* of them forced you? The ones in your ledger?'

'I never –'

'What crap!'

(No faith: case closed.)

Her voice had gone hoarse and gummy, no longer that of a schoolgirl. 'Anyway, don't go blaming it on me,' she said, and moved her sparkler to within lethal range of the bombs. 'I'm not the one who went after anything in a skirt. Or lied. Or kept a ledger under the mattress.' She lighted a fresh sparkler. 'And now you've got some fresh new bimbo.'

'Bimbo,' I said, 'would be incorrect.'

'It *is* correct. Get on your knees.'

'Pardon?'

'Your knees.'

'You aren't serious?'

'Down,' she said.

I studied her for a moment – this woman I had never known – and then suddenly, to my own astonishment, I found myself smiling. Mrs Kooshof was right: jealousy. Or close enough to offer a kind of consolation, a kind of revenge.

A door squeaked open inside me.

Did I love her? I did. Was she still sacred? She was not.

Lorna Sue looked at me hard.

One cannot be certain about such things, but perhaps she noted the shift inside me. A vein fluttered at her forehead. Slowly, she pushed up to her feet, moved back a step, and then transferred the hot end of the sparkler to the palm of her left hand.

I could smell the flesh cooking.

'I mean it, I'll blow you up,' she said. 'Everybody. Myself too. Don't think I'm not serious.'

'You always were.'

'Down.'

I shook my head. Amazing, but I heard myself uttering that daring, difficult, conclusive word, *No*.*

Lorna Sue gaped at me.

'We're not kids anymore,' I said. 'No kneeling. No, thanks. Just no. No more games.'

'This *isn't* a game!' she screamed. 'God, are you blind? I'm *burning* myself.'

'Blind is what I was.'

I turned.

I made my way to the stairs.

Then I turned back again.

For a man who lives by words, a man whose very being amounts to little more than language, it came as the ultimate

* Odd thing. The word was *no* – spoken quietly, barely a whisper – but it felt to me like a loud, liberating, sublimely heroic *yes*.

satisfaction – indeed, the only vengeance that could ever make a difference – to stop and square my shoulders and return to Lorna Sue the parting gift of a long, cold, reptilian stare.

'A piece of advice,' I said. (Imagine the thrill in my bones.) 'Grow up. Don't be a seven-year-old.'

In the end it was neither Herbie nor I who disarmed the former girl of my dreams. It was Mrs Robert Kooshof. She walked across the attic floor, took the sparkler from Lorna Sue's hand, extinguished it, then joined me at the top of the stairs.

Not a minute later we were on the sidewalk outside, heading home.

Which brings me, finally, to add a word in behalf of my steadfast companion, paramour, mistress, consort, and buxom bride-to-be.

To those tyrants of gender who would denigrate her, who would dare lift their noses and call Mrs Robert Kooshof spineless or submissive or wishy-washy – to all such blind, bewhiskered, man-hating ideologues I belligerently submit that there is something to be said for essential goodness. There is something to be said for decency. There is something to be said for tolerance and endurance and faith and forgiveness and rugged hope and never, never giving up.

She tossed the sparkler into the street.

Later she prepared breakfast for two.

Weak? A doormat?

'Do the dishes,' she said, 'then pack your bags. This is history, Thomas.'

37

Fiji

And so we reside for the present on a balmy, hospitable, out-of-the-way island somewhere southeast of Tampa, somewhere north of Venezuela, a spot on our planet whose precise latitude and longitude must for security reasons go undisclosed. Mrs Robert Kooshof makes pottery. I prune the bougainvillea, cultivate vegetables, fine-tune this personal record. In the evenings we consume fresh fish, a drink or two, and very often each other.

We have dwelled here nearly six months. Tomorrow is Christmas.

A new life, one could say. And a very good life, all considered, at least for the time being. We live in the hills above a lovely aqua bay, in what our leasing agent calls a 'villa' but that in fact is little more than a small, pink-painted prefab, of which there are far too many in these parts. There is a kiln out back, a garden that requires much fertilizer. We have few neighbors. A quarter mile down the slope, where the hills flatten out into tourist country, there is a modest parish town – more a village, actually – whose quaint, Frankish name I am not at liberty to reveal.

Beyond the town, along the beach to the west, is a thriving Club Med.

*   *   *

On weekdays Mrs Kooshof rises early. She walks down the gravel road that winds into town, thence to a tiny shop just off Rue du —, where she peddles her pottery under the somewhat fraudulent tag of 'native ware.' But give her credit. It is her dream, after all, and the dream has come true. She owns a half interest in the shop. She seems content. She wears colorful pareus and shell jewelry and often a blossom in her hair. She is tropic brown. Her clients are mostly widows and librarians, perhaps a few pensive newlyweds, all fresh off the cruise ships that ride at anchor in our pretty aqua bay.

Sometimes I come to sit on the porch in front of the shop. There is a trellis overhead. I sip coffee softened with milk. I compose my thoughts. I consult my internal dictionary. *Turtle*, I sometimes think. *Commitment. Substance. Roses. Pontiac. Cornfield. If. Lost. Sacred. Tycoon. Tampa.* Occasionally, should inspiration strike, I will jot down a memory or two, or a telling footnote to this volume. But for the most part I watch the aqua bay.

At noon, when the shop closes down for the standard island siesta, Mrs Robert Kooshof and I cross the street for lunch at a favorite café. We eat expensively. She is well-off, remember, and there is no reason to shortchange ourselves. In the same breath, however, I must mention that the tropical life has rendered us newly health conscious – two or three glasses of wine, not a drop more, accompanied by a piece of grilled Creole grouper. To date I have dropped twelve unflattering pounds. I sport a Coppertone physique, a salt-and-pepper beard, a suite of hand-tailored seersucker suits. (In this same regard, I might add, Mrs Kooshof has been urging that I try a mother-of-pearl earring. And who knows? On my deathbed I might very well comply.)

364

Over lunch we converse. Slowly but steadily, though not without moments of retrogression, I have begun to master the high art of listening, a development that in myriad ways has expanded my universe. I have learned, for instance, that my beloved's divorce is but a week from becoming final; that her abusive, inattentive, altogether spiteful husband will be receiving a financial settlement far beyond fair; that his parole has been approved; that he hits the street next Thursday; that for all his good fortune, he remains unhappy with me; that he vows vengeance; that the tycoon's leaden shoe has apparently been transferred to another foot. Our current exile, therefore, strikes me as foresighted.

Not that we plan to stay forever.

Another year. Three tops.

Mrs Kooshof has quite prudently taken her house off the market, and it is a near certainty that sooner or later we shall return to live there, upon the prairie of my youth, in the Rock Cornish Hen Capital of the World.

And why not? As good as nowhere. Isolation, it appears, has become the dominant motif of our lives.

Which in the end is for the better.

It is not so much escape I seek, although escape has its own neck-saving virtues, but rather, more fundamentally, it is to remove myself from the hurly-burly, to pause and take stock, to reflect upon the man I was, the man I am, the man I may become. I have learned some things. A 'flirt-bird,' yes – Lorna Sue's creative slang has been duly registered in my dictionary. Slightly too forward at times. Presumptuous, perhaps. Such personal concessions, of course, still have a tendency to stick in this old flirt-bird's craw, for I am not one to dwell on my deficits, yet it has become clear that I may have once or twice taken my love craving to an ungentlemanly extreme and that in the course of events I may have split a hair or two in justifying these appetites.

My love ledger, needless to say, is a thing of the past. Like the rest of the world – like you – I keep the records in my head.

I make progress with each languid hour.

In the heat of midday, after lunch, Mrs Robert Kooshof and I will often take a short stroll down to the bay, where we wet our feet, after which I escort her back to the shop, put a kiss to her lips, bid her a profitable afternoon, and then make my solitary way westward toward the pristine topless beaches of Club Med.

So then.

Like an invalid on the mend, hour to hour, I gradually reclaim my life.

But let it be said, loud and clear, that even an old flirt-bird can be taught new tricks. In recent weeks I have taken up seaside hair braiding – an honorable trade in this warm clime. Eight American dollars a head. Tips excluded. Chitchat gratis. The chartered aircraft arrive like clockwork from New York and Paris and Naples, week after exhilarating week, and I have yet to experience a shortage of silky tresses upon the club's immaculate and fertile beaches.

Do I miss academia?

I am a pig in heaven.

I specialize in corn rows. I envision a Rock Cornish Salon in my prairie future.

As of the moment, I must guiltily confess, Mrs Robert Kooshof knows none of this. She sniffs at my skin. She wonders. In the evenings, as we sit beneath the stars in our hilltop garden, she will often ask how this memoir is coming along, to which I reply, 'Slowly, slowly,' and then after a time she will sigh and say, 'Thomas, you don't touch them, do you?' And on those eerily clairvoyant occasions I will explain to her, with impeccable honesty, that my policy has always been (and always will be) strictly hands off.

True enough: the proud, brawny tomcat still struts within me. Untamed, thank the Lord, but learning how to love.

I lost a wife, I gained back a friend. Herbie has come to visit twice. He will return, I hope, one day soon. On his last stopover he reported that Lorna Sue and her tycoon are doing well. No fires of late. Her spells come and go. Basically she is happy. There is not a great deal of passion to the marriage, I am sad to learn, but the tycoon worships her and offers the everyday sacrifice of selfhood.

On his own part, Herbie says, he is contemplating a move northward. Toronto, he thinks. He wept a little when he told me this, for to renounce his vows as Lorna Sue's caretaker will amount to its own kind of divorce, a betrayal and forswearing, a breach of faith, an end to something both numinous and profane.

Later, though, he laughed.

'Toronto,' he said, and hugged me. We stood in the waiting area of our tiny island airport; his return flight was already boarding. 'So, Tom, what do you think? Maybe the priest-hood? Or maybe one of those long-legged ice skaters? Which will it be?'

'Maybe both,' said I.

When it occurs to me, which is primarily near the nocturnal hour of retirement, I have taken to addressing my bewitch-ing companion by her Christian, semi-Moorish name. The word *Donna* remains unwieldy on my tongue, like a donkey's awkward load, but given that next June we will become man and wife, and given the conventions of our modern epoch, I often relent under threat of withheld physical favors. She is insistent on this point. 'Mrs Robert Kooshof' will no longer do. (Decorum is out, familiarity is in, but my secret plan, if I can summon the stamina, is to *Donna* her to death. Sentence after sentence, phrase after windy phrase, I will simply hammer the wayward woman – Donna, pass the salt, Donna, have a heart – until that glorious day when civility returns to fashion.)

Meanwhile, we make wedding plans.

June, as I say. Garden ceremony. Pastel garb. Steel band. Herbie has agreed to serve as best man.

I look forward, as one can imagine, to dispatching a special invitation to Lorna Sue, who for an instant may contemplate her loss. Even more than that, however, I anticipate with a nostalgic tremble the arrival of old acquaintances from such remote locales as Naples and New York.

It will be a joyous day.

I am at work amending the standard vows.

A step forward, a half step back. An appropriate pace in this sundrenched zone.

As promised, I see a psychiatrist. I am diligent. I write no phony checks. Each Thursday, at 2:00 P.M. sharp, I plod into the ramshackle office of our island's single shrink, a jolly young lady of African descent and considerable insight. We sit out back sometimes, where chickens peck at the dust, and together, in calypso cadences, explore the intricate curlicues of my psyche. The gal speaks little English; I command the island patois not at all. 'Turtle,' I may intone, shaping the creature with my hands, even sketching an example in the dust, which will cause my sleek soul-guide to squeal with unabashed delight.

'Like you, mon!' she will exclaim. 'Big shell! Very slow! But live long forever!'

(She cannot contain the feminine flash in her eyes.)

She gives me a small, noxious pouch to wear near my heart, walks me to the road, judiciously banks my check the same afternoon.

*   *   *

Live long forever.

I hope so. But I am being chased, as you are, toward some dim day of judgment.

On the beach this morning I spotted Death Chant.

Tonight I will braid Mrs Robert Kooshof's hair. Confess all. Begin again.

And you.

It has been years now.

He is in Fiji, with another woman, and will not soon be returning.

But believe this: He loved you. He still does. He knows his transgression and feels it like a loosened tooth in his mouth on the morning of your anniversary, and on your autumn birthday, and when the snow does not come to Fiji on Christmas Eve. Believe too, that in those soft Pacific breezes, late at night, he wakes to think of you, hoping you are well, and that the image with which he finally finds reprieve is of someday returning to your door and knocking on it and begging admittance. A matter of faith. And if you can believe this, which is not beyond believing, imagine how your beauty would fill that doorway. Imagine staring that powerful new stare of yours, the one you have been practicing in your dreams. Imagine how you might chuckle, or shake your head, or just quietly say goodbye and close the door. And imagine, finally, how he would then comprehend – feel as you have felt, know as you have known – the meaning of the word *Fiji*.

Take heart.

Fiji, my lost princess, is but a state of mind. Embolden yourself. Brave the belief.

Bless you.